The proceeds from the sale of this book will be used to support the mission of Library of America, a nonprofit organization that champions the nation's cultural heritage by publishing America's greatest writing in authoritative new editions and providing resources for readers to explore this rich, living legacy.

# THE SUN ALSO RISES

THE LIBRARY OF AMERICA
CORRECTED TEXT

## ERNEST HEMINGWAY

Robert W. Trogdon, editor

LIBRARY OF AMERICA

# CONTENTS

The Sun Also Rises                                                        I

Appendix: Related Writings                                              261

JOURNALISM

The Mecca of Fakers Is French Capital                                   265

American Bohemians in Paris a Weird Lot                                 268

Bull Fighting Is Not a Sport—It Is a Tragedy                           272

World's Series of Bull Fighting a Mad,
    Whirling Carnival                                                    282

LETTERS

To F. Scott Fitzgerald, 1 July [1925]                                  297

To Gertrude Stein and Alice B. Toklas,
    [16] July 1925                                                      299

To Clarence Hemingway, 20 August [1925]                                301

To Horace Liveright, [c. 19 January 1926]                              303

To William B. Smith, Jr., and Harold Loeb,
    [18 February 1926]                                                  306

To Maxwell Perkins, 5 June 1926                                        308

To Maxwell Perkins, 21 August 1926                                     311

To Maxwell Perkins, 16 November 1926                                   314

Chronology                                                             321

Note on the Texts                                                      348

Notes                                                                  356

Publisher's Note

This new, corrected text of *The Sun Also Rises* presents the
first printing of the 1926 Scribner's edition, emended in con-
sultation with all extant versions of the novel, both published
and unpublished, including the holograph manuscript, held at
the John F. Kennedy Presidential Library and Museum, and
the typescript setting copy, held in the Clifton Waller Barrett
library in the Albert and Shirley Small Collections Library at
the University of Virginia. This edition was prepared for Library
of America by Robert W. Trogdon. See the Note on the Texts
for further discussion of this edition.

# THE SUN ALSO RISES

*This book is for* HADLEY

*And for* JOHN HADLEY NICANOR

"You are all a lost generation."

—GERTRUDE STEIN *in conversation*

"One generation passeth away, and another generation cometh; but the earth abideth forever . . . The sun also ariseth, and the sun goeth down, and hasteth to the place where he arose . . . The wind goeth toward the south, and turneth about unto the north; it whirleth about continually, and the wind returneth again according to his circuits. . . . All the rivers run into the sea; yet the sea is not full; unto the place from whence the rivers come, thither they return again."

—*Ecclesiastes*

# BOOK ONE

## CHAPTER ONE

**R**OBERT COHN was once middleweight boxing champion of Princeton. Do not think that I am very much impressed by that as a boxing title, but it meant a lot to Cohn. He cared nothing for boxing, in fact he disliked it, but he learned it painfully and thoroughly to counter-act the feeling of inferiority and shyness he had felt on being treated as a Jew at Princeton. There was a certain inner comfort in knowing he could knock down anybody who was snooty to him, although, being very shy and a thoroughly nice boy, he never fought except in the gym. He was Spider Kelly's star pupil. Spider Kelly taught all his young gentlemen to box like featherweights, no matter whether they weighed one hundred and five or two hundred and five pounds. But it seemed to fit Cohn. He was really very fast. He was so good that Spider promptly overmatched him and got his nose permanently flattened. This increased Cohn's distaste for boxing, but it gave him a certain satisfaction of some strange sort, and it certainly improved his nose. In his last year at Princeton he read too much and took to wearing spectacles. I never met anyone of his class who remembered him. They did not even remember that he was middleweight boxing champion.

I mistrust all frank and simple people, especially when their stories hold together, and I always had a suspicion that perhaps Robert Cohn had never been middleweight boxing champion, and that perhaps a horse had stepped on his face, or that maybe his mother had been frightened or seen something, or that he had, maybe, bumped into something as a young child, but I finally had somebody verify the story from Spider Kelly. Spider Kelly not only remembered Cohn. He had often wondered what had become of him.

Robert Cohn was a member, through his father, of one of the richest Jewish families in New York, and through his mother of one of the oldest. At the military school where he prepped for Princeton and played a very good end on the football team, no one had made him race-conscious. No one had ever made him feel he was a Jew, and hence any different from anybody else, until he went to Princeton. He was a nice boy, a friendly boy, and very shy, and it made him bitter. He took it out in boxing, and he came out of Princeton with painful self-consciousness and the flattened nose, and was married by the first girl who was nice to him. He was married five years, had three children, lost most of the fifty thousand dollars his father left him, the balance of the estate having gone to his mother, hardened into a rather unattractive mold under domestic unhappiness with a rich wife; and just when he had made up his mind to leave his wife she left him and went off with a miniature-painter. As he had been thinking for months about leaving his wife and had not done it because it would be too cruel to deprive her of himself, her departure was a very healthful shock.

The divorce was arranged and Robert Cohn went out to the Coast. In California he fell among literary people and, as he still had a little of the fifty thousand left, in a short time he was backing a review of the Arts. The review commenced publication in Carmel, California, and finished in Provincetown, Massachusetts. By that time Cohn, who had been regarded purely as an angel, and whose name had appeared on the editorial page merely as a member of the advisory board, had become the sole editor. It was his money and he discovered he liked the authority of editing. He was sorry when the magazine became too expensive and he had to give it up.

By that time, though, he had other things to worry about. He had been taken in hand by a lady who hoped to rise with the magazine. She was very forceful, and Cohn never had a chance of not being taken in hand. Also he was sure that he loved her. When this lady saw that the magazine was not going to rise, she became a little disgusted with Cohn and decided that she might as well get what there was to get while there was still something available, so she urged that they go to Europe where Cohn could write. They came to Europe, where the lady had been educated, and stayed three years. During these three years, the first spent in travel, the last two in Paris, Robert Cohn had two friends, Braddocks and myself. Braddocks was his literary friend. I was his tennis friend.

The lady who had him, her name was Frances, found toward the end of the second year that her looks were going, and her attitude toward Robert changed from one of careless posses-sion and exploitation to the absolute determination that he should marry her. During this time Robert's mother had settled an allowance on him, about three hundred dollars a month. During two years and a half I do not believe that Robert Cohn looked at another woman. He was fairly happy, except that, like many people living in Europe, he would rather have been in America, and he had discovered writing. He wrote a novel, and it was not really such a bad novel as the critics later called it, although it was a very poor novel. He read many books, played bridge, played tennis, and boxed at a local gymnasium.

I first became aware of his lady's attitude toward him one night after the three of us had dined together. We had dined at l'Avenue's and afterward went to the Café de Versailles for coffee. We had several *fines* after the coffee, and I said I must be going. Cohn had been talking about the two of us going off somewhere on a week-end trip. He wanted to get out of town and get in a good walk. I suggested we fly to Strasbourg and walk up to Saint Odile, or somewhere or other in Alsace. "I know a girl in Strasbourg who can show us the town," I said.

Somebody kicked me under the table. I thought it was accidental and went on: "She's been there two years and knows everything there is to know about the town. She's a swell girl."

I was kicked again under the table and, looking, saw Frances, Robert's lady, her chin lifting and her face hardening.

"Hell," I said, "why go to Strasbourg? We could go up to Bruges, or to the Ardennes."

Cohn looked relieved. I was not kicked again. I said good night and went out. Cohn said he wanted to buy a paper and would walk to the corner with me. "For God's sake," he said, "why did you say that about that girl in Strasbourg for? Didn't you see Frances?"

"No, why should I? If I know an American girl that lives in Strasbourg what the hell is it to Frances?"

"It doesn't make any difference. Any girl. I couldn't go, that would be all."

"Don't be silly."

"You don't know Frances. Any girl at all. Didn't you see the way she looked?"

"Oh, well," I said, "let's go to Senlis."

"Don't get sore."

"I'm not sore. Senlis is a good place and we can stay at the Grand Cerf and take a hike in the woods and come home."

"Good, that will be fine."

"Well, I'll see you tomorrow at the courts," I said.

"Good night, Jake," he said, and started back to the café.

"You forgot to get your paper," I said.

"That's so." He walked with me up to the kiosque at the corner. "You are not sore, are you, Jake?" He turned with the paper in his hand.

"No, why should I be?"

"See you at tennis," he said. I watched him walk back to the café holding his paper. I rather liked him and evidently she led him quite a life.

## CHAPTER TWO

Tʜᴀᴛ ᴡɪɴᴛᴇʀ Robert Cohn went over to America with
his novel, and it was accepted by a fairly good publisher. His going made an awful row I heard, and I think that
was where Frances lost him, because several women were nice
to him in New York, and when he came back he was quite
changed. He was more enthusiastic about America than ever,
and he was not so simple, and he was not so nice. The publishers had praised his novel pretty highly and it rather went to his
head. Then several women had put themselves out to be nice
to him, and his horizons had all shifted. For four years his horizon had been absolutely limited to his wife. For three years, or
almost three years, he had never seen beyond Frances. I am
sure he had never been in love in his life.

He had married on the rebound from the rotten time he had
in college, and Frances took him on the rebound from his dis-
covery that he had not been everything to his first wife. He was
not in love yet but he realized that he was an attractive quantity
to women, and that the fact of a woman caring for him and
wanting to live with him was not simply a divine miracle. This
changed him so that he was not so pleasant to have around.
Also, playing for higher stakes than he could afford in some
rather steep bridge games with his New York connections, he
had held cards and won several hundred dollars. It made him
rather vain of his bridge game, and he talked several times of

how a man could always make a living at bridge if he were ever forced to.

Then there was another thing. He had been reading W. H. Hudson. That sounds like an innocent occupation, but Cohn had read and reread *The Purple Land*. *The Purple Land* is a very sinister book if read too late in life. It recounts splendid imaginary amorous adventures of a perfect English gentleman in an intensely romantic land, the scenery of which is very well described. For a man to take it at thirty-four as a guide-book to what life holds is about as safe as it would be for a man of the same age to enter Wall Street direct from a French convent, equipped with a complete set of the more practical Alger books. Cohn, I believe, took every word of *The Purple Land* as literally as though it had been an R. G. Dun report. You understand me, he made some reservations, but on the whole the book to him was sound. It was all that was needed to set him off. I did not realize the extent to which it had set him off until one day he came into my office.

"Hello, Robert," I said. "Did you come in to cheer me up?"

"Would you like to go to South America, Jake?" he asked.

"No."

"Why not?"

"I don't know. I never wanted to go. Too expensive. You can see all the South Americans you want in Paris anyway."

"They're not the real South Americans."

"They look awfully real to me."

I had a boat train to catch with a week's mail stories, and only half of them written.

"Do you know any dirt?" I asked.

"No."

"None of your exalted connections getting divorces?"

"No; listen, Jake. If I handled both our expenses, would you go to South America with me?"

"Why me?"

"You can talk Spanish. And it would be more fun with two of us."

"No," I said, "I like this town and I go to Spain in the summertime."

"All my life I've wanted to go on a trip like that," Cohn said. He sat down. "I'll be too old before I can ever do it."

"Don't be a fool," I said. "You can go anywhere you want. You've got plenty of money."

"I know. But I can't get started."

"Cheer up," I said. "All countries look just like the moving pictures."

But I felt sorry for him. He had it badly.

"I can't stand it to think my life is going so fast and I'm not really living it."

"Nobody ever lives their life all the way up except bull-fighters."

"I'm not interested in bull-fighters. That's an abnormal life. I want to go back in the country in South America. We could have a great trip."

"Did you ever think about going to British East Africa to shoot?"

"No, I wouldn't like that."

"I'd go there with you."

"No, that doesn't interest me."

"That's because you never read a book about it. Go on and read a book all full of love affairs with the beautiful shiny black princesses."

"I want to go to South America."

He had a hard, Jewish, stubborn streak.

"Come on downstairs and have a drink."

"Aren't you working?"

"No," I said. We went down the stairs to the café on the ground floor. I had discovered that was the best way to get rid of friends. Once you had a drink all you had to say was: "Well, I've got to get back and get off some cables," and it was done. It is very important to discover graceful exits like that in the newspaper business, where it is such an important part of the ethics that you should never seem to be working. Anyway, we went downstairs to the bar and had a whiskey and soda. Cohn looked at the bottles in bins around the wall. "This is a good place," he said.

"There's a lot of liquor," I agreed.

"Listen, Jake," he leaned forward on the bar. "Don't you ever get the feeling that all your life is going by and you're not taking advantage of it? Do you realize you've lived nearly half the time you have to live already?"

"Yes, every once in a while."

"Do you know that in about thirty-five years more we'll be dead?"

"What the hell, Robert," I said. "What the hell."

"I'm serious."

"It's one thing I don't worry about," I said.

"You ought to."

"I've had plenty to worry about one time or other. I'm through worrying."

"Well, I want to go to South America."

"Listen, Robert, going to another country doesn't make any difference. I've tried all that. You can't get away from yourself by moving from one place to another. There's nothing to that."

"But you've never been to South America."

"South America hell! If you went there the way you feel now it would be exactly the same. This is a good town. Why don't you start living your life in Paris?"

"I'm sick of Paris, and I'm sick of the Quarter."

"Stay away from the Quarter. Cruise around by yourself and see what happens to you."

"Nothing happens to me. I walked alone all one night and nothing happened except a bicycle cop stopped me and asked to see my papers."

"Wasn't the town nice at night?"

"I don't care for Paris."

So there you were. I was sorry for him, but it was not a thing you could do anything about, because right away you ran up against the two stubbornnesses: South America could fix it and he did not like Paris. He got the first idea out of a book, and I suppose the second came out of a book too.

"Well," I said, "I've got to go upstairs and get off some cables."

"Do you really have to go?"

"Yes, I've got to get these cables off."

"Do you mind if I come up and sit around the office?"

"No, come on up."

He sat in the outer room and read the papers, and the Editor and Publisher and I worked hard for two hours. Then I sorted out the carbons, stamped on a by-line, put the stuff in a couple of big manila envelopes and rang for a boy to take them to the Gare St. Lazare. I went out into the other room and there was Robert Cohn asleep in the big chair. He was asleep with his head on his arms. I did not like to wake him up, but I wanted to lock the office and shove off. I put my hand on his shoulder.

He shook his head. "I can't do it," he said, and put his head deeper into his arms. "I can't do it. Nothing will make me do it."

"Robert," I said, and shook him by the shoulder. He looked up. He smiled and blinked.

"Did I talk out loud just then?"

"Something. But it wasn't clear."

"God, what a rotten dream!"

"Did the typewriter put you to sleep?"

"Guess so. I didn't sleep all last night."

"What was the matter?"

"Talking," he said.

I could picture it. I have a rotten habit of picturing the bedroom scenes of my friends. We went out to the Café Napolitain to have an *apéritif* and watch the evening crowd on the Boulevard.

## CHAPTER THREE

I T WAS a warm spring night and I sat at a table on the terrace of the Napolitain after Robert had gone, watching it get dark and the electric signs come on, and the red and green stop-and-go traffic signal, and the crowd going by, and the horse-cabs clippety-clopping along at the edge of the solid taxi traffic, and the *poules* going by, singly and in pairs, looking for the evening meal. I watched a good-looking girl walk past the table and watched her go up the street and lost sight of her, and watched another, and then saw the first one coming back again. She went by once more and I caught her eye, and she came over and sat down at the table. The waiter came up.

"Well, what will you drink?" I asked.

"Pernod."

"That's not good for little girls."

"Little girl yourself. Dites garçon, un Pernod."

"A Pernod for me, too."

"What's the matter?" she asked. "Going on a party?"

"Sure. Aren't you?"

"I don't know. You never know in this town."

"Don't you like Paris?"

"No."

"Why don't you go somewhere else?"

"Isn't anywhere else."

"You're happy, all right."

"Happy, hell!"

Pernod is greenish imitation absinthe. When you add water it turns milky. It tastes like licorice and it has a good uplift, but it drops you just as far. We sat and drank it, and the girl looked sullen.

"Well," I said, "are you going to buy me a dinner?"

She grinned and I saw why she made a point of not laughing. With her mouth closed she was a rather pretty girl. I paid for the saucers and we walked out to the street. I hailed a horse-cab and the driver pulled up at the curb. Settled back in the slow, smoothly rolling *fiacre* we moved up the Avenue de l'Opéra, passed the locked doors of the shops, their windows lighted, the Avenue broad and shiny and almost deserted. The cab passed the New York *Herald* bureau with the window full of clocks.

"What are all the clocks for?" she asked.

"They show the hour all over America."

"Don't kid me."

We turned off the Avenue up the Rue des Pyramides, through the traffic of the Rue de Rivoli, and through a dark gate into the Tuileries. She cuddled against me and I put my arm around her. She looked up to be kissed. She touched me with one hand and I put her hand away.

"Never mind."

"What's the matter? You sick?"

"Yes."

"Everybody's sick. I'm sick, too."

We came out of the Tuileries into the light and crossed the Seine and then turned up the Rue des Saints Pères.

"You oughtn't to drink Pernod if you're sick."

"You neither."

"It doesn't make any difference with me. It doesn't make any difference with a woman."

"What are you called?"

"Georgette. How are you called?"

"Jacob."

"That's a Flemish name."

"American too."

"You're not Flamand?"

"No, American."

"Good, I detest Flamands."

By this time we were at the restaurant. I called to the *cocher* to stop. We got out and Georgette did not like the looks of the place. "This is no great thing of a restaurant."

"No," I said. "Maybe you would rather go to Foyot's. Why don't you keep the cab and go on?"

I had picked her up because of a vague sentimental idea that it would be nice to eat with someone. It was a long time since I had dined with a *poule*, and I had forgotten how dull it could be. We went into the restaurant, passed Madame Lavigne at the desk and into a little room. Georgette cheered up a little under the food.

"It isn't bad here," she said. "It isn't chic, but the food is all right."

"Better than you eat in Liège."

"Brussels, you mean."

We had another bottle of wine and Georgette made a joke. She smiled and showed all her bad teeth, and we touched glasses. "You're not a bad type," she said. "It's a shame you're sick. We get on well. What's the matter with you, anyway?"

"I got hurt in the war," I said.

"Oh, that dirty war."

We would probably have gone on and discussed the war and agreed that it was in reality a calamity for civilization, and perhaps would have been better avoided. I was bored enough. Just then from the other room someone called: "Barnes! I say, Barnes! Jacob Barnes!"

"It's a friend calling me," I explained, and went out.

There was Braddocks at a big table with a party: Cohn, Frances Clyne, Mrs. Braddocks, several people I did not know.

"You're coming to the dance, aren't you?" Braddocks asked.

"What dance?"

"Why, the dancings. Don't you know we've revived them?" Mrs. Braddocks put in.

"You must come, Jake. We're all going," Frances said from the end of the table. She was tall and had a smile.

"Of course, he's coming," Braddocks said. "Come in and have coffee with us, Barnes."

"Right."

"And bring your friend," said Mrs. Braddocks laughing. She was a Canadian and had all their easy social graces.

"Thanks, we'll be in," I said. I went back to the small room.

"Who are your friends?" Georgette asked.

"Writers and artists."

"There are lots of those on this side of the river."

"Too many."

"I think so. Still, some of them make money."

"Oh, yes."

We finished the meal and the wine. "Come on," I said. "We're going to have coffee with the others."

Georgette opened her bag, made a few passes at her face as she looked in the little mirror, re-defined her lips with the lip-stick, and straightened her hat.

"Good," she said.

We went into the room full of people and Braddocks and the men at his table stood up.

"I wish to present my fiancée, Mademoiselle Georgette Leblanc," I said. Georgette smiled that wonderful smile, and we shook hands all round.

"Are you related to Georgette Leblanc, the singer?" Mrs. Braddocks asked.

"Connais pas," Georgette answered.

"But you have the same name," Mrs. Braddocks insisted cordially.

"No," said Georgette. "Not at all. My name is Hobin."

"But Mr. Barnes introduced you as Mademoiselle Georgette Leblanc. Surely he did," insisted Mrs. Braddocks, who in the excitement of talking French was liable to have no idea what she was saying.

"He's a fool," Georgette said.

"Oh, it was a joke, then," Mrs. Braddocks said.

"Yes," said Georgette. "To laugh at."

"Did you hear that, Henry?" Mrs. Braddocks called down the table to Braddocks. "Mr. Barnes introduced his fiancée as Mademoiselle Leblanc, and her name is actually Hobin."

"Of course, darling. Mademoiselle Hobin, I've known her for a very long time."

"Oh, Mademoiselle Hobin," Frances Clyne called, speaking French very rapidly and not seeming so proud and astonished as Mrs. Braddocks at its coming out really French. "Have you been in Paris long? Do you like it here? You love Paris, do you not?"

"Who's she?" Georgette turned to me. "Do I have to talk to her?"

She turned to Frances, sitting smiling, her hands folded, her head poised on her long neck, her lips pursed ready to start talking again.

"No, I don't like Paris. It's expensive and dirty."

"Really? I find it so extraordinarily clean. One of the cleanest cities in all Europe."

"I find it dirty."

"How strange! But perhaps you have not been here very long."

"I've been here long enough."

"But it does have nice people in it. One must grant that."

Georgette turned to me. "You have nice friends."

Frances was a little drunk and would have liked to have kept it up but the coffee came, and Lavigne with the liqueurs, and after that we all went out and started for Braddocks's dancing-club.

The dancing-club was a *bal musette* in the Rue de la Montagne Sainte Geneviève. Five nights a week the working people of the Pantheon quarter danced there. One night a week it was the dancing-club. On Monday nights it was closed. When we arrived it was quite empty, except for a policeman sitting near the door, the wife of the proprietor back of the zinc bar, and the proprietor himself. The daughter of the house came downstairs as we went in. There were long benches, and tables ran across the room, and at the far end a dancing-floor.

"I wish people would come earlier," Braddocks said. The daughter came up and wanted to know what we would drink. The proprietor got up on a high stool beside the dancing-floor and began to play the accordion. He had a string of bells around one of his ankles and beat time with his foot as he played. Everyone danced. It was hot and we came off the floor perspiring.

"My God," Georgette said. "What a box to sweat in!"

"It's hot."

"Hot, my God!"

"Take off your hat."

"That's a good idea."

Someone asked Georgette to dance, and I went over to the bar. It was really very hot and the accordion music was pleasant in the hot night. I drank a beer, standing in the doorway and getting the cool breath of wind from the street. Two taxis were coming down the steep street. They both stopped in front of the Bal. A crowd of young men, some in jerseys and some in their shirt-sleeves, got out. I could see their hands and newly washed, wavy hair in the light from the door. The policeman standing by the door looked at me and smiled. They came in. As they went in, under the light I saw white hands, wavy hair, white faces, grimacing, gesturing, talking. With them was Brett. She looked very lovely and she was very much with them.

One of them saw Georgette and said: "I do declare. There is an actual harlot. I'm going to dance with her, Lett. You watch me."

The tall, dark one, called Lett, said: "Don't you be rash."

The wavy blond one answered: "Don't you worry, dear." And with them was Brett.

I was very angry. Somehow they always made me angry. I know they are supposed to be amusing, and you should be tolerant, but I wanted to swing on one, any one, anything to shatter that superior, simpering composure. Instead, I walked down the street and had a beer at the bar at the next bal. The beer was not good and I had a worse cognac to take the taste out of my mouth. When I came back to the bal there was a crowd on the floor and Georgette was dancing with the tall blond youth, who danced big-hippily, carrying his head on one side, his eyes lifted as he danced. As soon as the music stopped another one of them asked her to dance. She had been taken up by them. I knew then that they would all dance with her. They are like that.

I sat down at a table. Cohn was sitting there. Frances was dancing. Mrs. Braddocks brought up somebody and introduced him as Roger Prescott. He was from New York by way of Chicago, and was a rising new novelist. He had some sort of an English accent. I asked him to have a drink.

"Thanks so much," he said, "I've just had one."

"Have another."

"Thanks, I will then."

We got the daughter of the house over and each had a *fine à l'eau.*

"You're from Kansas City, they tell me," he said.

"Yes."

"Do you find Paris amusing?"

"Yes."

"Really?"

I was a little drunk. Not drunk in any positive sense but just enough to be careless.

"For God's sake," I said, "yes. Don't you?"

"Oh, how charmingly you get angry," he said. "I wish I had that faculty."

I got up and walked over toward the dancing-floor. Mrs. Braddocks followed me. "Don't be cross with Roger," she said. "He's still only a child, you know."

"I wasn't cross," I said. "I just thought perhaps I was going to throw up."

"Your fiancée is having a great success," Mrs. Braddocks

looked out on the floor where Georgette was dancing in the arms of the tall, dark one, called Lett.

"Isn't she," I said.

"Rather," said Mrs. Braddocks.

Cohn came up. "Come on, Jake," he said. "Have a drink." We walked over to the bar. "What's the matter with you? You seem all worked up over something?"

"Nothing. This whole show makes me sick is all."

Brett came up to the bar.

"Hello, you chaps."

"Hello, Brett," I said. "Why aren't you tight?"

"Never going to get tight any more. I say, give a chap a brandy and soda."

She stood holding the glass and I saw Robert Cohn looking at her. He looked a great deal as his compatriot must have looked when he saw the promised land. Cohn, of course, was much younger. But he had that look of eager, deserving expectation.

Brett was damned good-looking. She wore a slip-over jersey sweater and a tweed skirt, and her hair was brushed back like a boy's. She started all that. She was built with curves like the hull of a racing yacht, and you missed none of it with that wool jersey.

"It's a fine crowd you're with, Brett," I said.

"Aren't they lovely? And you, my dear. Where did you get it?"

"At the Napolitain."

"And have you had a lovely evening?"

"Oh, priceless," I said.

Brett laughed. "It's wrong of you, Jake. It's an insult to all of us. Look at Frances there, and Jo."

This for Cohn's benefit.

"It's in restraint of trade," Brett said. She laughed again.

"You're wonderfully sober," I said.

"Yes. Aren't I. And when one's with the crowd I'm with, one can drink in such safety, too."

The music started and Robert Cohn said: "Will you dance this with me, Lady Brett?"

Brett smiled at him. "I've promised to dance this with Jacob," she laughed. "You've a hell of a biblical name, Jake."

"How about the next?" asked Cohn.

"We're going," Brett said. "We've a date up at Montmartre."

Dancing, I looked over Brett's shoulder and saw Cohn, standing at the bar, still watching her.

"You've made a new one there," I said to her.

"Don't talk about it. Poor chap. I never knew it till just now."

"Oh, well," I said. "I suppose you like to add them up."

"Don't talk like a fool."

"You do."

"Oh, well. What if I do?"

"Nothing," I said. We were dancing to the accordion and someone was playing the banjo. It was hot and I felt happy. We passed close to Georgette dancing with another one of them.

"What possessed you to bring her?"

"I don't know, I just brought her."

"You're getting damned romantic."

"No, bored."

"Now?"

"No, not now."

"Let's get out of here. She's well taken care of."

"Do you want to?"

"Would I ask you if I didn't want to?"

We left the floor and I took my coat off a hanger on the wall and put it on. Brett stood by the bar. Cohn was talking to her. I stopped at the bar and asked them for an envelope. The patronne found one. I took a fifty-franc note from my pocket, put it in the envelope, sealed it, and handed it to the patronne.

"If the girl I came with asks for me, will you give her this?" I said. "If she goes out with one of those gentlemen, will you save this for me?"

"C'est entendu, monsieur," the patronne said. "You go now? So early?"

"Yes," I said.

We started out the door. Cohn was still talking to Brett. She said good night and took my arm. "Good night, Cohn," I said. Outside in the street we looked for a taxi.

"You're going to lose your fifty francs," Brett said.

"Oh, yes."

"No taxis."

"We could walk up to the Pantheon and get one."

"Come on and we'll get a drink in the pub next door and send for one."

"You wouldn't walk across the street."

"Not if I could help it."

We went into the next bar and I sent a waiter for a taxi.

"Well," I said, "we're out away from them."

We stood against the tall zinc bar and did not talk and looked at each other. The waiter came and said the taxi was outside. Brett pressed my hand hard. I gave the waiter a franc and we went out. "Where should I tell him?" I asked.

"Oh, tell him to drive around."

I told the driver to go to the Parc Montsouris, and got in, and slammed the door. Brett was leaning back in the corner, her eyes closed. I got in and sat beside her. The cab started with a jerk.

"Oh, darling, I've been so miserable," Brett said.

## CHAPTER FOUR

THE TAXI went up the hill, passed the lighted square, then on into the dark, still climbing, then levelled out onto a dark street behind St. Etienne du Mont, went smoothly down the asphalt, passed the trees and the standing bus at the Place de la Contrescarpe, then turned onto the cobbles of the Rue Mouffetard. There were lighted bars and late open shops on each side of the street. We were sitting apart and we jolted close together going down the old street. Brett's hat was off. Her head was back. I saw her face in the lights from the open shops, then it was dark, then I saw her face clearly as we came out on the Avenue des Gobelins. The street was torn up and men were working on the car-tracks by the light of acetylene flares. Brett's face was white and the long line of her neck showed in the bright light of the flares. The street was dark again and I kissed her. Our lips were tight together and then she turned away and pressed against the corner of the seat, as far away as she could get. Her head was down.

"Don't touch me," she said. "Please don't touch me."

"What's the matter?"

"I can't stand it."

"Oh, Brett."

"You mustn't. You must know. I can't stand it, that's all. Oh, darling, please understand!"

"Don't you love me?"

"Love you? I simply turn all to jelly when you touch me."

"Isn't there anything we can do about it?"

She was sitting up now. My arm was around her and she was leaning back against me, and we were quite calm. She was looking into my eyes with that way she had of looking that made you wonder whether she really saw out of her own eyes. They would look on and on after everyone else's eyes in the world would have stopped looking. She looked as though there were nothing on earth she would not look at like that, and really she was afraid of so many things.

"And there's not a damn thing we could do," I said.

"I don't know," she said. "I don't want to go through that hell again."

"We'd better keep away from each other."

"But, darling, I have to see you. It isn't all that you know."

"No, but it always gets to be."

"That's my fault. Don't we pay for all the things we do, though?"

She had been looking into my eyes all the time. Her eyes had different depths, sometimes they seemed perfectly flat. Now you could see all the way into them.

"When I think of the hell I've put chaps through. I'm paying for it all now."

"Don't talk like a fool," I said. "Besides, what happened to me is supposed to be funny. I never think about it."

"Oh, no. I'll lay you don't."

"Well, let's shut up about it."

"I laughed about it too, myself, once." She wasn't looking at me. "A friend of my brother's came home that way from Mons. It seemed like a hell of a joke. Chaps never know anything, do they?"

"No," I said. "Nobody ever knows anything."

I was pretty well through with the subject. At one time or another I had probably considered it from most of its various angles, including the one that certain injuries or imperfections are a subject of merriment while remaining quite serious for the person possessing them.

"It's funny," I said. "It's very funny. And it's a lot of fun, too, to be in love."

"Do you think so?" her eyes looked flat again.

"I don't mean fun that way. In a way it's an enjoyable feeling."

"No," she said. "I think it's hell on earth."

"It's good to see each other."

"No. I don't think it is."

"Don't you want to?"

"I have to."

We were sitting now like two strangers. On the right was the Parc Montsouris. The restaurant where they have the pool of live trout and where you can sit and look out over the park was closed and dark. The driver leaned his head around.

"Where do you want to go?" I asked. Brett turned her head away.

"Oh, go to the Select."

"Café Select," I told the driver. "Boulevard Montparnasse." We drove straight down, turning around the Lion de Belfort that guards the passing Montrouge trams. Brett looked straight ahead. On the Boulevard Raspail, with the lights of Montparnasse in sight, Brett said, "Would you mind very much if I asked you to do something?"

"Don't be silly."

"Kiss me just once more before we get there."

When the taxi stopped I got out and paid. Brett came out

putting on her hat. She gave me her hand as she stepped down. Her hand was shaky. "I say, do I look too much of a mess?" She pulled her man's felt hat down and started in for the bar. Inside, against the bar and at tables, were most of the crowd who had been at the dance.

"Hello, you chaps," Brett said. "I'm going to have a drink."

"Oh, Brett! Brett!" the little Greek portrait-painter, who called himself a duke, and whom everybody called Zizi, pushed up to her. "I got something fine to tell you."

"Hello, Zizi," Brett said.

"I want you to meet a friend," Zizi said. A fat man came up. "Count Mippipopolous, meet my friend Lady Ashley."

"How do you do?" said Brett.

"Well, does your ladyship have a good time here in Paris?" asked Count Mippipopolous, who wore an elk's tooth on his watch-chain.

"Rather," said Brett.

"Paris is a fine town all right," said the count. "But I guess you have pretty big doings yourself over in London."

"Oh, yes," said Brett. "Enormous."

Braddocks called to me from a table. "Barnes," he said, "have a drink. That girl of yours got in a frightful row."

"What about?"

"Something the patronne's daughter said. A corking row. She was rather splendid, you know. Showed her yellow card and demanded the patronne's daughter's too. I say it was a row."

"What finally happened?"

"Oh, someone took her home. Not a bad-looking girl. Wonderful command of the idiom. Do stay and have a drink."

"No," I said. "I must shove off. Seen Cohn?"

"He went home with Frances," Mrs. Braddocks put in.

"Poor chap, he looks awfully down," Braddocks said.

"I dare say he is," said Mrs. Braddocks.

"I have to shove off," I said. "Good night."

I said good night to Brett at the bar. The count was buying champagne. "Will you take a glass of wine with us, sir?" he asked.

"No. Thanks awfully. I have to go."

"Really going?" Brett asked.

"Yes," I said. "I've got a rotten headache."

"I'll see you tomorrow?"

"Come in at the office."

"Hardly."

"Well, where will I see you?"

"Anywhere around five o'clock."

"Make it the other side of town then."

"Good. I'll be at the Crillon at five."

"Try and be there," I said.

"Don't worry," Brett said. "I've never let you down, have I?"

"Heard from Mike?"

"Letter today."

"Good night, sir," said the count.

I went out onto the sidewalk and walked down toward the Boulevard St. Michel, passed the tables of the Rotonde, still crowded, looked across the street at the Dome, its tables running out to the edge of the pavement. Someone waved at me from a table, I did not see who it was, and went on. I wanted to get home. The Boulevard Montparnasse was deserted. Lavigne's was closed tight, and they were stacking the tables outside the Closerie des Lilas. I passed Ney's statue standing among the new-leaved chestnut-trees in the arc-light. There was a faded purple wreath leaning against the base. I stopped and read the inscription: from the Bonapartist Groups, some date; I forget. He looked very fine, Marshal Ney in his top-boots, gesturing with his sword among the green new horse-chestnut leaves. My flat was just across the street, a little way down the Boulevard St. Michel.

There was a light in the concierge's room and I knocked on the door and she gave me my mail. I wished her good night and went upstairs. There were two letters and some papers. I looked at them under the gas-light in the dining-room. The letters were from the States. One was a bank statement. It showed a balance of $2,432.60. I got out my check-book and deducted four checks drawn since the first of the month, and discovered I had a balance of $1,832.60. I wrote this on the back of the statement. The other letter was a wedding announce-ment. Mr. and Mrs. Aloysius Kirby announce the marriage of their daughter Katherine—I knew neither the girl nor the man she was marrying. They must be circularizing the town. It was a funny name. I felt sure I could remember anybody with a name like Aloysius. It was a good Catholic name. There was a crest on the announcement. Like Zizi the Greek duke. And that count. The count was funny. Brett had a title, too. Lady Ashley. To hell with Brett. To hell with you, Lady Ashley.

I lit the lamp beside the bed, turned off the gas, and opened the wide windows. The bed was far back from the windows, and I sat with the windows open and undressed by the bed. Outside a night train, running on the street-car tracks, went by carrying vegetables to the markets. They were noisy at night when you could not sleep. Undressing, I looked at myself in the mirror of the big armoire beside the bed. That was a typically French way to furnish a room. Practical, too, I suppose. Of all the ways to be wounded. I suppose it was funny. I put on my pajamas and got into bed. I had the two bull-fight papers, and I took their wrappers off. One was orange. The other yellow. They would both have the same news, so whichever I read first would spoil the other. *Le Toril* was the better paper, so I started to read it. I read it all the way through, including the Petite Correspondence and the Cornigrams. I blew out the lamp. Perhaps I would be able to sleep.

My head started to work. The old grievance. Well, it was a rotten way to be wounded and flying on a joke front like the Italian. In the Italian hospital we were going to form a society. It had a funny name in Italian. I wonder what became of the others, the Italians. That was in the Ospedale Maggiore in Milano, Padiglione Ponte. The next building was the Padiglione Zonda. There was a statue of Ponte, or maybe it was Zonda. That was where the liaison colonel came to visit me. That was funny. That was about the first funny thing. I was all bandaged up. But they had told him about it. Then he made that wonderful speech: "You, a foreigner, an Englishman (any foreigner was an Englishman) have given more than your life." What a speech! I would like to have it illuminated to hang in the office. He never laughed. He was putting himself in my place, I guess. "Che mala fortuna! Che mala fortuna!"

I never used to realize it, I guess. I try and play it along and just not make trouble for people. Probably I never would have had any trouble if I hadn't run into Brett when they shipped me to England. I suppose she only wanted what she couldn't have. Well, people were that way. To hell with people. The Catholic Church had an awfully good way of handling all that. Good advice, anyway. Not to think about it. Oh, it was swell advice. Try and take it sometime. Try and take it.

I lay awake thinking and my mind jumping around. Then I

couldn't keep away from it, and I started to think about Brett and all the rest of it went away. I was thinking about Brett and my mind stopped jumping around and started to go in sort of smooth waves. Then all of a sudden I started to cry. Then after a while it was better and I lay in bed and listened to the heavy trams go by and way down the street, and then I went to sleep.

I woke up. There was a row going on outside. I listened and I thought I recognized a voice. I put on a dressing-gown and went to the door. The concierge was talking downstairs. She was very angry. I heard my name and called down the stairs.

"Is that you, Monsieur Barnes?" the concierge called.

"Yes. It's me."

"There's a species of woman here who's waked the whole street up. What kind of a dirty business at this time of night! She says she must see you. I've told her you're asleep."

Then I heard Brett's voice. Half asleep I had been sure it was Georgette. I don't know why. She could not have known my address.

"Will you send her up, please?"

Brett came up the stairs. I saw she was quite drunk. "Silly thing to do," she said. "Make an awful row. I say, you weren't asleep, were you?"

"What did you think I was doing?"

"Don't know. What time is it?"

I looked at the clock. It was half-past four.

"Had no idea what hour it was," Brett said. "I say, can a chap sit down? Don't be cross, darling. Just left the count. He brought me here."

"What's he like?" I was getting brandy and soda and glasses.

"Just a little," said Brett. "Don't try and make me drunk. The count? Oh, rather. He's quite one of us."

"Is he a count?"

"Here's how. I rather think so, you know. Deserves to be, anyhow. Knows hell's own amount about people. Don't know where he got it all. Owns a chain of sweet-shops in the States."

She sipped at her glass.

"Think he called it a chain. Something like that. Linked them all up. Told me a little about it. Damned interesting. He's one of us, though. Oh, quite. No doubt. One can always tell."

She took another drink.

"How do I buck on about all this. You don't mind, do you? He's putting up for Zizi, you know."

"Is Zizi really a duke, too?"

"I shouldn't wonder. Greek, you know. Rotten painter. I rather liked the count."

"Where did you go with him?"

"Oh, everywhere. He just brought me here now. Offered me ten thousand dollars to go to Biarritz with him. How much is that in pounds?"

"Around two thousand."

"Lot of money. I told him I couldn't do it. He was awfully nice about it. Told him I knew too many people in Biarritz."

Brett laughed.

"I say, you are slow on the uptake," she said. I had only sipped my brandy and soda. I took a long drink.

"That's better. Very funny," Brett said. "Then he wanted me to go to Cannes with him. Told him I knew too many people in Cannes. Monte Carlo. Told him I knew too many people in Monte Carlo. Told him I knew too many people everywhere. Quite true, too. So I asked him to bring me here."

She looked at me, her hand on the table, her glass raised. "Don't look like that," she said. "Told him I was in love with

you. True, too. Don't look like that. He was damn nice about
it. Wants to drive us out to dinner tomorrow night. Like to go?"

"Why not?"

"I'd better go now."

"Why?"

"Just wanted to see you. Damned silly idea. Want to get
dressed and come down? He's got the car just up the street."

"The count?"

"Himself. And a chauffeur in livery. Going to drive me around
and have breakfast in the Bois. Hampers. Got it all at Zelli's.
Dozen bottles of Mumms. Tempt you?"

"I have to work in the morning," I said. "I'm too far behind
you now to catch up and be any fun."

"Don't be an ass."

"Can't do it."

"Right. Send him a tender message?"

"Anything. Absolutely."

"Good night, darling."

"Don't be sentimental."

"You make me ill."

We kissed good night and Brett shivered. "I'd better go," she
said. "Good night, darling."

"You don't have to go."

"Yes."

We kissed again on the stairs and as I called for the cor-
don the concierge muttered something behind her door. I
went back upstairs and from the open window watched Brett
walking up the street to the big limousine drawn up to the
curb under the arc-light. She got in and it started off. I turned
around. On the table was an empty glass and a glass half-full
of brandy and soda. I took them both out to the kitchen and

poured the half-full glass down the sink. I turned off the gas in the dining-room, kicked off my slippers sitting on the bed, and got into bed. This was Brett that I had felt like crying about. Then I thought of her walking up the street and stepping into the car, as I had last seen her, and of course in a little while I felt like hell again. It is awfully easy to be hard-boiled about everything in the daytime but at night it is another thing.

## CHAPTER FIVE

I N THE morning I walked down the boulevard to the
Rue Soufflot for coffee and brioche. It was a fine morning. The horse-chestnut trees in the Luxembourg Gardens
were in bloom. There was the pleasant early-morning feeling
of a hot day. I read the papers with the coffee and then smoked
a cigarette. The flower-women were coming up from the market and arranging their daily stock. Students went by going up
to the law school, or down to the Sorbonne. The Boulevard
was busy with trams and people going to work. I got on an S
bus and rode down to the Madeleine, standing on the back
platform. From the Madeleine I walked along the Boulevard
des Capucines to the Opera, and up to my office. I passed the
man with the jumping frogs and the man with the boxer toys. I
stepped aside to avoid walking into the thread with which his
girl assistant manipulated the boxers. She was standing looking away, the thread in her folded hands. The man was urging
two tourists to buy. Three more tourists had stopped and were
watching. I walked on behind a man who was pushing a roller
that printed the name CINZANO on the sidewalk in damp
letters. All along people were going to work. It felt pleasant to
be going to work. I walked across the avenue and turned in to
my office.

Upstairs in the office I read the French morning papers,
smoked, and then sat at the typewriter and got off a good

morning's work. At eleven o'clock I went over to the Quai d'Orsay in a taxi and went in and sat with about a dozen correspondents, while the foreign-office mouthpiece, a young Nouvelle Revue Française diplomat in horn-rimmed spectacles, talked and answered questions for half an hour. The President of the Council was in Lyons making a speech, or, rather he was on his way back. Several people asked questions to hear themselves talk and there were a couple of questions asked by news service men who wanted to know the answers. There was no news. I shared a taxi back from the Quai d'Orsay with Woolsey and Krum.

"What do you do nights, Jake?" asked Krum. "I never see you around."

"Oh, I'm over in the Quarter."

"I'm coming over some night. The Dingo. That's the great place, isn't it?"

"Yes. That, or this new dive, the Select."

"I've meant to get over," said Krum. "You know how it is, though, with a wife and kids."

"Playing any tennis?" Woolsey asked.

"Well, no," said Krum. "I can't say I've played any this year. I've tried to get away, but Sundays it's always rained, and the courts are so damned crowded."

"The Englishmen all have Saturday off," Woolsey said.

"Lucky beggars," said Krum. "Well, I'll tell you. Someday I'm not going to be working for an agency. Then I'll have plenty of time to get out in the country."

"That's the thing to do. Live out in the country and have a little car."

"I've been thinking some about getting a car next year."

I banged on the glass. The chauffeur stopped. "Here's my street," I said. "Come in and have a drink."

"Thanks, old man," Krum said. Woolsey shook his head. "I've got to file that line he got off this morning."

I put a two-franc piece in Krum's hand.

"You're crazy, Jake," he said. "This is on me."

"It's all on the office, anyway."

"Nope. I want to get it."

I waved goodbye. Krum put his head out. "See you at the lunch on Wednesday."

"You bet."

I went to the office in the elevator. Robert Cohn was waiting for me. "Hello, Jake," he said. "Going out to lunch?"

"Yes. Let me see if there is anything new."

"Where will we eat?"

"Anywhere."

I was looking over my desk. "Where do you want to eat?"

"How about Wetzel's? They've got good hors d'oeuvres."

In the restaurant we ordered hors d'oeuvres and beer. The sommelier brought the beer, tall, beaded on the outside of the steins, and cold. There were a dozen different dishes of hors d'oeuvres.

"Have any fun last night?" I asked.

"No. I don't think so."

"How's the writing going?"

"Rotten. I can't get this second book going."

"That happens to everybody."

"Oh, I'm sure of that. It gets me worried, though."

"Thought any more about going to South America?"

"I mean that."

"Well, why don't you start off?"

"Frances."

"Well," I said, "take her with you."

"She wouldn't like it. That isn't the sort of thing she likes. She likes a lot of people around."

"Tell her to go to hell."

"I can't. I've got certain obligations to her."

He shoved the sliced cucumbers away and took a pickled herring.

"What do you know about Lady Brett Ashley, Jake?"

"Her name's Lady Ashley. Brett's her own name. She's a nice girl," I said. "She's getting a divorce and she's going to marry Mike Campbell. He's over in Scotland now. Why?"

"She's a remarkably attractive woman."

"Isn't she."

"There's a certain quality about her, a certain fineness. She seems to be absolutely fine and straight."

"She's very nice."

"I don't know how to describe the quality," Cohn said. "I suppose it's breeding."

"You sound as though you liked her pretty well."

"I do. I shouldn't wonder if I were in love with her."

"She's a drunk," I said. "She's in love with Mike Campbell, and she's going to marry him. He's going to be rich as hell some day."

"I don't believe she'll ever marry him."

"Why not?"

"I don't know. I just don't believe it. Have you known her a long time?"

"Yes," I said. "She was a V.A.D. in a hospital I was in during the war."

"She must have been just a kid then."

"She's thirty-four now."

"When did she marry Ashley?"

"During the war. Her own true love had just kicked off with the dysentery."

"You talk sort of bitter."

"Sorry. I didn't mean to. I was just trying to give you the facts."

"I don't believe she would marry anybody she didn't love."

"Well," I said. "She's done it twice."

"I don't believe it."

"Well," I said, "don't ask me a lot of fool questions if you don't like the answers."

"I didn't ask you that."

"You asked me what I knew about Brett Ashley."

"I didn't ask you to insult her."

"Oh, go to hell."

He stood up from the table his face white, and stood there white and angry behind the little plates of hors d'oeuvres.

"Sit down," I said. "Don't be a fool."

"You've got to take that back."

"Oh, cut out the prep-school stuff."

"Take it back."

"Sure. Anything. I never heard of Brett Ashley. How's that?"

"No. Not that. About me going to hell."

"Oh, don't go to hell," I said. "Stick around. We're just starting lunch."

Cohn smiled again and sat down. He seemed glad to sit down. What the hell would he have done if he hadn't sat down? "You say such damned insulting things, Jake."

"I'm sorry. I've got a nasty tongue. I never mean it when I say nasty things."

"I know it," Cohn said. "You're really about the best friend I have, Jake."

God help you, I thought. "Forget what I said," I said out loud. "I'm sorry."

"It's all right. It's fine. I was just sore for a minute."

"Good. Let's get something else to eat."

After we finished the lunch we walked up to the Café de la Paix and had coffee. I could feel Cohn wanted to bring up Brett again, but I held him off it. We talked about one thing and another, and I left him to come to the office.

# CHAPTER SIX

AT FIVE o'clock I was in the Hotel Crillon waiting for Brett. She was not there, so I sat down and wrote some letters. They were not very good letters but I hoped their being on Crillon stationery would help them. Brett did not turn up, so about quarter to six I went down to the bar and had a Jack Rose with George the barman. Brett had not been in the bar either, and so I looked for her upstairs on my way out, and took a taxi to the Café Select. Crossing the Seine I saw a string of barges being towed empty down the current, riding high, the bargemen at the sweeps as they came toward the bridge. The river looked nice. It was always pleasant crossing bridges in Paris.

The taxi rounded the statue of the inventor of the semaphore engaged in doing same, and turned up the Boulevard Raspail, and I sat back to let that part of the ride pass. The Boulevard Raspail always made dull riding. It was like a certain stretch on the P.L.M. between Fontainebleau and Montereau that always made me feel bored and dead and dull until it was over. I suppose it is some association of ideas that makes those dead places in a journey. There are other streets in Paris as ugly as the Boulevard Raspail. It is a street I do not mind walking down at all. But I cannot stand to ride along it. Perhaps I had read something about it once. That was the way Robert Cohn was about all of Paris. I wondered where Cohn got that incapacity to enjoy

Paris. Possibly from Mencken. Mencken hates Paris, I believe. So many young men get their likes and dislikes from Mencken.

The taxi stopped in front of the Rotonde. No matter what café in Montparnasse you ask a taxi-driver to bring you to from the right bank of the river, they always take you to the Rotonde. Ten years from now it will probably be the Dome. It was near enough, anyway. I walked past the sad tables of the Rotonde to the Select. There were a few people inside at the bar, and outside, alone, sat Harvey Stone. He had a pile of saucers in front of him, and he needed a shave.

"Sit down," said Harvey, "I've been looking for you."

"What's the matter?"

"Nothing. Just looking for you."

"Been out to the races?"

"No. Not since Sunday."

"What do you hear from the States?"

"Nothing. Absolutely nothing."

"What's the matter?"

"I don't know. I'm through with them. I'm absolutely through with them."

He leaned forward and looked me in the eye.

"Do you want to know something, Jake?"

"Yes."

"I haven't had anything to eat for five days."

I figured rapidly back in my mind. It was three days ago that Harvey had won two hundred francs from me shaking poker dice in the New York Bar.

"What's the matter?"

"No money. Money hasn't come," he paused. "I tell you it's strange, Jake. When I'm like this I just want to be alone. I want to stay in my own room. I'm like a cat."

I felt in my pocket.

"Would a hundred help you any, Harvey?"

"Yes."

"Come on. Let's go and eat."

"There's no hurry. Have a drink."

"Better eat."

"No. When I get like this I don't care whether I eat or not."

We had a drink. Harvey added my saucer to his own pile.

"Do you know Mencken, Harvey?"

"Yes. Why?"

"What's he like?"

"He's all right. He says some pretty funny things. Last time I had dinner with him we talked about Hergesheimer. 'The trouble is,' he said, 'he's a garter snapper.' That's not bad."

"That's not bad."

"He's through now," Harvey went on. "He's written about all the things he knows, and now he's on all the things he doesn't know."

"I guess he's all right," I said. "I just can't read him."

"Oh, nobody reads him now," Harvey said, "except the people that used to read the Alexander Hamilton Institute."

"Well," I said. "That was a good thing, too."

"Sure," said Harvey. So we sat and thought deeply for a while.

"Have another port?"

"All right," said Harvey.

"There comes Cohn," I said. Robert Cohn was crossing the street.

"That moron," said Harvey. Cohn came up to our table.

"Hello, you bums," he said.

"Hello, Robert," Harvey said. "I was just telling Jake here that you're a moron."

"What do you mean?"

"Tell us right off. Don't think. What would you rather do if you could do anything you wanted?"

Cohn started to consider.

"Don't think. Bring it right out."

"I don't know," Cohn said. "What's it all about, anyway?"

"I mean what would you rather do. What comes into your head first. No matter how silly it is."

"I don't know," Cohn said. "I think I'd rather play football again with what I know about handling myself, now."

"I misjudged you," Harvey said. "You're not a moron. You're only a case of arrested development."

"You're awfully funny, Harvey," Cohn said. "Some day somebody will push your face in."

Harvey Stone laughed. "You think so. They won't, though. Because it wouldn't make any difference to me. I'm not a fighter."

"It would make a difference to you if anybody did it."

"No, it wouldn't. That's where you make your big mistake. Because you're not intelligent."

"Cut it out about me."

"Sure," said Harvey. "It doesn't make any difference to me. You don't mean anything to me."

"Come on, Harvey," I said. "Have another porto."

"No," he said. "I'm going up the street and eat. See you later, Jake."

He walked out and up the street. I watched him crossing the street through the taxis, small, heavy, slowly sure of himself in the traffic.

"He always gets me sore," Cohn said. "I can't stand him."

"I like him," I said. "I'm fond of him. You don't want to get sore at him."

"I know it," Cohn said. "He just gets on my nerves."

"Write this afternoon?"

"No. I couldn't get it going. It's harder to do than my first book. I'm having a hard time handling it."

The sort of healthy conceit that he had when he returned from America early in the spring was gone. Then he had been sure of his work, only with these personal longings for adventure. Now the sureness was gone. Somehow I feel I have not shown Robert Cohn clearly. The reason is that until he fell in love with Brett, I never heard him make one remark that would, in any way, detach him from other people. He was nice to watch on the tennis-court, he had a good body, and he kept it in shape; he handled his cards well at bridge, and he had a funny sort of undergraduate quality about him. If he were in a crowd nothing he said stood out. He wore what used to be called polo shirts at school, and may be called that still, but he was not professionally youthful. I do not believe he thought about his clothes much. Externally he had been formed at Princeton. Internally he had been molded by the two women who had trained him. He had a nice, boyish sort of cheerfulness that had never been trained out of him, and I probably have not brought it out. He loved to win at tennis. He probably loved to win as much as Lenglen, for instance. On the other hand, he was not angry at being beaten. When he fell in love with Brett his tennis game went all to pieces. People beat him who had never had a chance with him. He was very nice about it.

Anyhow, we were sitting on the terrace of the Café Select, and Harvey Stone had just crossed the street.

"Come on up to the Lilas," I said.

"I have a date."

"What time?"

"Frances is coming here at seven-fifteen."

"There she is."

Frances Clyne was coming toward us from across the street. She was a very tall girl who walked with a great deal of movement. She waved and smiled. We watched her cross the street.

"Hello," she said, "I'm so glad you're here, Jake. I've been wanting to talk to you."

"Hello, Frances," said Cohn. He smiled.

"Why, hello, Robert. Are you here?" She went on, talking rapidly. "I've had the darndest time. This one"—shaking her head at Cohn—"didn't come home for lunch."

"I wasn't supposed to."

"Oh, I know. But you didn't say anything about it to the cook. Then I had a date myself, and Paula wasn't at her office. I went to the Ritz and waited for her, and she never came, and of course I didn't have enough money to lunch at the Ritz."

"What did you do?"

"Oh, went out, of course." She spoke in a sort of imitation joyful manner. "I always keep my appointments. No one keeps theirs, nowadays. I ought to know better. How are you, Jake, anyway?"

"Fine."

"That was a fine girl you had at the dance, and then went off with that Brett one."

"Don't you like her?" Cohn asked.

"I think she's perfectly charming. Don't you?"

Cohn said nothing.

"Look, Jake. I want to talk with you. Would you come over

with me to the Dome? You'll stay here, won't you, Robert? Come on, Jake."

We crossed the Boulevard Montparnasse and sat down at a table. A boy came up with the *Paris Times*, and I bought one and opened it.

"What's the matter, Frances?"

"Oh, nothing," she said, "except that he wants to leave me."

"How do you mean?"

"Oh, he told everyone that we were going to be married, and I told my mother and everyone, and now he doesn't want to do it."

"What's the matter?"

"He's decided he hasn't lived enough. I knew it would happen when he went to New York."

She looked up, very bright-eyed and trying to talk inconsequentially.

"I wouldn't marry him if he doesn't want to. Of course I wouldn't. I wouldn't marry him now for anything. But it does seem to me to be a little late now, after we've waited three years, and I've just gotten my divorce."

I said nothing.

"We were going to celebrate so, and instead we've just had scenes. It's so childish. We have dreadful scenes, and he cries and begs me to be reasonable, but he says he just can't do it."

"It's rotten luck."

"I should say it is rotten luck. I've wasted two years and a half on him now. And I don't know now if any man will ever want to marry me. Two years ago I could have married anybody I wanted, down at Cannes. All the old ones that wanted to marry somebody chic and settle down were crazy about me. Now I don't think I could get anybody."

"Sure, you could marry anybody."

"No, I don't believe it. And I'm fond of him, too. And I'd like to have children. I always thought we'd have children."

She looked at me very brightly. "I never liked children much, but I don't want to think I'll never have them. I always thought I'd have them and then like them."

"He's got children."

"Oh, yes. He's got children, and he's got money, and he's got a rich mother, and he's written a book, and nobody will publish my stuff, nobody at all. It isn't bad, either. And I haven't got any money at all. I could have had alimony, but I got the divorce the quickest way."

She looked at me again very brightly.

"It isn't right. It's my own fault and it's not, too. I ought to have known better. And when I tell him he just cries and says he can't marry. Why can't he marry? I'd be a good wife. I'm easy to get along with. I leave him alone. It doesn't do any good."

"It's a rotten shame."

"Yes, it is a rotten shame. But there's no use talking about it, is there? Come on, let's go back to the café."

"And of course there isn't anything I can do."

"No. Just don't let him know I talked to you. I know what he wants." Now for the first time she dropped her bright, terribly cheerful manner. "He wants to go back to New York alone, and be there when his book comes out so when a lot of little chickens like it. That's what he wants."

"Maybe they won't like it. I don't think he's that way. Really."

"You don't know him like I do, Jake. That's what he wants to do. I know it. I know it. That's why he doesn't want to marry. He wants to have a big triumph this fall all by himself."

"Want to go back to the café?"

"Yes. Come on."

We got up from the table—they had never brought us a drink —and started across the street toward the Select, where Cohn sat smiling at us from behind the marble-topped table.

"Well, what are you smiling at?" Frances asked him. "Feel pretty happy?"

"I was smiling at you and Jake with your secrets."

"Oh, what I've told Jake isn't any secret. Everybody will know it soon enough. I only wanted to give Jake a decent version."

"What was it? About your going to England?"

"Yes, about my going to England. Oh, Jake! I forgot to tell you. I'm going to England."

"Isn't that fine!"

"Yes, that's the way it's done in the very best families. Robert's sending me. He's going to give me two hundred pounds and then I'm going to visit friends. Won't it be lovely? The friends don't know about it, yet."

She turned to Cohn and smiled at him. He was not smiling now.

"You were only going to give me a hundred pounds, weren't you, Robert? But I made him give me two hundred. He's really very generous. Aren't you, Robert?"

I do not know how people could say such terrible things to Robert Cohn. There are people to whom you could not say insulting things. They give you a feeling that the world would be destroyed, would actually be destroyed before your eyes, if you said certain things. But here was Cohn taking it all. Here it was, all going on right before me, and I did not even feel an impulse to try and stop it. And this was friendly joking to what went on later.

"How can you say such things, Frances?" Cohn interrupted.

"Listen to him. I'm going to England. I'm going to visit friends. Ever visit friends that didn't want you? Oh, they'll have to take me, all right. 'How do you do, my dear? Such a long time since we've seen you. And how is your dear mother?' Yes, how is my dear mother? She put all her money into French war bonds. Yes, she did. Probably the only person in the world that did. 'And what about Robert?' or else very careful talking around Robert. 'You must be most careful not to mention him, my dear. Poor Frances has had a most unfortunate experience.' Won't it be fun, Robert? Don't you think it will be fun, Jake?"

She turned to me with that terribly bright smile. It was very satisfactory to her to have an audience for this.

"And where are you going to be, Robert? It's my own fault, all right. Perfectly my own fault. When I made you get rid of your little secretary on the magazine I ought to have known you'd get rid of me the same way. Jake doesn't know about that. Should I tell him?"

"Shut up, Frances, for God's sake."

"Yes, I'll tell him. Robert had a little secretary on the magazine. Just the sweetest little thing in the world, and he thought she was wonderful, and then I came along and he thought I was pretty wonderful, too. So I made him get rid of her, and he had brought her to Provincetown from Carmel when he moved the magazine, and he didn't even pay her fare back to the coast. All to please me. He thought I was pretty fine, then. Didn't you, Robert?

"You mustn't misunderstand, Jake, it was absolutely platonic with the secretary. Not even platonic. Nothing at all, really. It was just that she was so nice. And he did that just to please me. Well, I suppose that we that live by the sword shall perish by the sword. Isn't that literary, though? You want to remember that for your next book, Robert.

"You know Robert is going to get material for a new book. Aren't you, Robert? That's why he's leaving me. He's decided I don't film well. You see, he was so busy all the time that we were living together, writing on this book, that he doesn't remember anything about us. So now he's going out and get some new material. Well, I hope he gets something frightfully interesting.

"Listen, Robert, dear. Let me tell you something. You won't mind, will you? Don't have scenes with your young ladies. Try not to. Because you can't have scenes without crying, and then you pity yourself so much you can't remember what the other person's said. You'll never be able to remember any conversations that way. Just try and be calm. I know it's awfully hard. But remember, it's for literature. We all ought to make sacrifices for literature. Look at me. I'm going to England without a protest. All for literature. We must all help young writers. Don't you think so, Jake? But you're not a young writer. Are you, Robert? You're thirty-four. Still, I suppose that is young for a great writer. Look at Hardy. Look at Anatole France. He just died a little while ago. Robert doesn't think he's any good, though. Some of his French friends told him. He doesn't read French very well himself. He wasn't a good writer like you are, was he, Robert? Do you think he ever had to go and look for material? What do you suppose he said to his mistresses when he wouldn't marry them? I wonder if he cried, too? Oh, I've just thought of something." She put her gloved hand up to her lips. "I know the real reason why Robert won't marry me, Jake. It's just come to me. They've sent it to me in a vision in the Café Select. Isn't it mystic? Someday they'll put a tablet up. Like at Lourdes. Do you want to hear, Robert? I'll tell you. It's so simple. I wonder why I never thought about it. Why, you see, Robert's always wanted to have a mistress, and if he doesn't marry me, why, then he's had one. She was his mistress for over two years. See how it is? And if he marries me, like he's always promised he would, that would be the end of all the romance. Don't you think that's bright of me to figure that out? It's true, too. Look at him and see if it's not. Where are you going, Jake?"

"I've got to go in and see Harvey Stone a minute."

Cohn looked up as I went in. His face was white. Why did he sit there? Why did he keep on taking it like that?

As I stood against the bar looking out I could see them through the window. Frances was talking on to him, smiling brightly, looking into his face each time she asked: "Isn't it so, Robert?" Or maybe she did not ask that now. Perhaps she said something else. I told the barman I did not want anything to drink and went out through the side door. As I went out the door I looked back through the two thicknesses of glass and saw them sitting there. She was still talking to him. I went down a side street to the Boulevard Raspail. A taxi came along and I got in and gave the driver the address of my flat.

## CHAPTER SEVEN

$\text{A}$s I started up the stairs the concierge knocked on the glass of the door of her lodge, and as I stopped she came out. She had some letters and a telegram.

"Here is the post. And there was a lady here to see you."

"Did she leave a card?"

"No. She was with a gentleman. It was the one who was here last night. In the end I find she is very nice."

"Was she with a friend of mine?"

"I don't know. He was never here before. He was very large. Very, very large. She was very nice. Very, very nice. Last night she was, perhaps, a little—" She put her head on one hand and rocked it up and down. "I'll speak perfectly frankly, Monsieur Barnes. Last night I found her not so gentille. Last night I formed another idea of her. But listen to what I tell you. She is très, très gentille. She is of very good family. It is a thing you can see."

"They did not leave any word?"

"Yes. They said they would be back in an hour."

"Send them up when they come."

"Yes, Monsieur Barnes. And that lady, that lady there is someone. An eccentric, perhaps, but quelqu'une, quelqu'une!"

The concierge, before she became a concierge, had owned a drink-selling concession at the Paris race-courses. Her life-work lay in the pelouse, but she kept an eye on the people

of the pesage, and she took great pride in telling me which
of my guests were well brought up, which were of good family, who were sportsmen, a French word pronounced with the
accent on the men. The only trouble was that people who did
not fall into any of those three categories were very liable to be
told there was no one home, chez Barnes. One of my friends,
an extremely underfed-looking painter, who was obviously to
Madame Duzinell neither well brought up, of good family, nor
a sportsman, wrote me a letter asking if I could get him a pass
to get by the concierge so he could come up and see me occa-
sionally in the evenings.

I went up to the flat wondering what Brett had done to the
concierge. The wire was a cable from Bill Gorton, saying he
was arriving on the *France*. I put the mail on the table, went
back to the bedroom, undressed and had a shower. I was rubbing down when I heard the door-bell pull. I put on a bathrobe
and slippers and went to the door. It was Brett. Back of her was
the count. He was holding a great bunch of roses.

"Hello, darling," said Brett. "Aren't you going to let us in?"

"Come on. I was just bathing."

"Aren't you the fortunate man. Bathing."

"Only a shower. Sit down, Count Mippipopolous. What will
you drink?"

"I don't know whether you like flowers, sir," the count said,
"but I took the liberty of just bringing these roses."

"Here, give them to me." Brett took them. "Get me some
water in this, Jake." I filled the big earthenware jug with water
in the kitchen, and Brett put the roses in it, and placed them
in the center of the dining-room table.

"I say. We have had a day."

"You don't remember anything about a date with me at the Crillon?"

"No. Did we have one? I must have been blind."

"You were quite drunk, my dear," said the count.

"Wasn't I, though? And the count's been a brick, absolutely."

"You've got hell's own drag with the concierge now."

"I ought to have. Gave her two hundred francs."

"Don't be a damned fool."

"His," she said, and nodded at the count.

"I thought we ought to give her a little something for last night. It was very late."

"He's wonderful," Brett said. "He remembers everything that's happened."

"So do you, my dear."

"Fancy," said Brett. "Who'd want to. I say, Jake, do we get a drink?"

"You get it while I go in and dress. You know where it is."

"Rather."

While I dressed I heard Brett put down glasses and then a siphon, and then heard them talking. I dressed slowly, sitting on the bed. I felt tired and pretty rotten. Brett came in the room, a glass in her hand, and sat on the bed.

"What's the matter, darling? Do you feel rocky?"

She kissed me coolly on the forehead.

"Oh, Brett, I love you so much."

"Darling," she said. Then: "Do you want me to send him away?"

"No. He's nice."

"I'll send him away."

"No, don't."

"Yes, I'll send him away."

"You can't just like that."

"Can't I, though? You stay here. He's mad about me, I tell you."

She was gone out of the room. I lay face down on the bed. I was having a bad time. I heard them talking but I did not listen. Brett came in and sat on the bed.

"Poor old darling." She stroked my head.

"What did you say to him?" I was lying with my face away from her. I did not want to see her.

"Sent him for champagne. He loves to go for champagne."

Then later: "Do you feel better, darling? Is the head any better?"

"It's better."

"Lie quiet. He's gone to the other side of town."

"Couldn't we live together, Brett? Couldn't we just live together?"

"I don't think so. I'd just *tromper* you with everybody. You couldn't stand it."

"I stand it now."

"That would be different. It's my fault, Jake. It's the way I'm made."

"Couldn't we go off in the country for a while?"

"It wouldn't be any good. I'll go if you like. But I couldn't live quietly in the country. Not with my own true love."

"I know."

"Isn't it rotten? There isn't any use my telling you I love you."

"You know I love you."

"Let's not talk. Talking's all bilge. I'm going away from you, and then Michael's coming back."

"Why are you going away?"

"Better for you. Better for me."

"When are you going?"

"Soon as I can."

"Where?"

"San Sebastian."

"Can't we go together?"

"No. That would be a hell of an idea after we'd just talked it out."

"We never agreed."

"Oh, you know as well as I do. Don't be obstinate, darling."

"Oh, sure," I said. "I know you're right. I'm just low, and when I'm low I talk like a fool."

I sat up, leaned over, found my shoes beside the bed and put them on. I stood up.

"Don't look like that, darling."

"How do you want me to look?"

"Oh, don't be a fool. I'm going away tomorrow."

"Tomorrow?"

"Yes. Didn't I say so? I am."

"Let's have a drink, then. The count will be back."

"Yes. He should be back. You know he's extraordinary about buying champagne. It means any amount to him."

We went into the dining-room. I took up the brandy bottle and poured Brett a drink and one for myself. There was a ring at the bell-pull. I went to the door and there was the count. Behind him was the chauffeur carrying a basket of champagne.

"Where should I have him put it, sir?" asked the count.

"In the kitchen," Brett said.

"Put it in there, Henry," the count motioned. "Now go down and get the ice." He stood looking after the basket inside the kitchen door. "I think you'll find that's very good wine," he said.

"I know we don't get much of a chance to judge good wine in the States now, but I got this from a friend of mine that's in the business."

"Oh, you always have someone in the trade," Brett said.

"This fellow raises the grapes. He's got thousands of acres of them."

"What's his name?" asked Brett. "Veuve Cliquot?"

"No," said the count. "Mumms. He's a baron."

"Isn't it wonderful," said Brett. "We all have titles. Why haven't you a title, Jake?"

"I assure you, sir," the count put his hand on my arm. "It never does a man any good. Most of the time it costs you money."

"Oh, I don't know. It's damned useful sometimes," Brett said.

"I've never known it to do me any good."

"You haven't used it properly. I've had hell's own amount of credit on mine."

"Do sit down, count," I said. "Let me take that stick."

The count was looking at Brett across the table under the gas-light. She was smoking a cigarette and flicking the ashes on the rug. She saw me notice it.

"I say, Jake, I don't want to ruin your rugs. Can't you give a chap an ash-tray?"

I found some ash-trays and spread them around. The chauffeur came up with a bucket full of salted ice. "Put two bottles in it, Henry," the count called.

"Anything else, sir?"

"No. Wait down in the car." He turned to Brett and to me. "We'll want to ride out to the Bois for dinner?"

"If you like," Brett said. "I couldn't eat a thing."

"I always like a good meal," said the count.

"Should I bring the wine in, sir?" asked the chauffeur.

"Yes. Bring it in, Henry," said the count. He took out a heavy pigskin cigar-case and offered it to me. "Like to try a real American cigar?"

"Thanks," I said. "I'll finish the cigarette."

He cut off the end of his cigar with a gold cutter he wore on one end of his watch-chain.

"I like a cigar to really draw," said the count. "Half the cigars you smoke don't draw."

He lit the cigar, puffed at it, looking across the table at Brett. "And when you're divorced, Lady Ashley, then you won't have a title."

"No. What a pity."

"No," said the count. "You don't need a title. You got class all over you."

"Thanks. Awfully decent of you."

"I'm not joking you," the count blew a cloud of smoke. "You got the most class of anybody I ever seen. You got it. That's all."

"Nice of you," said Brett. "Mummy would be pleased. Couldn't you write it out, and I'll send it in a letter to her."

"I'd tell her, too," said the count. "I'm not joking you. I never joke people. Joke people and you make enemies. That's what I always say."

"You're right," Brett said. "You're terribly right. I always joke people and I haven't a friend in the world. Except Jake here."

"You don't joke him."

"That's it."

"Do you now?" asked the count. "Do you joke him?"

Brett looked at me and wrinkled up the corners of her eyes.

"No," she said. "I wouldn't joke him."

"See," said the count. "You don't joke him."

"This is a hell of a dull talk," Brett said. "How about some of that champagne?"

The count reached down and twirled the bottles in the shiny bucket. "It isn't cold, yet. You're always drinking, my dear. Why don't you just talk?"

"I've talked too ruddy much. I've talked myself all out to Jake."

"I should like to hear you really talk, my dear. When you talk to me you never finish your sentences at all."

"Leave 'em for you to finish. Let anyone finish them as they like."

"It is a very interesting system," the count reached down and gave the bottles a twirl. "Still I would like to hear you talk some time."

"Isn't he a fool?" Brett asked.

"Now," the count brought up a bottle. "I think this is cool."

I brought a towel and he wiped the bottle dry and held it up. "I like to drink champagne from magnums. The wine is better but it would have been too hard to cool." He held the bottle, looking at it. I put out the glasses.

"I say. You might open it," Brett suggested.

"Yes, my dear. Now I'll open it."

It was amazing champagne.

"I say that is wine," Brett held up her glass. "We ought to toast something. Here's to royalty."

"This wine is too good for toast-drinking, my dear. You don't want to mix emotions up with a wine like that. You lose the taste."

Brett's glass was empty.

"You ought to write a book on wines, count," I said.

"Mr. Barnes," answered the count, "all I want out of wines is to enjoy them."

"Let's enjoy a little more of this," Brett pushed her glass forward. The count poured very carefully. "There, my dear. Now you enjoy that slowly, and then you can get drunk."

"Drunk? Drunk?"

"My dear, you are charming when you are drunk."

"Listen to the man."

"Mr. Barnes," the count poured my glass full. "She is the only lady I have ever known who was as charming when she was drunk as when she was sober."

"You haven't been around much, have you?"

"Yes, my dear. I have been around very much. I have been around a very great deal."

"Drink your wine," said Brett. "We've all been around. I dare say Jake here has seen as much as you have."

"My dear, I am sure Mr. Barnes has seen a lot. Don't think I don't think so, sir. I have seen a lot, too."

"Of course you have, my dear," Brett said. "I was only ragging."

"I have been in seven wars and four revolutions," the count said.

"Soldiering?" Brett asked.

"Sometimes, my dear. And I have got arrow wounds. Have you ever seen arrow wounds?"

"Let's have a look at them."

The count stood up, unbuttoned his vest, and opened his shirt. He pulled up the undershirt onto his chest and stood, his chest black, and big stomach muscles bulging under the light.

"You see them?"

Below the line where his ribs stopped were two raised white welts. "See on the back where they come out." Above the small of the back were the same two scars, raised as thick as a finger.

"I say. Those are something."

"Clean through."

The count was tucking in his shirt.

"Where did you get those?" I asked.

"In Abyssinia. When I was twenty-one years old."

"What were you doing?" asked Brett. "Were you in the army?"

"I was on a business trip, my dear."

"I told you he was one of us. Didn't I?" Brett turned to me. "I love you, count. You're a darling."

"You make me very happy, my dear. But it isn't true."

"Don't be an ass."

"You see, Mr. Barnes, it is because I have lived very much that now I can enjoy everything so well. Don't you find it like that?"

"Yes. Absolutely."

"I know," said the count. "That is the secret. You must get to know the values."

"Doesn't anything ever happen to your values?" Brett asked.

"No. Not any more."

"Never fall in love?"

"Always," said the count. "I am always in love."

"What does that do to your values?"

"That, too, has got a place in my values."

"You haven't any values. You're dead, that's all."

"No, my dear. You're not right. I'm not dead at all."

We drank three bottles of the champagne and the count left the basket in my kitchen. We dined at a restaurant in the Bois. It was a good dinner. Food had an excellent place in the count's values. So did wine. The count was in fine form during the meal. So was Brett. It was a good party.

"Where would you like to go?" asked the count after dinner. We were the only people left in the restaurant. The two waiters were standing over against the door. They wanted to go home.

"We might go up on the hill," Brett said. "Haven't we had a splendid party?"

The count was beaming. He was very happy.

"You are very nice people," he said. He was smoking a cigar again. "Why don't you get married, you two?"

"We want to lead our own lives," I said.

"We have our careers," Brett said. "Come on. Let's get out of this."

"Have another brandy," the count said.

"Get it on the hill."

"No. Have it here where it is quiet."

"You and your quiet," said Brett. "What is it men feel about quiet?"

"We like it," said the count. "Like you like noise, my dear."

"All right," said Brett. "Let's have one."

"Sommelier!" the count called.

"Yes, sir."

"What is the oldest brandy you have?"

"Eighteen eleven, sir."

"Bring us a bottle."

"I say. Don't be ostentatious. Call him off, Jake."

"Listen, my dear. I get more value for my money in old brandy than in any other antiquities."

"Got many antiquities?"

"I got a houseful."

Finally we went up to Montmartre. Inside Zelli's it was

crowded, smoky, and noisy. The music hit you as you went in. Brett and I danced. It was so crowded we could barely move. The nigger drummer waved at Brett. We were caught in the jam, dancing in one place in front of him.

"Hahre you?"

"Great."

"Thaats good."

He was all teeth and lips.

"He's a great friend of mine," Brett said. "Damn good drummer."

The music stopped and we started toward the table where the count sat. Then the music started again and we danced. I looked at the count. He was sitting at the table smoking a cigar. The music stopped again.

"Let's go over."

Brett started toward the table. The music started and again we danced, tight in the crowd.

"You are a rotten dancer, Jake. Michael's the best dancer I know."

"He's splendid."

"He's got his points."

"I like him," I said. "I'm damned fond of him."

"I'm going to marry him," Brett said. "Funny. I haven't thought about him for a week."

"Don't you write him?"

"Not I. Never write letters."

"I'll bet he writes to you."

"Rather. Damned good letters, too."

"When are you going to get married?"

"How do I know? As soon as we can get the divorce. Michael's trying to get his mother to put up for it."

"Could I help you?"

"Don't be an ass. Michael's people have loads of money."

The music stopped. We walked over to the table. The count stood up.

"Very nice," he said. "You looked very, very nice."

"Don't you dance, count?" I asked.

"No. I'm too old."

"Oh, come off it," Brett said.

"My dear, I would do it if I would enjoy it. I enjoy to watch you dance."

"Splendid," Brett said. "I'll dance again for you sometime. I say. What about your little friend, Zizi?"

"Let me tell you. I support that boy, but I don't want to have him around."

"He is rather hard."

"You know I think that boy's got a future. But personally I don't want him around."

"Jake's rather the same way."

"He gives me the willys."

"Well," the count shrugged his shoulders. "About his future you can't ever tell. Anyhow, his father was a great friend of my father."

"Come on. Let's dance," Brett said.

We danced. It was crowded and close.

"Oh, darling," Brett said, "I'm so miserable."

I had that feeling of going through something that has all happened before. "You were happy a minute ago."

The drummer shouted: "You can't two time——"

"It's all gone."

"What's the matter?"

"I don't know. I just feel terribly."

". . . . . ." the drummer chanted. Then turned to his sticks.

"Want to go?"

I had the feeling as in a nightmare of it all being something repeated, something I had been through and that now I must go through again.

". . . . . ." the drummer sang softly.

"Let's go," said Brett. "You don't mind."

". . . . . ." the drummer shouted and grinned at Brett.

"All right," I said. We got out from the crowd. Brett went to the dressing-room.

"Brett wants to go," I said to the count. He nodded. "Does she? That's fine. You take the car. I'm going to stay here for a while, Mr. Barnes."

We shook hands.

"It was a wonderful time," I said. "I wish you would let me get this." I took a note out of my pocket.

"Mr. Barnes, don't be ridiculous," the count said.

Brett came over with her wrap on. She kissed the count and put her hand on his shoulder to keep him from standing up. As we went out the door I looked back and there were three girls at his table. We got into the big car. Brett gave the chauffeur the address of her hotel.

"No, don't come up," she said at the hotel. She had rung and the door was unlatched.

"Really?"

"No. Please."

"Good night, Brett," I said. "I'm sorry you feel rotten."

"Good night, Jake. Good night, darling. I won't see you again." We kissed standing at the door. She pushed me away. We kissed again. "Oh, don't!" Brett said.

She turned quickly and went into the hotel. The chauffeur

drove me around to my flat. I gave him twenty francs and he touched his cap and said, "Good night, sir," and drove off. I rang the bell. The door opened and I went upstairs and went to bed.

# BOOK TWO

## CHAPTER EIGHT

I DID NOT see Brett again until she came back from San Sebastian. One card came from her from there. It had a picture of the Concha, and said: "Darling. Very quiet and healthy. Love to all the chaps. Brett."

Nor did I see Robert Cohn again. I heard Frances had left for England and I had a note from Cohn saying he was going out in the country for a couple of weeks, he did not know where, but that he wanted to hold me to the fishing-trip in Spain we had talked about last winter. I could reach him always, he wrote, through his bankers.

Brett was gone, I was not bothered by Cohn's troubles, I rather enjoyed not having to play tennis, there was plenty of work to do, I went often to the races, dined with friends, and put in some extra time at the office getting things ahead so I could leave it in charge of my secretary when Bill Gorton and I should shove off to Spain the end of June. Bill Gorton arrived, put up a couple of days at the flat and went off to Vienna. He was very cheerful and said the States were wonderful. New York was wonderful. There had been a grand theatrical season and a whole crop of great young light heavyweights. Any one of them was a good prospect to grow up, put on weight and trim Dempsey. Bill was very happy. He had made a lot of money on his last book, and was going to make a lot more. We had a good time while he was in Paris, and then he went off to Vienna. He was coming back in three weeks and we would leave for Spain to get in some fishing and go to the fiesta at Pamplona. He wrote that Vienna was wonderful. Then a card from Budapest: "Jake, Budapest is wonderful." Then I got a wire: "Back on Monday."

Monday evening he turned up at the flat. I heard his taxi stop and went to the window and called to him; he waved and started upstairs carrying his bags. I met him on the stairs, and took one of the bags.

"Well," I said, "I hear you had a wonderful trip."

"Wonderful," he said. "Budapest is absolutely wonderful."

"How about Vienna?"

"Not so good, Jake. Not so good. It seemed better than it was."

"How do you mean?" I was getting glasses and a syphon.

"Tight, Jake. I was tight."

"That's strange. Better have a drink."

Bill rubbed his forehead. "Remarkable thing," he said. "Don't know how it happened. Suddenly it happened."

"Last long?"

"Four days, Jake. Lasted just four days."

"Where did you go?"

"Don't remember. Wrote you a postcard. Remember that perfectly."

"Do anything else?"

"Not so sure. Possible."

"Go on. Tell me about it."

"Can't remember. Tell you anything I could remember."

"Go on. Take that drink and remember."

"Might remember a little," Bill said. "Remember something

about a prize-fight. Enormous Vienna prize-fight. Had a nigger in it. Remember the nigger perfectly."

"Go on."

"Wonderful nigger. Looked like Tiger Flowers, only four times as big. All of a sudden everybody started to throw things. Not me. Nigger'd just knocked local boy down. Nigger put up his glove. Wanted to make a speech. Awful noble-looking nigger. Started to make a speech. Then local white boy hit him. Then he knocked white boy cold. Then everybody commenced to throw chairs. Nigger went home with us in our car. Couldn't get his clothes. Wore my coat. Remember the whole thing now. Big sporting evening."

"What happened?"

"Loaned the nigger some clothes and went around with him to try and get his money. Claimed nigger owed them money on account of wrecking hall. Wonder who translated? Was it me?"

"Probably it wasn't you."

"You're right. Wasn't me at all. Was another fellow. Think we called him the local Harvard man. Remember him now. Studying music."

"How'd you come out?"

"Not so good, Jake. Injustice everywhere. Promoter claimed nigger promised let local boy stay. Claimed nigger violated contract. Can't knock out Vienna boy in Vienna. 'My God, Mister Gorton,' said nigger, 'I didn't do nothing in there for forty minutes but try and let him stay. That white boy musta ruptured himself swinging at me. I never did hit him.'"

"Did you get any money?"

"No money, Jake. All we could get was nigger's clothes. Somebody took his watch, too. Splendid nigger. Big mistake to have come to Vienna. Not so good, Jake. Not so good."

"What became of the nigger?"

"Went back to Cologne. Lives there. Married. Got a family. Going to write me a letter and send me the money I loaned him. Wonderful nigger. Hope I gave him the right address."

"You probably did."

"Well, anyway, let's eat," said Bill. "Unless you want me to tell you some more travel stories."

"Go on."

"Let's eat."

We went downstairs and out onto the Boulevard St. Michel in the warm June evening.

"Where will we go?"

"Want to eat on the island?"

"Sure."

We walked down the Boulevard. At the juncture of the Rue Denfert-Rochereau with the Boulevard is a statue of two men in flowing robes.

"I know who they are." Bill eyed the monument. "Gentlemen who invented pharmacy. Don't try and fool me on Paris."

We went on.

"Here's a taxidermist's," Bill said. "Want to buy anything? Nice stuffed dog?"

"Come on," I said. "You're pie-eyed."

"Pretty nice stuffed dogs," Bill said. "Certainly brighten up your flat."

"Come on."

"Just one stuffed dog. I can take 'em or leave 'em alone. But listen, Jake. Just one stuffed dog."

"Come on."

"Mean everything in the world to you after you bought it.

Simple exchange of values. You give them money. They give you a stuffed dog."

"We'll get one on the way back."

"All right. Have it your own way. Road to hell paved with unbought stuffed dogs. Not my fault."

We went on.

"How'd you feel that way about dogs so sudden?"

"Always felt that way about dogs. Always been a great lover of stuffed animals."

We stopped and had a drink.

"Certainly like to drink," Bill said. "You ought to try it sometimes, Jake."

"You're about a hundred and forty-four ahead of me."

"Ought not to daunt you. Never be daunted. Secret of my success. Never been daunted. Never been daunted in public."

"Where were you drinking?"

"Stopped at the Crillon. George made me a couple of Jack Roses. George's a great man. Know the secret of his success? Never been daunted."

"You'll be daunted after about three more Pernods."

"Not in public. If I begin to feel daunted I'll go off by myself. I'm like a cat that way."

"When did you see Harvey Stone?"

"At the Crillon. Harvey was just a little daunted. Hadn't eaten for three days. Doesn't eat any more. Just goes off like a cat. Pretty sad."

"He's all right."

"Splendid. Wish he wouldn't keep going off like a cat, though. Makes me nervous."

"What'll we do tonight?"

"Doesn't make any difference. Only let's not get daunted. Suppose they got any hard-boiled eggs here? If they had hard-boiled eggs here we wouldn't have to go all the way down to the island to eat."

"Nix," I said. "We're going to have a regular meal."

"Just a suggestion," said Bill. "Want to start now?"

"Come on."

We started on again down the Boulevard. A horse-cab passed us. Bill looked at it.

"See that horse-cab? Going to have that horse-cab stuffed for you for Christmas. Going to give all my friends stuffed animals. I'm a nature writer."

A taxi passed, someone in it waved, then banged for the driver to stop. The taxi backed up to the curb. In it was Brett.

"Beautiful lady," said Bill. "Going to kidnap us."

"Hullo!" Brett said. "Hullo!"

"This is Bill Gorton. Lady Ashley."

Brett smiled at Bill. "I say I'm just back. Haven't bathed even. Michael comes in tonight."

"Good. Come on and eat with us, and we'll all go to meet him."

"Must clean myself."

"Oh, rot! Come on."

"Must bathe. He doesn't get in till nine."

"Come and have a drink, then, before you bathe."

"Might do that. Now you're not talking rot."

We got in the taxi. The driver looked around.

"Stop at the nearest bistro," I said.

"We might as well go to the Closerie," Brett said. "I can't drink these rotten brandies."

"Closerie des Lilas."

Brett turned to Bill.

"Have you been in this pestilential city long?"

"Just got in today from Budapest."

"How was Budapest?"

"Wonderful. Budapest was wonderful."

"Ask him about Vienna."

"Vienna," said Bill, "is a strange city."

"Very much like Paris," Brett smiled at him, wrinkling the corners of her eyes.

"Exactly," Bill said. "Very much like Paris at this moment."

"You *have* a good start."

Sitting out on the terrasse of the Lilas Brett ordered a whiskey and soda, I took one, too, and Bill took another Pernod.

"How are you, Jake?"

"Great," I said. "I've had a good time."

Brett looked at me. "I was a fool to go away," she said. "One's an ass to leave Paris."

"Did you have a good time?"

"Oh, all right. Interesting. Not frightfully amusing."

"See anybody?"

"No, hardly anybody. I never went out."

"Didn't you swim?"

"No. Didn't do a thing."

"Sounds like Vienna," Bill said.

Brett wrinkled up the corners of her eyes at him.

"So that's the way it was in Vienna."

"It was like everything in Vienna."

Brett smiled at him again.

"You've a nice friend, Jake."

"He's all right," I said. "He's a taxidermist."

"That was in another country," Bill said. "And besides all the animals were dead."

"One more," Brett said, "and I must run. Do send the waiter for a taxi."

"There's a line of them. Right out in front."

"Good."

We had the drink and put Brett into her taxi.

"Mind you're at the Select around ten. Make him come. Michael will be there."

"We'll be there," Bill said. The taxi started and Brett waved.

"Quite a girl," Bill said. "She's damned nice. Who's Michael?"

"The man she's going to marry."

"Well, well," Bill said. "That's always just the stage I meet anybody. What'll I send them? Think they'd like a couple of stuffed race-horses?"

"We better eat."

"Is she really Lady something or other?" Bill asked in the taxi on our way down to the Ile Saint Louis.

"Oh, yes. In the stud-book and everything."

"Well, well."

We ate dinner at Madame Lecomte's restaurant on the far side of the island. It was crowded with Americans and we had to stand up and wait for a place. Someone had put it in the American Women's Club list as a quaint restaurant on the Paris quais as yet untouched by Americans, so we had to wait forty-five minutes for a table. Bill had eaten at the restaurant in 1918, and right after the armistice, and Madame Lecomte made a great fuss over seeing him.

"Doesn't get us a table, though," Bill said. "Grand woman, though."

We had a good meal, a roast chicken, new green beans, mashed potatoes, a salad, and some apple pie and cheese.

"You've got the world here all right," Bill said to Madame Lecomte. She raised her hand. "Oh, my God!"

"You'll be rich."

"I hope so."

After the coffee and a *fine* we got the bill, chalked up the same as ever on a slate, that was doubtless one of the "quaint" features, paid it, shook hands, and went out.

"You never come here anymore, Monsieur Barnes," Madame Lecomte said.

"Too many compatriots."

"Come at lunch-time. It's not crowded then."

"Good. I'll be down soon."

We walked along under the trees that grew out over the river on the Quai d'Orléans side of the island. Across the river were the broken walls of old houses that were being torn down.

"They're going to cut a street through."

"They would," Bill said.

We walked on and circled the island. The river was dark and a bateau mouche went by, all bright with lights, going fast and quiet up and out of sight under the bridge. Down the river was Notre Dame squatting against the night sky. We crossed to the left bank of the Seine by the wooden foot-bridge from the Quai de Bethune, and stopped on the bridge and looked down the river at Notre Dame. Standing on the bridge the island looked dark, the houses were high against the sky, and the trees were shadows.

"It's pretty grand," Bill said. "God, I love to get back."

We leaned on the wooden rail of the bridge and looked up the river to the lights of the big bridges. Below the water was smooth and black. It made no sound against the piles of the bridge. A man and a girl passed us. They were walking with their arms around each other.

We crossed the bridge and walked up the Rue du Cardinal Lemoine. It was steep walking, and we went all the way up to the Place Contrescarpe. The arc-light shone through the leaves of the trees in the square, and underneath the trees was an S bus ready to start. Music came out of the door of the Negre Joyeux. Through the window of the Café Aux Amateurs I saw the long zinc bar. Outside on the terrasse working people were drinking. In the open kitchen of the Amateurs a girl was cooking potato-chips in oil. There was an iron pot of stew. The girl ladled some onto a plate for an old man who stood holding a bottle of red wine in one hand.

"Want to have a drink?"

"No," said Bill. "I don't need it."

We turned to the right off the Place Contrescarpe, walking along smooth narrow streets with high old houses on both sides. Some of the houses jutted out toward the street. Others were cut back. We came onto the Rue du Pot de Fer and followed it along until it brought us to the rigid north and south of the Rue Saint Jacques and then walked south, past Val de Grâce, set back behind the courtyard and the iron fence, to the Boulevard du Port Royal.

"What do you want to do?" I asked. "Go up to the café and see Brett and Mike?"

"Why not."

We walked along Port Royal until it became Montparnasse, and then on past the Lilas, Lavigne's, and all the little cafés, Damoy's, crossed the street to the Rotonde, past its lights and tables to the Select.

Michael came toward us from the tables. He was tanned and healthy-looking.

"Hel-lo, Jake," he said. "Hel-lo! Hel-lo! How are you, old lad?"

"You look very fit, Mike."

"Oh, I am, I'm frightfully fit. I've done nothing but walk. Walk all day long. One drink a day with my mother at tea."

Bill had gone in to the bar. He was standing talking with Brett, who was sitting on a high stool, her legs crossed. She had no stockings on.

"It's good to see you, Jake," Michael said. "I'm a little tight, you know. Amazing, isn't it. Did you see my nose?"

There was a patch of dried blood on the bridge of his nose.

"An old lady's bags did that," Mike said. "I reached up to help her with them and they fell on me."

Brett gestured at him from the bar with her cigarette-holder and wrinkled the corners of her eyes.

"An old lady," said Mike. "Her bags *fell* on me.

"Let's go in and see Brett. I say, she is a piece. You *are* a lovely lady, Brett. Where did you get that hat?"

"Chap bought it for me. Don't you like it?"

"It's a dreadful hat. Do get a good hat."

"Oh, we've so much money now," Brett said. "I say, haven't you met Bill yet? You *are* a lovely host, Jake."

She turned to Mike. "This is Bill Gorton. This drunkard is Mike Campbell. Mr. Campbell is an undischarged bankrupt."

"Aren't I, though. You know I met my ex-partner yesterday in London. Chap who did me in."

"What did he say?"

"Bought me a drink. I thought I might as well take it. I say, Brett, you *are* a lovely piece. Don't you think she's beautiful?"

"Beautiful. With this nose?"

"It's a lovely nose. Go on, point it at me. Isn't she a lovely piece?"

"Couldn't we have kept the man in Scotland?"

"I say, Brett, let's turn in early."

"Don't be indecent, Michael. Remember there are ladies at this bar."

"Isn't she a lovely piece? Don't you think so, Jake?"

"There's a fight tonight," Bill said. "Like to go?"

"Fight," said Mike. "Who's fighting?"

"Ledoux and somebody."

"He's very good, Ledoux," Mike said. "I'd like to see it, rather" —he was making an effort to pull himself together—"but I can't go. I have a date with this thing here. I say, Brett, do get a new hat."

Brett pulled the felt hat down far over one eye and smiled out from under it. "You two run along to the fight. I'll have to be taking Mr. Campbell home directly."

"I'm not tight," Mike said. "Perhaps just a little. I say, Brett, you are a lovely piece."

"Go on to the fight," Brett said. "Mr. Campbell's getting difficult. What are these outbursts of affection, Michael?"

"I say, you are a lovely piece."

We said good night. "I'm sorry I can't go," Mike said. Brett laughed. I looked back from the door. Mike had one hand on the bar and was leaning toward Brett, talking. Brett was looking at him quite coolly, but the corners of her eyes were smiling.

Outside on the pavement I said: "Do you want to go to the fight?"

"Sure," said Bill. "If we don't have to walk."

"Mike was pretty excited about his girl friend," I said in the taxi.

"Well," said Bill. "You can't blame him such a hell of a lot."

## CHAPTER NINE

THE LEDOUX–KID FRANCIS fight was the night of the 20th of June. It was a good fight. The morning after the fight I had a letter from Robert Cohn, written from Hendaye. He was having a very quiet time, he said, bathing, playing some golf and much bridge. Hendaye had a splendid beach, but he was anxious to start on the fishing-trip. When would I be down? If I would buy him a double-tapered line he would pay me when I came down.

That same morning I wrote Cohn from the office that Bill and I would leave Paris on the 25th unless I wired him otherwise, and would meet him at Bayonne, where we could get a bus over the mountains to Pamplona. The same evening about seven o'clock I stopped in at the Select to see Michael and Brett. They were not there, and I went over to the Dingo. They were inside sitting at the bar.

"Hello, darling," Brett put out her hand.

"Hello, Jake," Mike said. "I understand I was tight last night."

"Weren't you, though," Brett said. "Disgraceful business."

"Look," said Mike, "when do you go down to Spain? Would you mind if we came down with you?"

"It would be grand."

"You wouldn't mind, really? I've been at Pamplona, you know. Brett's mad to go. You're sure we wouldn't just be a bloody nuisance?"

"Don't talk like a fool."

"I'm a little tight, you know. I wouldn't ask you like this if I weren't. You're sure you don't mind?"

"Oh, shut up, Michael," Brett said. "How can the man say he'd mind now? I'll ask him later."

"But you don't mind, do you?"

"Don't ask that again unless you want to make me sore. Bill and I go down on the morning of the 25th."

"By the way, where is Bill?" Brett asked.

"He's out at Chantilly dining with some people."

"He's a good chap."

"Splendid chap," said Mike. "He is, you know."

"You don't remember him," Brett said.

"I do. Remember him perfectly. Look, Jake, we'll come down the night of the 25th. Brett can't get up in the morning."

"Indeed not!"

"If our money comes and you're sure you don't mind."

"It will come, all right. I'll see to that."

"Tell me what tackle to send for."

"Get two or three rods with reels, and lines, and some flies."

"I won't fish," Brett put in.

"Get two rods, then, and Bill won't have to buy one."

"Right," said Mike. "I'll send a wire to the keeper."

"Won't it be splendid," Brett said. "Spain! We *will* have fun."

"The 25th. When is that?"

"Saturday."

"We *will* have to get ready."

"I say," said Mike, "I'm going to the barber's."

"I must bathe," said Brett. "Walk up to the hotel with me, Jake. Be a good chap."

"We *have* got the loveliest hotel," Mike said. "I think it's a brothel!"

"We left our bags here at the Dingo when we got in and they asked us at this hotel if we wanted a room for the afternoon only. Seemed frightfully pleased we were going to stay all night."

"*I* believe it's a brothel," Mike said. "And *I* should know."

"Oh, shut it and go and get your hair cut."

Mike went out. Brett and I sat on at the bar.

"Have another?"

"Might."

"I needed that," Brett said.

We walked up the Rue Delambre.

"I haven't seen you since I've been back," Brett said.

"No."

"How *are* you, Jake?"

"Fine."

Brett looked at me. "I say," she said, "is Robert Cohn going on this trip?"

"Yes. Why?"

"Don't you think it will be a bit rough on him?"

"Why should it?"

"Who did you think I went down to San Sebastian with?"

"Congratulations," I said.

We walked along.

"What did you say that for?"

"I don't know. What would you like me to say?"

We walked along and turned a corner.

"He behaved rather well, too. He gets a little dull."

"Does he?"

"I rather thought it would be good for him."

"You might take up social service."

"Don't be nasty."

"I won't."

"Didn't you really know?"

"No," I said. "I guess I didn't think about it."

"Do you think it will be too rough on him?"

"That's up to him," I said. "Tell him you're coming. He can always not come."

"I'll write him and give him a chance to pull out of it."

I did not see Brett again until the night of the 24th of June.

"Did you hear from Cohn?"

"Rather. He's keen about it."

"My God!"

"I thought it was rather odd myself."

"Says he can't wait to see me."

"Does he think you're coming alone?"

"No. I told him we were all coming down together. Michael and all."

"He's wonderful."

"Isn't he."

They expected their money the next day. We arranged to meet at Pamplona. They would go directly to San Sebastian and take the train from there. We would all meet at the Montoya in Pamplona. If they did not turn up on Monday at the latest we would go on ahead up to Burguete in the mountains, to start fishing. There was a bus to Burguete. I wrote out an itinerary so they could follow us.

Bill and I took the morning train from the Gare d'Orsay. It was a lovely day, not too hot, and the country was beautiful from the start. We went back into the diner and had breakfast.

Leaving the dining-car I asked the conductor for tickets for the first service.

"Nothing until the fifth."

"What's this?"

There were never more than two servings of lunch on that train, and always plenty of places for both of them.

"They're all reserved," the dining-car conductor said. "There will be a fifth service at three-thirty."

"This is serious," I said to Bill.

"Give him ten francs."

"Here," I said. "We want to eat in the first service."

The conductor put the ten francs in his pocket.

"Thank you," he said. "I would advise you gentlemen to get some sandwiches. All the places for the first four services were reserved at the office of the company."

"You'll go a long way, brother," Bill said to him in English. "I suppose if I'd given you five francs you would have advised us to jump off the train."

"*Comment?*"

"Go to hell!" said Bill. "Get the sandwiches made and a bottle of wine. You tell him, Jake."

"And send it up to the next car." I described where we were.

In our compartment were a man and his wife and their young son.

"I suppose you're Americans, aren't you?" the man asked. "Having a good trip?"

"Wonderful," said Bill.

"That's what you want to do. Travel while you're young. Mother and I always wanted to get over, but we had to wait a while."

"You could have come over ten years ago, if you'd wanted to," the wife said. "What you always said was: 'See America first!' I will say we've seen a good deal, take it one way and another."

"Say, there's plenty of Americans on this train," the husband said. "They've got seven cars of them from Dayton, Ohio. They've been on a pilgrimage to Rome, and now they're going down to Biarritz and Lourdes."

"So, that's what they are. Pilgrims. Goddam Puritans," Bill said.

"What part of the States you boys from?"

"Kansas City," I said. "He's from Chicago."

"You both going to Biarritz?"

"No. We're going fishing in Spain."

"Well, I never cared for it, myself. There's plenty that do out where I come from, though. We got some of the best fishing in the state of Montana. I've been out with the boys, but I never cared for it any."

"Mighty little fishing you did on them trips," his wife said.

He winked at us.

"You know how the ladies are. If there's a jug goes along, or a case of beer, they think it's hell and damnation."

"That's the way men are," his wife said to us. She smoothed her comfortable lap. "I voted against prohibition to please him, and because I like a little beer in the house, and then he talks that way. It's a wonder they ever find anyone to marry them."

"Say," said Bill, "do you know that gang of Pilgrim Fathers have cornered the dining-car until half past three this afternoon?"

"How do you mean? They can't do a thing like that."

"You try and get seats."

"Well, mother, it looks as though we better go back and get another breakfast."

She stood up and straightened her dress.

"Will you boys keep an eye on our things? Come on, Hubert."

They all three went up to the wagon restaurant. A little while after they were gone a steward went through announcing the first service, and pilgrims, with their priests, commenced filing down the corridor. Our friend and his family did not come back. A waiter passed in the corridor with our sandwiches and the bottle of Chablis, and we called him in.

"You're going to work today," I said.

He nodded his head. "They start now, at ten-thirty."

"When do we eat?"

"Huh! When do I eat?"

He left two glasses for the bottle, and we paid him for the sandwiches and tipped him.

"I'll get the plates," he said, "or bring them with you."

We ate the sandwiches and drank the Chablis and watched the country out of the window. The grain was just beginning to ripen and the fields were full of poppies. The pastureland was green, and there were fine trees, and sometimes big rivers and chateaux off in the trees.

At Tours we got off and bought another bottle of wine, and when we got back in the compartment the gentleman from Montana and his wife and his son, Hubert, were sitting comfortably.

"Is there good swimming in Biarritz?" asked Hubert.

"That boy's just crazy till he can get in the water," his mother said. "It's pretty hard on youngsters travelling."

"There's good swimming," I said. "But it's dangerous when it's rough."

"Did you get a meal?" Bill asked.

"We sure did. We set right there when they started to come in, and they must have just thought we were in the party. One of the waiters said something to us in French, and then they just sent three of them back."

"They thought we were snappers, all right," the man said. "It certainly shows you the power of the Catholic Church. It's a pity you boys ain't Catholics. You could get a meal, then, all right."

"I am," I said. "That's what makes me so sore."

Finally at a quarter past four we had lunch. Bill had been rather difficult at the last. He buttonholed a priest who was coming back with one of the returning streams of pilgrims.

"When do us Protestants get a chance to eat, father?"

"I don't know anything about it. Haven't you got tickets?"

"It's enough to make a man join the Klan," Bill said. The priest looked back at him.

Inside the dining-car the waiters served the fifth successive table d'hôte meal. The waiter who served us was soaked through. His white jacket was purple under the arms.

"He must drink a lot of wine."

"Or wear purple undershirts."

"Let's ask him."

"No. He's too tired."

The train stopped for half an hour at Bordeaux and we went out through the station for a little walk. There was not time to get in to the town. Afterward we passed through the Landes and watched the sun set. There were wide fire-gaps cut through the pines, and you could look up them like avenues and see wooded hills way off. About seven-thirty we had dinner and watched the country through the open window in the diner. It was all sandy pine country full of heather. There were little clearings with houses in them, and once in a while we passed a sawmill. It got dark and we could feel the country hot and sandy and dark outside of the window, and about nine o'clock we got into Bayonne. The man and his wife and Hubert all shook hands with us. They were going on to La Négresse to change for Biarritz.

"Well, I hope you have lots of luck," he said.

"Be careful about those bull-fights."

"Maybe we'll see you at Biarritz," Hubert said.

We got off with our bags and rod-cases and passed through the dark station and out to the lights and the line of cabs and hotel buses. There, standing with the hotel runners, was Robert Cohn. He did not see us at first. Then he started forward.

"Hello, Jake. Have a good trip?"

"Fine," I said. "This is Bill Gorton."

"How are you?"

"Come on," said Robert. "I've got a cab." He was a little near-sighted. I had never noticed it before. He was looking at Bill, trying to make him out. He was shy, too.

"We'll go up to my hotel. It's all right. It's quite nice."

We got into the cab, and the cabman put the bags up on the seat beside him and climbed up and cracked his whip, and we drove over the dark bridge and into the town.

"I'm awfully glad to meet you," Robert said to Bill. "I've heard so much about you from Jake and I've read your books. Did you get my line, Jake?"

The cab stopped in front of the hotel, and we all got out and went in. It was a nice hotel, and the people at the desk were very cheerful, and we each had a good small room.

## CHAPTER TEN

I N THE morning it was bright, and they were sprinkling the streets of the town, and we all had breakfast in a café. Bayonne is a nice town. It is like a very clean Spanish town and it is on a big river. Already, so early in the morning, it was very hot on the bridge across the river. We walked out on the bridge and then took a walk through the town.

I was not at all sure Mike's rods would come from Scotland in time, so we hunted a tackle store and finally bought a rod for Bill upstairs over a dry goods store. The man who sold the tackle was out, and we had to wait for him to come back. Finally he came in, and we bought a pretty good rod cheap and two landing-nets.

We went out into the street again and took a look at the cathedral. Cohn made some remark about it being a very good example of something or other, I forget what. It seemed like a nice cathedral, nice and dim, like Spanish churches. Then we went up past the old fort and out to the local Syndicat d'Initiative office, where the bus was supposed to start from. There they told us the bus service did not start until the 1st of July. We found out at the tourist office what we ought to pay for a motor-car to Pamplona and hired one at a big garage just around the corner from the Municipal Theater for four hundred francs. The car was to pick us up at the hotel in forty minutes, and we stopped at the café on the square where we had eaten breakfast and had a beer. It was hot, but the town had a cool, fresh, early-morning smell and it was pleasant sitting in the café. A breeze started to blow, and you could feel that the air came from the sea. There were pigeons out in the square, and the houses were a yellow, sun-baked color, and I did not want to leave the café. But we had to go to the hotel to get our bags packed and pay the bill. We paid for the beers, we matched and I think Cohn paid, and went up to the hotel. It was only sixteen francs apiece for Bill and me, with ten per cent added for the service, and we had the bags sent down and waited for Robert Cohn. While we were waiting I saw a cockroach on the parquet floor that must have been at least three inches long. I pointed him out to Bill and then put my shoe on him. We agreed he must have just come in from the garden. It was really an awfully clean hotel.

Cohn came down, finally, and we all went out to the car. It was a big, closed car, with a driver in a white duster with blue collar and cuffs, and we had him put the back of the car down. He piled in the bags and we started off up the street and out of the town. We passed some lovely gardens and had a good look back at the town, and then we were out in the country, green and rolling, and the road climbing all the time. We passed lots of Basques with oxen, or cattle, hauling carts along the road, and nice farmhouses, low roofs, and all white-plastered. In the Basque country the land all looks very rich and green and the houses and villages look well-off and clean. Every village had a pelota court and on some of them kids were playing in the hot sun. There were signs on the walls of the churches saying it was forbidden to play pelota against them, and the houses in the villages had red tiled roofs, and then the road turned off and commenced to climb and we were going way up close along a hillside, with a valley below and hills stretched off back toward the sea. You couldn't see the sea. It was too far away. You could see only hills and more hills, and you knew where the sea was.

We crossed the Spanish frontier. There was a little stream and a bridge, and Spanish carabineers, with patent-leather Bonaparte hats, and short guns on their backs, on one side, and on the other fat Frenchmen in Kepis and mustaches. They only opened one bag and took the passports in and looked at them. There was a general store and inn on each side of the line. The chauffeur had to go in and fill out some papers about the car and we got out and went over to the stream to see if there were any trout. Bill tried to talk some Spanish to one of the carabineers, but it did not go very well. Robert Cohn asked, pointing with his finger, if there were any trout in the stream, and the carabineer said yes, but not many.

I asked him if he ever fished, and he said no, that he didn't care for it.

Just then an old man with long, sunburned hair and beard, and clothes that looked as though they were made of gunny-sacking, came striding up to the bridge. He was carrying a long staff, and he had a kid slung on his back, tied by the four legs, the head hanging down.

The carabineer waved him back with his sword. The man turned without saying anything, and started back up the white road into Spain.

"What's the matter with the old one?" I asked.

"He hasn't got any passport."

I offered the guard a cigarette. He took it and thanked me.

"What will he do?" I asked.

The guard spat in the dust.

"Oh, he'll just wade across the stream."

"Do you have much smuggling?"

"Oh," he said, "they go through."

The chauffeur came out, folding up the papers and putting them in the inside pocket of his coat. We all got in the car and it started up the white dusty road into Spain. For a while the country was much as it had been; then, climbing all the time, we crossed the top of a Col, the road winding back and forth on itself, and then it was really Spain. There were long brown mountains and a few pines and far-off forests of beech-trees on some of the mountainsides. The road went along the summit of the Col, and then dropped down, and the driver had to honk, and slow up, and turn out to avoid running into two donkeys that were sleeping in the road. We came down out of the mountains and through an oak forest, and there were white cattle grazing in the forest. Down below there were grassy plains and clear streams, and then we crossed a stream and went through a gloomy little village, and started to climb again. We climbed up and up and crossed another high Col and turned along it, and the road ran down to the right, and we saw a whole new range of mountains off to the south, all brown and baked-looking and furrowed in strange shapes.

After a while we came out of the mountains, and there were trees along both sides of the road, and a stream and ripe fields of grain, and the road went on, very white and straight ahead, and then lifted to a little rise, and off on the left was a hill with an old castle, with buildings close around it and a field of grain going right up to the walls and shifting in the wind. I was up in front with the driver and I turned around. Robert Cohn was asleep, but Bill looked and nodded his head. Then we crossed a wide plain, and there was a big river off on the right shining in the sun from between the line of trees, and away off you could see the plateau of Pamplona rising out of the plain, and the walls of the city, and the great brown cathedral, and the broken skyline of the other churches. In back of the plateau were the mountains, and every way you looked there were other mountains, and ahead the road stretched out white across the plain going toward Pamplona.

We came into the town on the other side of the plateau, the road slanting up steeply and dustily with shade-trees on the sides, and then levelling out through the new part of town they are building up outside the old walls. We passed the bull-ring, high and white and concrete-looking in the sun, and then came into the big square by a side street and stopped in front of the Hotel Montoya.

The driver helped us down with the bags. There was a crowd of kids watching the car, and the square was hot, and the trees were green, and the flags hung on their staffs, and it was good to get out of the sun and under the shade of the arcade that runs all the way around the square. Montoya was glad to see us, and shook hands and gave us good rooms looking out on the square, and then we washed and cleaned up and went downstairs in the dining-room for lunch. The driver stayed for lunch, too, and afterward we paid him and he started back to Bayonne.

There are two dining-rooms in the Montoya. One is upstairs on the second floor and looks out on the square. The other is down one floor below the level of the square and has a door that opens on the back street that the bulls pass along when they run through the streets early in the morning on their way to the ring. It is always cool in the downstairs dining-room and we had a very good lunch. The first meal in Spain was always a shock

with the hors d'oeuvres, an egg course, two meat courses, vegetables, salad, and dessert and fruit. You have to drink plenty
of wine to get it all down. Robert Cohn tried to say he did
not want any of the second meat course, but we would not
interpret for him, and so the waitress brought him something
else as a replacement, a plate of cold meats, I think. Cohn had
been rather nervous ever since we had met at Bayonne. He did
not know whether we knew Brett had been with him at San
Sebastian, and it made him rather awkward.

"Well," I said, "Brett and Mike ought to get in tonight."

"I'm not sure they'll come," Cohn said.

"Why not?" Bill said. "Of course they'll come."

"They're always late," I said.

"I rather think they're not coming," Robert Cohn said.

He said it with an air of superior knowledge that irritated
both of us.

"I'll bet you fifty pesetas they're here tonight," Bill said. He
always bets when he is angered, and so he usually bets foolishly.

"I'll take it," Cohn said. "Good. You remember it, Jake. Fifty
pesetas."

"I'll remember it myself," Bill said. I saw he was angry and
wanted to smooth him down.

"It's a sure thing they'll come," I said. "But maybe not tonight."

"Want to call it off?" Cohn asked.

"No. Why should I? Make it a hundred if you like."

"All right. I'll take that."

"That's enough," I said. "Or you'll have to make a book and
give me some of it."

"I'm satisfied," Cohn said. He smiled. "You'll probably win it
back at bridge, anyway."

"You haven't got it yet," Bill said.

We went out to walk around under the arcade to the Café Iruña for coffee. Cohn said he was going over and get a shave.

"Say," Bill said to me, "have I got any chance on that bet?"

"You've got a rotten chance. They've never been on time anywhere. If their money doesn't come it's a cinch they won't get in tonight."

"I was sorry as soon as I opened my mouth. But I had to call him. He's all right, I guess, but where does he get this inside stuff? Mike and Brett fixed it up with us about coming down here."

I saw Cohn coming over across the square.

"Here he comes."

"Well, let him not get superior and Jewish."

"The barber shop's closed," Cohn said. "It's not open till four."

We had coffee at the Iruña, sitting in comfortable wicker chairs looking out from the cool of the arcade at the big square. After a while Bill went to write some letters and Cohn went over to the barber-shop. It was still closed, so he decided to go up to the hotel and get a bath, and I sat out in front of the café and then went for a walk in the town. It was very hot, but I kept on the shady side of the streets and went through the market and had a good time seeing the town again. I went to the Ayuntamiento and found the old gentleman who subscribes for the bull-fight tickets for me every year, and he had gotten the money I sent him from Paris and renewed my subscriptions, so that was all set. He was the archivist, and all the archives of the town were in his office. That has nothing to do with the story. Anyway his office had a green baize door and a big wooden door, and when I went out I left him sitting among the archives that covered all the walls, and I shut both the doors, and as I went out of the building into the street the porter stopped me to brush off my coat.

"You must have been in a motor-car," he said.

The back of the collar and the upper part of the shoulders were gray with dust.

"From Bayonne."

"Well, well," he said. "I knew you were in a motor-car from the way the dust was." So I gave him two copper coins.

At the end of the street I saw the cathedral and walked up toward it. The first time I ever saw it I thought the facade was ugly but I liked it now. I went inside. It was dim and dark and the pillars went high up, and there were people praying, and it smelt of incense, and there were some wonderful big windows. I knelt and started to pray and prayed for everybody I thought of, Brett and Mike and Bill and Robert Cohn and myself, and all the bull-fighters, separately for the ones I liked, and lumping all the rest, then I prayed for myself again, and while I was praying for myself I found I was getting sleepy, so I prayed that the bull-fights would be good and that it would be a fine fiesta, and that we would get some fishing. I wondered if there was anything else I might pray for, and I thought I would like to have some money, so I prayed that I would make a lot of money, and then I started to think how I would make it, and thinking of making money reminded me of the count, and I started wondering about where he was, and regretting I hadn't seen him since that night in Montmartre, and about something funny Brett told me about him, and as all the time I was kneeling with my forehead on the wood in front of me, and was thinking of myself as praying, I was a little ashamed, and regretted that I was such a rotten Catholic, but realized there was nothing I could do about it, at least for a while, and maybe never, but that anyway it was a grand religion, and I only wished I felt religious and maybe I would the next time; and then I was out in the hot sun on the steps of the cathedral, and the forefingers and the thumb of my right hand were still damp, and I felt them dry in the sun. The sunlight was hot and hard, and I crossed over beside some buildings, and walked back along side streets to the hotel.

At dinner that night we found that Robert Cohn had taken a bath, had had a shave and a haircut and a shampoo, and something put on his hair afterward to make it stay down. He was nervous, and I did not try to help him any. The train was due in at nine o'clock from San Sebastian, and, if Brett and Mike were coming, they would be on it. At twenty minutes to nine we were not half through dinner. Robert Cohn got up from the table and said he would go to the station. I said I would go with him, just to devil him. Bill said he would be damned if he would leave his dinner. I said we would be right back.

We walked to the station. I was enjoying Cohn's nervousness. I hoped Brett would be on the train. At the station the train was late, and we sat on a baggage-truck and waited outside in the dark. I have never seen a man in civil life as nervous as Robert Cohn—nor as eager. I was enjoying it. It was lousy to enjoy it, but I felt lousy. Cohn had a wonderful quality of bringing out the worst in anybody.

After a while we heard the train-whistle way off below on the other side of the plateau, and then we saw the headlight coming up the hill. We went inside the station and stood with a crowd of people just back of the gates, and the train came in and stopped, and everybody started coming out through the gates.

They were not in the crowd. We waited till everybody had gone through and out of the station and gotten into buses, or taken cabs, or were walking with their friends or relatives through the dark into the town.

"I knew they wouldn't come," Robert said. We were going back to the hotel.

"I thought they might," I said.

Bill was eating fruit when we came in and finishing a bottle of wine.

"Didn't come, eh?"

"No."

"Do you mind if I give you that hundred pesetas in the morning, Cohn?" Bill asked. "I haven't changed any money here yet."

"Oh, forget about it," Robert Cohn said. "Let's bet on something else. Can you bet on bull-fights?"

"You could," Bill said, "but you don't need to."

"It would be like betting on the war," I said. "You don't need any economic interest."

"I'm very curious to see them," Robert said.

Montoya came up to our table. He had a telegram in his hand. "It's for you." He handed it to me.

It read: "STOPPED NIGHT SAN SEBASTIAN."

"It's from them," I said. I put it in my pocket. Ordinarily I should have handed it over.

"They've stopped over in San Sebastian," I said. "Send their regards to you."

Why I felt that impulse to devil him I do not know. Of course I do know. I was blind, unforgivingly jealous of what had happened to him. The fact that I took it as a matter of course did not alter that any. I certainly did hate him. I do not think I ever really hated him until he had that little spell of superiority at lunch—that and when he went through all that barbering. So I put the telegram in my pocket. The telegram came to me, anyway.

"Well," I said. "We ought to pull out on the noon bus for Burguete. They can follow us if they get in tomorrow night."

There were only two trains up from San Sebastian, an early morning train and the one we had just met.

"That sounds like a good idea," Cohn said.

"The sooner we get on the stream the better."

"It's all one to me when we start," Bill said. "The sooner the better."

We sat in the Iruña for a while and had coffee and then took a little walk out to the bull-ring and across the field and under the trees at the edge of the cliff and looked down at the river in the dark, and I turned in early. Bill and Cohn stayed out in the café quite late, I believe, because I was asleep when they came in.

In the morning I bought three tickets for the bus to Burguete. It was scheduled to leave at two o'clock. There was nothing earlier. I was sitting over at the Iruña reading the papers when I saw Robert Cohn coming across the square. He came up to the table and sat down in one of the wicker chairs.

"This is a comfortable café," he said. "Did you have a good night, Jake?"

"I slept like a log."

"I didn't sleep very well. Bill and I were out late, too."

"Where were you?"

"Here. And after it shut we went over to that other café. The old man there speaks German and English."

"The Café Suizo."

"That's it. He seems like a nice old fellow. I think it's a better café than this one."

"It's not so good in the daytime," I said. "Too hot. By the way, I got the bus tickets."

"I'm not going up today. You and Bill go on ahead."

"I've got your ticket."

"Give it to me. I'll get the money back."

"It's five pesetas."

Robert Cohn took out a silver five-peseta piece and gave it to me.

"I ought to stay," he said. "You see I'm afraid there's some sort of misunderstanding."

"Why," I said. "They may not come here for three or four days now if they start on parties at San Sebastian."

"That's just it," said Robert. "I'm afraid they expected to meet me at San Sebastian, and that's why they stopped over."

"What makes you think that?"

"Well, I wrote suggesting it to Brett."

"Why in hell didn't you stay there and meet them, then?" I started to say, but I stopped. I thought that idea would come to him by itself, but I do not believe it ever did.

He was being confidential now and it was giving him pleasure to be able to talk with the understanding that I knew there was something between him and Brett.

"Well, Bill and I will go up right after lunch," I said.

"I wish I could go. We've been looking forward to this fishing all winter." He was being sentimental about it. "But I ought to stay. I really ought. As soon as they come I'll bring them right up."

"Let's find Bill."

"I want to go over to the barber-shop."

"See you at lunch."

I found Bill up in his room. He was shaving.

"Oh, yes, he told me all about it last night," Bill said. "He's a great little confider. He said he had a date with Brett at San Sebastian."

"The lying bastard!"

"Oh, no," said Bill. "Don't get sore. Don't get sore at this stage of the trip. How did you ever happen to know this fellow, anyway?"

"Don't rub it in."

Bill looked around, half-shaved, and then went on talking into the mirror while he lathered his face.

"Didn't you send him with a letter to me in New York last winter? Thank God, I'm a travelling man. Haven't you got some more Jewish friends you could bring along?" He rubbed his chin with his thumb, looked at it, and then started scraping again.

"You've got some fine ones yourself."

"Oh, yes. I've got some darbs. But not alongside of this Robert Cohn. The funny thing is he's nice, too. I like him. But he's just so awful."

"He can be damn nice."

"I know it. That's the terrible part."

I laughed.

"Yes. Go on and laugh," said Bill. "You weren't out with him last night until two o'clock."

"Was he very bad?"

"Awful. What's all this about him and Brett, anyway? Did she ever have anything to do with him?"

He raised his chin up and pulled it from side to side.

"Sure. She went down to San Sebastian with him."

"What a damn-fool thing to do. Why did she do that?"

"She wanted to get out of town and she can't go anywhere alone. She said she thought it would be good for him."

"What bloody fool things people do. Why didn't she go off with some of her own people? Or you?"—he slurred that over —"or me? Why not me?" He looked at his face carefully in the glass, put a big dab of lather on each cheek-bone. "It's an honest face. It's a face any woman would be safe with."

"She'd never seen it."

"She should have. All women should see it. It's a face that ought to be thrown on every screen in the country. Every woman ought to be given a copy of this face as she leaves the altar. Mothers should tell their daughters about this face. My son"—he pointed the razor at me—"go west with this face and grow up with the country."

He ducked down to the bowl, rinsed his face with cold water, put on some alcohol, and then looked at himself carefully in the glass, pulling down his long upper lip.

"My God!" he said, "isn't it an awful face?"

He looked in the glass.

"And as for this Robert Cohn," Bill said, "he makes me sick, and he can go to hell, and I'm damn glad he's staying here so we won't have him fishing with us."

"You're damn right."

"We're going trout fishing. We're going trout fishing in the Irati River, and we're going to get tight now at lunch on the wine of the country, and then take a swell bus ride."

"Come on. Let's go over to the Iruña and start," I said.

## CHAPTER ELEVEN

I T WAS baking hot in the square when we came out after lunch with our bags and the rod-case to go to Burguete. People were on top of the bus, and others were climbing up a ladder. Bill went up and Robert sat beside Bill to save a place for me, and I went back in the hotel to get a couple of bottles of wine to take with us. When I came out the bus was crowded. Men and women were sitting on all the baggage and boxes on top, and the women all had their fans going in the sun. It certainly was hot. Robert climbed down and I fitted into the place he had saved on the one wooden seat that ran across the top.

Robert Cohn stood in the shade of the arcade waiting for us to start. A Basque with a big leather wine-bag in his lap lay across the top of the bus in front of our seat, leaning back against our legs. He offered the wine-skin to Bill and to me, and when I tipped it up to drink he imitated the sound of a klaxon motor-horn so well and so suddenly that I spilled some of the wine, and everybody laughed. He apologized and made me take another drink. He made the klaxon again a little later, and it fooled me the second time. He was very good at it. The Basques liked it. The man next to Bill was talking to him in Spanish and Bill was not getting it, so he offered the man one of the bottles of wine. The man waved it away. He said it was too hot and he had drunk too much at lunch. When Bill offered the bottle the second time he took a long drink, and then the bottle went all over that part of the bus. Everyone took a drink very politely, and then they made us cork it up and put it away. They all wanted us to drink from their leather wine-bottles. They were peasants going up into the hills.

Finally, after a couple more false klaxons, the bus started, and Robert Cohn waved goodbye to us, and all the Basques waved goodbye to him. As soon as we started out on the road outside of town it was cool. It felt nice riding high up and close under the trees. The bus went quite fast and made a good breeze, and as we went out along the road with the dust powdering the trees and down the hill, we had a fine view, back through the trees, of the town rising up from the bluff above the river. The Basque lying against my knees pointed out the view with the neck of the wine-bottle and winked at us. He nodded his head.

"Pretty nice, eh?"

"These Basques are swell people," Bill said.

The Basque lying against my legs was tanned the color of saddle-leather. He wore a black smock like all the rest. There were wrinkles in his tanned neck. He turned around and offered his wine-bag to Bill. Bill handed him one of our bottles. The Basque wagged a forefinger at him and handed the bottle back, slapping in the cork with the palm of his hand. He shoved the wine-bag up.

"Arriba! Arriba!" he said. "Lift it up."

Bill raised the wine-skin and let the stream of wine spurt out and into his mouth, his head tipped back. When he stopped drinking and tipped the leather bottle down a few drops ran down his chin.

"No! No!" several Basques said. "Not like that." One

snatched the bottle away from the owner, who was himself about to give a demonstration. He was a young fellow and he held the wine-bottle at full arms' length and raised it high up, squeezing the leather bag with his hand so the stream of wine hissed into his mouth. He held the bag out there, the wine making a flat, hard trajectory into his mouth, and he kept on swallowing smoothly and regularly.

"Hey!" the owner of the bottle shouted. "Whose wine is that?"

The drinker waggled his little finger at him and smiled at us with his eyes. Then he bit the stream off sharp, made a quick lift with the wine-bag and lowered it down to the owner. He winked at us. The owner shook the wine-skin sadly.

We passed through a town and stopped in front of the posada, and the driver took on several packages. Then we started on again, and outside the town the road commenced to mount. We were going through farming country with rocky hills that sloped down into the fields. The grain-fields went up the hill-sides. Now as we went higher there was a wind blowing the grain. The road was white and dusty, and the dust rose under the wheels and hung in the air behind us. The road climbed up into the hills and left the rich grain-fields below. Now there were only patches of grain on the bare hillsides and on each side of the water-courses. We turned sharply out to the side of the road to give room to pass to a long string of six mules, fol-lowing one after the other, hauling a high-hooded wagon loaded with freight. The wagon and the mules were covered with dust. Close behind was another string of mules and another wagon. This was loaded with lumber, and the arriero driving the mules leaned back and put on the thick wooden brakes as we passed.

Up here the country was quite barren and the hills were rocky and hard-baked clay furrowed by the rain.

We came around a curve into a town, and on both sides opened out a sudden green valley. A stream went through the center of the town and fields of grapes touched the houses.

The bus stopped in front of a posada and many of the passengers got down, and a lot of the baggage was unstrapped from the roof from under the big tarpaulins and lifted down. Bill and I got down and went into the posada. There was a low, dark room with saddles and harness, and hay-forks made of white wood, and clusters of canvas rope-soled shoes and hams and slabs of bacon and white garlics and long sausages hanging from the roof. It was cool and dusky, and we stood in front of a long wooden counter with two women behind it serving drinks. Behind them were shelves stacked with supplies and goods.

We each had an aguardiente and paid forty centimes for the two drinks. I gave the woman fifty centimes to make a tip, and she gave me back the copper piece, thinking I had misunderstood the price.

Two of our Basques came in and insisted on buying a drink. So they bought a drink, and then we bought a drink, and then they slapped us on the back and bought another drink. Then we bought, and then we all went out into the sunlight and the heat, and climbed back on top of the bus. There was plenty of room now for everyone to sit on the seat, and the Basque who had been lying on the tin roof now sat between us. The woman who had been serving drinks came out wiping her hands on her apron and talked to somebody inside the bus. Then the driver came out swinging two flat leather mail-pouches and climbed up, and everybody waving we started off.

The road left the green valley at once, and we were up in the hills again. Bill and the wine-bottle Basque were having a conversation. A man leaned over from the other side of the seat and asked in English: "You're Americans?"

"Sure."

"I been there," he said. "Forty years ago."

He was an old man, as brown as the others, with the stubble of a white beard.

"How was it?"

"What you say?"

"How was America?"

"Oh, I was in California. It was fine."

"Why did you leave?"

"What you say?"

"Why did you come back here?"

"Oh! I come back to get married. I was going to go back but my wife she don't like to travel. Where you from?"

"Kansas City."

"I been there," he said. "I been in Chicago, St. Louis, Kansas City, Denver, Los Angeles, Salt Lake City."

He named them carefully.

"How long were you over?"

"Fifteen years. Then I come back and got married."

"Have a drink?"

"All right," he said. "You can't get this in America, eh?"

"There's plenty if you can pay for it."

"What you come over here for?"

"We're going to the fiesta at Pamplona."

"You like the bull-fights?"

"Sure. Don't you?"

"Yes," he said. "I guess I like them."

Then after a little:

"Where you go now?"

"Up to Burguete to fish."

"Well," he said, "I hope you catch something."

He shook hands and turned around to the back seat again. The other Basques had been impressed. He sat back comfortably and smiled at me when I turned around to look at the country. But the effort of talking American seemed to have tired him. He did not say anything after that.

The bus climbed steadily up the road. The country was barren and rocks stuck up through the clay. There was no grass beside the road. Looking back we could see the country spread out below. Far back the fields were squares of green and brown on the hillsides. Making the horizon were the brown mountains. They were strangely shaped. As we climbed higher the horizon kept changing. As the bus ground slowly up the road we could see other mountains coming up in the south. Then the road came over the crest, flattened out, and went into a forest. It was a forest of cork oaks, and the sun came through the trees in patches, and there were cattle grazing back in the trees. We went through the forest and the road came out and turned along a rise of land, and out ahead of us was a rolling green plain, with dark mountains beyond it. These were not like the brown, heat-baked mountains we had left behind. These were wooded and there were clouds coming down from them. The green plain stretched off. It was cut by fences and the white of the road showed through the trunks of a double line of trees that crossed the plain toward the north. As we came to the edge of the rise we saw the red roofs and white houses of Burguete ahead strung out on the plain, and away off on the shoulder of the first dark mountain was the gray metal-sheathed roof of the monastery of Roncevalles.

"There's Roncevaux," I said.

"Where?"

"Way off there where the mountain starts."

"It's cold up here," Bill said.

"It's high," I said. "It must be twelve hundred meters."

"It's awful cold," Bill said.

The bus levelled down onto the straight line of road that ran to Burguete. We passed a crossroads and crossed a bridge over a stream. The houses of Burguete were along both sides of the road. There were no side streets. We passed the church and the school-yard, and the bus stopped. We got down and the driver handed down our bags and the rod-case. A carabineer in his cocked hat and yellow leather cross-straps came up.

"What's in there?" he pointed to the rod-case. I opened it and showed him. He asked to see our fishing permits and I got them out. He looked at the date and then waved us on.

"Is that all right?" I asked.

"Yes. Of course."

We went up the street, past the white-washed stone houses, families sitting in their doorways watching us, to the inn.

The fat woman who ran the inn came out from the kitchen and shook hands with us. She took off her spectacles, wiped them, and put them on again. It was cold in the inn and the wind was starting to blow outside. The woman sent a girl upstairs with us to show the room. There were two beds, a washstand, a clothes chest and a big, framed steel-engraving of Nuestra Señora de Roncesvalles. The wind was blowing against the shutters. The room was on the north side of the inn. We washed, put on sweaters, and came downstairs into the dining-room. It had a stone floor, low ceiling, and was oak-paneled. The shutters were all up and it was so cold you could see your breath.

"My God!" said Bill. "It can't be this cold tomorrow. I'm not going to wade a stream in this weather."

There was an upright piano in the far corner of the room beyond the wooden tables and Bill went over and started to play.

"I got to keep warm," he said.

I went out to find the woman and ask her how much the room and board was. She put her hands under her apron and looked away from me.

"Twelve pesetas."

"Why, we only paid that in Pamplona."

She did not say anything, just took off her glasses and wiped them on her apron.

"That's too much," I said. "We didn't pay more than that at a big hotel."

"We've put in a bathroom."

"Haven't you got anything cheaper?"

"Not in the summer. Now is the big season."

We were the only people in the inn. Well, I thought, it's only a few days.

"Is the wine included?"

"Oh, yes."

"Well," I said. "It's all right."

I went back to Bill. He blew his breath at me to show how cold it was, and went on playing. I sat at one of the tables and looked at the pictures on the wall. There was one panel of rabbits, dead, one of pheasants, also dead, and one panel of dead ducks. The panels were all dark and smoky-looking. There was a cupboard full of liqueur bottles. I looked at them all. Bill was still playing. "How about a hot rum punch?" he said. "This isn't going to keep me warm permanently."

I went out and told the woman what a rum punch was and how to make it. In a few minutes a girl brought a stone pitcher, steaming, into the room. Bill came over from the piano and we drank the hot punch and listened to the wind.

"There isn't too much rum in that."

I went over to the cupboard and brought the rum bottle and poured a half-tumblerful into the pitcher.

"Direct action," said Bill. "It beats legislation."

The girl came in and laid the table for supper.

"It blows like hell up here," Bill said.

The girl brought in a big bowl of hot vegetable soup and the wine. We had fried trout afterward and some sort of a stew and a big bowl full of wild strawberries. We did not lose money on the wine, and the girl was shy but nice about bringing it. The old woman looked in once and counted the empty bottles.

After supper we went upstairs and smoked and read in bed to keep warm. Once in the night I woke and heard the wind blowing. It felt good to be warm and in bed.

# CHAPTER TWELVE

**W**HEN I WOKE in the morning I went to the window and looked out. It had cleared and there were no clouds on the mountains. Outside under the window were some carts and an old diligence, the wood of the roof cracked and split by the weather. It must have been left from the days before the motor-buses. A goat hopped up on one of the carts and then to the roof of the diligence. He jerked his head at the other goats below and when I waved at him he bounded down.

Bill was still sleeping, so I dressed, put on my shoes outside in the hall, and went downstairs. No one was stirring downstairs, so I unbolted the door and went out. It was cool outside in the early morning and the sun had not yet dried the dew that had come when the wind died down. I hunted around in the shed behind the inn and found a sort of mattock, and went down toward the stream to try and dig some worms for bait. The stream was clear and shallow but it did not look trouty. On the grassy bank where it was damp I drove the mattock into the earth and loosened a chunk of sod. There were worms underneath. They slid out of sight as I lifted the sod and I dug carefully and got a good many. Digging at the edge of the damp ground I filled two empty tobacco-tins with worms and sifted dirt onto them. The goats watched me dig.

When I went back into the inn the woman was down in the kitchen, and I asked her to get coffee for us, and that we wanted a lunch. Bill was awake and sitting on the edge of the bed.

"I saw you out of the window," he said. "Didn't want to interrupt you. What were you doing? Burying your money?"

"You lazy bum!"

"Been working for the common good? Splendid. I want you to do that every morning."

"Come on," I said. "Get up."

"What? Get up? I never get up."

He climbed into bed and pulled the sheet up to his chin.

"Try and argue me into getting up."

I went on looking for the tackle and putting it all together in the tackle-bag.

"Aren't you interested?" Bill asked.

"I'm going down and eat."

"Eat? Why didn't you say eat? I thought you just wanted me to get up for fun. Eat? Fine. Now you're reasonable. You go out and dig some more worms and I'll be right down."

"Oh, go to hell!"

"Work for the good of all." Bill stepped into his underclothes. "Show irony and pity."

I started out of the room with the tackle-bag, the nets, and the rod-case.

"Hey! come back!"

I put my head in the door.

"Aren't you going to show a little irony and pity?"

I thumbed my nose.

"That's not irony."

As I went downstairs I heard Bill singing, "Irony and Pity. When you're feeling ——. Oh, Give them Irony and Give them Pity. Oh, give them Irony. When they're feeling —— Just a little irony. Just a little pity. ——" He kept on singing until he came downstairs. The tune was: "The Bells are Ringing for Me and My Gal." I was reading a week-old Spanish paper.

"What's all this irony and pity?"

"What? Don't you know about Irony and Pity?"

"No. Who got it up?"

"Everybody. They're mad about it in New York. It's just like the Fratellinis used to be."

The girl came in with the coffee and buttered toast. Or, rather, it was bread toasted and buttered.

"Ask her if she's got any jam," Bill said. "Be ironical with her."

"Have you got any jam?"

"That's not ironical. I wish I could talk Spanish."

The coffee was good and we drank it out of big bowls. The girl brought in a glass dish of raspberry jam.

"Thank you."

"Hey! that's not the way," Bill said. "Say something ironical. Make some crack about Primo de Rivera."

"I could ask her what kind of a jam they think they've gotten into in the Riff."

"Poor," said Bill. "Very poor. You can't do it. That's all. You don't understand irony. You have no pity. Say something pitiful."

"Robert Cohn."

"Not so bad. That's better. Now why is Cohn pitiful? Be ironic."

He took a big gulp of coffee.

"Aw, hell!" I said. "It's too early in the morning."

"There you go. And you claim you want to be a writer, too. You're only a newspaper man. An expatriated newspaper man. You ought to be ironical the minute you get out of bed. You ought to wake up with your mouth full of pity."

"Go on," I said. "Who did you get this stuff from?"

"Everybody. Don't you read? Don't you ever see anybody? You know what you are? You're an expatriate. Why don't you live in New York? Then you'd know these things. What do you want me to do? Come over here and tell you every year?"

"Take some more coffee," I said.

"Good. Coffee is good for you. It's the caffeine in it. Caffeine, we are here. Caffeine puts a man on her horse and a woman in his grave. You know what's the trouble with you? You're an expatriate. One of the worst type. Haven't you heard that? Nobody that ever left their own country ever wrote anything worth printing. Not even in the newspapers."

He drank the coffee.

"You're an expatriate. You've lost touch with the soil. You get precious. Fake European standards have ruined you. You drink yourself to death. You become obsessed by sex. You spend all your time talking, not working. You are an expatriate, see? You hang around cafés."

"It sounds like a swell life," I said. "When do I work?"

"You don't work. One group claims women support you. Another group claims you're impotent."

"No," I said. "I just had an accident."

"Never mention that," Bill said. "That's the sort of thing that can't be spoken of. That's what you ought to work up into a mystery. Like Henry James's bicycle."

He had been going splendidly, but he stopped. I was afraid he thought he had hurt me with that crack about being impotent. I wanted to start him again.

"It wasn't a bicycle," I said. "He was riding horse-back."

"I heard it was a tricycle."

"Well," I said. "A plane is sort of like a tricycle. The joystick works the same way."

"But you don't pedal it."

"No," I said, "I guess you don't pedal it."

"Let's lay off that," Bill said.

"All right. I was just standing up for the tricycle."

"I think he's a good writer, too," Bill said. "And you're a hell of a good guy. Anybody ever tell you you were a good guy?"

"I'm not a good guy."

"Listen. You're a hell of a good guy, and I'm fonder of you than anybody on earth. I couldn't tell you that in New York. It'd mean I was a faggot. That was what the Civil War was about. Abraham Lincoln was a faggot. He was in love with General Grant. So was Jefferson Davis. Lincoln just freed the slaves on a bet. The Dred Scott case was framed by the Anti-Saloon League. Sex explains it all. The Colonel's Lady and Judy O'Grady are Lesbians under their skin."

He stopped.

"Want to hear some more?"

"Shoot," I said.

"I don't know any more. Tell you some more at lunch."

"Old Bill," I said.

"You bum!"

We packed the lunch and two bottles of wine in the rucksack, and Bill put it on. I carried the rod-case and the landing-nets slung over my back. We started up the road and then went across a meadow and found a path that crossed the fields and went toward the woods on the slope of the first hill. We walked across the fields on the sandy path. The fields were rolling and grassy and the grass was short from the sheep grazing.

The cattle were up in the hills. We heard their bells in the woods.

The path crossed a stream on a foot-log. The log was surfaced off, and there was a sapling bent across for a rail. In the flat pool beside the stream tadpoles spotted the sand. We went up a steep bank and across the rolling fields. Looking back we saw Burguete, white houses and red roofs, and the white road with a truck going along it and the dust rising.

Beyond the fields we crossed another faster-flowing stream. A sandy road led down to the ford and beyond into the woods. The path crossed the stream on another foot-log below the ford, and joined the road, and we went into the woods.

It was a beech wood and the trees were very old. Their roots bulked above the ground and the branches were twisted. We walked on the road between the thick trunks of the old beeches and the sunlight came through the leaves in light patches on the grass. The trees were big, and the foliage was thick but it was not gloomy. There was no undergrowth, only the smooth grass, very green and fresh, and the big gray trees well spaced as though it were a park.

"This is country," Bill said.

The road went up a hill and we got into thick woods, and the road kept on climbing. Sometimes it dipped down but rose again steeply. All the time we heard the cattle in the woods. Finally, the road came out on the top of the hills. We were on the top of the height of land that was the highest part of the range of wooded hills we had seen from Burguete. There were wild strawberries growing on the sunny side of the ridge in a little clearing in the trees.

Ahead the road came out of the forest and went along the

shoulder of the ridge of hills. The hills ahead were not wooded, and there were great fields of yellow gorse. Way off we saw the steep bluffs, dark with trees and jutting with gray stone, that marked the course of the Irati River.

"We have to follow this road along the ridge, cross these hills, go through the woods on the far hills, and come down to the Irati valley," I pointed out to Bill.

"That's a hell of a hike."

"It's too far to go and fish and come back the same day, comfortably."

"Comfortably. That's a nice word. We'll have to go like hell to get there and back and have any fishing at all."

It was a long walk and the country was very fine, but we were tired when we came down the steep road that led out of the wooded hills into the valley of the Rio de la Fabrica.

The road came out from the shadow of the woods into the hot sun. Ahead was a river-valley. Beyond the river was a steep hill. There was a field of buckwheat on the hill. We saw a white house under some trees on the hillside. It was very hot and we stopped under some trees beside a dam that crossed the river.

Bill put the pack against one of the trees and we jointed up the rods, put on the reels, tied on leaders, and got ready to fish.

"You're sure this thing has trout in it?" Bill asked.

"It's full of them."

"I'm going to fish a fly. You got any McGintys?"

"There's some in there."

"You going to fish bait?"

"Yeah. I'm going to fish the dam here."

"Well, I'll take the fly-book, then." He tied on a fly. "Where'd I better go? Up or down?"

"Down is the best. They're plenty up above, too."

Bill went down the bank.

"Take a worm can."

"No, I don't want one. If they won't take a fly I'll just flick it around."

Bill was down below watching the stream.

"Say," he called up against the noise of the dam. "How about putting the wine in that spring up the road?"

"All right," I shouted. Bill waved his hand and started down the stream. I found the two wine-bottles in the pack, and carried them up the road to where the water of a spring flowed out of an iron pipe. There was a board over the spring and I lifted it and, knocking the corks firmly into the bottles, lowered them down into the water. It was so cold my hand and wrist felt numbed. I put back the slab of wood, and hoped nobody would find the wine.

I got my rod that was leaning against the tree, took the bait-can and landing-net, and walked out onto the dam. It was built to provide a head of water for driving logs. The gate was up, and I sat on one of the squared timbers and watched the smooth apron of water before the river tumbled into the falls. In the white water at the foot of the dam it was deep. As I baited up, a trout shot up out of the white water into the falls and was carried down. Before I could finish baiting, another trout jumped at the falls, making the same lovely arc and disappearing into the water that was thundering down. I put on a good-sized sinker and dropped into the white water close to the edge of the timbers of the dam.

I did not feel the first trout strike. When I started to pull up I felt that I had one and brought him, fighting and bending the rod almost double, out of the boiling water at the foot of the falls, and swung him up and onto the dam. He was a good trout, and I banged his head against the timber so that he quivered out straight, and then slipped him into my bag.

While I had him on, several trout had jumped at the falls. As soon as I baited up and dropped in again I hooked another and brought him in the same way. In a little while I had six. They were all about the same size. I laid them out, side by side, all their heads pointing the same way, and looked at them. They were beautifully colored and firm and hard from the cold water. It was a hot day, so I slit them all and shucked out the insides, gills and all, and tossed them over across the river. I took the trout ashore, washed them in the cold, smoothly heavy water above the dam, and then picked some ferns, and packed them all in the bag, three trout on a layer of ferns, then another layer of ferns then three more trout, and then covered them with ferns. They looked nice in the ferns, and now the bag was bulky, and I put it in the shade of the tree.

It was very hot on the dam, so I put my worm-can in the shade with the bag, and got a book out of the pack and settled down under the tree to read until Bill should come up for lunch.

It was a little past noon and there was not much shade, but I sat against the trunk of two of the trees that grew together, and read. The book was something by A.E.W. Mason, and I was reading a wonderful story about a man who had been frozen in the Alps and then fallen into a glacier and disappeared, and his bride was going to wait twenty-four years exactly for his body to come out on the moraine, while her true love waited too, and they were still waiting when Bill came up.

"Get any?" he asked. He had his rod and his bag and his net all in one hand, and he was sweating. I hadn't heard him come up, because of the noise from the dam.

"Six. What did you get?"

Bill sat down, opened up his bag, laid a big trout on the grass. He took out three more, each one a little bigger than the last, and laid them side by side in the shade from the tree. His face was sweaty and happy.

"How are yours?"

"Smaller."

"Let's see them."

"They're packed."

"How big are they really?"

"They're all about the size of your smallest."

"You're not holding out on me?"

"I wish I were."

"Get them all on worms?"

"Yes."

"You lazy bum!"

Bill put the trout in the bag and started for the river, swinging the open bag. He was wet from the waist down and I knew he must have been wading the stream.

I walked up the road and got out the two bottles of wine. They were cold. Moisture beaded on the bottles as I walked back to the trees. I spread the lunch on a newspaper, and uncorked one of the bottles and leaned the other against a tree. Bill came up drying his hands, his bag plump with ferns.

"Let's see that bottle," he said. He pulled the cork and tipped up the bottle and drank. "Whew! That makes my eyes ache."

"Let's try it."

The wine was icy cold and tasted faintly rusty.

"That's not such filthy wine," Bill said.

"The cold helps it," I said.

We unwrapped the little parcels of lunch.

"Chicken."

"There's hard-boiled eggs."

"Find any salt?"

"First the egg," said Bill. "Then the chicken. Even Bryan could see that."

"He's dead. I read it in the paper yesterday."

"No. Not really?"

"Yes. Bryan's dead."

Bill laid down the egg he was peeling.

"Gentlemen," he said, and unwrapped a drumstick from a piece of newspaper. "I reverse the order. For Bryan's sake. As a tribute to the Great Commoner. First the chicken; then the egg."

"Wonder what day God created the chicken?"

"Oh," said Bill, sucking the drumstick, "how should we know? We should not question. Our stay on earth is not for long. Let us rejoice and believe and give thanks."

"Eat an egg."

Bill gestured with the drumstick in one hand and the bottle of wine in the other.

"Let us rejoice in our blessings. Let us utilize the fowls of the air. Let us utilize the product of the vine. Will you utilize a little, brother?"

"After you, brother."

Bill took a long drink.

"Utilize a little, brother," he handed me the bottle. "Let us not doubt, brother. Let us not pry into the holy mysteries of the hen-coop with simian fingers. Let us accept on faith and simply say—I want you to join with me in saying—What shall we say, brother?" He pointed the drumstick at me and went on. "Let me tell you. We will say, and I for one am proud to say—and I want you to say with me, on your knees, brother. Let no man be ashamed to kneel here in the great out-of-doors. Remember the woods were God's first temples. Let us kneel and say: 'Don't eat that Lady—that's Mencken.'"

"Here," I said. "Utilize a little of this."

We uncorked the other bottle.

"What's the matter?" I said. "Didn't you like Bryan?"

"I loved Bryan," said Bill. "We were like brothers."

"Where did you know him?"

"He and Mencken and I all went to Holy Cross together."

"And Frankie Frisch."

"It's a lie. Frankie Frisch went to Fordham."

"Well," I said, "I went to Loyola with Bishop Manning."

"It's a lie," Bill said. "I went to Loyola with Bishop Manning myself."

"You're cock-eyed," I said.

"On wine?"

"Why not?"

"It's the humidity," Bill said. "They ought to take this damn humidity away."

"Have another shot."

"Is this all we've got?"

"Only the two bottles."

"Do you know what you are?" Bill looked at the bottle affectionately.

"No," I said.

"You're in the pay of the Anti-Saloon League."

"I went to Notre Dame with Wayne B. Wheeler."

"It's a lie," said Bill. "I went to Austin Business College with Wayne B. Wheeler. He was class president."

"Well," I said, "the saloon must go."

"You're right there, old classmate," Bill said. "The saloon must go, and I will take it with me."

"You're cock-eyed."

"On wine?"

"On wine."

"Well, maybe I am."

"Want to take a nap?"

"All right."

We lay with our heads in the shade and looked up into the trees.

"You asleep?"

"No," Bill said. "I was thinking."

I shut my eyes. It felt good lying on the ground.

"Say," Bill said, "what about this Brett business?"

"What about it?"

"Were you ever in love with her?"

"Sure."

"For how long?"

"Off and on for a hell of a long time."

"Oh, hell!" Bill said. "I'm sorry, fella."

"It's all right," I said. "I don't give a damn anymore."

"Really?"

"Really. Only I'd a hell of a lot rather not talk about it."

"You aren't sore I asked you?"

"Why the hell should I be?"

"I'm going to sleep," Bill said. He put a newspaper over his face.

"Listen, Jake," he said, "are you really a Catholic?"

"Technically."

"What does that mean?"

"I don't know."

"All right, I'll go to sleep now," he said. "Don't keep me awake by talking so much."

I went to sleep, too. When I woke up Bill was packing the rucksack. It was late in the afternoon and the shadow from the trees was long and went out over the dam. I was stiff from sleeping on the ground.

"What did you do? Wake up?" Bill asked. "Why didn't you spend the night?" I stretched and rubbed my eyes.

"I had a lovely dream," Bill said. "I don't remember what it was about, but it was a lovely dream."

"I don't think I dreamt."

"You ought to dream," Bill said. "All our biggest business men have been dreamers. Look at Ford. Look at President Coolidge. Look at Rockefeller. Look at Jo Davidson."

I disjointed my rod and Bill's and packed them in the rod-case. I put the reels in the tackle-bag. Bill had packed the rucksack and we put one of the trout-bags in. I carried the other.

"Well," said Bill, "have we got everything?"

"The worms."

"Your worms. Put them in there."

He had the pack on his back and I put the worm-cans in one of the outside flap pockets.

"You got everything now?"

I looked around on the grass at the foot of the elm-trees.

"Yes."

We started up the road into the woods. It was a long walk home to Burguete, and it was dark when we came down across the fields to the road, and along the road between the houses of the town, their windows lighted, to the inn.

We stayed five days at Burguete and had good fishing. The nights were cold and the days were hot, and there was always a breeze even in the heat of the day. It was hot enough so that it felt good to wade in a cold stream, and the sun dried you when you came out and sat on the bank. We found a stream with a pool deep enough to swim in. In the evenings we played three-handed bridge with an Englishman named Harris, who had walked over from Saint Jean Pied de Port and was stopping at the inn for the fishing. He was very pleasant and went with us twice to the Irati River. There was no word from Robert Cohn nor from Brett and Mike.

## CHAPTER THIRTEEN

ONE MORNING I went down to breakfast and the
Englishman, Harris, was already at the table. He
was reading the paper through spectacles. He looked up and
smiled.

"Good morning," he said. "Letter for you. I stopped at the
post and they gave it me with mine."

The letter was at my place at the table, leaning against a
coffee-cup. Harris was reading the paper again. I opened the
letter. It had been forwarded from Pamplona. It was dated San
Sebastian, Sunday:

Dear Jake,

We got here Friday, Brett passed out on the train, so brought
her here for 3 days rest with old friends of ours. We go to Montoya Hotel Pamplona Tuesday, arriving at I don't know what
hour. Will you send a note by the bus to tell us what to do to
rejoin you all on Wednesday? All our love and sorry to be late,
but Brett was really done in and will be quite all right by Tues.
and is practically so now. I know her so well and try to look after
her but it's not so easy. Love to all the chaps,

Michael.

"What day of the week is it?" I asked Harris.

"Wednesday, I think. Yes, quite. Wednesday. Wonderful how
one loses track of the days up here in the mountains."

"Yes. We've been here nearly a week."

"I hope you're not thinking of leaving?"

"Yes. We'll go in on the afternoon bus, I'm afraid."

"What a rotten business. I had hoped we'd all have another go at the Irati together."

"We have to go *into* Pamplona. We're meeting people there."

"What rotten luck for me. We've had a jolly time here at Burguete."

"Come on in to Pamplona. We can play some bridge there, and there's going to be a damned fine fiesta."

"I'd like to. Awfully nice of you to ask me. I'd best stop on here, though. I've not much more time to fish."

"You want those big ones in the Irati."

"I say, I do, you know. They're enormous trout there."

"I'd like to try them once more."

"Do. Stop over another day. Be a good chap."

"We really have to get into town," I said.

"What a pity."

After breakfast Bill and I were sitting warming in the sun on a bench out in front of the inn and talking it over. I saw a girl coming up the road from the center of the town. She stopped in front of us and took a telegram out of the leather wallet that hung against her skirt.

"Por ustedes?"

I looked at it. The address was: "Barnes, Burguete."

"Yes. It's for us."

She brought out a book for me to sign, and I gave her a couple of coppers. The telegram was in Spanish: "Vengo Jueves Cohn."

I handed it to Bill.

"What does the word Cohn mean?" he asked.

"What a lousy telegram!" I said. "He could send ten words for the same price. 'I come Thursday.' That gives you a lot of dope, doesn't it?"

"It gives you all the dope that's of interest to Cohn."

"We're going in, anyway," I said. "There's no use trying to move Brett and Mike out here and back before the fiesta. Should we answer it?"

"We might as well," said Bill. "There's no need for us to be snooty."

We walked up to the post-office and asked for a telegraph blank.

"What will we say?" Bill asked.

"'Arriving tonight.' That's enough."

We paid for the message and walked back to the inn. Harris was there and the three of us walked up to Roncevalles. We went through the monastery.

"It's a remarkable place," Harris said, when we came out. "But you know I'm not much on those sort of places."

"Me either," Bill said.

"It's a remarkable place, though," Harris said. "I wouldn't not have seen it. I'd been intending coming up each day."

"It isn't the same as fishing, though, is it?" Bill asked. He liked Harris.

"I say not."

We were standing in front of the old chapel of the monastery.

"Isn't that a pub across the way?" Harris asked. "Or do my eyes deceive me?"

"It has the look of a pub," Bill said.

"It looks to me like a pub," I said.

"I say," said Harris, "let's utilize it." He had taken up utilizing from Bill.

We had a bottle of wine apiece. Harris would not let us pay. He talked Spanish quite well, and the inn-keeper would not take our money.

"I say. You don't know what it's meant to me to have you chaps up here."

"We've had a grand time, Harris."

Harris was a little tight.

"I say. Really you don't know how much it means. I've not had much fun since the war."

"We'll fish together again, some time. Don't you forget it, Harris."

"We must. We *have* had such a jolly good time."

"How about another bottle around?"

"Jolly good idea," said Harris.

"This is mine," said Bill. "Or we don't drink it."

"I wish you'd let me pay for it. It *does* give me pleasure, you know."

"This is going to give me pleasure," Bill said.

The inn-keeper brought in the fourth bottle. We had kept the same glasses. Harris lifted his glass.

"I say. You know this does utilize well."

Bill slapped him on the back.

"Good old Harris."

"I say. You know my name isn't really Harris. It's Wilson-Harris. All one name. With a hyphen, you know."

"Good old Wilson-Harris," Bill said. "We call you Harris because we're so fond of you."

"I say, Barnes. You don't know what this all means to me."

"Come on and utilize another glass," I said.

"Barnes. Really, Barnes, you can't know. That's all."

"Drink up, Harris."

We walked back down the road from Roncevalles with Harris between us. We had lunch at the inn and Harris went with us to the bus. He gave us his card, with his address in London and his club and his business address, and as we got on the bus he handed us each an envelope. I opened mine and there were a dozen flies in it. Harris had tied them himself. He tied all his own flies.

"I say, Harris—" I began.

"No, no!" he said. He was climbing down from the bus. "They're not first-rate flies at all. I only thought if you fished them some time it might remind you of what a good time we had."

The bus started. Harris stood in front of the post-office. He waved. As we started along the road he turned and walked back toward the inn.

"Say, wasn't that Harris nice?" Bill said.

"I think he really did have a good time."

"Harris? You bet he did."

"I wish he'd come into Pamplona."

"He wanted to fish."

"Yes. You couldn't tell how English would mix with each other, anyway."

"I suppose not."

We got into Pamplona late in the afternoon and the bus stopped in front of the Hotel Montoya. Out in the plaza they were stringing electric-light wires to light the plaza for the fiesta. A few kids came up when the bus stopped, and a custom officer for the town made all the people getting down from the bus open their bundles on the sidewalk. We went into the hotel and on the stairs I met Montoya. He shook hands with us, smiling in his embarrassed way.

"Your friends are here," he said.

"Mr. Campbell?"

"Yes. Mr. Cohn and Mr. Campbell and Lady Ashley."

He smiled as though there were something I would hear about.

"When did they get in?"

"Yesterday. I've saved you the rooms you had."

"That's fine. Did you give Mr. Campbell the room on the plaza?"

"Yes. All the rooms we looked at."

"Where are our friends now?"

"I think they went to the pelota."

"And how about the bulls?"

Montoya smiled. "Tonight," he said. "Tonight at seven o'clock they bring in the Villar bulls, and tomorrow come the Miuras. Do you all go down?"

"Oh, yes. They've never seen a desencajonada."

Montoya put his hand on my shoulder.

"I'll see you there."

He smiled again. He always smiled as though bull-fighting were a very special secret between the two of us; a rather shocking but really very deep secret that we knew about. He always smiled as though there were something lewd about the secret to outsiders, but that it was something that we understood. It would not do to expose it to people who would not understand.

"Your friend, is he aficionado, too?" Montoya smiled at Bill.

"Yes. He came all the way from New York to see the San Fermines."

"Yes?" Montoya politely disbelieved. "But he's not aficionado like you."

He put his hand on my shoulder again embarrassedly.

"Yes," I said. "He's a real aficionado."

"But he's not aficionado like you are."

Aficion means passion. An aficionado is one who is passionate about the bull-fights. All the good bull-fighters stayed at Montoya's hotel; that is, those with aficion stayed there. The commercial bull-fighters stayed once, perhaps, and then did not come back. The good ones came each year. In Montoya's room were their photographs. The photographs were dedicated to Juanito Montoya or to his sister. The photographs of bull-fighters Montoya had really believed in were framed. Photographs of bull-fighters who had been without aficion Montoya kept in a drawer of his desk. They often had the most flattering inscriptions. But they did not mean anything. One day Montoya took them all out and dropped them in the waste-basket. He did not want them around.

We often talked about bulls and bull-fighters. I had stopped at the Montoya for several years. We never talked for very long at a time. It was simply the pleasure of discovering what we each felt. Men would come in from distant towns and before they left Pamplona stop and talk for a few minutes with Montoya about bulls. These men were aficionados. Those who were aficionados could always get rooms even when the hotel was full. Montoya introduced me to some of them. They were always very polite at first, and it amused them very much that I should be an American. Somehow it was taken for granted that an American could not have aficion. He might simulate it or confuse it with excitement, but he could not really have it. When they saw that I had aficion, and there was no password, no set questions that could bring it out, rather it was a sort of oral spiritual examination with the questions always a little on the defensive and never apparent, there was this same embar-

rassed putting the hand on the shoulder, or a "Buen hombre."
But nearly always there was the actual touching. It seemed as
though they wanted to touch you to make it certain.

Montoya could forgive anything of a bull-fighter who had
aficion. He could forgive attacks of nerves, panic, bad unex-
plainable actions, all sorts of lapses. For one who had aficion
he could forgive anything. At once he forgave me all my friends.
Without his ever saying anything they were simply a little
something shameful between us, like the spilling open of the
horses in bull-fighting.

Bill had gone upstairs as we came in, and I found him washing and changing in his room.

"Well," he said, "talk a lot of Spanish?"

"He was telling me about the bulls coming in tonight."

"Let's find the gang and go down."

"All right. They'll probably be at the café."

"Have you got tickets?"

"Yes. I got them for all the unloadings."

"What's it like?" He was pulling his cheek before the glass,
looking to see if there were unshaved patches under the line
of the jaw.

"It's pretty good," I said. "They let the bulls out of the cages
one at a time, and they have steers in the corral to receive
them and keep them from fighting, and the bulls tear in at the
steers and the steers run around like old maids trying to quiet
them down."

"Do they ever gore the steers?"

"Sure. Sometimes they go right after them and kill them."

"Can't the steers do anything?"

"No. They're trying to make friends."

"What do they have them in for?"

"To quiet down the bulls and keep them from breaking their horns against the stone walls, or goring each other."

"Must be swell being a steer."

We went down the stairs and out of the door and walked across the square toward the Café Iruña. There were two lonely looking ticket-houses standing in the square. Their windows, marked SOL, SOL Y SOMBRA, and SOMBRA, were shut. They would not open until the day before the fiesta.

Across the square the white wicker tables and chairs of the Iruña extended out beyond the Arcade to the edge of the street. I looked for Brett and Mike at the tables. There they were. Brett and Mike and Robert Cohn. Brett was wearing a Basque beret. So was Mike. Robert Cohn was bare-headed and wearing his spectacles. Brett saw us coming and waved. Her eyes crinkled up as we came up to the table.

"Hello, you chaps!" she called.

Brett was happy. Mike had a way of getting an intensity of feeling into shaking hands. Robert Cohn shook hands because we were back.

"Where the hell have you been?" I asked.

"I brought them up here," Cohn said.

"What rot," Brett said. "We'd have gotten here earlier if you hadn't come."

"You'd never have gotten here."

"What rot! You chaps are brown. Look at Bill."

"Did you get good fishing?" Mike asked. "We wanted to join you."

"It wasn't bad. We missed you."

"I wanted to come," Cohn said, "but I thought I ought to bring them."

"You bring us. What rot."

"Was it really good?" Mike asked. "Did you take many?"

"Some days we took a dozen apiece. There was an English-man up there."

"Named Harris," Bill said. "Ever know him, Mike? He was in the war, too."

"Fortunate fellow," Mike said. "What times we had. How I wish those dear days were back."

"Don't be an ass."

"Were you in the war, Mike?" Cohn asked.

"Was I not."

"He was a very distinguished soldier," Brett said. "Tell them about the time your horse bolted down Piccadilly."

"I'll not. I've told that four times."

"You never told me," Robert Cohn said.

"I'll not tell that story. It reflects discredit on me."

"Tell them about your medals."

"I'll not. That story reflects great discredit on me."

"What story's that?"

"Brett will tell you. She tells all the stories that reflect dis-credit on me."

"Go on. Tell it, Brett."

"Should I?"

"I'll tell it myself."

"What medals have you got, Mike?"

"I haven't got any medals."

"You must have some."

"I suppose I've the usual medals. But I never sent in for them. One time there was this whopping big dinner and the Prince of Wales was to be there, and the cards said medals will be worn. So naturally I had no medals, and I stopped at my tailor's and he was impressed by the invitation, and I thought that's a good piece of business, and I said to him: 'You've got to fix me up with some medals.' He said: 'What medals, sir?' And I said: 'Oh, any medals. Just give me a few medals.' So he said: 'What medals *have* you, sir?' And I said: 'How should I know?' Did he think I spent all my time reading the bloody gazette? 'Just give me a good lot. Pick them out yourself.' So he got me some medals, you know, miniature medals, and handed me the box, and I put it in my pocket and forgot it. Well, I went to the dinner, and it was the night they'd shot Henry Wilson, so the prince didn't come and the king didn't come, and no one wore any medals, and all these coves were busy taking off their medals, and I had mine in my pocket."

He stopped for us to laugh.

"Is that all?"

"That's all. Perhaps I didn't tell it right."

"You didn't," said Brett. "But no matter."

We were all laughing.

"Ah, yes," said Mike. "I know now. It was a damn dull dinner, and I couldn't stick it, so I left. Later on in the evening I found the box in my pocket. What's this? I said. Medals? Bloody military medals? So I cut them all off their backing—you know, they put them on a strip—and gave them all around. Gave one to each girl. Form of souvenir. They thought I was hell's own shakes of a soldier. Give away medals in a night club. Dashing fellow."

"Tell the rest," Brett said.

"Don't you think that was funny?" Mike asked. We were all laughing. "It was. I swear it was. Any rate, my tailor wrote me and wanted the medals back. Sent a man around. Kept on writing for months. Seems some chap had left them to be cleaned.

Frightfully military cove. Set hell's own store by them." Mike paused. "Rotten luck for the tailor," he said.

"You don't mean it," Bill said. "I should think it would have been grand for the tailor."

"Frightfully good tailor. Never believe it to see me now," Mike said. "I used to pay him a hundred pounds a year just to keep him quiet. So he wouldn't send me any bills. Frightful blow to him when I went bankrupt. It was right after the medals. Gave his letters rather a bitter tone."

"How did you go bankrupt?" Bill asked.

"Two ways," Mike said. "Gradually and then suddenly."

"What brought it on?"

"Friends," said Mike. "I had a lot of friends. False friends. Then I had creditors, too. Probably had more creditors than anybody in England."

"Tell them about in the court," Brett said.

"I don't remember," Mike said. "I was just a little tight."

"Tight!" Brett exclaimed. "You were blind!"

"Extraordinary thing," Mike said. "Met my former partner the other day. Offered to buy me a drink."

"Tell them about your learned counsel," Brett said.

"I will not," Mike said. "My learned counsel was blind, too. I say this is a gloomy subject. Are we going down and see these bulls unloaded or not?"

"Let's go down."

We called the waiter, paid, and started to walk through the town. I started off walking with Brett, but Robert Cohn came up and joined her on the other side. The three of us walked along, past the Ayuntamiento with the banners hung from the balcony, down past the market and down past the steep street that led to the bridge across the Arga. There were many people walking to go and see the bulls, and carriages drove down the hill and across the bridge, the drivers, the horses, and the whips rising above the walking people in the street. Across the bridge we turned up a road to the corrals. We passed a wine-shop with a sign in the window: Good Wine 30 Centimes A Liter.

"That's where we'll go when funds get low," Brett said.

The woman standing in the door of the wine-shop looked at us as we passed. She called to someone in the house and three girls came to the window and stared. They were staring at Brett.

At the gate of the corrals two men took tickets from the people that went in. We went in through the gate. There were trees inside and a low, stone house. At the far end was the stone wall of the corrals, with apertures in the stone that were like loopholes running all along the face of each corral. A ladder led up to the top of the wall, and people were climbing up the ladder and spreading down to stand on the walls that separated the two corrals. As we came up to the ladder, walking across the grass under the trees, we passed the big, gray painted cages with the bulls in them. There was one bull in each travelling-box. They had come by train from a bull-breeding ranch in Castile, and had been unloaded off flat-cars at the station and brought up here to be let out of their cages into the corrals. Each cage was stencilled with the name and the brand of the bull-breeder.

We climbed up and found a place on the wall looking down into the corral. The stone walls were whitewashed, and there was straw on the ground and wooden feed-boxes and water-troughs set against the wall.

"Look up there," I said.

Beyond the river rose the plateau of the town. All along the

old walls and ramparts people were standing. The three lines of
fortifications made three black lines of people. Above the walls
there were heads in the windows of the houses. At the far end
of the plateau boys had climbed into the trees.

"They must think something is going to happen," Brett said.

"They want to see the bulls."

Mike and Bill were on the other wall across the pit of the corral. They waved to us. People who had come late were standing behind us, pressing against us when other people crowded
them.

"Why don't they start?" Robert Cohn asked.

A single mule was hitched to one of the cages and dragged
it up against the gate in the corral wall. The men shoved and
lifted it with crowbars into position against the gate. Men were
standing on the wall ready to pull up the gate of the corral and
then the gate of the cage. At the other end of the corral a gate
opened and two steers came in, swaying their heads and trotting, their lean flanks swinging. They stood together at the far
end, their heads toward the gate where the bull would enter.

"They don't look happy," Brett said.

The men on top of the wall leaned back and pulled up the
door of the corral. Then they pulled up the door of the cage.

I leaned way over the wall and tried to see into the cage. It
was dark. Someone rapped on the cage with an iron bar. Inside
something seemed to explode. The bull, striking into the wood
from side to side with his horns, made a great noise. Then I
saw a dark muzzle and the shadow of horns, and then, with a
clattering on the wood in the hollow box, the bull charged and
came out into the corral, skidding with his forefeet in the straw
as he stopped, his head up, the great hump of muscle on his
neck swollen tight, his body muscles quivering as he looked up

at the crowd on the stone walls. The two steers backed away against the wall, their heads sunken, their eyes watching the bull.

The bull saw them and charged. A man shouted from behind one of the boxes and slapped his hat against the planks, and the bull, before he reached the steer, turned, gathered himself and charged where the man had been, trying to reach him behind the planks with a half-dozen quick, searching drives with the right horn.

"My God, isn't he beautiful?" Brett said. We were looking right down on him.

"Look how he knows how to use his horns," I said. "He's got a left and a right just like a boxer."

"Not really?"

"You watch."

"It goes too fast."

"Wait. There'll be another one in a minute."

They had backed up another cage into the entrance. In the far corner a man, from behind one of the plank shelters, attracted the bull, and while the bull was facing away the gate was pulled up and a second bull came out into the corral.

He charged straight for the steers and two men ran out from behind the planks and shouted, to turn him. He did not change his direction and the men shouted: "Hah! Hah! Toro!" and waved their arms; the two steers turned sideways to take the shock, and the bull drove into one of the steers.

"Don't look," I said to Brett. She was watching, fascinated.

"Fine," I said. "If it doesn't buck you."

"I saw it," she said. "I saw him shift from his left to his right horn."

"Damn good!"

The steer was down now, his neck stretched out, his head twisted, he lay the way he had fallen. Suddenly the bull left off and made for the other steer which had been standing at the far end, his head swinging, watching it all. The steer ran awkwardly and the bull caught him, hooked him lightly in the flank, and then turned away and looked up at the crowd on the walls, his crest of muscle rising. The steer came up to him and made as though to nose at him and the bull hooked perfunctorily. The next time he nosed at the steer and then the two of them trotted over to the other bull.

When the next bull came out, all three, the two bulls and the steer, stood together, their heads side by side, their horns against the newcomer. In a few minutes the steer picked the new bull up, quieted him down, and made him one of the herd. When the last two bulls had been unloaded the herd were all together.

The steer who had been gored had gotten to his feet and stood against the stone wall. None of the bulls came near him, and he did not attempt to join the herd.

We climbed down from the wall with the crowd, and had a last look at the bulls through the loopholes in the wall of the corral. They were all quiet now, their heads down. We got a carriage outside and rode up to the café. Mike and Bill came in half an hour later. They had stopped on the way for several drinks.

We were sitting in the café.

"That's an extraordinary business," Brett said.

"Will those last ones fight as well as the first?" Robert Cohn asked. "They seemed to quiet down awfully fast."

"They all know each other," I said. "They're only dangerous when they're alone, or only two or three of them together."

"What do you mean, dangerous?" Bill said. "They all looked dangerous to me."

"They only want to kill when they're alone. Of course, if you went in there you'd probably detach one of them from the herd, and he'd be dangerous."

"That's too complicated," Bill said. "Don't you ever detach me from the herd, Mike."

"I say," Mike said, "they *were* fine bulls, weren't they? Did you see their horns?"

"Did I not," said Brett. "I had no idea what they were like."

"Did you see the one hit that steer?" Mike asked. "That was extraordinary."

"It's no life being a steer," Robert Cohn said.

"Don't you think so?" Mike said. "I would have thought you'd loved being a steer, Robert."

"What do you mean, Mike?"

"They lead such a quiet life. They never say anything and they're always hanging about so."

We were embarrassed. Bill laughed. Robert Cohn was angry. Mike went on talking.

"I should think you'd love it. You'd never have to say a word. Come on, Robert. Do say something. Don't just sit there."

"I said something, Mike. Don't you remember? About the steers."

"Oh, say something more. Say something funny. Can't you see we're all having a good time here?"

"Come off it, Michael. You're drunk," Brett said.

"I'm not drunk. I'm quite serious. *Is* Robert Cohn going to follow Brett around like a steer all the time?"

"Shut up, Michael. Try and show a little breeding."

"Breeding be damned. Who has any breeding, anyway,

except the bulls? Aren't the bulls lovely? Don't you like them, Bill? Why don't you say something, Robert? Don't sit there looking like a bloody funeral. What if Brett did sleep with you? She's slept with lots of better people than you."

"Shut up," Cohn said. He stood up. "Shut up, Mike."

"Oh, don't stand up and act as though you were going to hit me. That won't make any difference to me. Tell me, Robert. Why do you follow Brett around like a poor bloody steer? Don't you know you're not wanted? I know when I'm not wanted. Why don't you know when you're not wanted? You came down to San Sebastian where you weren't wanted, and followed Brett around like a bloody steer. Do you think that's right?"

"Shut up. You're drunk."

"Perhaps I am drunk. Why aren't you drunk? Why don't you ever get drunk, Robert? You know you didn't have a good time at San Sebastian because none of our friends would invite you on any of the parties. You can't blame them hardly. Can you? I asked them to. They wouldn't do it. You can't blame them, now. Can you? Now, answer me. Can you blame them?"

"Go to hell, Mike."

"I can't blame them. Can you blame them? Why do you follow Brett around? Haven't you any manners? How do you think it makes *me* feel?"

"You're a splendid one to talk about manners," Brett said. "You've such lovely manners."

"Come on, Robert," Bill said.

"What do you follow her around for?"

Bill stood up and took hold of Cohn.

"Don't go," Mike said. "Robert Cohn's going to buy a drink."

Bill went off with Cohn. Cohn's face was sallow. Mike went on talking. I sat and listened for a while. Brett looked disgusted.

"I say, Michael, you might not be such a bloody ass," she interrupted. "I'm not saying he's not right, you know." She turned to me.

The emotion left Mike's voice. We were all friends together.

"I'm not so damn drunk as I sounded," he said.

"I know you're not," Brett said.

"We're none of us sober," I said.

"I didn't say anything I didn't mean."

"But you put it so badly," Brett laughed.

"He was an ass, though. He came down to San Sebastian where he damn well wasn't wanted. He hung around Brett and just *looked* at her. It made me damned well sick."

"He did behave very badly," Brett said.

"Mark you. Brett's had affairs with men before. She tells me all about everything. She gave me this chap Cohn's letters to read. I wouldn't read them."

"Damned noble of you."

"No, listen, Jake. Brett's gone off with men. But they weren't ever Jews, and they didn't come and hang about afterward."

"Damned good chaps," Brett said. "It's all rot to talk about it. Michael and I understand each other."

"She gave me Robert Cohn's letters. I wouldn't read them."

"You wouldn't read any letters, darling. You wouldn't read mine."

"I can't read letters," Mike said. "Funny, isn't it?"

"You can't read anything."

"No. You're wrong there. I read quite a bit. I read when I'm at home."

"You'll be writing next," Brett said. "Come on, Michael. Do buck up. You've got to go through with this thing now. He's here. Don't spoil the fiesta."

"Well, let him behave, then."

"He'll behave. I'll tell him."

"You tell him, Jake. Tell him either he must behave or get out."

"Yes," I said, "it would be nice for me to tell him."

"Look, Brett. Tell Jake what Robert calls you. That *is* perfect, you know."

"Oh, no. I can't."

"Go on. We're all friends. Aren't we all friends, Jake?"

"I can't tell him. It's too ridiculous."

"I'll tell him."

"You won't, Michael. Don't be an ass."

"He calls her Circe," Mike said. "He claims she turns men into swine. Damn good. I wish I were one of these literary chaps."

"He'd be good, you know," Brett said. "He writes a good letter."

"I know," I said. "He wrote me from San Sebastian."

"That was nothing," Brett said. "He can write a damned amusing letter."

"She made me write that. She was supposed to be ill."

"I damned well was, too."

"Come on," I said, "we must go in and eat."

"How should I meet Cohn?" Mike said.

"Just act as though nothing had happened."

"It's quite all right with me," Mike said. "I'm not embarrassed."

"If he says anything, just say you were tight."

"Quite. And the funny thing is I think I was tight."

"Come on," Brett said. "Are these poisonous things paid for? I must bathe before dinner."

We walked across the square. It was dark and all around the square were the lights from the cafés under the arcades. We walked across the gravel under the trees to the hotel.

They went upstairs and I stopped to speak with Montoya.

"Well, how did you like the bulls?" he asked.

"Good. They were nice bulls."

"They're all right"—Montoya shook his head—"but they're not too good."

"What didn't you like about them?"

"I don't know. They just didn't give me the feeling that they were so good."

"I know what you mean."

"They're all right."

"Yes. They're all right."

"How did your friends like them?"

"Fine."

"Good," Montoya said.

I went upstairs. Bill was in his room standing on the balcony looking out at the square. I stood beside him.

"Where's Cohn?"

"Upstairs in his room."

"How does he feel?"

"Like hell, naturally. Mike was awful. He's terrible when he's tight."

"He wasn't so tight."

"The hell he wasn't. I know what we had before we came to the café."

"He sobered up afterward."

"Good. He was terrible. I don't like Cohn, God knows, and I think it was a silly trick for him to go down to San Sebastian, but nobody has any business to talk like Mike."

"How'd you like the bulls?"

"Grand. It's grand the way they bring them out."

"Tomorrow come the Miuras."

"When does the fiesta start?"

"Day after tomorrow."

"We've got to keep Mike from getting so tight. That kind of stuff is terrible."

"We'd better get cleaned up for supper."

"Yes. That will be a pleasant meal."

"Won't it."

As a matter of fact, supper was a pleasant meal. Brett wore a black, sleeveless evening dress. She looked quite beautiful. Mike acted as though nothing had happened. I had to go up and bring Robert Cohn down. He was reserved and formal, and his face was still taut and sallow, but he cheered up finally. He could not stop looking at Brett. It seemed to make him happy. It must have been pleasant for him to see her looking so lovely, and know he had been away with her and that everyone knew it. They could not take that away from him. Bill was very funny. So was Michael. They were good together.

It was like certain dinners I remember from the war. There was much wine, an ignored tension, and a feeling of things coming that you could not prevent happening. Under the wine I lost the disgusted feeling and was happy. It seemed they were all such nice people.

## CHAPTER FOURTEEN

I DO NOT know what time I got to bed. I remember undressing, putting on a bathrobe, and standing out on the balcony. I knew I was quite drunk, and when I came in I put on the light over the head of the bed and started to read. I was reading a book by Turgenieff. Probably I read the same two pages over several times. It was one of the stories in *A Sportsman's Sketches*. I had read it before, but it seemed quite new. The country became very clear and the feeling of pressure in my head seemed to loosen. I was very drunk and I did not want to shut my eyes because the room would go round and round. If I kept on reading that feeling would pass.

I heard Brett and Robert Cohn come up the stairs. Cohn said good night outside the door and went on up to his room. I heard Brett go into the room next door. Mike was already in bed. He had come in with me an hour before. He woke as she came in, and they talked together. I heard them laugh. I turned off the light and tried to go to sleep. It was not necessary to read anymore. I could shut my eyes without getting the wheeling sensation. But I could not sleep. There is no reason why because it is dark you should look at things differently from when it is light. The hell there isn't!

I figured that all out once, and for six months I never slept with the electric light off. That was another bright idea. To hell with women, anyway. To hell with you, Brett Ashley.

Women made such swell friends. Awfully swell. In the first place, you had to be in love with a woman to have a basis of friendship. I had been having Brett for a friend. I had not been thinking about her side of it. I had been getting something for nothing. That only delayed the presentation of the bill. The bill always came. That was one of the swell things you could count on.

I thought I had paid for everything. Not like the woman pays and pays and pays. No idea of retribution or punishment. Just exchange of values. You gave up something and got something else. Or you worked for something. You paid some way for everything that was any good. I paid my way into enough things that I liked, so that I had a good time. Either you paid by learning about them, or by experience, or by taking chances, or by money. Enjoying living was learning to get your money's worth and knowing when you had it. You could get your money's worth. The world was a good place to buy in. It seemed like a fine philosophy. In five years, I thought, it will seem just as silly as all the other fine philosophies I've had.

Perhaps that wasn't true, though. Perhaps as you went along you did learn something. I did not care what it was all about. All I wanted to know was how to live in it. Maybe if you found out how to live in it you learned from that what it was all about.

I wished Mike would not behave so terribly to Cohn, though. Mike was a bad drunk. Brett was a good drunk. Bill was a good drunk. Cohn was never drunk. Mike was unpleasant after he passed a certain point. I liked to see him hurt Cohn. I wished he would not do it, though, because afterward it made me disgusted at myself. That was morality; things that made you disgusted afterward. No, that must be immorality. That was a large statement. What a lot of bilge I could think up at night. What rot, I could hear Brett say it. What rot! When you were with English you got into the habit of using English expressions in your thinking. The English spoken language— the upper classes, anyway—must have fewer words than the Eskimo. Of course I didn't know anything about the Eskimo. Maybe the Eskimo was a fine language. Say the Cherokee. I didn't know anything about the Cherokee, either. The English talked with inflected phrases. One phrase to mean everything. I liked them, though. I liked the way they talked. Take Harris. Still Harris was not the upper classes.

I turned on the light again and read. I read the Turgenieff. I knew that now, reading it in the oversensitized state of my mind after much too much brandy, I would remember it somewhere, and afterward it would seem as though it had really happened to me. I would always have it. That was another good thing you paid for and then had. Sometime along toward daylight I went to sleep.

The next two days in Pamplona were quiet, and there were no more rows. The town was getting ready for the fiesta. Work-men put up the gate-posts that were to shut off the side streets when the bulls were released from the corrals and came run-ning through the streets in the morning on their way to the ring. The workmen dug holes and fitted in the timbers, each timber numbered for its regular place. Out on the plateau beyond the town employees of the bull-ring exercised pica-dor horses, galloping them stiff-legged on the hard, sun baked fields behind the bull-ring. The big gate of the bull-ring was open, and inside the amphitheater was being swept. The ring was rolled and sprinkled, and carpenters replaced weakened or cracked planks in the barrera. Standing at the edge of the smooth rolled sand you could look up in the empty stands and see old women sweeping out the boxes.

Outside, the fence that led from the last street of the town to the entrance of the bull-ring was already in place and made a long pen; the crowd would come running down with the bulls behind them on the morning of the day of the first bull-fight. Out across the plain, where the horse and cattle fair would be, some gypsies had camped under the trees. The wine and aguardiente sellers were putting up their booths. One booth advertised ANIS DEL TORO. The cloth sign hung against the planks in the hot sun. In the big square that was the center of the town there was no change yet. We sat in the white wicker chairs on the terrasse of the café and watched the motor-buses come in and unload peasants from the country coming in to the market, and we watched the buses fill up and start out with peasants sitting with their saddle-bags full of the things they had bought in the town. The tall gray motor-buses were the only life of the square except for the pigeons and the man with a hose who sprinkled the gravelled square and watered the streets.

In the evening was the paseo. For an hour after dinner every-one, all the good-looking girls, the officers from the garrison, all the fashionable people of the town, walked in the street on one side of the square while the café tables filled with the regular after-dinner crowd.

During the morning I usually sat in the café and read the Madrid papers and then walked in the town or out into the country. Sometimes Bill went along. Sometimes he wrote in his room. Robert Cohn spent the mornings studying Spanish or trying to get a shave at the barber-shop. Brett and Mike never got up until noon. We all had a vermouth at the café. It was a quiet life and no one was drunk. I went to church a couple of times, once with Brett. She said she wanted to hear me go to confession, but I told her that not only was it impossible but it was not as interesting as it sounded, and, besides, it would be in a language she did not know. We met Cohn as we came out of church, and although it was obvious he had followed us, yet he was very pleasant and nice, and we all three went for a walk out to the gypsy camp, and Brett had her fortune told.

It was a good morning, there were high white clouds above the mountains. It had rained a little in the night and it was fresh and cool on the plateau, and there was a wonderful view. We all felt good and we felt healthy, and I felt quite friendly to Cohn. You could not be upset about anything on a day like that.

That was the last day before the fiesta.

## CHAPTER FIFTEEN

A T NOON of Sunday, the 6th of July, the fiesta exploded. There is no other way to describe it. People had been coming in all day from the country, but they were assimilated in the town and you did not notice them. The square was as quiet in the hot sun as on any other day. The peasants were in the outlying wine-shops. There they were drinking, getting ready for the fiesta. They had come in so recently from the plains and the hills that it was necessary that they make their shifting in values gradually. They could not start in paying café prices. They got their money's worth in the wine-shops. Money still had a definite value in hours worked and bushels of grain sold. Late in the fiesta it would not matter what they paid, nor where they bought.

Now on the day of the starting of the fiesta of San Fermin they had been in the wine-shops of the narrow streets of the town since early morning. Going down the streets in the morning on the way to mass in the cathedral, I heard them singing through the open doors of the shops. They were warming up. There were many people at the eleven o'clock mass. San Fermin is also a religious festival.

I walked down the hill from the cathedral and up the street to the café on the square. It was a little before noon. Robert Cohn and Bill were sitting at one of the tables. The marble-topped tables and the white wicker chairs were gone. They were replaced by cast-iron tables and severe folding chairs. The café was like a battleship stripped for action. Today the waiters did not leave you alone all morning to read without asking if you wanted to order something. A waiter came up as soon as I sat down.

"What are you drinking?" I asked Bill and Robert.

"Sherry," Cohn said.

"Jerez," I said to the waiter.

Before the waiter brought the sherry the rocket that announced the fiesta went up in the square. It burst and there was a gray ball of smoke high up above the Theatre Gayarre, across on the other side of the plaza. The ball of smoke hung in the sky like a shrapnel burst, and as I watched, another rocket came up to it, trickling smoke in the bright sunlight. I saw the bright flash as it burst and another little cloud of smoke appeared. By the time the second rocket had burst there were so many people in the arcade, that had been empty a minute before, that the waiter, holding the bottle high up over his head, could hardly get through the crowd to our table. People were coming into the square from all sides, and down the street we heard the pipes and the fifes and the drums coming. They were playing the *riau-riau* music, the pipes shrill and the drums pounding, and behind them came the men and boys dancing. When the fifers stopped they all crouched down in the street, and when the reed-pipes and the fifes shrilled, and the flat, dry, hollow drums tapped it out again, they all went up in the air dancing. In the crowd you saw only the heads and shoulders of the dancers going up and down.

In the square a man, bent over, was playing on a reed-pipe, and a crowd of children were following him shouting and pulling at his clothes. He came out of the square, the children following him, and piped them past the café and down a side street. We saw his blank pockmarked face as he went by, piping, the children close behind him shouting and pulling at him.

"He must be the village idiot," Bill said. "My God! look at that!"

Down the street came dancers. The street was solid with dancers, all men. They were all dancing in time behind their own fifers and drummers. They were a club of some sort, and all wore workmen's blue smocks, and red handkerchiefs around their necks, and carried a great banner on two poles. The banner danced up and down with them as they came down surrounded by the crowd.

"Hurray for Wine! Hurray for the Foreigners!" was painted on the banner.

"Where are the foreigners?" Robert Cohn asked.

"We're the foreigners," Bill said.

All the time rockets were going up. The café tables were all full now. The square was emptying of people and the crowd was filling the cafés.

"Where's Brett and Mike?" Bill asked.

"I'll go and get them," Cohn said.

"Bring them here."

The fiesta was really started. It kept up day and night for seven days. The dancing kept up, the drinking kept up, the noise went on. The things that happened could only have happened during a fiesta. Everything became quite unreal finally and it seemed as though nothing could have any consequences. It seemed out of place to think of consequences during the fiesta. All during the fiesta you had the feeling, even when it was quiet, that you had to shout any remark to make it heard. It was the same feeling about any action. It was a fiesta and it went on for seven days.

That afternoon was the big religious procession. San Fermin was translated from one church to another. In the procession were all the dignitaries, civil and religious. We could not see them because the crowd was too great. Ahead of the formal procession and behind it danced the *riau-riau* dancers. There was one mass of yellow shirts dancing up and down in the crowd. All we could see of the procession through the closely pressed people that crowded all the side streets and curbs were the great giants, cigar-store Indians, thirty feet high, Moors, a King and Queen, whirling and waltzing solemnly to the *riau-riau*.

They were all standing outside the chapel where San Fermin and the dignitaries had passed in leaving a guard of soldiers, the giants, with the men who danced in them standing beside their resting frames, and the dwarfs moving with their whacking bladders through the crowd. We started inside and there was a smell of incense and people filing back into the church, but Brett was stopped just inside the door because she had no hat, so we went out again and along the street that ran back from the chapel into town. The street was lined on both sides with people keeping their place at the curb for the return of the procession. Some dancers formed a circle around Brett and started to dance. They wore big wreaths of white garlics around their necks. They took Bill and me by the arms and put us in the circle. Bill started to dance, too. They were all chanting. Brett wanted to dance but they did not want her to. They wanted her as an image to dance around. When the song ended with the sharp *riau-riau!* they rushed us into a wine-shop.

We stood at the counter. They had Brett seated on a wine-cask. It was dark in the wine-shop and full of men singing, hard-voiced singing. Back of the counter they drew the wine from casks. I put down money for the wine, but one of the men picked it up and put it back in my pocket.

"I want a leather wine-bottle," Bill said.

"There's a place down the street," I said. "I'll go get a couple."

The dancers did not want me to go out. Three of them were sitting on the high wine-cask beside Brett, teaching her to drink out of the wine-skins. They had hung a wreath of garlics around her neck. Someone insisted on giving her a glass. Somebody was teaching Bill a song. Singing it into his ear. Beating time on Bill's back.

I explained to them that I would be back. Outside in the street I went down the street looking for the shop that made leather wine-bottles. The crowd was packed on the sidewalks and many of the shops were shuttered, and I could not find it. I walked as far as the church, looking on both sides of the street. Then I asked a man and he took me by the arm and led me to it. The shutters were up but the door was open.

Inside it smelled of fresh tanned leather and hot tar. A man was stencilling completed wine-skins. They hung from the roof in bunches. He took one down, blew it up, screwed the nozzle tight, and then jumped on it.

"See! It doesn't leak."

"I want another one, too. A big one."

He took down a big one that would hold a gallon or more from the roof. He blew it up, his cheeks puffing ahead of the wine-skin, and stood on the bota holding on to a chair.

"What are you going to do? Sell them in Bayonne?"

"No. Drink out of them."

He slapped me on the back.

"Good man. Eight pesetas for the two. The lowest price."

The man who was stencilling the new ones and tossing them into a pile stopped.

"It's true," he said. "Eight pesetas is cheap."

I paid and went out and along the street back to the wine-shop. It was darker than ever inside and very crowded. I did not see Brett and Bill, and someone said they were in the back room. At the counter the girl filled the two wine-skins for me. One held two liters. The other held five liters. Filling them both cost three pesetas sixty centimes. Someone at the counter, that I had never seen before, tried to pay for the wine, but I finally paid for it myself. The man who had wanted to pay then bought me a drink. He would not let me buy one in return, but said he would take a rinse of the mouth from the new wine-bag. He tipped the big six-liter bag up and squeezed it so the wine hissed against the back of his throat.

"All right," he said, and handed back the bag.

In the back room Brett and Bill were sitting on barrels surrounded by the dancers. Everybody had his arms on everybody else's shoulders, and they were all singing. Mike was sitting at a table with several men in their shirt-sleeves eating from a bowl of tuna fish, chopped onions and vinegar. They were all drinking wine and mopping up the oil and vinegar with pieces of bread.

"Hello, Jake. Hello!" Mike called. "Come here. I want you to meet my friends. We're all having an hors-d'oeuvre."

I was introduced to the people at the table. They supplied their names to Mike and sent for a fork for me.

"Stop eating their dinner, Michael," Brett shouted from the wine-barrels.

"I don't want to eat up your meal," I said when someone handed me a fork.

"Eat," he said. "What do you think it's here for?"

I unscrewed the nozzle of the big wine-bottle and handed it around. Everyone took a drink, tipping the wine-skin at arm's length.

Outside, above the singing, we could hear the music of the procession going by.

"Isn't that the procession?" Mike asked.

"Nada," someone said. "It's nothing. Drink up. Lift the bottle."

"Where did they find you?" I asked Mike.

"Someone brought me here," Mike said. "They said you were here."

"Where's Cohn?"

"He's passed out," Brett called. "They've put him away somewhere."

"Where is he?"

"I don't know."

"How should we know," Bill said. "I think he's dead."

"He's not dead," Mike said. "I know he's not dead. He's just passed out on Anis del Mono."

As he said Anis del Mono one of the men at the table looked up, brought out a bottle from inside his smock, and handed it to me.

"No," I said. "No thanks!"

"Yes. Yes. Arriba! Up with the bottle!"

I took a drink. It tasted of licorice and warmed all the way. I could feel it warming in my stomach.

"Where the hell is Cohn?"

"I don't know," Mike said. "I'll ask. Where is the drunken comrade?" he asked in Spanish.

"You want to see him?"

"Yes," I said.

"Not me," said Mike. "This gent."

The Anis del Mono man wiped his mouth and stood up.

"Come on."

In a back room Robert Cohn was sleeping quietly on some wine-casks. It was almost too dark to see his face. They had covered him with a coat and another coat was folded under his head. Around his neck and on his chest was a big wreath of twisted garlics.

"Let him sleep," the man whispered. "He's all right."

Two hours later Cohn appeared. He came into the front room still with the wreath of garlics around his neck. The Spaniards shouted when he came in. Cohn wiped his eyes and grinned.

"I must have been sleeping," he said.

"Oh, not at all," Brett said.

"You were only dead," Bill said.

"Aren't we going to go and have some supper?" Cohn asked.

"Do you want to eat?"

"Yes. Why not? I'm hungry."

"Eat those garlics, Robert," Mike said. "I say. Do eat those garlics."

Cohn stood there. His sleep had made him quite all right.

"Do let's go and eat," Brett said. "I must get a bath."

"Come on," Bill said. "Let's translate Brett to the hotel."

We said goodbye to many people and shook hands with many people and went out. Outside it was dark.

"What time is it do you suppose?" Cohn asked.

"It's tomorrow," Mike said. "You've been asleep two days."

"No," said Cohn, "what time is it?"

"It's ten o'clock."

"What a lot we've drunk."

"You mean what a lot *we've* drunk. You went to sleep."

Going down the dark streets to the hotel we saw the sky-rockets going up in the square. Down the side streets that led to the square we saw the square solid with people, those in the center all dancing.

It was a big meal at the hotel. It was the first meal of the prices being doubled for the fiesta, and there were several new courses. After the dinner we were out in the town. I remember resolving that I would stay up all night to watch the bulls go through the streets at six o'clock in the morning, and being so sleepy that I went to bed around four o'clock. The others stayed up.

My own room was locked and I could not find the key, so I went upstairs and slept on one of the beds in Cohn's room. The fiesta was going on outside in the night, but I was too sleepy for it to keep me awake. When I woke it was the sound of the rocket exploding that announced the release of the bulls from the corrals at the edge of town. They would race through the streets and out to the bull-ring. I had been sleeping heavily and I woke feeling I was too late. I put on a coat of Cohn's and went out on the balcony. Down below the narrow street was empty. All the balconies were crowded with people. Suddenly a crowd came down the street. They were all running, packed close together. They passed along and up the street toward the bull-ring and behind them came more men running faster, and then some stragglers who were really running. Behind them was a little bare space, and then the bulls, galloping, tossing their heads up and down. It all went out of sight around the corner. One man fell, rolled to the gutter, and lay quiet. But the bulls went right on and did not notice him. They were all running together.

After they went out of sight a great roar came from the bull-ring. It kept on. Then finally the pop of the rocket that meant the bulls had gotten through the people in the ring and into the corrals. I went back in the room and got into bed. I had been standing on the stone balcony in bare feet. I knew our crowd must have all been out at the bull-ring. Back in bed, I went to sleep.

Cohn woke me when he came in. He started to undress and went over and closed the window because the people on the balcony of the house just across the street were looking in.

"Did you see the show?" I asked.

"Yes. We were all there."

"Anybody get hurt?"

"One of the bulls got into the crowd in the ring and tossed six or eight people."

"How did Brett like it?"

"It was all so sudden there wasn't any time for it to bother anybody."

"I wish I'd been up."

"We didn't know where you were. We went to your room but it was locked."

"Where did you stay up?"

"We danced at some club."

"I got sleepy," I said.

"My gosh! I'm sleepy now," Cohn said. "Doesn't this thing ever stop?"

"Not for a week."

Bill opened the door and put his head in.

"Where were you, Jake?"

"I saw them go through from the balcony. How was it?"

"Grand."

"Where you going?"

"To sleep."

No one was up before noon. We ate at tables set out under the arcade. The town was full of people. We had to wait for a table. After lunch we went over to the Iruña. It had filled up, and as the time for the bull-fight came it got fuller, and the tables were crowded closer. There was a close, crowded hum that came every day before the bull-fight. The café did not make this same noise at any other time, no matter how crowded it was. This hum went on, and we were in it and a part of it.

I had taken six seats for all the fights. Three of them were barreras, the first row at the ring-side, and three were sobrepuertos, seats with wooden backs, half-way up the amphitheatre. Mike thought Brett had best sit high up for her first time, and Cohn wanted to sit with them. Bill and I were going to sit in the barreras, and I gave the extra ticket to a waiter to sell. Bill said something to Cohn about what to do and how to look so he would not mind the horses. Bill had seen one season of bull-fights.

"I'm not worried about how I'll stand it. I'm only afraid I may be bored," Cohn said.

"You think so?"

"Don't look at the horses, after the bull hits them," I said to Brett. "Watch the charge and see the picador try and keep the bull off, but then don't look again until the horse is dead if it's been hit."

"I'm a little nervy about it," Brett said. "I'm worried whether I'll be able to go through with it all right."

"You'll be all right. There's nothing but that horse part that will bother you, and they're only in for a few minutes with each bull. Just don't watch when it's bad."

"She'll be all right," Mike said. "I'll look after her."

"I don't think you'll be bored," Bill said.

"I'm going over to the hotel to get the glasses and the wine-skin," I said. "See you back here. Don't get cock-eyed."

"I'll come along," Bill said. Brett smiled at us.

We walked around through the arcade to avoid the heat of the square.

"That Cohn gets me," Bill said. "He's got this Jewish superiority so strong that he thinks the only emotion he'll get out of the fight will be being bored."

"We'll watch him with the glasses," I said.

"Oh, to hell with him!"

"He spends a lot of time there."

"I want him to stay there."

In the hotel on the stairs we met Montoya.

"Come on," said Montoya. "Do you want to meet Pedro Romero?"

"Fine," said Bill. "Let's go see him."

We followed Montoya up a flight and down the corridor.

"He's in room number eight," Montoya explained. "He's getting dressed for the bull-fight."

Montoya knocked on the door and opened it. It was a gloomy room with a little light coming in from the window on the narrow street. There were two beds separated by a monastic partition. The electric light was on. The boy stood very straight and unsmiling in his bull-fighting clothes. His jacket hung over the back of a chair. They were just finishing winding his sash. His black hair shone under the electric light. He wore a white linen shirt and the sword-handler finished his sash and stood up and stepped back. Pedro Romero nodded, seeming very far away and dignified when we shook hands. Montoya said something about what great aficionados we were, and that we wanted to wish him luck. Romero listened very seriously. Then he turned to me. He was the best-looking boy I have ever seen.

"You go to the bull-fight," he said in English.

"You know English," I said, feeling like an idiot.

"No," he answered, and smiled.

One of three men who had been sitting on the beds came up and asked us if we spoke French. "Would you like me to interpret for you? Is there anything you would like to ask Pedro Romero?"

We thanked him. What was there that you would like to ask? The boy was nineteen years old, alone except for his sword-handler and the three hangers-on, and the bull-fight was to commence in twenty minutes. We wished him "Mucha suerte," shook hands, and went out. He was standing, straight and handsome and altogether by himself, alone in the room with the hangers-on as we shut the door.

"He's a fine boy, don't you think so?" Montoya asked.

"He's a good-looking kid," I said.

"He looks like a torero," Montoya said. "He has the type."

"He's a fine boy."

"We'll see how he is in the ring," Montoya said.

We found the big leather wine-bottle leaning against the wall in my room, took it and the field-glasses, locked the door, and went downstairs.

It was a good bull-fight. Bill and I were very excited about Pedro Romero. Montoya was sitting about ten places away.

After Romero had killed his first bull Montoya caught my eye and nodded his head. This was a real one. There had not been a real one for a long time. Of the other two matadors, one was very fair and the other was passable. But there was no comparison with Romero, although neither of his bulls was much.

Several times during the bull-fight I looked up at Mike and Brett and Cohn, with the glasses. They seemed to be all right. Brett did not look upset. All three were leaning forward on the concrete railing in front of them.

"Let me take the glasses," Bill said.

"Does Cohn look bored?" I asked.

"That kike!"

Outside the ring, after the bull-fight was over, you could not move in the crowd. We could not make our way through but had to be moved with the whole thing, slowly, as a glacier, back to town. We had that disturbed emotional feeling that always comes after a bull-fight and the feeling of elation that comes after a good bull-fight. The fiesta was going on. The drums pounded and the pipe music was shrill, and everywhere the flow of the crowd was broken by patches of dancers. The dancers were in a crowd, so you did not see the intricate play of the feet. All you saw was the heads and shoulders going up and down, up and down. Finally, we got out of the crowd and made for the café. The waiter saved chairs for the others, and we each ordered an absinthe and watched the crowd in the square and the dancers.

"What do you suppose that dance is?" Bill asked.

"It's a sort of jota."

"They're not all the same," Bill said. "They dance differently to all the different tunes."

"It's swell dancing."

In front of us on a clear part of the street a company of boys were dancing. The steps were very intricate and their faces were intent and concentrated. They all looked down while they danced. Their rope-soled shoes tapped and spatted on the pavement. The toes touched. The heels touched. The balls of the feet touched. Then the music broke wildly and the step was finished and they were all dancing on up the street.

"Here come the gentry," Bill said.

They were crossing the street.

"Hello, men," I said.

"Hello, gents!" said Brett. "You saved us seats? How nice."

"I say," Mike said, "that Romero what'shisname is somebody. Am I wrong?"

"Oh, isn't he lovely," Brett said. "And those green trousers."

"Brett never took her eyes off them."

"I say, I must borrow your glasses tomorrow."

"How did it go?"

"Wonderfully! Simply perfect. I say, it is a spectacle!"

"How about the horses?"

"I couldn't help looking at them."

"She couldn't take her eyes off them," Mike said. "She's an extraordinary wench."

"They do have some rather awful things happen to them," Brett said. "I couldn't look away, though."

"Did you feel all right?"

"I didn't feel badly at all."

"Robert Cohn did," Mike put in. "You were quite green, Robert."

"The first horse did bother me," Cohn said.

"You weren't bored, were you?" asked Bill.

Cohn laughed.

"No. I wasn't bored. I wish you'd forgive me that."

"It's all right," Bill said, "so long as you weren't bored."

"He didn't look bored," Mike said. "I thought he was going to be sick."

"I never felt that bad. It was just for a minute."

"*I* thought he was going to be sick. You weren't bored, were you, Robert?"

"Let up on that, Mike. I said I was sorry I said it."

"He was, you know. He was positively green."

"Oh, shove it along, Michael."

"You mustn't ever get bored at your first bull-fight, Robert," Mike said. "It might make such a mess."

"Oh, shove it along, Michael," Brett said.

"He said Brett was a sadist," Mike said. "Brett's not a sadist. She's just a lovely, healthy wench."

"Are you a sadist, Brett?" I asked.

"Hope not."

"He said Brett was a sadist just because she has a good, healthy stomach."

"Won't be healthy long."

Bill got Mike started on something else than Cohn. The waiter brought the absinthe glasses.

"Did you really like it?" Bill asked Cohn.

"No, I can't say I liked it. I think it's a wonderful show."

"Gad, yes! What a spectacle!" Brett said.

"I wish they didn't have the horse part," Cohn said.

"They're not important," Bill said. "After a while you never notice anything disgusting."

"It is a bit strong just at the start," Brett said. "There's a dreadful moment for me just when the bull starts for the horse."

"The bulls were fine," Cohn said.

"They were very good," Mike said.

"I want to sit down below, next time." Brett drank from her glass of absinthe.

"She wants to see the bull-fighters close by," Mike said.

"They are something," Brett said. "That Romero lad is just a child."

"He's a damned good-looking boy," I said. "When we were up in his room I never saw a better-looking kid."

"How old do you suppose he is?"

"Nineteen or twenty."

"Just imagine it."

The bull-fight on the second day was much better than on the first. Brett sat between Mike and me at the barrera, and Bill and Cohn went up above. Romero was the whole show. I do not think Brett saw any other bull-fighter. No one else did either, except the hard-shelled technicians. It was all Romero. There were two other matadors, but they did not count. I sat beside Brett and explained to Brett what it was all about. I told her about watching the bull, not the horse, when the bulls charged the picadors, and got her to watching the picador place the point of his pic so that she saw what it was all about, so that it became more something that was going on with a definite end, and less of a spectacle with unexplained horrors. I had her watch how Romero took the bull away from a fallen horse with his cape, and how he held him with the cape and turned him, smoothly and suavely, never wasting the bull. She saw how Romero avoided every brusque movement and saved his bulls for the last when he wanted them, not winded and discomposed but smoothly worn down. She saw how close Romero always worked to the bull, and I pointed out to her the tricks the other bull-fighters used to make it look as though they were working closely. She saw why she liked Romero's cape-work and why she did not like the others.

Romero never made any contortions, always it was straight and pure and natural in line. The others twisted themselves like corkscrews, their elbows raised, and leaned against the flanks of the bull after his horns had passed, to give a faked look of danger. Afterward, all that was faked turned bad and gave an unpleasant feeling. Romero's bull-fighting gave real emotion, because he kept the absolute purity of line in his movements and always quietly and calmly let the horns pass him close each time. He did not have to emphasize their closeness. Brett saw how something that was beautiful done close to the bull was ridiculous if it were done a little way off. I told her how since the death of Joselito all the bull-fighters had been developing a technique that simulated this appearance of danger in order to give a fake emotional feeling, while the bull-fighter was really safe. Romero had the old thing, the holding of his purity of line through the maximum of exposure, while he dominated the bull by making him realize he was unattainable, while he prepared him for the killing.

"I've never seen him do an awkward thing," Brett said.

"You won't until he gets frightened," I said.

"He'll never be frightened," Mike said. "He knows too damned much."

"He knew everything when he started. The others can't ever learn what he was born with."

"And God, what looks," Brett said.

"I believe, you know, that she's falling in love with this bull-fighter chap," Mike said.

"I wouldn't be surprised."

"Be a good chap, Jake. Don't tell her anything more about him. Tell her how they beat their old mothers."

"Tell me what drunks they are."

"Oh, frightful," Mike said. "Drunk all day and spend all their time beating their poor old mothers."

"He looks that way," Brett said.

"Doesn't he," I said.

They had hitched the mules to the dead bull and then the whips cracked, the men ran, and the mules, straining forward, their legs pushing, broke into a gallop, and the bull, one horn up, his head on its side, swept a swath smoothly across the sand and out the red gate.

"This next is the last one."

"Not really," Brett said. She leaned forward on the *barrera*. Romero waved his picadors to their places, then stood, his cape against his chest, looking across the ring to where the bull would come out.

After it was over we went out and were pressed tight in the crowd.

"These bull-fights are hell on one," Brett said. "I'm limp as a rag."

"Oh, you'll get a drink," Mike said.

The next day Pedro Romero did not fight. It was Miura bulls, and a very bad bull-fight. The next day there was no bull-fight scheduled. But all day and all night the fiesta kept on.

## CHAPTER SIXTEEN

I N THE morning it was raining. A fog had come over the mountains from the sea. You could not see the tops of the mountains. The plateau was dull and gloomy, and the shapes of the trees and the houses were changed. I walked out beyond the town to look at the weather. The bad weather was coming over the mountains from the sea.

The flags in the square hung wet from the white poles and the banners were wet and hung damp against the front of the houses, and in between the steady drizzle the rain came down and drove everyone under the arcades and made pools of water in the square, and the streets wet and dark and deserted; yet the fiesta kept up without any pause. It was only driven under cover.

The covered seats of the bull-ring had been crowded with people sitting out of the rain watching the concourse of Basque and Navarrais dancers and singers, and afterward the Val Carlos dancers in their costumes danced down the street in the rain, the drums sounding hollow and damp, and the chiefs of the bands riding ahead on their big, heavy-footed horses, their costumes wet, the horses' coats wet in the rain. The crowd was in the cafés and the dancers came in, too, and sat, their tight-wound white legs under the tables, shaking the water from their belled caps, and spreading their red and purple jackets over the chairs to dry. It was raining hard outside.

I left the crowd in the café and went over to the hotel to get shaved for dinner. I was shaving in my room when there was a knock on the door.

"Come in," I called.

Montoya walked in.

"How are you?" he said.

"Fine," I said.

"No bulls today."

"No," I said, "nothing but rain."

"Where are your friends?"

"Over at the Iruña."

Montoya smiled his embarrassed smile.

"Look," he said. "Do you know the American ambassador?"

"Yes," I said. "Everybody knows the American ambassador."

"He's here in town, now."

"Yes," I said. "Everybody's seen them."

"I've seen them, too," Montoya said. He didn't say anything. I went on shaving.

"Sit down," I said. "Let me send for a drink."

"No, I have to go."

I finished shaving and put my face down into the bowl and washed it with cold water. Montoya was standing there looking more embarrassed.

"Look," he said. "I've just had a message from them at the Grand Hotel that they want Pedro Romero and Marcial Lalanda to come over for coffee tonight after dinner."

"Well," I said, "it can't hurt Marcial any."

"Marcial has been in San Sebastian all day. He drove over in a car this morning with Marquez. I don't think they'll be back tonight."

Montoya stood embarrassed. He wanted me to say something.

"Don't give Romero the message," I said.

"You think so?"

"Absolutely."

Montoya was very pleased.

"I wanted to ask you because you were an American," he said.

"That's what I'd do."

"Look," said Montoya. "People take a boy like that. They don't know what he's worth. They don't know what he means. Any foreigner can flatter him. They start this Grand Hotel business, and in one year they're through."

"Like Algabeno," I said.

"Yes, like Algabeno."

"They're a fine lot," I said. "There's one American woman down here now that collects bull-fighters."

"I know. They only want the young ones."

"Yes," I said. "The old ones get fat."

"Or crazy like Gallo."

"Well," I said, "it's easy. All you have to do is not give him the message."

"He's such a fine boy," said Montoya. "He ought to stay with his own people. He shouldn't mix in that stuff."

"Won't you have a drink?" I asked.

"No," said Montoya, "I have to go." He went out.

I went downstairs and out the door and took a walk around through the arcades around the square. It was still raining. I looked in at the Iruña for the gang and they were not there, so I walked on around the square and back to the hotel. They were eating dinner in the downstairs dining-room.

They were well ahead of me and it was no use trying to catch them. Bill was buying shoe-shines for Mike. Bootblacks opened the street door and each one Bill called over and started to work on Mike.

"This is the eleventh time my boots have been polished," Mike said. "I say, Bill is an ass."

The bootblacks had evidently spread the report. Another came in.

"Limpia botas?" he said to Bill.

"No," said Bill. "For this señor."

The bootblack knelt down beside the one at work and started on Mike's free shoe that shone already in the electric light.

"Bill's a yell of laughter," Mike said.

I was drinking red wine, and so far behind them that I felt a little uncomfortable about all this shoe-shining. I looked around the room. At the next table was Pedro Romero. He stood up when I nodded, and asked me to come over and meet a friend. His table was beside ours, almost touching. I met the friend, a Madrid bull-fight critic, a little man with a drawn face. I told Romero how much I liked his work, and he was very pleased. We talked Spanish and the critic knew a little French. I reached to our table for my wine-bottle, but the critic took my arm. Romero laughed.

"Drink here," he said in English.

He was very bashful about his English, but he was really very pleased with it, and as we went on talking he brought out words he was not sure of, and asked me about them. He was anxious to know the English for *Corrida de toros*, the exact translation. Bull-fight he was suspicious of. I explained that bull-fight in Spanish was the *lidia* of a *toro*. The Spanish word *corrida* means in English the running of bulls—the French translation is *Course de taureaux*. The critic put that in. There is no Spanish word for bull-fight.

Pedro Romero said he had learned a little English in Gibraltar. He was born in Ronda. That is not far above Gibraltar. He started bull-fighting in Malaga in the bull-fighting school there. He had only been at it three years. The bull-fight critic joked him about the number of *Malagueño* expressions he used. He was nineteen years old, he said. His older brother was with him as a banderillero, but he did not live in this hotel. He lived in a smaller hotel with the other people who worked for Romero. He asked me how many times I had seen him in the ring. I told him only three. It was really only two, but I did not want to explain after I had made the mistake.

"Where did you see me the other time? In Madrid?"

"Yes," I lied. I had read the accounts of his two appearances in Madrid in the bull-fight papers, so I was all right.

"The first or the second time?"

"The first."

"I was very bad," he said. "The second time I was better. You remember?" He turned to the critic.

He was not at all embarrassed. He talked of his work as something altogether apart from himself. There was nothing conceited or braggartly about him.

"I like it very much that you like my work," he said. "But you haven't seen it yet. Tomorrow if I get a good bull, I will try and show it to you."

When he said this he smiled, anxious that neither the bull-fight critic nor I would think he was boasting.

"I am anxious to see it," the critic said. "I would like to be convinced."

"He doesn't like my work much." Romero turned to me. He was serious.

The critic explained that he liked it very much, but that so far it had been incomplete.

"Wait till tomorrow if a good one comes out."

"Have you seen the bulls for tomorrow?" the critic asked me.

"Yes. I saw them unloaded."

Pedro Romero leaned forward.

"What did you think of them?"

"Very nice," I said. "About twenty-six arrobas. Very short horns. Haven't you seen them?"

"Oh, yes," said Romero.

"They won't weigh twenty-six arrobas," said the critic.

"No," said Romero.

"They've got bananas for horns," the critic said.

"*You* call them bananas?" asked Romero. He turned to me and smiled. "You wouldn't call them bananas?"

"No," I said. "They're horns all right."

"They're very short," said Pedro Romero. "Very, very short. Still, they aren't bananas."

"I say, Jake," Brett called from the next table, "you *have* deserted us."

"Just temporarily," I said. "We're talking bulls."

"You *are* superior."

"Tell him that bulls have no balls," Mike shouted. He was drunk.

Romero looked at me inquiringly.

"Drunk," I said. "Borracho! Muy borracho!"

"You might introduce your friends," Brett said. She had not stopped looking at Pedro Romero. I asked them if they would like to have coffee with us. They both stood up. Romero's face was very brown. He had very nice manners.

I introduced them all around and they started to sit down, but there was not enough room, so we all moved over to the big table by the wall to have coffee. Mike ordered a bottle of Fundador and glasses for everybody. There was a lot of drunken talking.

"Tell him I think writing is lousy," Bill said. "Go on, tell him. Tell him I'm ashamed of being a writer."

Pedro Romero was sitting beside Brett and listening to her.

"Go on. Tell him!" Bill said.

Romero looked up smiling.

"This gentleman," I said, "is a writer."

Romero was impressed. "This other one, too," I said, pointing at Cohn.

"He looks like Villalta," Romero said, looking at Bill. "Rafael, doesn't he look like Villalta?"

"I can't see it," the critic said.

"Really," Romero said in Spanish. "He looks a lot like Villalta. What does the drunken one do?"

"Nothing."

"Is that why he drinks?"

"No. He's waiting to marry this lady."

"Tell him bulls have no balls!" Mike shouted, very drunk, from the other end of the table.

"What does he say?"

"He's drunk."

"Jake," Mike called. "Tell him bulls have no balls!"

"You understand?" I said.

"Yes."

I was sure he didn't, so it was all right.

"Tell him Brett wants to see him put on those green pants."

"Pipe down, Mike."

"Tell him Brett is dying to know how he can get into those pants."

"Pipe down."

During this Romero was fingering his glass and talking with Brett. Brett was talking French and he was talking Spanish and a little English, and laughing.

Bill was filling the glasses.

"Tell him Brett wants to come into—"

"Oh, pipe down, Mike, for Christ's sake!"

Romero looked up smiling. "Pipe down! I know that," he said.

Just then Montoya came into the room. He started to smile at me, then he saw Pedro Romero with a big glass of cognac in his hand, sitting laughing between me and a woman with bare shoulders, at a table full of drunks. He did not even nod.

Montoya went out of the room. Mike was on his feet proposing a toast. "Let's all drink to—" he began. "Pedro Romero," I said. Everybody stood up. Romero took it very seriously, and we touched glasses and drank it down, I rushing it a little because Mike was trying to make it clear that that was not at all what he was going to drink to. But it went off all right, and Pedro Romero shook hands with everyone and he and the critic went out together.

"My God! he's a lovely boy," Brett said. "And how I would love to see him get into those clothes. He must use a shoe-horn."

"I started to tell him," Mike began. "And Jake kept interrupting me. Why do you interrupt me? Do you think you talk Spanish better than I do?"

"Oh, shut up, Mike! Nobody interrupted you."

"No, I'd like to get this settled." He turned away from me. "Do you think you amount to something, Cohn? Do you think you belong here among us? People who are out to have a good time? For God's sake don't be so noisy, Cohn!"

"Oh, cut it out, Mike," Cohn said.

"Do you think Brett wants you here? Do you think you add to the party? Why don't you say something?"

"I said all I had to say the other night, Mike."

"I'm not one of you literary chaps." Mike stood shakily and leaned against the table. "I'm not clever. But I do know when I'm not wanted. Why don't you see when you're not wanted, Cohn? Go away. Go away, for God's sake. Take that sad Jewish face away. Don't you think I'm right?"

He looked at us.

"Sure," I said. "Let's all go over to the Iruña."

"No. Don't you think I'm right? I love that woman."

"Oh, don't start that again. Do shove it along, Michael," Brett said.

"Don't you think I'm right, Jake?"

Cohn still sat at the table. His face had the sallow, yellow look it got when he was insulted, but somehow he seemed to be enjoying it. The childish, drunken heroics of it. It was his affair with a lady of title.

"Jake," Mike said. He was almost crying. "You know I'm right. Listen, you!" He turned to Cohn: "Go away! Go away now!"

"But I won't go, Mike," said Cohn.

"Then I'll make you!" Mike started toward him around the table. Cohn stood up and took off his glasses. He stood waiting, his face sallow, his hands fairly low, proudly and firmly waiting for the assault, ready to do battle for his lady love.

I grabbed Mike. "Come on to the café," I said. "You can't hit him here in the hotel."

"Good!" said Mike. "Good idea!"

We started off. I looked back as Mike stumbled up the stairs and saw Cohn putting his glasses on again. Bill was sitting at the table pouring another glass of Fundador. Brett was sitting looking straight ahead at nothing.

Outside on the square it had stopped raining and the moon was trying to get through the clouds. There was a wind blowing. The military band was playing and the crowd was massed on the far side of the square where the fireworks specialist and his son were trying to send up fire balloons. A balloon would start up jerkily, on a great bias, and be torn by the wind or blown against the houses of the square. Some fell into the crowd. The magnesium flared and the fireworks exploded and chased about in the crowd. There was no one dancing in the square. The gravel was too wet.

Brett came out with Bill and joined us. We stood in the crowd and watched Don Manuel Orquito, the fireworks king, standing on a little platform, carefully starting the balloons with sticks, standing above the heads of the crowd to launch the balloons off into the wind. The wind brought them all down, and Don Manuel Orquito's face was sweaty in the light of his complicated fireworks that fell into the crowd and charged and chased, sputtering and cracking, between the legs of the people. The people shouted as each new luminous paper bubble careened, caught fire, and fell.

"They're razzing Don Manuel," Bill said.

"How do you know he's Don Manuel?" Brett said.

"His name's on the program. Don Manuel Orquito, the pirotecnico of esta ciudad."

"Globos illuminados," Mike said. "A collection of globos illuminados. That's what the paper said."

The wind blew the band music away.

"I say, I wish one would go up," Brett said. "That Don Manuel chap is furious."

"He's probably worked for weeks fixing them to go off, spelling out 'Hail to San Fermin,'" Bill said.

"Globos illuminados," Mike said. "A bunch of bloody globos illuminados."

"Come on," said Brett. "We can't stand here."

"Her ladyship wants a drink," Mike said.

"How you know things," Brett said.

Inside, the café was crowded and very noisy. No one noticed us come in. We could not find a table. There was a great noise going on.

"Come on, let's get out of here," Bill said.

Outside the paseo was going on under the arcade. There were some English and Americans from Biarritz in sport clothes scattered at the tables. Some of the women stared at the people going by with lorgnons. We had acquired, at some time, a friend of Bill's from Biarritz. She was staying with another girl at the Grand Hotel. The other girl had a headache and had gone to bed.

"Here's the pub," Mike said. It was the Bar Milano, a small, tough bar where you could get food and where they danced in the back room. We all sat down at a table and ordered a bottle of Fundador. The bar was not full. There was nothing going on.

"This is a hell of a place," Bill said.

"It's too early."

"Let's take the bottle and come back later," Bill said. "I don't want to sit here on a night like this."

"Let's go and look at the English," Mike said. "I love to look at the English."

"They're awful," Bill said. "Where did they all come from?"

"They come from Biarritz," Mike said. "They come to see the last day of the quaint little Spanish festa."

"I'll festa them," Bill said.

"You're an extraordinarily beautiful girl." Mike turned to Bill's friend. "When did you come here?"

"Come off it, Michael."

"I say, she *is* a lovely girl. Where have I been? Where have I been looking all this while? You're a lovely thing. *Have* we met? Come along with me and Bill. We're going to festa the English."

"I'll festa them," Bill said. "What the hell are they doing at this fiesta?"

"Come on," Mike said. "Just us three. We're going to festa the bloody English. I hope you're not English? I'm Scotch. I hate the English. I'm going to festa them. Come on, Bill."

Through the window we saw them, all three arm in arm, going toward the café. Rockets were going up in the square.

"I'm going to sit here," Brett said.

"I'll stay with you," Cohn said.

"Oh, don't!" Brett said. "For God's sake, go off somewhere. Can't you see Jake and I want to talk?"

"I didn't," Cohn said. "I thought I'd sit here because I felt a little tight."

"What a hell of a reason for sitting with anyone. If you're tight, go to bed. Go on to bed."

"Was I rude enough to him?" Brett asked. Cohn was gone. "My God! I'm so sick of him!"

"He doesn't add much to the gayety."

"He depresses me so."

"He's behaved very badly."

"Damned badly. He had a chance to behave so well."

"He's probably waiting just outside the door now."

"Yes. He would. You know I do know how he feels. He can't believe it didn't mean anything."

"I know."

"Nobody else would behave as badly. Oh, I'm so sick of the whole thing. And Michael. Michael's been lovely, too."

"It's been damned hard on Mike."

"Yes. But he didn't need to be a swine."

"Everybody behaves badly," I said. "Give them the proper chance."

"You wouldn't behave badly." Brett looked at me.

"I'd be as big an ass as Cohn," I said.

"Darling, don't let's talk a lot of rot."

"All right. Talk about anything you like."

"Don't be difficult. You're the only person I've got, and I feel rather awful tonight."

"You've got Mike."

"Yes, Mike. Hasn't he been pretty."

"Well," I said, "it's been damned hard on Mike, having Cohn around and seeing him with you."

"Don't I know it, darling? Please don't make me feel any worse than I do."

Brett was nervous as I had never seen her before.

She kept looking away from me and looking ahead at the wall.

"Want to go for a walk?"

"Yes. Come on."

I corked up the Fundador bottle and gave it to the bartender.

"Let's have one more drink of that," Brett said. "My nerves are rotten."

We each drank a glass of the smooth amontillado brandy.

"Come on," said Brett.

As we came out the door I saw Cohn walk out from under the arcade.

"He *was* there," Brett said.

"He can't be away from you."

"Poor devil!"

"I'm not sorry for him. I hate him, myself."

"I hate him, too," she shivered. "I hate his damned suffering."

We walked arm in arm down the side street away from the crowd and the lights of the square. The street was dark and wet, and we walked along it to the fortifications at the edge of town. We passed wine-shops with light coming out from their doors onto the black, wet street, and sudden bursts of music.

"Want to go in?"

"No."

We walked out across the wet grass and onto the stone wall of the fortifications. I spread a newspaper on the stone and Brett sat down. Across the plain it was dark, and we could see the mountains. The wind was high up and took the clouds across the moon. Below us were the dark pits of the fortifications. Behind were the trees and the shadow of the cathedral, and the town silhouetted against the moon.

"Don't feel bad," I said.

"I feel like hell," Brett said. "Don't let's talk."

We looked out at the plain. The long lines of trees were dark in the moonlight. There were the lights of a car on the road climbing the mountain. Up on the top of the mountain we saw the lights of the fort. Below to the left was the river. It was high from the rain, and black and smooth. Trees were dark along the banks. We sat and looked out. Brett stared straight ahead. Suddenly she shivered.

"It's cold."

"Want to walk back?"

"Through the park."

We climbed down. It was clouding over again. In the park it was dark under the trees.

"Do you still love me, Jake?"

"Yes," I said.

"Because I'm a goner," Brett said.

"How?"

"I'm a goner. I'm mad about the Romero boy. I'm in love with him, I think."

"I wouldn't be if I were you."

"I can't help it. I'm a goner. It's tearing me all up inside."

"Don't do it."

"I can't help it. I've never been able to help anything."

"You ought to stop it."

"How can I stop it? I can't stop things. Feel that?"

Her hand was trembling.

"I'm like that all through."

"You oughtn't to do it."

"I can't help it. I'm a goner now, anyway. Don't you see the difference?"

"No."

"I've got to do something. I've got to do something I really want to do. I've lost my self-respect."

"You don't have to do that."

"Oh, darling, don't be difficult. What do you think it's meant to have that damned Jew about, and Mike the way he's acted?"

"Sure."

"I can't just stay tight all the time."

"No."

"Oh, darling, please stay by me. Please stay by me and see me through this."

"Sure."

"I don't say it's right. It is right though for me. God knows, I've never felt such a bitch."

"What do you want me to do?"

"Come on," Brett said. "Let's go and find him."

Together we walked down the gravel path in the park in the dark, under the trees and then out from under the trees and past the gate into the street that led into town.

Pedro Romero was in the café. He was at a table with other bull-fighters and bull-fight critics. They were smoking cigars. When we came in they looked up. Romero smiled and bowed. We sat down at a table half-way down the room.

"Ask him to come over and have a drink."

"Not yet. He'll come over."

"I can't look at him."

"He's nice to look at," I said.

"I've always done just what I wanted."

"I know."

"I do feel such a bitch."

"Well," I said.

"My God!" said Brett, "the things a woman goes through."

"Yes?"

"Oh, I do feel such a bitch."

I looked across at the table. Pedro Romero smiled. He said something to the other people at his table, and stood up. He came over to our table. I stood up and we shook hands.

"Won't you have a drink?"

"You must have a drink with me," he said. He seated himself, asking Brett's permission without saying anything. He had very nice manners. But he kept on smoking his cigar. It went well with his face.

"You like cigars?" I asked.

"Oh, yes. I always smoke cigars."

It was part of his system of authority. It made him seem older. I noticed his skin. It was clear and smooth and very brown. There was a triangular scar on his cheek-bone. I saw he was watching Brett. He felt there was something between them. He must have felt it when Brett gave him her hand. He was being very careful. I think he was sure, but he did not want to make any mistake.

"You fight tomorrow," I said.

"Yes," he said. "Algabeno was hurt today in Madrid. Did you hear?"

"No," I said. "Badly?"

He shook his head.

"Nothing. Here," he showed his hand. Brett reached out and spread the fingers apart.

"Oh!" he said in English, "you tell fortunes?"

"Sometimes. Do you mind?"

"No. I like it." He spread his hand flat on the table. "Tell me I live for always, and be a millionaire."

He was still very polite, but he was surer of himself. "Look," he said, "do you see any bulls in my hand?"

He laughed. His hand was very fine and the wrist was small.

"There are thousands of bulls," Brett said. She was not at all nervous now. She looked lovely.

"Good," Romero laughed. "At a thousand duros apiece," he said to me in Spanish. "Tell me some more."

"It's a good hand," Brett said. "I think he'll live a long time."

"Say it to me. Not to your friend."

"I said you'd live a long time."

"I know it," Romero said. "I'm never going to die."

I tapped with my finger-tips on the table. Romero saw it. He shook his head.

"No. Don't do that. The bulls are my best friends."

I translated to Brett.

"You kill your friends?" she asked.

"Always," he said in English, and laughed. "So they don't kill me." He looked at her across the table.

"You know English well."

"Yes," he said. "Pretty well, sometimes. But I must not let anybody know. It would be very bad, a torero who speaks English."

"Why?" asked Brett.

"It would be bad. The people would not like it. Not yet."

"Why not?"

"They would not like it. Bull-fighters are not like that."

"What are bull-fighters like?"

He laughed and tipped his hat down over his eyes and changed the angle of his cigar and the expression of his face.

"Like at the table," he said. I glanced over. He had mimicked exactly the expression of Nacional. He smiled, his face natural again. "No. I must forget English."

"Don't forget it, yet," Brett said.

"No?"

"No."

"All right."

He laughed again.

"I would like a hat like that," Brett said.

"Good. I'll get you one."

"Right. See that you do."

"I will. I'll get you one tonight."

I stood up. Romero rose, too.

"Sit down," I said. "I must go and find our friends and bring them here."

He looked at me. It was a final look to ask if it were understood. It was understood all right.

"Sit down," Brett said to him. "You must teach me Spanish."

He sat down and looked at her across the table. I went out. The hard-eyed people at the bull-fighter table watched me go. It was not pleasant. When I came back and looked in the café, twenty minutes later, Brett and Pedro Romero were gone. The coffee-glasses and our three empty cognac-glasses were on the table. A waiter came with a cloth and picked up the glasses and mopped off the table.

# CHAPTER SEVENTEEN

OUTSIDE THE Bar Milano I found Bill and Mike and Edna. Edna was the girl's name.

"We've been thrown out," Edna said.

"By the police," said Mike. "There's some people in there that don't like me."

"I've kept them out of four fights," Edna said. "You've got to help me."

Bill's face was red.

"Come back in, Edna," he said. "Go on in there and dance with Mike."

"It's silly," Edna said. "There'll just be another row."

"Damned Biarritz swine," Bill said.

"Come on," Mike said. "After all, it's a pub. They can't occupy a whole pub."

"Good old Mike," Bill said. "Damned English swine come here and insult Mike and try and spoil the fiesta."

"They're so bloody," Mike said. "I hate the English."

"They can't insult Mike," Bill said. "Mike is a swell fellow. They can't insult Mike. I won't stand it. Who cares if he is a damn bankrupt?" His voice broke.

"Who cares?" Mike said. "I don't care. Jake doesn't care. Do *you* care?"

"No," Edna said. "Are you a bankrupt?"

"Of course I am. You don't care, do you, Bill?"

Bill put his arm around Mike's shoulder.

"I wish to hell I was a bankrupt. I'd show those bastards."

"They're just English," Mike said. "It never makes any difference what the English say."

"The dirty swine," Bill said. "I'm going to clean them out."

"Bill," Edna looked at me. "Please don't go in again, Bill. They're so stupid."

"That's it," said Mike. "They're stupid. I knew that was what it was."

"They can't say things like that about Mike," Bill said.

"Do you know them?" I asked Mike.

"No. I never saw them. They say they know me."

"I won't stand it," Bill said.

"Come on. Let's go over to the Suizo," I said.

"They're a bunch of Edna's friends from Biarritz," Bill said.

"They're simply stupid," Edna said.

"One of them's Charley Blackman, from Chicago," Bill said.

"I was never in Chicago," Mike said.

Edna started to laugh and could not stop.

"Take me away from here," she said, "you bankrupts."

"What kind of a row was it?" I asked Edna. We were walking across the square to the Suizo. Bill was gone.

"I don't know what happened, but someone had the police called to keep Mike out of the back room. There were some people that had known Mike at Cannes. What's the matter with Mike?"

"Probably he owes them money," I said. "That's what people usually get bitter about."

In front of the ticket-booths out in the square there were two lines of people waiting. They were sitting on chairs or crouched on the ground with blankets and newspapers around them.

They were waiting for the wickets to open in the morning to buy tickets for the bull-fight. The night was clearing and the moon was out. Some of the people in the line were sleeping.

At the Café Suizo we had just sat down and ordered Fundador when Robert Cohn came up.

"Where's Brett?" he asked.

"I don't know."

"She was with you."

"She must have gone to bed."

"She's not."

"I don't know where she is."

His face was sallow under the light. He was standing up.

"Tell me where she is."

"Sit down," I said. "I don't know where she is."

"The hell you don't!"

"You can shut your face."

"Tell me where Brett is."

"I'll not tell you a damn thing."

"You know where she is."

"If I did I wouldn't tell you."

"Oh, go to hell, Cohn," Mike called from the table. "Brett's gone off with the bull-fighter chap. They're on their honeymoon."

"You shut up."

"Oh, go to hell!" Mike said languidly.

"Is that where she is?" Cohn turned to me.

"Go to hell!"

"She was with you. Is that where she is?"

"Go to hell!"

"I'll make you tell me"—he stepped forward—"you damned pimp."

I swung at him and he ducked. I saw his face duck sideways in the light. He hit me and I sat down on the pavement. As I started to get on my feet he hit me twice. I went down backward under a table. I tried to get up and felt I did not have any legs. I felt I must get on my feet and try and hit him. Mike helped me up. Someone poured a carafe of water on my head. Mike had an arm around me, and I found I was sitting on a chair. Mike was pulling at my ears.

"I say, you were cold," Mike said.

"Where the hell were you?"

"Oh, I was around."

"You didn't want to mix in it?"

"He knocked Mike down, too," Edna said.

"He didn't knock me out," Mike said. "I just lay there."

"Does this happen every night at your fiestas?" Edna asked. "Wasn't that Mr. Cohn?"

"I'm all right," I said. "My head's a little wobbly."

There were several waiters and a crowd of people standing around.

"Vaya!" said Mike. "Get away. Go on."

The waiters moved the people away.

"It was quite a thing to watch," Edna said. "He must be a boxer."

"He is."

"I wish Bill had been here," Edna said. "I'd like to have seen Bill knocked down, too. I've always wanted to see Bill knocked down. He's so big."

"I was hoping he would knock down a waiter," Mike said, "and get arrested. I'd like to see Mr. Robert Cohn in jail."

"No," I said.

"Oh, no," said Edna. "You don't mean that."

"I do, though," Mike said. "I'm not one of these chaps likes being knocked about. I never play games, even."

Mike took a drink.

"I never liked to hunt, you know. There was always the danger of having a horse fall on you. How do you feel, Jake?"

"All right."

"You're nice," Edna said to Mike. "Are you really a bankrupt?"

"I'm a tremendous bankrupt," Mike said. "I owe money to everybody. Don't you owe any money?"

"Tons."

"I owe everybody money," Mike said. "I borrowed a hundred pesetas from Montoya tonight."

"The hell you did," I said.

"I'll pay it back," Mike said. "I always pay everything back."

"That's why you're a bankrupt, isn't it?" Edna said.

I stood up. I had heard them talking from a long way away. It all seemed like some bad play.

"I'm going over to the hotel," I said. Then I heard them talking about me.

"Is he all right?" Edna asked.

"We'd better walk with him."

"I'm all right," I said. "Don't come. I'll see you all later."

I walked away from the café. They were sitting at the table. I looked back at them and at the empty tables. There was a waiter sitting at one of the tables with his head in his hands.

Walking across the square to the hotel everything looked new and changed. I had never seen the trees before. I had never seen the flagpoles before, nor the front of the theater. It was all different. I felt as I felt once coming home from an out-of-town football game. I was carrying a suitcase with my football things in it, and I walked up the street from the station in the town I had lived in all my life and it was all new. They were raking the lawns and burning leaves in the road, and I stopped for a long time and watched. It was all strange. Then I went on, and my feet seemed to be a long way off, and everything seemed to come from a long way off, and I could hear my feet walking a great distance away. I had been kicked in the head early in the game. It was like that crossing the square. It was like that going up the stairs in the hotel. Going up the stairs took a long time, and I had the feeling that I was carrying my suitcase. There was a light in the room. Bill came out and met me in the hall.

"Say," he said, "go up and see Cohn. He's been in a jam, and he's asking for you."

"The hell with him."

"Go on. Go on up and see him."

I did not want to climb another flight of stairs.

"What are you looking at me that way for?"

"I'm not looking at you. Go on up and see Cohn. He's in bad shape."

"You were drunk a little while ago," I said.

"I'm drunk now," Bill said. "But you go up and see Cohn. He wants to see you."

"All right," I said. It was just a matter of climbing more stairs. I went on up the stairs carrying my phantom suitcase. I walked down the hall to Cohn's room. The door was shut and I knocked.

"Who is it?"

"Barnes."

"Come in, Jake."

I opened the door and went in, and set down my suitcase. There was no light in the room. Cohn was lying, face down, on the bed in the dark.

"Hello, Jake."

"Don't call me Jake."

I stood by the door. It was just like this that I had come home. Now it was a hot bath that I needed. A deep, hot bath, to lie back in.

"Where's the bathroom?" I asked.

Cohn was crying. There he was, face down on the bed, crying. He had on a white polo shirt, the kind he'd worn at Princeton.

"I'm sorry, Jake. Please forgive me."

"Forgive you, hell."

"Please forgive me, Jake."

I did not say anything. I stood there by the door.

"I was crazy. You must see how it was."

"Oh, that's all right."

"I couldn't stand it about Brett."

"You called me a pimp."

I did not care. I wanted a hot bath. I wanted a hot bath in deep water.

"I know. Please don't remember it. I was crazy."

"That's all right."

He was crying. His voice was funny. He lay there in his white shirt on the bed in the dark. His polo shirt.

"I'm going away in the morning."

He was crying without making any noise.

"I just couldn't stand it about Brett. I've been through hell,

Jake. It's been simply hell. When I met her down here Brett treated me as though I were a perfect stranger. I just couldn't stand it. We lived together at San Sebastian. I suppose you know it. I can't stand it anymore."

He lay there on the bed.

"Well," I said, "I'm going to take a bath."

"You were the only friend I had, and I loved Brett so."

"Well," I said, "so long."

"I guess it isn't any use," he said. "I guess it isn't any damn use."

"What?"

"Everything. Please say you forgive me, Jake."

"Sure," I said. "It's all right."

"I felt so terribly. I've been through such hell, Jake. Now everything's gone. Everything."

"Well," I said, "so long. I've got to go."

He rolled over, sat on the edge of the bed, and then stood up.

"So long, Jake," he said. "You'll shake hands, won't you?"

"Sure. Why not."

We shook hands. In the dark I could not see his face very well.

"Well," I said, "see you in the morning."

"I'm going away in the morning."

"Oh, yes," I said.

I went out. Cohn was standing in the door of the room.

"Are you all right, Jake?" he asked.

"Oh, yes," I said. "I'm all right."

I could not find the bathroom. After a while I found it. There was a deep stone tub. I turned on the taps and the water would not run. I sat down on the edge of the bath-tub. When I got up to go I found I had taken off my shoes. I hunted for them and found them and carried them downstairs. I found my room and went inside and undressed and got into bed.

I woke with a headache and the noise of the bands going by in the street. I remembered I had promised to take Bill's friend Edna to see the bulls go through the street and into the ring. I dressed and went downstairs and out into the cold early morning. People were crossing the square, hurrying toward the bull-ring. Across the square were the two lines of men in front of the ticket-booths. They were still waiting for the tickets to go on sale at seven o'clock. I hurried across the street to the café. The waiter told me that my friends had been there and gone.

"How many were they?"

"Two gentlemen and a lady."

That was all right. Bill and Mike were with Edna. She had been afraid last night they would pass out. That was why I was to be sure to take her. I drank the coffee and hurried with the other people toward the bull-ring. I was not groggy now. There was only a bad headache. Everything looked sharp and clear, and the town smelt of the early morning.

The stretch of ground from the edge of the town to the bull-ring was muddy. There was a crowd all along the fence that led to the ring, and the outside balconies and the top of the bull-ring were solid with people. I heard the rocket and I knew I could not get into the ring in time to see the bulls come in, so I shoved through the crowd to the fence. I was pushed close against the planks of the fence. Between the two fences of the runway the police were clearing the crowd along. They walked or trotted on into the bull-ring. Then people commenced to come running. A drunk slipped and fell. Two policemen grabbed him and rushed him over to the fence. The crowd were running fast now. There was a great shout from the crowd, and putting my head through between the boards I saw the bulls just coming out of the street into the long running pen. They were going fast and gaining on the crowd. Just then another drunk started out from the fence with a blouse in his hands. He wanted to do capework with the bulls. The two policemen tore out, collared him, one hit him with a club, and they dragged him against the fence and stood flattened out against the fence as the last of the crowd and the bulls went by. There were so many people running ahead of the bulls that the mass thickened and slowed up going through the gate into the ring, and as the bulls passed, galloping together, heavy, muddy-sided, horns swinging, one shot ahead, caught a man in the running crowd in the back and lifted him in the air. Both the man's arms were by his sides, his head went back as the horn went in, and the bull lifted him and then dropped him. The bull picked another man running in front, but the man disappeared into the crowd, and the crowd was through the gate and into the ring with the bulls behind them. The red door of the ring went shut, the crowd on the outside balconies of the bull-ring were pressing through to the inside, there was a shout, then another shout.

The man who had been gored lay face down in the trampled mud. People climbed over the fence, and I could not see the man because the crowd was so thick around him. From inside the ring came the shouts. Each shout meant a charge by some bull into the crowd. You could tell by the degree of intensity in the shout how bad a thing it was that was happening. Then the rocket went up that meant the steers had gotten the bulls out of the ring and into the corrals. I left the fence and started back toward the town.

Back in the town I went to the café to have a second coffee and some buttered toast. The waiters were sweeping out the café and mopping off the tables. One came over and took my order.

"Anything happen at the encierro?"

"I didn't see it all. One man was badly cogida."

"Where?"

"Here." I put one hand on the small of my back and the other on my chest, where it looked as though the horn must have come through. The waiter nodded his head and swept the crumbs from the table with his cloth.

"Badly cogida," he said. "All for sport. All for pleasure."

He went away and came back with the long-handled coffee and milk pots. He poured the milk and coffee. It came out of the long spouts in two streams into the big cup. The waiter nodded his head.

"Badly cogida through the back," he said. He put the pots down on the table and sat down in the chair at the table. "A big horn wound. All for fun. Just for fun. What do you think of that?"

"I don't know."

"That's it. All for fun. Fun, you understand."

"You're not an aficionado?"

"Me? What are bulls? Animals. Brute animals." He stood up and put his hand on the small of his back. "Right through the back. A cornada right through the back. For fun—you understand."

He shook his head and walked away, carrying the coffee-pots. Two men were going by in the street. The waiter shouted to them. They were grave-looking. One shook his head. "Muerto!" he called.

The waiter nodded his head. The two men went on. They were on some errand. The waiter came over to my table.

"You hear? Muerto. Dead. He's dead. With a horn through him. All for morning fun. Es muy flamenco."

"It's bad."

"Not for me," the waiter said. "No fun in that for me."

Later in the day we learned that the man who was killed was named Vicente Girones, and came from near Tafalla. The next day in the paper we read that he was twenty-eight years old, and had a farm, a wife, and two children. He had continued to come to the fiesta each year after he was married. The next day his wife came in from Tafalla to be with the body, and the day after there was a service in the chapel of San Fermin, and the coffin was carried to the railway-station by members of the dancing and drinking society of Tafalla. The drums marched ahead, and there was music on the fifes, and behind the men who carried the coffin walked the wife and two children. . . . Behind them marched all the members of the dancing and drinking societies of Pamplona, Estella, Tafalla, and Sanguesa who could stay over for the funeral. The coffin was loaded into the baggage-car of the train, and the widow and the two children rode, sitting, all three together, in an open third-class railway-carriage. The train started with a jerk, and then ran smoothly, going down grade around the edge of the plateau and out into the fields of grain that blew in the wind on the plain on the way to Tafalla.

The bull who killed Vicente Girones was named Bocanegra, was Number 118 of the bull-breeding establishment of Sanchez Taberno, and was killed by Pedro Romero as the third bull of that same afternoon. His ear was cut by popular acclamation and given to Pedro Romero, who, in turn, gave it to Brett, who wrapped it in a handkerchief belonging to myself, and left both ear and handkerchief, along with a number of Muratti cigarette-stubs, shoved far back in the drawer of the bed-table that stood beside her bed in the Hotel Montoya, in Pamplona.

Back in the hotel, the night watchman was sitting on a bench inside the door. He had been there all night and was very sleepy. He stood up as I came in. Three of the waitresses came in at the same time. They had been to the morning show at the bull-ring. They went upstairs laughing. I followed them upstairs and went into my room. I took off my shoes and lay down on the bed. The window was open onto the balcony and the sunlight was bright in the room. I did not feel sleepy. It must have been half past three o'clock when I had gone to bed and the bands had waked me at six. My jaw was sore on both sides. I felt it with my thumb and fingers. That damn Cohn. He should have hit somebody the first time he was insulted, and then gone away. He was so sure that Brett loved him. He was going to stay, and true love would conquer all. Someone knocked on the door.

"Come in."

It was Bill and Mike. They sat down on the bed.

"Some encierro," Bill said. "Some encierro."

"I say, weren't you there?" Mike asked. "Ring for some beer, Bill."

"What a morning!" Bill said. He mopped off his face. "My God! what a morning! And here's old Jake. Old Jake, the human punching-bag."

"What happened inside?"

"Good God!" Bill said, "what happened, Mike?"

"There were these bulls coming in," Mike said. "Just ahead

of them was the crowd, and some chap tripped and brought the whole lot of them down."

"And the bulls all came in right over them," Bill said.

"I heard them yell."

"That was Edna," Bill said.

"Chaps kept coming out and waving their shirts."

"One bull went along the barrera and hooked everybody over."

"They took about twenty chaps to the infirmary," Mike said.

"What a morning!" Bill said. "The damn police kept arresting chaps that wanted to go and commit suicide with the bulls."

"The steers took them in in the end," Mike said.

"It took about an hour."

"It was really about a quarter of an hour," Mike objected.

"Oh, go to hell," Bill said. "You've been in the war. It was two hours and a half for me."

"Where's that beer?" Mike asked.

"What did you do with the lovely Edna?"

"We took her home just now. She's gone to bed."

"How did she like it?"

"Fine. We told her it was just like that every morning."

"She was impressed," Mike said.

"She wanted us to go down in the ring, too," Bill said. "She likes action."

"I said it wouldn't be fair to my creditors," Mike said.

"What a morning," Bill said. "And what a night!"

"How's your jaw, Jake?" Mike asked.

"Sore," I said.

Bill laughed.

"Why didn't you hit him with a chair?"

"You can talk," Mike said. "He'd have knocked you out, too. I never saw him hit me. I rather think I saw him just before, and then quite suddenly I was sitting down in the street, and Jake was lying under a table."

"Where did he go afterward?" I asked.

"Here she is," Mike said. "Here's the beautiful lady with the beer."

The chambermaid put the tray with the beer-bottles and glasses down on the table.

"Now bring up three more bottles," Mike said.

"Where did Cohn go after he hit me?" I asked Bill.

"Don't you know about that?" Mike was opening a beer-bottle. He poured the beer into one of the glasses, holding the glass close to the bottle.

"Really?" Bill asked.

"Why he went in and found Brett and the bull-fighter chap in the bull-fighter's room, and then he massacred the poor, bloody bull-fighter."

"No."

"Yes."

"What a night!" Bill said.

"He nearly killed the poor, bloody bull-fighter. Then Cohn wanted to take Brett away. Wanted to make an honest woman of her, I imagine. Damned touching scene."

He took a long drink of the beer.

"He is an ass."

"What happened?"

"Brett gave him what for. She told him off. I think she was rather good."

"I'll bet she was," Bill said.

"Then Cohn broke down and cried, and wanted to shake hands with the bull-fighter fellow. He wanted to shake hands with Brett, too."

"I know. He shook hands with me."

"Did he? Well, they weren't having any of it. The bull-fighter fellow was rather good. He didn't say much, but he kept getting up and getting knocked down again. Cohn couldn't knock him out. It must have been damned funny."

"Where did you hear all this?"

"Brett. I saw her this morning."

"What happened finally?"

"It seems the bull-fighter fellow was sitting on the bed. He'd been knocked down about fifteen times, and he wanted to fight some more. Brett held him and wouldn't let him get up. He was weak, but Brett couldn't hold him, and he got up. Then Cohn said he wouldn't hit him again. Said he couldn't do it. Said it would be wicked. So the bull-fighter chap sort of rather staggered over to him. Cohn went back against the wall.

"'So you won't hit me?'

"'No,' said Cohn. 'I'd be ashamed to.'

"So the bull-fighter fellow hit him just as hard as he could in the face, and then sat down on the floor. He couldn't get up, Brett said. Cohn wanted to pick him up and carry him to the bed. He said if Cohn helped him he'd kill him, and he'd kill him anyway this morning if Cohn wasn't out of town. Cohn was crying, and Brett had told him off, and he wanted to shake hands. I've told you that before."

"Tell the rest," Bill said.

"It seems the bull-fighter chap was sitting on the floor. He was waiting to get strength enough to get up and hit Cohn again. Brett wasn't having any shaking hands, and Cohn was crying and telling her how much he loved her, and she was telling him not to be a ruddy ass. Then Cohn leaned down to shake hands with the bull-fighter fellow. No hard feelings, you know. All for forgiveness. And the bull-fighter chap hit him in the face again."

"That's quite a kid," Bill said.

"He ruined Cohn," Mike said. "You know I don't think Cohn will ever want to knock people about again."

"When did you see Brett?"

"This morning. She came in to get some things. She's looking after this Romero lad."

He poured out another bottle of beer.

"Brett's rather cut up. But she loves looking after people. That's how we came to go off together. She was looking after me."

"I know," I said.

"I'm rather drunk," Mike said. "I think I'll *stay* rather drunk. This is all awfully amusing, but it's not too pleasant. It's not too pleasant for me."

He drank off the beer.

"I gave Brett what for, you know. I said if she would go about with Jews and bull-fighters and such people, she must expect trouble." He leaned forward. "I say, Jake, do you mind if I drink that bottle of yours? She'll bring you another one."

"Please," I said. "I wasn't drinking it, anyway."

Mike started to open the bottle. "Would you mind opening it?" I pressed up the wire fastener and poured it for him.

"You know," Mike went on, "Brett was rather good. She's always rather good. I gave her a fearful hiding about Jews and bull-fighters and all those sort of people, and do you know what she said: 'Yes. I've had such a hell of a happy life with the British aristocracy!'"

He took a drink.

"That was rather good. Ashley, chap she got the title from, was a sailor, you know. Ninth baronet. When he came home he wouldn't sleep in a bed. Always made Brett sleep on the floor. Finally, when he got really bad, he used to tell her he'd kill her. Always slept with a loaded service revolver. Brett used to take the shells out when he'd gone to sleep. She hasn't had an absolutely happy life, Brett. Damned shame, too. She enjoys things so."

He stood up. His hand was shaky.

"I'm going in the room. Try and get a little sleep."

He smiled.

"We go too long without sleep in these fiestas. I'm going to start now and get plenty of sleep. Damn bad thing not to get sleep. Makes you frightfully nervy."

"We'll see you at noon at the Iruña," Bill said.

Mike went out the door. We heard him in the next room.

He rang the bell and the chambermaid came and knocked at the door.

"Bring up half a dozen bottles of beer and a bottle of Fundador," Mike told her.

"Si, señorito."

"I'm going to bed," Bill said. "Poor old Mike. I had a hell of a row about him last night."

"Where? At that Milano place?"

"Yes. There was a fellow there that had helped pay Brett and Mike out of Cannes, once. He was damned nasty."

"I know the story."

"I didn't. Nobody ought to have a right to say things about Mike."

"That's what makes it bad."

"They oughtn't to have any right. I wish to hell they didn't have any right. I'm going to bed."

"Was anybody killed in the ring?"

"I don't think so. Just badly hurt."

"A man was killed outside in the runway."

"Was there?" said Bill.

## CHAPTER EIGHTEEN

AT NOON we were all at the café. It was crowded. We were eating shrimps and drinking beer. The town was crowded. Every street was full. Big motor-cars from Biarritz and San Sebastian kept driving up and parking around the square. They brought people for the bull-fight. Sight-seeing cars came up, too. There was one with twenty-five English-women in it. They sat in the big, white car and looked through their glasses at the fiesta. The dancers were all quite drunk. It was the last day of the fiesta.

The fiesta was solid and unbroken, but the motor-cars and tourist-cars made little islands of onlookers. When the cars emptied, the onlookers were absorbed into the crowd. You did not see them again except as sport clothes, odd-looking at a table among the closely packed peasants in black smocks. The fiesta absorbed even the Biarritz English so that you did not see them unless you passed close to a table. All the time there was music in the street. The drums kept on pounding and the pipes were going. Inside the cafés men with their hands gripping the table, or on each other's shoulders, were singing the hard-voiced singing.

"Here comes Brett," Bill said. I looked and saw her coming through the crowd in the square, walking, her head up, as though the fiesta were being staged in her honor, and she found it pleasant and amusing.

"Hello, you chaps!" she said. "I say, I *have* a thirst."

"Get another big beer," Bill said to the waiter.

"Shrimps?"

"Is Cohn gone?" Brett asked.

"Yes," Bill said. "He hired a car."

The beer came. Brett started to lift the glass mug and her hand shook. She saw it and smiled, and leaned forward and took a long sip.

"Good beer."

"Very good," I said. I was nervous about Mike. I did not think he had slept. He must have been drinking all the time, but he seemed to be under control.

"I heard Cohn had hurt you, Jake," Brett said.

"No. Knocked me out. That was all."

"I say, he did hurt Pedro Romero," Brett said. "He hurt him most badly."

"How is he?"

"He'll be all right. He won't go out of the room."

"Does he look badly?"

"Very. He was really hurt. I told him I wanted to pop out and see you chaps for a minute."

"Is he going to fight?"

"Rather. I'm going with you, if you don't mind."

"How's your boy friend?" Mike asked. He had not listened to anything that Brett had said.

"Brett's got a bull-fighter," he said. "She had a Jew named Cohn, but he turned out badly."

Brett stood up.

"I am not going to listen to that sort of rot from you, Michael."

"How's your boy friend?"

"Damned well," Brett said. "Watch him this afternoon."

"Brett's got a bull-fighter," Mike said. "A beautiful, bloody bull-fighter."

"Would you mind walking over with me? I want to talk to you, Jake."

"Tell him all about your bull-fighter," Mike said. "Oh, to hell with your bull-fighter!" He tipped the table so that all the beers and the dish of shrimps went over in a crash.

"Come on," Brett said. "Let's get out of this."

In the crowd crossing the square I said: "How is it?"

"I'm not going to see him after lunch until the fight. His people come in and dress him. They're very angry about me, he says."

Brett was radiant. She was happy. The sun was out and the day was bright.

"I feel altogether changed," Brett said. "You've no idea, Jake."

"Anything you want me to do?"

"No, just go to the fight with me."

"We'll see you at lunch?"

"No. I'm eating with him."

We were standing under the arcade at the door of the hotel. They were carrying tables out and setting them up under the arcade.

"Want to take a turn out to the park?" Brett asked. "I don't want to go up yet. I fancy he's sleeping."

We walked along past the theatre and out of the square and along through the barracks of the fair, moving with the crowd between the lines of booths. We came out on a cross street that led to the Paseo de Sarasate. We could see the crowd walking there, all the fashionably dressed people. They were making the turn at the upper end of the park.

"Don't let's go there," Brett said. "I don't want staring at just now."

We stood in the sunlight. It was hot and good after the rain and the clouds from the sea.

"I hope the wind goes down," Brett said. "It's very bad for him."

"So do I."

"He says the bulls are all right."

"They're good."

"Is that San Fermin's?"

Brett looked at the yellow wall of the chapel.

"Yes. Where the show started on Sunday."

"Let's go in. Do you mind? I'd rather like to pray a little for him or something."

We went in through the heavy leather door that moved very lightly. It was dark inside. Many people were praying. You saw them as your eyes adjusted themselves to the half-light. We knelt at one of the long wooden benches. After a little I felt Brett stiffen beside me, and saw she was looking straight ahead.

"Come on," she whispered throatily. "Let's get out of here. Makes me damned nervous."

Outside in the hot brightness of the street Brett looked up at the tree-tops in the wind. The praying had not been much of a success.

"Don't know why I get so nervy in church," Brett said. "Never does me any good."

We walked along.

"I'm damned bad for a religious atmosphere," Brett said. "I've the wrong type of face."

"You know," Brett said, "I'm not worried about him at all. I just feel happy about him."

"Good."

"I wish the damn wind would drop, though."

"It's liable to go down by five o'clock."

"Let's hope."

"You might pray," I laughed.

"Never does me any good. I've never gotten anything I prayed for. Have you?"

"Oh, yes."

"Oh, rot," said Brett. "Maybe it works for some people, though. You don't look very religious, Jake."

"I'm pretty religious."

"Oh, rot," said Brett. "Don't start proselyting today. Today's going to be bad enough as it is."

It was the first time I had seen her in the old happy, careless way since before she went off with Cohn. We were back again in front of the hotel. All the tables were set now, and already several were filled with people eating.

"Do look after Mike," Brett said. "Don't let him get too bad."

"Your frients haff gone upstairs," the German maitre d'hôtel said in English. He was a continual eavesdropper. Brett turned to him:

"Thank you so much. Have you anything else to say?"

"No, ma'am."

"Good," said Brett.

"Save us a table for three," I said to the German. He smiled his dirty little pink-and-white smile.

"Iss madam eating here?"

"No," Brett said.

"Den I think a tabul for two will be enuff."

"Don't talk to him," Brett said. "Mike must have been in bad shape," she said on the stairs. We passed Montoya on the stairs. He bowed and did not smile.

"I'll see you at the café," Brett said. "Thank you, so much, Jake."

We had stopped at the floor our rooms were on. She went straight down the hall and into Romero's room. She did not knock. She simply opened the door, went in, and closed it behind her.

I stood in front of the door of Mike's room and knocked. There was no answer. I tried the knob and it opened. Inside the room was in great disorder. All the bags were opened and clothing was strewn around. There were empty bottles beside the bed. Mike lay on the bed looking like a death mask of himself. He opened his eyes and looked at me.

"Hello, Jake," he said very slowly. "I'm getting a lit tle sleep. I've want ed a lit tle sleep for a long time."

"Let me cover you over."

"No. I'm quite warm."

"Don't go. I have n't got ten to sleep yet."

"You'll sleep, Mike. Don't worry, boy."

"Brett's got a bull-fighter," Mike said. "But her Jew has gone away."

He turned his head and looked at me.

"Damned good thing, what?"

"Yes. Now go to sleep, Mike. You ought to get some sleep."

"I'm just start ing. I'm go ing to get a lit tle sleep."

He shut his eyes. I went out of the room and turned the door to quietly. Bill was in my room reading the paper.

"See Mike?"

"Yes."

"Let's go and eat."

"I won't eat downstairs with that German head waiter. He was damned snotty when I was getting Mike upstairs."

"He was snotty to us, too."

"Let's go out and eat in the town."

We went down the stairs. On the stairs we passed a girl coming up with a covered tray.

"There goes Brett's lunch," Bill said.

"And the kid's," I said.

Outside on the terrace under the arcade the German head waiter came up. His red cheeks were shiny. He was being polite.

"I haff a tabul for two for you gentlemen," he said.

"Go sit at it," Bill said. We went on out across the street.

We ate at a restaurant in a side street off the square. They were all men eating in the restaurant. It was full of smoke and drinking and singing. The food was good and so was the wine. We did not talk much. Afterward we went to the café and watched the fiesta come to the boiling-point. Brett came over soon after lunch. She said she had looked in the room and that Mike was asleep.

When the fiesta boiled over and toward the bull-ring we went with the crowd. Brett sat at the ringside between Bill and me. Directly below us was the callejon, the passageway between the stands and the red fence of the barrera. Behind us the concrete stands filled solidly. Out in front, beyond the red fence, the sand of the ring was smooth-rolled and yellow. It looked a little heavy from the rain, but it was dry in the sun and firm and smooth. The sword-handlers and bull-ring servants came down the callejon carrying on their shoulders the wicker baskets of fighting capes and muletas. They were bloodstained and compactly folded and packed in the baskets. The sword-handlers opened the heavy leather sword-cases so the red wrapped hilts of the sheaf of swords showed as the leather case leaned against the fence. They unfolded the dark-stained red flannel of the muletas and fixed batons in them to spread the stuff and give the matador something to hold. Brett watched it all. She was absorbed in the professional details.

"He's his name stencilled on all the capes and muletas," she said. "Why do they call them muletas?"

"I don't know."

"I wonder if they ever launder them."

"I don't think so. It might spoil the color."

"The blood must stiffen them," Bill said.

"Funny," Brett said. "How one doesn't mind the blood."

Below in the narrow passage of the callejon the sword-handlers arranged everything. All the seats were full. Above, all the boxes were full. There was not an empty seat except in the President's box. When he came in the fight would start. Across the smooth sand, in the high doorway that led into the corrals, the bull-fighters were standing, their arms furled in their capes, talking, waiting for the signal to march in across the arena. Brett was watching them with the glasses.

"Here, would you like to look?"

I looked through the glasses and saw the three matadors. Romero was in the center, Belmonte on his left, Marcial on his right. Back of them were their people, and behind the banderilleros, back in the passageway and in the open space of the corral I saw the picadors. Romero was wearing a black suit. His tri-cornered hat was low down over his eyes. I could not see his face clearly under the hat, but it looked badly marked. He was looking straight ahead. Marcial was smoking a cigarette guardedly, holding it in his hand. Belmonte looked ahead, his face wan and yellow, his long wolf jaw out. He was looking at nothing. Neither he nor Romero seemed to have anything in common with the others. They were all alone. The President came in; there was handclapping above us in the grand stand, and I handed the glasses to Brett. There was applause. The music started. Brett looked through the glasses.

"Here, take them," she said.

Through the glasses I saw Belmonte speak to Romero. Marcial straightened up and dropped his cigarette, and, looking straight ahead, their heads back, their free arms swinging, the three matadors walked out. Behind them came all the procession, opening out, all striding in step, all the capes furled, everybody with free arms swinging, and behind rode the picadors, their pics rising like lances. Behind all came the two trains of mules and the bull-ring servants. The matadors bowed, holding their hats on, before the President's box, and then came over to the barrera below us. Pedro Romero took off his heavy gold-brocaded cape and handed it over the fence to his sword-handler. He said something to the sword-handler. Close below us we saw Romero's lips were puffed, both eyes were discolored. His face was discolored and swollen. The sword-handler took the cape, looked up at Brett, and came over to us and handed up the cape.

"Spread it out in front of you," I said.

Brett leaned forward. The cape was heavy and smoothly stiff with gold. The sword-handler looked back, shook his head, and said something. A man beside me leaned over toward Brett.

"He doesn't want you to spread it," he said. "You should fold it and keep it in your lap."

Brett folded the heavy cape.

Romero did not look up at us. He was speaking to Belmonte. Belmonte had sent his formal cape over to some friends. He looked across at them and smiled, his wolf smile that was only with the mouth. Romero leaned over the barrera and asked for the water-jug. The sword-handler brought it and Romero poured water over the percale of his fighting-cape, and then scuffed the lower folds in the sand with his slippered foot.

"What's that for?" Brett asked.

"To give it weight in the wind."

"His face looks bad," Bill said.

"He feels very badly," Brett said. "He should be in bed."

The first bull was Belmonte's. Belmonte was very good. But because he got thirty thousand pesetas and people had stayed in line all night to buy tickets to see him, the crowd demanded that he should be more than very good. Belmonte's great attraction is working close to the bull. In bull-fighting they speak of the terrain of the bull and the terrain of the bull-fighter. As long as a bull-fighter stays in his own terrain he is comparatively safe. Each time he enters into the terrain of the bull he is in great danger. Belmonte, in his best days, worked always in the terrain of the bull. This way he gave the sensation of coming tragedy. People went to the corrida to see Belmonte, to be given tragic sensations, and perhaps to see the death of Belmonte. Fifteen years ago they said if you wanted to see Belmonte you should go quickly while he was still alive. Since then he has killed more than a thousand bulls. When he retired the legend grew up about how his bull-fighting had been, and when he came out of retirement the public were disappointed because no real man could work as close to the bulls as Belmonte was supposed to have done, not, of course, even Belmonte.

Also Belmonte imposed conditions and insisted that his

bulls should not be too large, nor too dangerously armed with horns, and so the element that was necessary to give the sensation of tragedy was not there, and the public, who wanted three times as much from Belmonte, who was sick with a fistula, as Belmonte had ever been able to give, felt defrauded and cheated, and Belmonte's jaw came further out in contempt, and his face turned yellower, and he moved with greater difficulty as his pain increased, and finally the crowd were actively against him, and he was utterly contemptuous and indifferent. He had meant to have a great afternoon and instead it was an afternoon of sneers, shouted insults, and finally a volley of cushions and pieces of bread and vegetables thrown down at him in the plaza where he had had his greatest triumphs. His jaw only went further out. Sometimes he turned to smile that toothed, long-jawed, lipless smile when he was called something particularly insulting, and always the pain that any movement produced grew stronger and stronger, until finally his yellow face was parchment color, and after his second bull was dead and the throwing of bread and cushions was over, after he had saluted the President with the same wolf-jawed smile and contemptuous eyes, and handed his sword over the barrera to be wiped and put back in its case, he passed through into the callejon and leaned on the barrera below us, his head on his arms, not seeing, not hearing anything, only going through his pain. When he looked up, finally, he asked for a drink of water. He swallowed a little, rinsed his mouth, spat the water, took his cape and went back into the ring.

Because they were against Belmonte the public were for Romero. From the moment he left the barrera and went toward the bull they applauded him. Belmonte watched Romero, too, watched him always without seeming to. He paid no attention to Marcial. Marcial was the sort of thing he knew all about. He had come out of retirement to compete with Marcial, knowing it was a competition gained in advance. He had expected to compete with Marcial and the other stars of the decadence of bull-fighting, and he knew that the sincerity of his own bull-fighting would be so set off by the false aesthetics of the bull-fighters of the decadent period that he would only have to be in the ring. His return from retirement had been spoiled by Romero. Romero did always, smoothly, calmly, and beautifully, what he, Belmonte, could only bring himself to do now sometimes. The crowd felt it, even the people from Biarritz, even the American ambassador saw it, finally. It was a competition that Belmonte would not enter because it would lead only to a bad horn wound or death. Belmonte was no longer well enough. He no longer had his greatest moments in the bull-ring. He was not sure that there were any great moments. Things were not the same and now life only came in flashes. He had flashes of the old greatness with his bulls, but they were not of value because he had discounted them in advance when he had picked the bulls out for their safety, getting out of a motor and leaning on a fence, looking over at the herd on the ranch of his friend the bull-breeder. So he had two small, manageable bulls without much horns, and when he felt the greatness again coming, just a little of it through the pain that was always with him, it had been discounted and sold in advance, and it did not give him a good feeling. It was the greatness, but it did not make bull-fighting wonderful to him anymore.

Pedro Romero had the greatness. He loved bull-fighting, and I think he loved the bulls, and I think he loved Brett. Everything of which he could control the locality he did in front of her all that afternoon. Never once did he look up. He made it stronger that way, and did it for himself, too, as well as for her. Because he did not look up to ask if it pleased he did it all for himself inside, and it strengthened him, and yet he did it for her, too. But he did not do it for her at any loss to himself. He gained by it all through the afternoon.

His first "quite" was directly below us. The three matadors take the bull in turn after each charge he makes at a picador. Belmonte was the first. Marcial was the second. Then came Romero. The three of them were standing at the left of the horse. The picador, his hat down over his eyes, the shaft of his pic angling sharply toward the bull, kicked in the spurs and held them and with the reins in his left hand walked the horse forward toward the bull. The bull was watching. Seemingly he watched the white horse, but really he watched the triangular steel point of the pic. Romero, watching, saw the bull start to turn his head. He did not want to charge. Romero flicked his cape so the color caught the bull's eye. The bull charged with the reflex, charged, and found not the flash of color but a white horse, and a man leaned far over the horse, shot the steel point of the long hickory shaft into the hump of muscle on the bull's shoulder, and pulled his horse sideways as he pivoted on the pic, making a wound, enforcing the iron into the bull's shoulder, making him bleed for Belmonte.

The bull did not insist under the iron. He did not really want to get at the horse. He turned and the group broke apart and Romero was taking him out with his cape. He took him out softly and smoothly, and then stopped and, standing squarely in front of the bull, offered him the cape. The bull's tail went up and he charged, and Romero moved his arms ahead of the bull, wheeling, his feet firmed. The dampened, mud-weighted cape swung open and full as a sail fills, and Romero pivoted with it just ahead of the bull. At the end of the pass they were facing each other again. Romero smiled. The bull wanted it again, and Romero's cape filled again, this time on the other side. Each time he let the bull pass so close that the man and the bull and the cape that filled and pivoted ahead of the bull were all one sharply etched mass. It was all so slow and so con- trolled. It was as though he were rocking the bull to sleep. He made four veronicas like that, and finished with a half-veronica that turned his back on the bull and came away toward the applause, his hand on his hip, his cape on his arm, and the bull watching his back going away.

In his own bulls he was perfect. His first bull did not see well. After the first two passes with the cape Romero knew exactly how bad the vision was impaired. He worked accordingly. It was not brilliant bull-fighting. It was only perfect bull-fighting. The crowd wanted the bull changed. They made a great row. Nothing very fine could happen with a bull that could not see the lures, but the President would not order him replaced.

"Why don't they change him?" Brett asked.

"They've paid for him. They don't want to lose their money."

"It's hardly fair to Romero."

"Watch how he handles a bull that can't see the color."

"It's the sort of thing I don't like to see."

It was not nice to watch if you cared anything about the person who was doing it. With the bull who could not see the colors of the capes, or the scarlet flannel of the muleta, Romero had to make the bull consent with his body. He had to get so close that the bull saw his body, and would start for it, and then shift the bull's charge to the flannel and finish out the pass in the classic manner. The Biarritz crowd did not like it. They thought Romero was afraid, and that was why he gave that little sidestep each time as he transferred the bull's charge from his own body to the flannel. They preferred Belmonte's imitation of himself or Marcial's imitation of Belmonte. There were three of them in the row behind us.

"What's he afraid of the bull for? The bull's so dumb he only goes after the cloth."

"He's just a young bull-fighter. He hasn't learned it yet."

"But I thought he was fine with the cape before."

"Probably he's nervous now."

Out in the center of the ring, all alone, Romero was going on with the same thing, getting so close that the bull could see him plainly, offering the body, offering it again a little closer, the bull watching dully, then so close that the bull thought he had him, offering again and finally drawing the charge and then, just before the horns came, giving the bull the red cloth to follow with that little, almost imperceptible, jerk that so offended the critical judgement of the Biarritz bull-fight experts.

"He's going to kill now," I said to Brett. "The bull's still strong. He wouldn't wear himself out."

Out in the center of the ring Romero profiled in front of the bull, drew the sword out from the folds of the muleta, rose on his toes, and sighted along the blade. The bull charged as Romero charged. Romero's left hand dropped the muleta over the bull's muzzle to blind him, his left shoulder went forward between the horns as the sword went in, and for just an instant he and the bull were one, Romero way out over the bull, the right arm extended high up to where the hilt of the sword had gone in between the bull's shoulders. Then the figure was broken. There was a little jolt as Romero came clear, and then he was standing, one hand up, facing the bull, his shirt ripped out from under his sleeve, the white blowing in the wind, and the bull, the red sword hilt tight between his shoulders, his head going down and his legs settling.

"There he goes," Bill said.

Romero was close enough so the bull could see him. His hand still up, he spoke to the bull. The bull gathered himself, then his head went forward and he went over slowly, then all over, suddenly, four feet in the air.

They handed the sword to Romero, and carrying it blade down, the muleta in his other hand, he walked over to in front of the President's box, bowed, straightened and came over to the barrera and handed over the sword and muleta.

"Bad one," said the sword-handler.

"He made me sweat," said Romero. He wiped off his face. The sword-handler handed him the water-jug. Romero wiped his lips. It hurt him to drink out of the jug. He did not look up at us.

Marcial had a big day. They were still applauding him when Romero's last bull came in. It was the bull that had sprinted out and killed the man in the morning running.

During Romero's first bull his hurt face had been very noticeable. Everything he did showed it. All the concentration of the awkwardly delicate working with the bull that could not see well brought it out. The fight with Cohn had not touched his spirit but his face had been smashed and his body hurt. He was wiping all that out now. Each thing that he did with this bull wiped that out a little cleaner. It was a good bull, a big bull, and with horns, and it turned and recharged easily and surely. He was what Romero wanted in bulls.

When he had finished his work with the muleta and was ready to kill, the crowd made him go on. They did not want the bull killed yet, they did not want it to be over. Romero went on. It was like a course in bull-fighting. All the passes he linked up, all completed, all slow, templed and smooth. There were no tricks and no mystifications. There was no brusqueness. And each pass as it reached the summit gave you a sudden ache inside. The crowd did not want it ever to be finished.

The bull was squared on all four feet to be killed, and Romero killed directly below us. He killed not as he had been forced to by the last bull, but as he wanted to. He profiled directly in front of the bull, drew the sword out of the folds of the muleta and sighted along the blade. The bull watched him. Romero spoke to the bull and tapped one of his feet. The bull charged and Romero waited for the charge, the muleta held low, sighting along the blade, his feet firm. Then without taking a step forward, he became one with the bull, the sword was in high between the shoulders, the bull had followed the low-swung flannel, that disappeared as Romero lurched clear to the left, and it was over. The bull tried to go forward, his legs commenced to settle, he swung from side to side, hesitated, then went down on his knees, and Romero's older brother leaned forward behind him and drove a short knife into the bull's neck at the base of the horns. The first time he missed. He drove the knife in again, and the bull went over, twitching and rigid. Romero's brother, holding the bull's horn in one hand, the knife in the other, looked up at the President's box. Handkerchiefs were waving all over the bull-ring. The President looked down from the box and waved his handkerchief. The brother cut the notched black ear from the dead bull and trotted over with it to Romero. The bull lay heavy and black on the sand, his tongue out. Boys were running toward him from all parts of the arena, making a little circle around him. They were starting to dance around the bull.

Romero took the ear from his brother and held it up toward the President. The President bowed and Romero, running to get ahead of the crowd, came toward us. He leaned up against the barrera and gave the ear to Brett. He nodded his head and smiled. The crowd were all about him. Brett held down the cape.

"You liked it?" Romero called.

Brett did not say anything. They looked at each other and smiled. Brett had the ear in her hand.

"Don't get bloody," Romero said, and grinned. The crowd wanted him. Several boys shouted at Brett. The crowd was the boys, the dancers, and the drunks. Romero turned and tried to get through the crowd. They were all around him trying to lift him and put him on their shoulders. He fought and twisted away, and started running, in the midst of them, toward the exit. He did not want to be carried on people's shoulders. But they held him and lifted him. It was uncomfortable and his legs were spraddled and his body was very sore. They were lifting him and all running toward the gate. He had his hand on somebody's shoulder. He looked around at us apologetically. The crowd, running, went out the gate with him.

We all three went back to the hotel. Brett went upstairs. Bill and I sat in the downstairs dining-room and ate some hard-boiled eggs and drank several bottles of beer. Belmonte came down in his street clothes with his manager and two other men. They sat at the next table and ate. Belmonte ate very little. They were leaving on the seven o'clock train for Barcelona. Belmonte wore a blue-striped shirt and a dark suit, and ate soft-boiled eggs. The others ate a big meal. Belmonte did not talk. He only answered questions.

Bill was tired after the bull-fight. So was I. We both took

a bull-fight very hard. We sat and ate the eggs and I watched Belmonte and the people at his table. The men with him were tough-looking and businesslike.

"Come on over to the café," Bill said. "I want an absinthe."

It was the last day of the fiesta. Outside it was beginning to be cloudy again. The square was full of people and the fireworks experts were making up their set pieces for the night and covering them over with beech branches. Boys were watching. We passed stands of rockets with long bamboo stems. Outside the café there was a great crowd. The music and the dancing were going on. The giants and the dwarfs were passing.

"Where's Edna?" I asked Bill.

"I don't know."

We watched the beginning of the evening of the last night of the fiesta. The absinthe made everything seem better. I drank it without sugar in the dripping glass, and it was pleasantly bitter.

"I feel sorry about Cohn," Bill said. "He had an awful time."

"Oh, to hell with Cohn," I said.

"Where do you suppose he went?"

"Up to Paris."

"What do you suppose he'll do?"

"Oh, to hell with him."

"What do you suppose he'll do?"

"Pick up with his old girl, probably."

"Who was his old girl?"

"Somebody named Frances."

We had another absinthe.

"When do you go back?" I asked.

"Tomorrow."

After a little while Bill said: "Well, it was a swell fiesta."

"Yes," I said; "something doing all the time."

"You wouldn't believe it. It's like a wonderful nightmare."

"Sure," I said. "I'd believe anything. Including nightmares."

"What's the matter? Feel low?"

"Low as hell."

"Have another absinthe. Here, waiter! Another absinthe for this señor."

"I feel like hell," I said.

"Drink that," said Bill. "Drink it slow."

It was beginning to get dark. The fiesta was going on. I began to feel drunk but I did not feel any better.

"How do you feel?"

"I feel like hell."

"Have another?"

"It won't do any good."

"Try it. You can't tell; maybe this is the one that gets it. Hey, waiter! Another absinthe for this señor!"

I poured the water directly into it and stirred it instead of letting it drip. Bill put in a lump of ice. I stirred the ice around with a spoon in the brownish, cloudy mixture.

"How is it?"

"Fine."

"Don't drink it fast that way. It will make you sick."

I set down the glass. I had not meant to drink it fast.

"I feel tight."

"You ought to."

"That's what you wanted, wasn't it?"

"Sure. Get tight. Get over your damn depression."

"Well, I'm tight. Is that what you want?"

"Sit down."

"I won't sit down," I said. "I'm going over to the hotel."

I was very drunk. I was drunker than I ever remembered

having been. At the hotel I went upstairs. Brett's door was open. I put my head in the room. Mike was sitting on the bed. He waved a bottle.

"Jake," he said. "Come in, Jake."

I went in and sat down. The room was unstable unless I looked at some fixed point.

"Brett, you know. She's gone off with the bull-fighter chap."

"No."

"Yes. She looked for you to say goodbye. They went on the seven o'clock train."

"Did they?"

"Bad thing to do," Mike said. "She shouldn't have done it."

"No."

"Have a drink? Wait while I ring for some beer."

"I'm drunk," I said. "I'm going in and lie down."

"Are you blind? I was blind myself."

"Yes," I said, "I'm blind."

"Well, bung-o," Mike said. "Get some sleep, old Jake."

I went out the door and into my own room and lay on the bed. The bed went sailing off and I sat up in bed and looked at the wall to make it stop. Outside in the square the fiesta was going on. It did not mean anything. Later Bill and Mike came in to get me to go down and eat with them. I pretended to be asleep.

"He's asleep. Better let him alone."

"He's blind as a tick," Mike said. They went out.

I got up and went to the balcony and looked out at the dancing in the square. The world was not wheeling anymore. It was just very clear and bright, and inclined to blur at the edges. I washed, brushed my hair. I looked strange to myself in the glass, and went downstairs to the dining-room.

"Here he is!" said Bill. "Good old Jake! I knew you wouldn't pass out."

"Hello, you old drunk," Mike said.

"I got hungry and woke up."

"Eat some soup," Bill said.

The three of us sat at the table, and it seemed as though about six people were missing.

# BOOK THREE

## CHAPTER NINETEEN

IN THE morning it was all over. The fiesta was finished. I woke about nine o'clock, had a bath, dressed, and went downstairs. The square was empty and there were no people on the streets. A few children were picking up rocket-sticks in the square. The cafés were just opening and the waiters were carrying out the comfortable white wicker chairs and arranging them around the marble-topped tables in the shade of the arcade. They were sweeping the streets and sprinkling them with a hose.

I sat in one of the wicker chairs and leaned back comfortably. The waiter was in no hurry to come. The white-paper announcements of the unloading of the bulls and the big schedules of special trains were still up on the pillars of the arcade. A waiter wearing a blue apron came out with a bucket of water and a cloth, and commenced to tear down the notices, pulling the paper off in strips and washing and rubbing away the paper that stuck to the stone. The fiesta was over.

I drank a coffee and after a while Bill came over. I watched him come walking across the square. He sat down at the table and ordered a coffee.

"Well," he said, "it's all over."

"Yes," I said. "When do you go?"

"I don't know. We better get a car, I think. Aren't you going back to Paris?"

"No. I can stay away another week. I think I'll go to San Sebastian."

"I want to get back."

"What's Mike going to do?"

"He's going to Saint Jean de Luz."

"Let's get a car and all go as far as Bayonne. You can get the train up from there tonight."

"Good. Let's go after lunch."

"All right. I'll get the car."

We had lunch and paid the bill. Montoya did not come near us. One of the maids brought the bill. The car was outside. The chauffeur piled and strapped the bags on top of the car and put them in beside him in the front seat and we got in. The car went out of the square, along through the side streets, out under the trees and down the hill and away from Pamplona. It did not seem like a very long ride. Mike had a bottle of Fundador. I only took a couple of drinks. We came over the mountains and out of Spain and down the white roads and through the overfoliaged, wet, green, Basque country, and finally into Bayonne. We left Bill's baggage at the station, and he bought a ticket to Paris. His train left at seven-ten. We came out of the station. The car was standing out in front.

"What shall we do about the car?" Bill asked.

"Oh, bother the car," Mike said. "Let's just keep the car with us."

"All right," Bill said. "Where shall we go?"

"Let's go to Biarritz and have a drink."

"Old Mike the spender," Bill said.

We drove in to Biarritz and left the car outside a very Ritz place. We went into the bar and sat on high stools and drank a whiskey and soda.

"That drink's mine," Mike said.

"Let's roll for it."

So we rolled poker dice out of a deep leather dice-cup. Bill was out first roll. Mike lost to me and handed the bartender a hundred-franc note. The whiskeys were twelve francs apiece. We had another round and Mike lost again. Each time he gave the bartender a good tip. In a room off the bar there was a good jazz band playing. It was a pleasant bar. We had another round. I went out on the first roll with four kings. Bill and Mike rolled. Mike won the first roll with four jacks. Bill won the second. On the final roll Mike had three kings and let them stay. He handed the dice-cup to Bill. Bill rattled them and rolled, and there were three kings, an ace, and a queen.

"It's yours, Mike," Bill said. "Old Mike, the gambler."

"I'm so sorry," Mike said. "I can't get it."

"What's the matter?"

"I've no money," Mike said. "I'm stony. I've just twenty francs. Here, take twenty francs."

Bill's face sort of changed.

"I just had enough to pay Montoya. Damned lucky to have it, too."

"I'll cash you a check," Bill said.

"That's damned nice of you, but you see I can't write checks."

"What are you going to do for money?"

"Oh, some will come through. I've two weeks allowance should be here. I can live on tick at this pub in Saint Jean."

"What do you want to do about the car?" Bill asked me. "Do you want to keep it on?"

"It doesn't make any difference. Seems sort of idiotic."

"Come on, let's have another drink," Mike said.

"Fine. This one is on me," Bill said. "Has Brett any money?" He turned to Mike.

"I shouldn't think so. She put up most of what I gave to old Montoya."

"She hasn't any money with her?" I asked.

"I shouldn't think so. She never has any money. She gets five hundred quid a year and pays three hundred and fifty of it in interest to Jews."

"I suppose they get it at the source," said Bill.

"Quite. They're not really Jews. We just call them Jews. They're Scotsmen, I believe."

"Hasn't she any at all with her?" I asked.

"I hardly think so. She gave it all to me when she left."

"Well," Bill said, "we might as well have another drink."

"Damned good idea," Mike said. "One never gets anywhere by discussing finances."

"No," said Bill. Bill and I rolled for the next two rounds. Bill lost and paid. We went out to the car.

"Anywhere you'd like to go, Mike?" Bill asked.

"Let's take a drive. It might do my credit good. Let's drive about a little."

"Fine. I'd like to see the coast. Let's drive down toward Hendaye."

"I haven't any credit along the coast."

"You can't ever tell," said Bill.

We drove out along the coast road. There was the green of the headlands, the white, red-roofed villas, patches of forest, and the ocean very blue with the tide out and the water curling far out along the beach. We drove through Saint Jean de Luz and passed through villages farther down the coast. Back of the rolling country we were going through we saw the mountains we had come over from Pamplona. The road went on ahead. Bill looked at his watch. It was time for us to go back. He knocked on the glass and told the driver to turn around. The driver backed the car out into the grass to turn it. In back of us were the woods, below a stretch of meadow, then the sea.

At the hotel where Mike was going to stay in Saint Jean we stopped the car and he got out. The chauffeur carried in his bags. Mike stood by the side of the car.

"Goodbye, you chaps," Mike said. "It was a damned fine fiesta."

"So long, Mike," Bill said.

"I'll see you around," I said.

"Don't worry about money," Mike said. "You can pay for the car, Jake, and I'll send you my share."

"So long, Mike."

"So long, you chaps. You've been damned nice."

We all shook hands. We waved from the car to Mike. He stood in the road watching. We got to Bayonne just before the train left. A porter carried Bill's bags in from the consigne. I went as far as the inner gate to the tracks.

"So long, fella," Bill said.

"So long, kid!"

"It was swell. I've had a swell time."

"Will you be in Paris?"

"No. I have to sail on the 17th. So long, fella!"

"So long, old kid!"

He went in through the gate to the train. The porter went ahead with the bags. I watched the train pull out. Bill was at one of the windows. The window passed, the rest of the train passed, and the tracks were empty. I went outside to the car.

"How much do we owe you?" I asked the driver. The price to Bayonne had been fixed at a hundred and fifty pesetas.

"Two hundred pesetas."

"How much more will it be if you drive me to San Sebastian on your way back?"

"Fifty pesetas."

"Don't kid me."

"Thirty-five pesetas."

"It's not worth it," I said. "Drive me to the Hotel Panier Fleuri."

At the hotel I paid the driver and gave him a tip. The car was powdered with dust. I rubbed the rod-case through the dust. It seemed the last thing that connected me with Spain and the fiesta. The driver put the car in gear and went down the street. I watched it turn off to take the road to Spain. I went into the hotel and they gave me a room. It was the same room I had slept in when Bill and Cohn and I were in Bayonne. That seemed a very long time ago. I washed, changed my shirt, and went out in the town.

At a newspaper kiosque I bought a copy of the New York *Herald* and sat in a café to read it. It felt strange to be in France again. There was a safe, suburban feeling. I wished I had gone up to Paris with Bill, except that Paris would have meant more fiesta-ing. I was through with fiestas for a while. It would be quiet in San Sebastian. The season does not open there until August. I could get a good hotel room and read and swim. There was a fine beach there. There were wonderful trees along the promenade above the beach, and there were many children sent down with their nurses before the season opened. In the evening there would be band concerts under the trees across from the Café Marinas. I could sit in the Marinas and listen.

"How does one eat inside?" I asked the waiter. Inside the café was a restaurant.

"Well. Very well. One eats very well."

"Good."

I went in and ate dinner. It was a big meal for France but it seemed very carefully apportioned after Spain. I drank a bottle of wine for company. It was a Château Margaux. It was pleasant to be drinking slowly and to be tasting the wine and to be drinking alone. A bottle of wine was good company. Afterward I had coffee. The waiter recommended a Basque liqueur called Izzarra. He brought in the bottle and poured a liqueur-glass full. He said Izzarra was made of the flowers of the Pyrenees. The veritable flowers of the Pyrenees. It looked like hair-oil and smelled like Italian *strega*. I told him to take the flowers of the Pyrenees away and bring me a *vieux marc*. The *marc* was good. I had a second *marc* after the coffee.

The waiter seemed a little offended about the flowers of the Pyrenees, so I overtipped him. That made him happy. It felt comfortable to be in a country where it is so simple to make people happy. You can never tell whether a Spanish waiter will thank you. Everything is on such a clear financial basis in France. It is the simplest country to live in. No one makes things complicated by becoming your friend for any obscure reason. If you want people to like you you have only to spend a little money. I spent a little money and the waiter liked me. He appreciated my valuable qualities. He would be glad to see me back. I would dine there again sometime and he would be glad to see me, and would want me at his table. It would be a sincere liking because it would have a sound basis. I was back in France.

Next morning I tipped everyone a little too much at the hotel to make more friends, and left on the morning train for San Sebastian. At the station I did not tip the porter more than I should because I did not think I would ever see him again. I only wanted a few good French friends in Bayonne to make me welcome in case I should come back there again. I knew that if they remembered me their friendship would be loyal.

At Irun we had to change trains and show passports. I hated to leave France. Life was so simple in France. I felt I was a fool to be going back into Spain. In Spain you could not tell about anything. I felt like a fool to be going back into it, but I stood in line with my passport, opened my bags for the customs, bought a ticket, went through a gate, climbed onto the train, and after forty minutes and eight tunnels I was at San Sebastian.

Even on a hot day San Sebastian has a certain early-morning quality. The trees seem as though their leaves were never quite dry. The streets feel as though they had just been sprinkled. It is always cool and shady on certain streets on the hottest day. I went to a hotel in the town where I had stopped before, and they gave me a room with a balcony that opened out above the roofs of the town. There was a green mountainside beyond the roofs.

I unpacked my bags and stacked my books on the table beside the head of the bed, put out my shaving things, hung up some clothes in the big armoire, and made up a bundle for the laundry. Then I took a shower in the bathroom and went down to lunch. Spain had not changed to summer-time, so I was early. I set my watch again. I had recovered an hour by coming to San Sebastian.

As I went into the dining-room the concierge brought me a police bulletin to fill out. I signed it and asked him for two telegraph forms, and wrote a message to the Hotel Montoya, telling them to forward all mail and telegrams for me to this address. I calculated how many days I would be in San Sebastian and then wrote out a wire to the office asking them to hold mail, but forward all wires for me to San Sebastian for six days. Then I went in and had lunch.

After lunch I went up to my room, read a while, and went to sleep. When I woke it was half past four. I found my swimming-suit, wrapped it with a comb in a towel, and went down-stairs and walked up the street to the Concha. The tide was about half-way out. The beach was smooth and firm, and the sand yellow. I went into a bathing-cabin, undressed, put on my suit, and walked across the smooth sand to the sea. The sand was warm under bare feet. There were quite a few people in the water and on the beach. Out beyond where the headlands of the Concha almost met to form the harbor there was a white line of breakers and the open sea. Although the tide was going out, there were a few slow rollers. They came in like undulations in the water, gathered weight of water, and then broke smoothly on the warm sand. I waded out. The water was cold. As a roller came I dove, swam out under water, and came to the surface with all the chill gone. I swam out to the raft, pulled myself up, and lay on the hot planks. A boy and girl were at the other end. The girl had undone the top strap of her bathing-suit and was browning her back. The boy lay face downward on the raft and talked to her. She laughed at things he said, and turned her brown back in the sun. I lay on the raft in the sun until I was dry. Then I tried several dives. I dove deep once, swimming down to the bottom. I swam with my eyes open and it was green and dark. The raft made a dark shadow. I came out of water beside the raft, pulled up, dove once more, holding it for length, and then swam ashore. I lay on the beach

until I was dry, then went into the bathing-cabin, took off my
suit, sloshed myself with fresh water, and rubbed dry.

I walked around the harbor under the trees to the casino,
and then up one of the cool streets to the Café Marinas. There
was an orchestra playing inside the café and I sat out on the
terrace and enjoyed the fresh coolness in the hot day, and had
a glass of lemon-juice and shaved ice and then a long whiskey
and soda. I sat in front of the Marinas for a long time and read
and watched the people, and listened to the music.

Later when it began to get dark, I walked around the harbor
and out along the promenade, and finally back to the hotel
for supper. There was a bicycle-race on, the Tour du Pays
Basque, and the riders were stopping that night in San Sebastian. In the dining-room, at one side, there was a long table of
bicycle-riders, eating with their trainers and managers. They
were all French and Belgians, and paid close attention to their
meal, but they were having a good time. At the head of the
table were two good-looking French girls, with much Rue du
Faubourg Montmartre chic. I could not make out whom they
belonged to. They all spoke in slang at the long table and there
were many private jokes and some jokes at the far end that
were not repeated when the girls asked to hear them. The next
morning at five o'clock the race resumed with the last lap,
San Sebastian–Bilbao. The bicycle-riders drank much wine,
and were burned and browned by the sun. They did not take
the race seriously except among themselves. They had raced
among themselves so often that it did not make much difference who won. Especially in a foreign country. The money
could be arranged.

The man who had a matter of two minutes lead in the race
had an attack of boils, which were very painful. He sat on the

small of his back. His neck was very red and the blond hairs were sunburned. The other riders joked him about his boils. He tapped on the table with his fork.

"Listen," he said, "tomorrow my nose is so tight on the handle-bars that the only thing touches those boils is a lovely breeze."

One of the girls looked at him down the table, and he grinned and turned red. The Spaniards, they said, did not know how to pedal.

I had coffee out on the terrasse with the team manager of one of the big bicycle manufacturers. He said it had been a very pleasant race, and would have been worth watching if Bottechia had not abandoned it at Pamplona. The dust had been bad, but in Spain the roads were better than in France. Bicycle road-racing was the only sport in the world, he said. Had I ever followed the Tour de France? Only in the papers. The Tour de France was the greatest sporting event in the world. Following and organizing the road races had made him know France. Few people know France. All spring and all summer and all fall he spent on the road with bicycle road-racers. Look at the number of motor-cars now that followed the riders from town to town in a road race. It was a rich country and more *sportif* every year. It would be the most *sportif* country in the world. It was bicycle road-racing did it. That and football. He knew France. *La France Sportive.* He knew road-racing. We had a cognac. After all, though, it wasn't bad to get back to Paris. There is only one Paname. In all the world, that is. Paris is the town the most *sportif* in the world. Did I know the *Chope de Negre*? Did I not. I would see him there some time. I certainly would. We would drink another *fine* together. We certainly would. They started at six o'clock less a quarter in the morning. Would I be

up for the depart? I would certainly try to. Would I like him
to call me? It was very interesting. I would leave a call at the
desk. He would not mind calling me. I could not let him take
the trouble. I would leave a call at the desk. We said goodbye
until the next morning.

In the morning when I awoke the bicycle-riders and their
following cars had been on the road for three hours. I had
coffee and the papers in bed and then dressed and took my
bathing-suit down to the beach. Everything was fresh and
cool and damp in the early morning. Nurses in uniform and
in peasant costume walked under the trees with children. The
Spanish children were beautiful. Some bootblacks sat together
under a tree talking to a soldier. The soldier had only one arm.
The tide was in and there was a good breeze and a surf on the
beach.

I undressed in one of the bath-cabins, crossed the narrow
line of beach and went into the water. I swam out, trying to
swim through the rollers, but having to dive sometimes. Then
in the quiet water I turned and floated. Floating I saw only the
sky, and felt the drop and lift of the swells. I swam back to the
surf and coasted in, face down, on a big roller, then turned
and swam, trying to keep in the trough and not have a wave
break over me. It made me tired, swimming in the trough, and
I turned and swam out to the raft. The water was buoyant and
cold. It felt as though you could never sink. I swam slowly, it
seemed like a long swim with the high tide, and then pulled up
on the raft and sat, dripping, on the boards that were becoming hot in the sun. I looked around at the bay, the old town,
the casino, the line of trees along the promenade, and the big
hotels with their white porches and gold-lettered names. Off
on the right, almost closing the harbor, was a green hill with a

castle. The raft rocked with the motion of the water. On the other side of the narrow gap that led into the open sea was another high headland. I thought I would like to swim across the bay but I was afraid of cramp.

I sat in the sun and watched the bathers on the beach. They looked very small. After a while I stood up, gripped with my toes on the edge of the raft as it tipped with my weight, and dove cleanly and deeply, to come up through the lightening water, blew the salt water out of my head, and swam slowly and steadily in to shore.

After I was dressed and had paid for the bath-cabin, I walked back to the hotel. The bicycle-racers had left several copies of *L'Auto* around, and I gathered them up in the reading-room and took them out and sat in an easy chair in the sun to read about and catch up on French sporting life. While I was sitting there the concierge came out with a blue envelope in his hand.

"A telegram for you, sir."

I poked my finger along under the fold that was fastened down, spread it open, and read it. It had been forwarded from Paris:

COULD YOU COME HOTEL MONTANA MADRID AM RATHER IN TROUBLE BRETT.

I tipped the concierge and read the message again. A postman was coming along the sidewalk. He turned in the hotel. He had a big moustache and looked very military. He came out of the hotel again. The concierge was just behind him.

"Here's another telegram for you, sir."

"Thank you," I said.

I opened it. It was forwarded from Pamplona.

COULD YOU COME HOTEL MONTANA MADRID
AM RATHER IN TROUBLE BRETT.

The concierge stood there waiting for another tip, probably.
"What time is there a train for Madrid?"

"It left at nine this morning. There is a slow train at eleven,
and the Sud Express at ten tonight."

"Get me a berth on the Sud Express. Do you want the money
now?"

"Just as you wish," he said. "I will have it put on the bill."

"Do that."

Well, that meant San Sebastian all shot to hell. I suppose,
vaguely, I had expected something of the sort. I saw the concierge standing in the doorway.

"Bring me a telegram form, please."

He brought it, and I took out my fountain-pen and printed:
Lady Ashley Hotel Montana Madrid Arriving Sud Express
Tomorrow Love Jake.

That seemed to handle it. That was it. Send a girl off with
one man. Introduce her to another to go off with him. Now go
and bring her back. And sign the wire with love. That was it all
right. I went in to lunch.

I did not sleep much that night on the Sud Express. In the
morning I had breakfast in the dining-car and watched the
rock and pine country between Avila and Escorial. I saw the
Escorial out of the window, gray and long and cold in the sun,
and did not give a damn about it. I saw Madrid come up over
the plain, a compact white sky-line on the top of a little cliff
away off across the sun-hardened country.

The Norte station in Madrid is the end of the line. All trains
finish there. They don't go on anywhere. Outside were cabs

and taxis and a line of hotel runners. It was like a country town. I took a taxi and we climbed up through the gardens, by the empty palace and the unfinished church on the edge of the cliff, and on up until we were in the high, hot, modern town. The taxi coasted down a smooth street to the Puerta del Sol, and then through the traffic and out into the Carrera San Jeronimo. All the shops had their awnings down against the heat. The windows on the sunny side of the street were shuttered. The taxi stopped at the curb. I saw the sign HOTEL MONTANA on the second floor. The taxi-driver carried the bags in and left them by the elevator. I could not make the elevator work, so I walked up. On the second floor up was a cut brass sign: HOTEL MONTANA. I rang and no one came to the door. I rang again and a maid with a sullen face opened the door.

"Is Lady Ashley here?" I asked.

She looked at me dully.

"Is an Englishwoman here?"

She turned and called someone inside. A very fat woman came to the door. Her hair was gray and stiffly oiled in scallops around her face. She was short and commanding.

"Muy buenos," I said. "Is there an Englishwoman here? I would like to see this English lady."

"Muy buenos. Yes, there is a female English. Certainly you can see her if she wishes to see you."

"She wishes to see me."

"The chica will ask her."

"It is very hot."

"It is very hot in the summer in Madrid."

"And how cold in winter."

"Yes, it is very cold in winter."

Did I want to stay myself in person in the Hotel Montana?

Of that as yet I was undecided, but it would give me pleasure if my bags were brought up from the ground floor in order that they might not be stolen. Nothing was ever stolen in the Hotel Montana. In other fondas, yes. Not here. No. The personages of this establishment were rigidly selected. I was happy to hear it. Nevertheless I would welcome the upbringal of my bags.

The maid came in and said that the female English wanted to see the male English now, at once.

"Good," I said. "You see. It is as I said."

"Clearly."

I followed the maid's back down a long, dark corridor. At the end she knocked on a door.

"Hello," said Brett. "Is it you, Jake?"

"It's me."

"Come in. Come in."

I opened the door. The maid closed it after me. Brett was in bed. She had just been brushing her hair and held the brush in her hand. The room was in that disorder produced only by those who have always had servants.

"Darling!" Brett said.

I went over to the bed and put my arms around her. She kissed me, and while she kissed me I could feel she was thinking of something else. She was trembling in my arms. She felt very small.

"Darling! I've had such a hell of a time."

"Tell me about it."

"Nothing to tell. He only left yesterday. I made him go."

"Why didn't you keep him?"

"I don't know. It isn't the sort of thing one does. I don't think I hurt him any."

"You were probably damn good for him."

"He shouldn't be living with anyone. I realized that right away."

"No."

"Oh, hell!" she said, "let's not talk about it. Let's never talk about it."

"All right."

"It was rather a knock his being ashamed of me. He was ashamed of me for a while, you know."

"No."

"Oh, yes. They ragged him about me at the café, I guess. He wanted me to grow my hair out. Me, with long hair. I'd look so like hell."

"It's funny."

"He said it would make me more womanly. I'd look a fright."

"What happened?"

"Oh, he got over that. He wasn't ashamed of me long."

"What was it about being in trouble?"

"I didn't know whether I could make him go, and I didn't have a sou to go away and leave him. He tried to give me a lot of money, you know. I told him I had scads of it. He knew that was a lie. I couldn't take his money, you know."

"No."

"Oh, let's not talk about it. There were some funny things, though. Do give me a cigarette."

I lit the cigarette.

"He learned his English as a waiter in Gib."

"Yes."

"He wanted to marry me, finally."

"Really?"

"Of course. I can't even marry Mike."

"Maybe he thought that would make him Lord Ashley."

"No. It wasn't that. He really wanted to marry me. So I couldn't go away from him, he said. He wanted to make it sure I could never go away from him. After I'd gotten more womanly, of course."

"You ought to feel set up."

"I do. I'm all right again. He's wiped out that damned Cohn."

"Good."

"You know I'd have lived with him if I hadn't seen it was bad for him. We got along damned well."

"Outside of your personal appearance."

"Oh, he'd have gotten used to that."

She put out the cigarette.

"I'm thirty-four, you know. I'm not going to be one of these bitches that ruins children."

"No."

"I'm not going to be that way. I feel rather good, you know. I feel rather set up."

"Good."

She looked away. I thought she was looking for another cigarette. Then I saw she was crying. I could feel her crying. Shaking and crying. She wouldn't look up. I put my arms around her.

"Don't let's ever talk about it. Please don't let's ever talk about it."

"Dear Brett."

"I'm going back to Mike." I could feel her crying as I held her close. "He's so damned nice and he's so awful. He's my sort of thing."

She would not look up. I stroked her hair. I could feel her shaking.

"I won't be one of those bitches," she said. "But, oh, Jake, please let's never talk about it."

We left the Hotel Montana. The woman who ran the hotel would not let me pay the bill. The bill had been paid.

"Oh, well. Let it go," Brett said. "It doesn't matter now."

We rode in a taxi down to the Palace Hotel, left the bags, arranged for berths on the Sud Express for the night, and went into the bar of the hotel for a cocktail. We sat on high stools at the bar while the barman shook the Martinis in a large nickelled shaker.

"It's funny what a wonderful gentility you get in the bar of a big hotel," I said.

"Barmen and jockeys are the only people who are polite anymore."

"No matter how vulgar a hotel is, the bar is always nice."

"It's odd."

"Bartenders have always been fine."

"You know," Brett said, "it's quite true. He is only nineteen. Isn't it amazing?"

We touched the two glasses as they stood side by side on the bar. They were coldly beaded. Outside the curtained window was the summer heat of Madrid.

"I like an olive in a Martini," I said to the barman.

"Right you are, sir. There you are."

"Thanks."

"I should have asked, you know."

The barman went far enough up the bar so that he would not hear our conversation. Brett had sipped from the Martini as it stood, on the wood. Then she picked it up. Her hand was steady enough to lift it after that first sip.

"It's good. Isn't it a nice bar."

"They're all nice bars."

"You know I didn't believe it at first. He was born in 1905. I was in school in Paris, then. Think of that."

"Anything you want me to think about it?"

"Don't be an ass. *Would* you buy a lady a drink?"

"We'll have two more Martinis."

"As they were before, sir?"

"They were very good." Brett smiled at him.

"Thank you, ma'am."

"Well, bung-o," Brett said.

"Bung-o!"

"You know," Brett said, "he'd only been with two women before. He never cared about anything but bull-fighting."

"He's got plenty of time."

"I don't know. He thinks it was me. Not the show in general."

"Well, it was you."

"Yes. It was me."

"I thought you weren't going to ever talk about it."

"How can I help it?"

"You'll lose it if you talk about it."

"I just talk around it. You know I feel rather damned good, Jake."

"You should."

"You know it makes one feel rather good deciding not to be a bitch."

"Yes."

"It's sort of what we have instead of God."

"Some people have God," I said. "Quite a lot."

"He never worked very well with me."

"Should we have another Martini?"

The barman shook up two more Martinis and poured them out into fresh glasses.

"Where will we have lunch?" I asked Brett. The bar was cool. You could feel the heat outside through the window.

"Here?" asked Brett.

"It's rotten here in the hotel. Do you know a place called Botin's?" I asked the barman.

"Yes, sir. Would you like to have me write out the address?"

"Thank you."

We lunched upstairs at Botin's. It is one of the best restaurants in the world. We had roast young suckling pig and drank *rioja alta*. Brett did not eat much. She never ate much. I ate a very big meal and drank three bottles of *rioja alta*.

"How do you feel, Jake?" Brett asked. "My God! what a meal you've eaten."

"I feel fine. Do you want a dessert?"

"Lord, no."

Brett was smoking.

"You like to eat, don't you?" she said.

"Yes," I said. "I like to do a lot of things."

"What do you like to do?"

"Oh," I said, "I like to do a lot of things. Don't you want a dessert?"

"You asked me that once," Brett said.

"Yes," I said. "So I did. Let's have another bottle of *rioja alta*."

"It's very good."

"You haven't drunk much of it," I said.

"I have. You haven't seen."

"Let's get two bottles," I said. The bottles came. I poured a little in my glass, then a glass for Brett, then filled my glass. We touched glasses.

"Bung-o!" Brett said. I drank my glass and poured out another. Brett put her hand on my arm.

"Don't get drunk, Jake," she said. "You don't have to."

"How do you know?"

"Don't," she said. "You'll be all right."

"I'm not getting drunk," I said. "I'm just drinking a little wine. I like to drink wine."

"Don't get drunk," she said. "Jake, don't get drunk."

"Want to go for a ride?" I said. "Want to ride through the town?"

"Right," Brett said. "I haven't seen Madrid. I should see Madrid."

"I'll finish this," I said.

Downstairs we came out through the first-floor dining-room to the street. A waiter went for a taxi. It was hot and bright. Up the street was a little square with trees and grass where there were taxis parked. A taxi came up the street, the waiter hanging out at the side. I tipped him and told the driver where to drive, and got in beside Brett. The driver started up the street. I settled back. Brett moved close to me. We sat close against each other. I put my arm around her and she rested against me comfortably. It was very hot and bright, and the houses looked sharply white. We turned out onto the Gran Via.

"Oh, Jake," Brett said, "we could have had such a damned good time together."

Ahead was a mounted policeman in khaki directing traffic. He raised his baton. The car slowed suddenly pressing Brett against me.

"Yes," I said. "Isn't it pretty to think so."

THE END

# APPENDIX

JOURNALISM

# THE MECCA OF FAKERS IS
# FRENCH CAPITAL

P ARIS.—Paris is the Mecca of the bluffers and fakers in every line of endeavor from music to prizefighting. You find more famous American dancers who have never been heard of in America; more renowned Russian dancers who are disclaimed by the Russians; and more champion prizefighters who were preliminary boys before they crossed the ocean, per square yard in Paris than anywhere else in the world.

This state of affairs exists because of the extreme provinciality of the French people, and because of the gullibility of the French press. Everyone in Canada knows the names of half a dozen French soldiers and statesmen, but no one in France could give you the name of a Canadian general or statesman or tell you who was the present head of the Canadian government. By no one I mean none of the ordinary people; shop keepers, hotel owners and general bourgeois class. For example, my *femme de ménage* was horrified yesterday when I told her there was a Prohibition in Canada and the States. "Why have we never heard of it?" she asked. "Has it just been a law? What then does a man drink?"

An American girl was recently billed at the Paris music halls as "America's best known and best loved dancer." None of the recent arrivals in Paris from the States had ever heard of her, but Parisians flocked to see the American "Star." Later it came out that she had a small part in a U.S. musical show some years ago.

Russians have inundated the city. They can get away with almost anything, because it is easy for a Russian to claim that he was anything he may want to say, in Russia; there is no way to check up on Russian reputations at present. So we have great Russian dancers, great Russian pianists, flutists, composers, and organists—all equally bad.

Jack Clifford, who styled himself the colored light-heavyweight champion of the United States and Canada, was a recent nine-days' wonder in France. He avoided meeting any fighters and demanded tremendous sums to box, but announced his willingness to meet Carpentier if a suitable purse was offered. No American had ever heard of him—but the Europeans swallowed him whole.

Clifford met his downfall in Vienna, where a third-rate Austrian pugilist, with an unpronounceable name, punished him so badly that the fight was halted in the third round to save the Negro from further punishment. Clifford had been on the floor most of the evening and did not show even an amateur's knowledge of fighting. The crowd, which had paid several baskets of kronen apiece to see the American black champion, attempted to lynch Clifford with the ropes cut from the ring, but the Negro was saved by the police and left Vienna that night.

At present a familiar figure to those Torontonians who attend boxing matches is basking in the pleasant spotlight of European publicity. It is none other than Soldier Jones. Jones is being hailed by the Paris papers as "the heavyweight champion of Canada, the man who has never been knocked off his feet, the winner of eighty-five fights by knockouts and the best fighter that Canada has ever produced."

Jones is at present in England, where he is being groomed for a fight with Beckett, but his manager has sent press dope over to Paris, where it is being published by the English papers and avidly copied by the French.

Torontonians who recall what happened one night last year, when this same Soldier Jones abandoned caution so far as to enter the ring with Harry Greb, will be able to form their own opinions of how easy it is to become a "champion" abroad. The only rule seems to be that you must choose to be a champion of some very distant country and then stay away from that country. That is the way the fiddlers, fighters, painters and dancers are doing.

*Toronto Daily Star*
March 25, 1922

## AMERICAN BOHEMIANS IN PARIS
## A WEIRD LOT

P ARIS.—The scum of Greenwich Village, New York, has been skimmed off and deposited in large ladles on that section of Paris adjacent to the Café Rotonde. New scum, of course, has risen to take the place of the old, but the oldest scum, the thickest scum and the scummiest scum has come across the ocean, somehow, and with its afternoon and evening levees has made the Rotonde the leading Latin Quarter showplace for tourists in search of atmosphere.

It is a strange-acting and strange-looking breed that crowd the tables of the Café Rotonde. They have all striven so hard for a careless individuality of clothing that they have achieved a sort of uniformity of eccentricity. A first look into the smoky, high-ceilinged, table-crammed interior of the Rotonde gives you the same feeling that hits you as you step into the bird-house at the zoo. There seems to be a tremendous, raucous, many-pitched squawking going on, broken up by many waiters who fly around through the smoke like so many black and white magpies. The tables are full—they are always full —someone is moved down and crowded together, something is knocked over, more people come in at the swinging door, another black and white waiter pivots between tables toward the door and, having shouted your order at his disappearing back, you look around you at individual people.

You can only see a certain number of individuals at the Rotonde on one night. When you have reached your quota you are quite aware that you must go. There is a perfectly definite moment when you know you have seen enough of the Rotonde's inmates and must leave. If you want to know how definite it is, try and eat your way through a jug of soured molasses. To some people the feeling that you cannot go on will come at the first mouthful. Others are hardier. But there is a limit for all normal people. For the people who crowd together around the tables of the Café Rotonde do something very definite to that premier seat of the emotions, the stomach.

For the first dose of Rotonde individuals you might observe a short, dumpy woman with newly blond hair, cut Old-Dutch-Cleanser fashion, a face like a pink enameled ham and fat fingers that reach out of the long blue silk sleeves of a Chinese-looking smock. She is sitting hunched forward over the table, smoking a cigarette in a two-foot holder, and her flat face is absolutely devoid of any expression.

She is looking flatly at her masterpiece that is hung on the white plaster wall of the café, along with some 3,000 others, as part of the Rotonde's salon for customers only. Her master-piece looks like a red mince pie descending the stairs, and the adoring, though expressionless, painter spends every afternoon and evening seated at the table before it in a devout attitude.

After you have finished looking at the painter and her work you can turn your head a little and see a big, light-haired woman sitting at a table with three young men. The big woman is wear-ing a picture hat of the "Merry Widow" period and is making jokes and laughing hysterically. The three young men laugh whenever she does. The waiter brings the bill, the big woman pays it, settles her hat on her head with slightly unsteady hands,

and she and the three young men go out together. She is laughing again as she goes out of the door. Three years ago she came
to Paris with her husband from a little town in Connecticut,
where they had lived and he had painted with increasing success for ten years. Last year he went back to America alone.

Those are two of the twelve hundred people who jam the
Rotonde. You can find anything you are looking for at the
Rotonde—except serious artists. The trouble is that people
who go on a tour of the Latin Quarter look in at the Rotonde
and think they are seeing an assembly of the great artists of
Paris. I want to correct that in a very public manner, for the
artists of Paris who are turning out creditable work resent and
loathe the Rotonde crowd.

The fact that there are twelve francs for a dollar brought over
the Rotonders, along with a good many other people, and if the
exchange ever gets back to normal they will all have to go back
to America. They are nearly all loafers expending the energy
that an artist puts into his creative work in talking about what
they are going to do and condemning the work of all artists
who have gained any degree of recognition. By talking about
art they obtain the same satisfaction that the real artist does in
his work. That is very pleasant, of course, but they insist upon
posing as artists.

Since the good old days when Charles Baudelaire led a purple lobster on a leash through the same old Latin Quarter, there
has not been much good poetry written in cafés. Even then I
suspect that Baudelaire parked the lobster with the concierge
down on the first floor, put the chloroform bottle corked on
the washstand and sweated and carved at the *Fleurs du Mal*
alone with his ideas and his paper as all artists have worked
before and since. But the gang that congregates at the corner of

the Boulevard Montparnasse and the Boulevard Raspail have no time to work at anything else; they put in a full day at the Rotonde.

*Toronto Star Weekly*

March 25, 1922

## BULL FIGHTING IS NOT A SPORT—
## IT IS A TRAGEDY

I T WAS spring in Paris and everything looked just a little too beautiful. Mike and I decided to go to Spain. Strater drew us a fine map of Spain on the back of a menu of the Strix restaurant. On the same menu he wrote the name of a restaurant in Madrid where the specialty is young suckling pig roasted, the name of the pensione on the Via San Jerónimo where the bullfighters live, and sketched a plan showing where the Grecos are hung in the Prado.

Fully equipped with this menu and our old clothes, we started for Spain. Our objective—to see bullfights.

We left Paris one morning and got off the train at Madrid the next noon. We saw our first bullfight at 4:30 that afternoon. It took about two hours to get tickets. We finally got them from scalpers for twenty-five pesetas apiece. The bullring was entirely sold out. We had barrera seats. These, the scalper explained in Spanish and broken French, were the first row of the ringside, directly under the royal box, and immediately opposite where the bulls would come out.

We asked him if he didn't have any less distinguished seats for somewhere around twelve pesetas, but he was sold out. So we paid the fifty pesetas for the two tickets, and with the tickets in our pockets sat out on the sidewalk in front of a big café near the Puerta del Sol. It was very exciting, sitting out in front

of a café your first day in Spain with a ticket in your pocket
that meant that rain or shine you were going to see a bullfight
in an hour and a half. In fact, it was so exciting that we started
out for the bullring on the outskirts of the city in about half an
hour.

The bullring or Plaza de Toros was a big, tawny brick amphitheater standing at the end of a street in an open field. The
yellow and red Spanish flag was floating over it. Carriages
were driving up and people getting out of buses. There was
a great crowd of beggars around the entrance. Men were selling water out of big terra-cotta water bottles. Kids sold fans,
canes, roasted salted almonds in paper spills, fruit and slabs
of ice cream. The crowd was gay and cheerful but all intent
on pushing toward the entrance. Mounted civil guards with
patent-leather cocked hats and carbines slung over their back
sat their horses like statues, and the crowd flowed through.

Inside they all stood around in the bullring, talking and looking up in the grandstand at the girls in the boxes. Some of
the men had field glasses in order to look better. We found
our seats and the crowd began to leave the ring and get into
the rows of concrete seats. The ring was circular—that sounds
foolish, but a boxing ring is square—with a sand floor. Around
it was a red board fence—just high enough for a man to be able
to vault over it. Between the board fence, which is called the
barrera, and the first row of seats ran a narrow alleyway. Then
came the seats which were just like a football stadium except
that around the top ran a double circle of boxes.

Every seat in the amphitheater was full. The arena was
cleared. Then on the far side of the arena out of the crowd, four
heralds in medieval costume stood up and blew a blast on their

trumpets. The band crashed out, and from the entrance on the far side of the ring four horsemen in black velvet with ruffs around their necks rode out into the white glare of the arena. The people on the sunny side were baking in the heat and fanning themselves. The whole sol side was a flicker of fans.

Behind the four horsemen came the procession of the bullfighters. They had been all formed in ranks in the entranceway ready to march out, and as the music started they came. In the front rank walked the three espadas, or toreros, who would have charge of the killing of the six bulls of the afternoon.

They came walking out in heavily brocaded yellow and black costumes, the familiar "toreador" suit, heavy with gold embroidery, cape, jacket, shirt and collar, knee breeches, pink stockings, and low pumps. Always at bullfights, afterward the incongruity of those pink stockings used to strike me. Just behind the three principals—and after your first bullfight you do not look at their costumes but their faces—marched the teams, or cuadrillas. They are dressed in the same way but not as gorgeously as the matadors.

Back of the teams ride the picadors. Big, heavy, brown-faced men in wide flat hats, carrying lances like long window poles. They are astride horses that make Spark Plug look as trim and sleek as a King's Plate winner. Back of the pics come the gaily harnessed mule teams and the red-shirted monos, or bullring servants.

The bullfighters march in across the sand to the president's box. They march with easy professional stride, swinging along, not in the least theatrical except for their clothes. They all have the easy grace and slight slouch of the professional athlete. From their faces they might be major league ball players. They salute the president's box and then spread out along the barrera, exchanging their heavy brocaded capes for the fighting capes that have been laid along the red fence by the attendants.

We leaned forward over the barrera. Just below us the three matadors of the afternoon were leaning against the fence talking. One lighted a cigarette. He was a short, clear-skinned gypsy, Gitanillo, in a wonderful gold brocaded jacket, his short pigtail sticking out under his black cocked hat.

"He's not very fancy," a young man in a straw hat, with obviously American shoes, who sat on my left, said.

"But he sure knows bulls, that boy. He's a great killer."

"You're an American, aren't you?" asked Mike.

"Sure," the boy grinned. "But I know this gang. That's Gitanillo. You want to watch him. The kid with the chubby face is Chicuelo. They say he doesn't really like bullfighting, but the town's crazy about him. The one next to him is Villalta. He's the great one."

I had noticed Villalta. He was straight as a lance and walked like a young wolf. He was talking and smiling at a friend who leaned over the barrera. Upon his tanned cheekbone was a big patch of gauze held on with adhesive tape.

"He got gored last week at Málaga," said the American.

The American, whom later we were to learn to know and love as the Gin Bottle King, because of a great feat of arms performed at an early hour of the morning with a container of Mr. Gordon's celebrated product as his sole weapon in one of the four most dangerous situations I have ever seen, said: "The show's going to begin."

Out in the arena the picadors had galloped their decrepit horses around the ring, sitting straight and stiff in their rocking-chair saddles. Now all but three had ridden out of the ring. These three were huddled against the red painted fence of the barrera. Their horses backed against the fence, one eye bandaged, their lances at rest.

In rode two of the marshals in the velvet jackets and white ruffs. They galloped up to the president's box, swerved and saluted, doffing their hats and bowing low. From the box an object came hurtling down. One of the marshals caught it in his plumed hat.

"The key to the bullpen," said the Gin Bottle King.

The two horsemen whirled and rode across the arena. One of them tossed the key to a man in torero costume, they both saluted with a wave of their plumed hats, and had gone from the ring. The big gate was shut and bolted. There was no more entrance. The ring was complete.

The crowd had been shouting and yelling. Now it was dead silent. The man with the key stepped toward an iron-barred, low, red door and unlocked the great sliding bar. The door swung open. The man hid behind it. Inside it was dark.

Then, ducking his head as he came up out of the dark pen, a bull came into the arena. He came out all in a rush, big, black and white, weighing over a ton, and moving with a soft gallop. Just as he came out the sun seemed to dazzle him for an instant. He stood as though he were frozen, his great crest of muscle up, firmly planted, his eyes looking around, his horns pointed forward, black and white and sharp as porcupine quills. Then he charged. And as he charged, I suddenly saw what bullfighting is all about.

For the bull was absolutely unbelievable. He seemed like some great prehistoric animal, absolutely deadly and absolutely vicious. And he was silent. He charged silently and with a soft, galloping rush. When he turned he turned on his four feet like a cat. When he charged the first thing that caught his eye was the picador on one of the wretched horses. The picador dug his spurs into the horse and they galloped away. The bull came on in his rush, refused to be shaken off, and in full gallop crashed into the animal from the side, ignored the horse, drove one of his horns high into the thigh of the picador, and tore him, saddle and all, off the horse's back.

The bull went on without pausing to worry the picador lying on the ground. The next picador was sitting on his horse braced to receive the shock of the charge, his lance ready. The bull hit him sideways on, and horse and rider went high up in the air in a kicking mass and fell across the bull's back. As they came down the bull charged into them. The dough-faced kid, Chicuelo, vaulted over the fence, ran toward the bull and flapped his cape into the bull's face. The bull charged the cape and Chicuelo dodged backward and had the bull clear in the arena.

Without an instant's hesitation, the bull charged Chicuelo. The kid stood his ground, simply swung back on his heels and floated his cape like a ballet dancer's skirt into the bull's face as he passed.

"Olé!"—pronounced Oh-Lay!—roared the crowd.

The bull whirled and charged again. Without moving, Chicuelo repeated the performance. His legs rigid, just withdrawing his body from the rush of the bull's horns and floating the cape out with that beautiful swing.

Again the crowd roared. The Kid did this seven times. Each time the bull missed him by inches. Each time he gave the bull a free shot at him. Each time the crowd roared. Then he flopped the cape once at the bull at the finish of a pass, swung it around behind him and walked away from the bull to the barrera.

"He's the boy with the cape all right," said the Gin Bottle King. "That swing he did with the cape's called a veronica."

The chubby-faced Kid who did not like bullfighting and had just done the seven wonderful veronicas was standing against the fence just below us. His face glistened with sweat in the sun but was almost expressionless. His eyes were looking out across the arena where the bull was standing making up his mind to charge a picador. He was studying the bull because a few minutes later it would be his duty to kill him, and once he went out with his thin, red-hilted sword and his piece of red cloth to kill the bull in the final set it would be him or the bull. There are no drawn battles in bullfighting.

I am not going to describe the rest of that afternoon in detail. It was the first bullfight I ever saw, but it was not the best. The best was in the little town of Pamplona high up in the hills of Navarre, and came weeks later. Up in Pamplona, where they have held six days of bullfighting each year since A.D. 1126, and where the bulls race through the streets of the town each morning at six o'clock with half the town running ahead of them. Pamplona, where every man and boy in town is an amateur bullfighter and where there is an amateur fight each morning that is attended by 20,000 people in which the amateur fighters are all unarmed and there is a casualty list at least equal to a Dublin election. But Pamplona, with the best bullfight and the wild tale of the amateur fights, comes in the second chapter.

I am not going to apologize for bullfighting. It is a survival of the days of the Roman Colosseum. But it does need some explanation. Bullfighting is not a sport. It was never supposed to be. It is a tragedy. A very great tragedy. The tragedy is the death of the bull. It is played in three definite acts.

The Gin Bottle King—who, by the way, does not drink gin —told us a lot of this that first night as we sat in the upstairs room of the little restaurant that made a specialty of roast young suckling pig, roasted on an oak plank and served with a mushroom tortilla and vino rojo. The rest we learned later at the bullfighters' pensione in the Via San Jerónimo, where one of the bullfighters had eyes exactly like a rattlesnake.

Much of it we learned in the sixteen fights we saw in different parts of Spain from San Sebastian to Granada.

At any rate bullfighting is not a sport. It is a tragedy, and it symbolizes the struggle between man and the beasts. There are usually six bulls to a fight. A fight is called a corrida de toros. Fighting bulls are bred like race-horses, some of the oldest breeding establishments being several hundred years old. A good bull is worth about $2,000. They are bred for speed, strength and viciousness. In other words a good fighting bull is an absolutely incorrigible bad bull.

Bullfighting is an exceedingly dangerous occupation. In the sixteen fights I saw there were only two in which there was no one badly hurt. On the other hand it is very remunerative. A popular espada gets $5,000 for his afternoon's work. An unpopular espada though may not get $500. Both run the same risks. It is a good deal like Grand Opera for the really great matadors except they run the chance of being killed every time they cannot hit high C.

No one at any time in the fight can approach the bull except directly from the front. That is where the danger comes. There are also all sorts of complicated passes that must be done with the cape, each requiring as much technique as a champion billiard player. And underneath it all is the necessity for playing the old tragedy in the absolutely custom-bound, law-laid-down way. It must all be done gracefully, seemingly effortlessly and always with dignity. The worst criticism the Spaniards ever make of a bullfighter is that his work is "vulgar."

The three absolute acts of the tragedy are first the entry of the bull when the picadors receive the shock of his attacks and attempt to protect their horses with their lances. Then the horses go out and the second act is the planting of the banderillos. This is one of the most interesting and difficult parts but among the easiest for a new bullfight fan to appreciate in technique. The banderillos are three-foot, gaily colored darts with a small fishhook prong in the end. The man who is going to plant them walks out into the arena alone with the bull. He lifts the banderillos at arm's length and points them toward the bull. Then he calls "Toro! Toro!" The bull charges and the banderillero rises to his toes, bends in a curve forward and, just as the bull is about to hit him, drops the darts into the bull's hump just back of his horns.

They must go in evenly, one on each side. They must not be shoved, or thrown or stuck in from the side. This is the first time the bull has been completely baffled, there is the prick of the darts that he cannot escape and there are no horses for him to charge into. But he charges the man again and again and each time he gets a pair of the long banderillos that hang from his hump by their tiny barbs and flop like porcupine quills.

Last is the death of the bull, which is in the hands of the matador who has had charge of the bull since his first attack. Each matador has two bulls in the afternoon. The death of the bull is most formal and can only be brought about in one way, directly from the front by the matador, who must receive the bull in full charge and kill him with a sword thrust between the shoulders just back of the neck and between the horns. Before killing the bull he must first do a series of passes with the muleta, a piece of red cloth about the size of a large napkin. With the muleta, the torero must show his complete mastery of the bull, must make the bull miss him again and again by inches, before he is allowed to kill him. It is in this phase that most of the fatal accidents occur.

The word "toreador" is obsolete Spanish and is never used. The torero is usually called an espada, or swordsman. He must be proficient in all three acts of the fight. In the first he uses the cape and does veronicas and protects the picadors by taking the bull out and away from them when they are spilled to the ground. In the second act he plants the banderillos. In the third act he masters the bull with the muleta and kills him.

Few toreros excel in all three departments. Some, like young Chicuelo, are unapproachable in their capework. Others like the late Joselito are wonderful banderilleros. Only a few are great killers. Most of the greatest killers are gypsies.

*Toronto Star Weekly*
October 20, 1923

# WORLD'S SERIES OF BULL FIGHTING
## A MAD, WHIRLING CARNIVAL

I N PAMPLONA, a white-walled, sun-baked town high up in the hills of Navarre, is held in the first two weeks of July each year the world series of bullfighting.

Bullfight fans from all Spain jam into the little town. Hotels double their prices and fill every room. The cafés under the wide arcades that run around the Plaza de la Constitución have every table crowded, the tall Pilgrim Father sombreros of Andalusia sitting over the same table with straw hats from Madrid and the flat blue Basque caps of Navarre and the Basque country.

Really beautiful girls, gorgeous, bright shawls over their shoulders, dark, dark-eyed, black lace mantillas over their hair, walk with their escorts in the crowds that pass from morning until night along the narrow walk that runs between inner and outer belts of café tables under the shade of the arcade out of the white glare of the Plaza de la Constitución. All day and all night there is dancing in the streets. Bands of blue-shirted peasants whirl and lift and swing behind a drum, fife and reed instruments in the ancient Basque Riau-Riau dances. And at night there is the throb of the big drums and the military band as the whole town dances in the great open square of the Plaza.

We landed at Pamplona at night. The streets were solid with people dancing. Music was pounding and throbbing. Fireworks were being set off from the big public square. All the carnivals I have ever seen paled in comparison. A rocket exploded over our heads with a blinding burst and the stick came swirling and whishing down. Dancers, snapping their fingers and whirling in perfect time through the crowd, bumped into us before we could get our bags down from the top of the station bus. Finally I got the bags through the crowd to the hotel.

We had wired and written for rooms two weeks ahead. Nothing had been saved. We were offered a single room with a single bed opening onto the kitchen ventilator shaft for seven dollars a day apiece. There was a big row with the landlady, who stood in front of her desk with her hands on her hips, and her broad Indian face perfectly placid, and told us in a few words of French and much Basque Spanish that she had to make all her money for the whole year in the next ten days. That people would come and that people would have to pay what she asked. She could show us a better room for ten dollars apiece. We said it would be preferable to sleep in the streets with the pigs. The landlady agreed that might be possible. We said we preferred it to such a hotel. All perfectly amicable. The landlady considered. We stood our ground. Mrs. Hemingway sat down on our rucksacks.

"I can get you a room in a house in the town. You can eat here," said the landlady.

"How much?"

"Five dollars."

We started off through the dark, narrow, carnival-mad streets with a boy carrying our rucksacks. It was a lovely big room in an old Spanish house with walls thick as a fortress. A cool, pleasant room, with a red tile floor and two big, comfortable beds set back in an alcove. A window opened on to an iron-grilled porch out over the street. We were very comfortable.

All night long the wild music kept up in the street below. Several times in the night there was a wild roll of drumming, and I got out of bed and across the tiled floor to the balcony. But it was always the same. Men, blue-shirted, bareheaded, whirling and floating in a wild fantastic dance down the street behind the rolling drums and shrill fifes.

Just at daylight there was a crash of music in the street below. Real military music. Herself was up, dressed, at the window.

"Come on," she said. "They're all going somewhere." Down below the street was full of people. It was five o'clock in the morning. They were all going in one direction. I dressed in a hurry and we started after them.

The crowd was all going toward the great public square. People were pouring into it from every street and moving out of it toward the open country we could see through the narrow gaps in the high walls.

"Let's get some coffee," said Herself.

"Do you think we've got time? Hey, what's going to happen?" I asked a newsboy.

"Encierro," he said scornfully. "The encierro commences at six o'clock."

"What's the encierro?" I asked him.

"Oh, ask me tomorrow," he said, and started to run. The entire crowd was running now.

"I've got to have my coffee. No matter what it is," Herself said.

The waiter poured two streams of coffee and milk into the glass out of his big kettles. The crowd were still running, coming from all the streets that fed into the Plaza.

"What is this encierro anyway?" Herself asked, gulping the coffee.

"All I know is that they let the bulls out into the streets."

We started out after the crowd. Out of a narrow gate into a great yellow open space of country with the new concrete bull-ring standing high and white and black with people. The yellow and red Spanish flag blowing in the early-morning breeze. Across the open and once inside the bullring, we mounted to the top looking toward the town. It cost a peseta to go up to the top. All the other levels were free. There were easily twenty thousand people there. Everyone jammed on the outside of the big concrete amphitheater, looking toward the yellow town with the bright red roofs, where a long wooden pen ran from the entrance of the city gate across the open, bare ground to the bullring.

It was really a double wooden fence, making a long entry from the main street of the town into the bullring itself. It made a runway about two hundred and fifty yards long. People were jammed solid on each side of it. Looking up it toward the main street.

Then far away there was a dull report.

"They're off," everybody shouted.

"What is it?" I asked a man next to me who was leaning far out over the concrete rail.

"The bulls! They have released them from the corrals on the far side of the city. They are racing through the city."

"Whew," said Herself. "What do they do that for?"

Then down the narrow fenced-in runway came a crowd of men and boys running. Running as hard as they could go. The gate feeding into the bullring was opened and they all ran pell-mell under the entrance levels into the ring. Then there came another crowd. Running even harder. Straight up the long pen from the town.

"Where are the bulls?" asked Herself.

Then they came in sight. Eight bulls galloping along, full tilt, heavyset, black, glistening, sinister, their horns bare, tossing their heads. And running with them, three steers with bells on their necks. They ran in a solid mass, and ahead of them sprinted, tore, ran and bolted the rear guard of the men and boys of Pamplona who had allowed themselves to be chased through the streets for a morning's pleasure.

A boy in his blue shirt, red sash, white canvas shoes, with the inevitable leather wine bottle hung from his shoulders, stumbled as he sprinted down the straightaway. The first bull lowered his head and made a jerky, sideways toss. The boy crashed up against the fence and lay there limp, the herd running solidly together passed him up. The crowd roared.

Everybody made a dash for the inside of the ring, and we got into a box just in time to see the bulls come into the ring filled with men. The men ran in a panic to each side. The bulls, still bunched solidly together, ran straight with the trained steers across the ring and into the entrance that led to the pens.

That was the entry. Every morning during the bullfighting festival of San Fermin at Pamplona, the bulls that are to fight in the afternoon are released from their corrals at six o'clock in the morning and race through the main street of the town for a mile and a half to the pen. The men who run ahead of them do it for the fun of the thing. It has been going on each year since a couple of hundred years before Columbus had his historic interview with Queen Isabella in the camp outside of Granada.

There are two things in favor of there being no accidents.

First, that fighting bulls are not aroused and vicious when they are together. Second, that the steers are relied upon to keep them moving.

Sometimes things go wrong, a bull will be detached from the herd as they pile through into the pen and with his crest up, a ton of speed and viciousness, his needle-sharp horns lowered, will charge again and again into the packed mass of men and boys in the bullring. There is no place for the men to get out of the ring. It is too jammed for them to climb over the barrera or red fence that rims the field. They have to stay in and take it. Eventually the steers get the bull out of the ring and into the pen. He may wound or kill thirty men before they can get him out. No armed men are allowed to oppose him. That is the chance the Pamplona bullfight fans take every morning during the Feria. It is the Pamplona tradition of giving the bulls a final shot at everyone in town before they enter the pens. They will not leave until they come out into the glare of the arena to die in the afternoon.

Consequently Pamplona is the toughest bullfight town in the world. The amateur fight that comes immediately after the bulls have entered the pens proves that. Every seat in the great amphitheater is packed. About three hundred men, with capes, odd pieces of cloth, old shirts, anything that will imitate a bullfighter's cape, are singing and dancing in the arena. There is a shout, and the bullpen opens. Out comes a young bull just as fast as he can come. On his horns are leather knobs to prevent his goring anyone. He charges and hits a man. Tosses him high in the air, and the crowd roars. The man comes down on the ground, and the bull goes for him, bumping him with his head. Worrying him with his horns. Several amateur bullfighters are flopping their capes in his face to make the bull charge and leave the man on the ground. The bull charges and bags another man. The crowd roars with delight.

Then the bull will turn like a cat and get somebody who has been acting very brave about ten feet behind him. Then he will toss a man over the fence. Then he picks out one man and follows him in a wild twisting charge through the entire crowd until he bags him. The barrera is packed with men and boys sitting along the top, and the bull decides to clear them all off. He goes along, hooking carefully with his horn and dropping them off with a toss of his horns like a man pitching hay.

Each time the bull bags someone the crowd roars with joy. Most of it is home-talent stuff. The braver the man has been or the more elegant pass he has attempted with his cape before the bull gets him, the more the crowd roars. No one is armed. No one hurts or plagues the bull in any way. A man who grabbed the bull by the tail and tried to hang on was hissed and booed by the crowd and the next time he tried it was knocked down by another man in the bullring. No one enjoys it all more than the bull.

As soon as he shows signs of tiring from his charges, the two old steers, one brown and the other looking like a big Holstein, come trotting in and alongside the young bull, who falls in behind them like a dog and follows them meekly on a tour of the arena and then out.

Another comes right in, and the charging and tossing, the ineffectual cape-waving, and wonderful music are repeated right over again. But always different. Some of the animals in this morning amateur fight are steers. Fighting bulls from the best strain who had some imperfection or other in build so they could never command the high prices paid for combat animals, $2,000 to $3,000 apiece. But there is nothing lacking in their fighting spirit.

The show comes off every morning. Everybody in town turns out at five thirty when the military bands go through the streets. Many of them stay up all night for it. We didn't miss one, and it is *quelque* sporting event that will get us both up at five thirty o'clock in the morning for six days running.

As far as I know, we were the only English-speaking people in Pamplona during the Feria of last year.

There were three minor earthquakes while we were there. Terrific cloudbursts in the mountains and the Ebro River flooded out Zaragoza. For two days the bullring was under water and the corrida had to be suspended for the first time in over a hundred years. That was during the middle of the fair. Everyone was desperate. On the third day it looked gloomier than ever, poured rain all morning, and then at noon the clouds rolled away up across the valley, the sun came out bright and hot and baking and that afternoon there was the greatest bull-fight I will perhaps ever see.

There were rockets going up into the air and the arena was nearly full when we got into our regular seats. The sun was hot and baking. Over on the other side we could see the bullfighters standing ready to come in. All wearing their oldest clothes because of the heavy, muddy going in the arena. We picked out the three matadors of the afternoon with our glasses. Only one of them was new. Olmos, a chubby-faced, jolly-looking man, something like Tris Speaker. The others we had seen often before. Maera, dark, spare and deadly looking, one of the very greatest toreros of all time. The third, young Algabeno, the son of a famous bullfighter, a slim young Andalusian with a charming Indian-looking face. All were wearing the suits they had probably started bullfighting with, too tight, old fashioned, outmoded.

There was the procession of entrance, the wild bullfight music played, the preliminaries were quickly over, the picadors retired along the red fence with their horses, the heralds sounded their trumpets and the door of the bullpen swung open. The bull came out in a rush, saw a man standing near the barrera and charged him. The man vaulted over the fence and the bull charged the barrera. He crashed into the fence in full charge and ripped a two-by-eight plank solidly out in a splintering smash. He broke his horn doing it and the crowd called for a new bull. The trained steers trotted in, the bull fell in meekly behind them, and the three of them trotted out of the arena.

The next bull came in with the same rush. He was Maera's bull and, after perfect cape play, Maera planted the banderillos. Maera is Herself's favorite bullfighter. And if you want to keep any conception of yourself as a brave, hard, perfectly balanced, thoroughly competent man in your wife's mind, never take her to a real bullfight. I used to go into the amateur fights in the morning to try and win back a small amount of her esteem but the more I discovered that bullfighting required a great quantity of a certain type of courage of which I had an almost complete lack, the more it became apparent that any admiration she might ever redevelop for me would have to be simply an antidote to the real admiration for Maera and Villalta. You cannot compete with bullfighters on their own ground. If anywhere. The only way most husbands are able to keep any drag with their wives at all is that, first there are only a limited

number of bullfighters, second there are only a limited number
of wives who have ever seen bullfights.

Maera planted his first pair of banderillos sitting down on
the edge of the little step-up that runs around the barrera. He
snarled at the bull and as the animal charged, leaned back tight
against the fence and as the horns struck on either side of him,
swung forward over the brute's head and planted the two darts
in his hump. He planted the next pair, same way, so near to us
we could have leaned over and touched him. Then he went out
to kill the bull and, after he had made absolutely unbelievable
passes with the little red cloth of the muleta, drew up his sword
and as the bull charged, Maera thrust. The sword shot out of
his hand and the bull caught him. He went up in the air on the
horns of the bull and then came down. Young Algabeno flopped
his cape in the bull's face. The bull charged him and Maera
staggered to his feet. But his wrist was sprained.

With his wrist sprained, so that every time he raised it to
sight for a thrust it brought beads of sweat out on his face,
Maera tried again and again to make his death thrust. He lost
his sword again and again, picked it up with his left hand from
the mud floor of the arena and transferred it to the right for
the thrust. Finally he made it and the bull went over. The bull
nearly got him twenty times. As he came in to stand up under
us at the barrera side, his wrist was swollen to twice normal
size. I thought of prizefighters I had seen quit because they had
hurt their hands.

There was almost no pause while the mules galloped in and
hitched on to the first bull and dragged him out and the second came in with a rush. The picadors took the first shock of

him with their bull lances. There was the snort and charge, the shock and the mass against the sky, the wonderful defense by the picador with his lance that held off the bull, and then Rosario Olmos stepped out with his cape.

Once he flopped the cape at the bull and floated it around in an easy graceful swing. Then he tried the same swing, the classic "veronica," and the bull caught him at the end of it. Instead of stopping at the finish, the bull charged on in. He caught Olmos squarely with his horn, hoisted him high in the air. He fell heavily and the bull was on top of him, driving his horns again and again into him. Olmos lay on the sand, his head on his arms. One of his teammates was flopping his cape madly in the bull's face. The bull lifted his head for an instant and charged and got his man. Just one terrific toss. Then he whirled and chased a man just in back of him toward the bar-rera. The man was running full tilt and as he put his hand on the fence to vault it the bull had him and caught him with his horn, shooting him way up into the crowd. He rushed toward the fallen man he had tossed who was getting to his feet and all alone Algabeno met him with the cape. Once, twice, three times he made the perfect, floating, slow swing with the cape, perfectly, graceful, debonair, back on his heels, baffling the bull. And he had command of the situation. There never was such a scene at any world series game.

There are no substitute matadors allowed. Maera was fin-ished. His wrist could not lift a sword for weeks. Olmos had been gored badly through the body. It was Algabeno's bull. This one and the next five.

He handled them all. Did it all. Cape play easy, graceful, confident. Beautiful work with the muleta. And serious, deadly killing. Five bulls he killed, one after the other, and each one was a separate problem to be worked out with death. At the end there was nothing debonair about him. It was only a question if he would last through or if the bulls would get him. They were all very wonderful bulls.

"He is a very great kid," said Herself. "He is only twenty."

"I wish we knew him," I said.

"Maybe we will some day," she said. Then considered a moment. "He will probably be spoiled by then."

They make twenty thousand a year.

That was just three months ago. It seems in a different century now, working in an office. It is a very long way from the sunbaked town of Pamplona, where the men race through the streets in the mornings ahead of the bulls to the morning ride to work on a Bay-Caledonia car. But it is only fourteen days by water to Spain and there is no need for a castle. There is always that room at 5 Calle de Eslava, and a son, if he is to redeem the family reputation as a bullfighter, must start very early.

*Toronto Star Weekly*
October 27, 1923

# LETTERS

## To F. Scott Fitzgerald, 1 July [1925]

Burguete, Navarra

July 1—

Dear Scott—

We are going in to Pamplona tomorrow. Been trout fishing here. How are you? And how is Zelda?

I am feeling better than I've ever felt—havent drunk any thing but wine since I left Paris. God it has been wonderful country. But you hate country. All right omit description of country. I wonder what your idea of heaven would be— A beautiful vacuum filled with wealthy monogamists, all powerful and members of the best families all drinking themselves to death. And hell would probably [be] an ugly vacuum full of poor polygamists unable to obtain booze or with chronic stomach disorders that they called secret sorrows.

To me heaven would be a big bull ring with me holding two barrera seats and a trout stream outside that no one else was allowed to fish in and two lovely houses in the town; one where I would have my wife and children and be monogamous and love them truly and well and the other where I would have my nine beautiful mistresses on 9 different floors and one house would be fitted up with special copies of the Dial printed on soft tissue and kept in the toilets on every floor and in the other house we would use the American Mercury and the New Republic. Then there would be a fine church like in Pamplona where I could go and be confessed on the way from one house to the other and I would get on my horse and ride out with my son to my bull ranch named Hacienda Hadley and toss coins to all my illegitimate children that lined the road. I would write out at the Hacienda and send my son in to lock the chastity belts onto my mistresses because someone had just galloped up with the news that a notorious monogamist named Fitzgerald had been seen riding toward the town at the head of a company of strolling drinkers.

Well anyway were going into town tomorrow early in the morning. Write me at the / Hotel Quintana

Pamplona

Spain

Or dont you like to write letters. I do because it's such a swell way to keep from working and yet feel you've done something.

So Long and love to Zelda from us both—

Yours,

Ernest

## To Gertrude Stein and Alice B. Toklas, [16] July 1925

July 15 1925
Hotel Aguilar
Carrera San Jeronimo, 37
Madrid.

Dear Friends—

We have had a fine time and no bad hot weather and seen Belmonte cogida-ed, and he is not so bad, and had a bull dedicated to us and Hadley got the ear given to her and wrapped it up in a handkerchief which, thank God was Don Stewarts. I tell her she ought to throw it away or cut it up into pieces and send them in letters to her friends in St. Louis but she wont let it go and it is doing very nicely.

Madrid is nice now and we have good rooms and pensione for 10 pesetas a day. They have re-built and re-hung the Prado —probably on Bob McAlmon's complaint and it is very fine. Hadley is there now and I'm going down when I finish this. Last night we went to a nocturnal and this afternoon is the Big Corrida de la Prensa with Freg—Villalta, Litri and Niño de la Palma. The last two are the great new phenomenons and Niño mano a mano with Belmonte made Belmonte look cheap. He did everything Belmonte did and did it better—kidding him—all the adornos and desplantes and all. Then he stepped out all by himself without any tricks—suave, templando with the cape, smooth and slow—splendid banderillos and started with 5 naturales with the muleta—beautiful complete faena all linked up and then killed perfectly.

He comes from Ronda and everybody in Spain is crazy about him—except of course those that can't stand him. But they were lined up all night before his first appearance in Madrid. We've seen him 4 times and will see him 4 more at Valencia. His giving Hadley his cape to hold etc. is quite efficacious at keeping her from worrying about Bumby. He is in great shape Marie writes and plays with all the kids and talks more all the time.

How is the proof coming and have you been fishing?

We found our best stream which was full of trout last year ruined by logging and running logs down—all the pools cleaned out—trout killed. We go to Valencia on the 21st and will be there till the 2nd of August at <u>Poste Restante</u>. Travelling 3rd class it hasnt been expensive and is very funny. Coming down from Pamplona there was a kid whose father raised wine near Tafalla and he was bringing big sample jugs down to Madrid to sell wine and of course every body was offering drinks to everybody else and he got inspired and opened jug after jug and 3 compartments including 2 priests and 4 Guardia Civil got very tight including unfortunately myself and I either lost or gave away our tickets and became worried or as worried as I could get as we got near Madrid but the Guardia Civil got us through all right with no tickets at all. It was the best party almost I've ever been on. Spaniards are the only people. Hadley and the priests talked Latin. It was very fine.

Love to you from us both,

Always yours

Hemingway.

## To Clarence Hemingway, 20 August [1925]

Aug 20—

4 am.

Dear Dad—

Thanks for the Int. Book Reviews, the Forest and Streams and your good letter.

Just got back from Spain yesterday. Splendid trip. Have been swimming nearly every day. Been working day and night and done about 60,000 words on a novel About 15,000 more to do. Am going to start in again after writing you.

Boni and Liveright have sent the jacket of my book and it looks very good.

We had no luck fishing this summer. The wonderful stream we got so many out of last summer was ruined by logging. Fish killed, pools destroyed, dams broken down. Made me feel sick.

Saw 24 bull fights and was in the ring several times.

It must have been fun on that trip across the straights. The motor car takes the wildness out of the country very quickly.

We would like to come over next summer and Hadley and I take a camping trip to one of the small trout rivers on the North shore of Lake Superior. We could get our equipment and go up from Windemere to the Soo and then around. I was thinking of the Steel River.

Both my legs have begun to bother me quite a bit and I imagine by the time I'm 40 or so if I don't keep them pretty well going and in good shape I'll have quite a bit of trouble.

I'm glad Mother is painting if she likes it. I haven't seen any of her work at all.

It is fine that Leicester is getting to be a good fisherman. I do not know anything that can give a person more enjoyment through life.

I have missed the fishing this year very much.

It's a shame I haven't written oftener but I've been working terribly hard on 2 different jobs and moving around Spain all the time. I started a letter to you and one to Mother in Pamplona but never finished them. We were at Valencia, Madrid, Saragossa and San Sebastian. Well good luck and love to all the folks. <u>Best</u> always to you,

Yours,<br>Ernie

Love to Ura and tell her I'll write her.

We're going to be forced out of here maybe but I'll let you know if there's any change of address.

*To Horace Liveright,* [c. 19 January 1926]

Dear Mr. Liveright:

I have your letter of December 30th rejecting Torrents of Spring. About two weeks ago I cabled you to deliver the manuscript of Torrents of Spring to Donald Ogden Stewart at the Yale Club. I hope you have done this.

As Torrents of Spring is my second completed book and as I submitted it to you and as you did not exercise your option to publish it; according to my contract with you your option on my third book then lapses. This is quite clear and open and shut. There was nothing in the contract about what order books should be submitted, whether the second book was to be a collection of short stories, a satire, a humorous book or a novel. The contract said one of my next three books must be a full length novel. There was nothing in the contract which said that a full length novel must be the second book which I submitted to you. On the other hand the contract is quite explicit that if you do not exercise your option to publish the 2nd book within 60 days of the receipt of the manuscript your option lapses and if your option lapses on the 2nd book it lapses on the 3rd book. There can be no doubt on this point. ~~There is no obligation~~

I did not submit The Torrents of Spring to you in the hope that you would turn it down. I consider it a good book and John Dos Passos, Louis Bromfield and Scott Fitzgerald, who are people of different tastes are enthusiastic about it. Your turning it down was your own affair. You say that everyone in your office was opposed to it and I may perhaps remind you that your office also was opposed to In Our Time and turned it down after discussion. Later you reversed this decision yourself. Your office was also enthusiastic about a novel of Harold Loeb's called Doodab which I believe did not prove to be a wow even as a succés d'estime. But how, because your office turns down my books, ~~as fast as I write them~~ you can expect to continue to hold an option on my future books, when that option has, by contract, lapsed I do not see.

I therefore regard myself free to give The Torrents of Spring and my future books to the publisher who offers me the best terms. I have already received offers for the Torrents of Spring and The Sun Also Rises, which I am still working on, from several publishers. I have not approached these publishers. They have heard of the books from friends who have seen the manuscript and in whose judgement they place some confidence.

I am going to be writing for some time and you cannot expect me to have looked with enthusiasm to a continual rejection of whatever I write by your office force, partners and associates, because they do not believe it to be a guaranteed best seller. I know that publishers are not in business for their health but I also know that I will pay my keep to, and eventually make a great deal of money, for, any publisher. And I most assuredly have not given a right to Boni and Liveright to reject my books and still keep an option on any future big money makers that may come: all for $200.

I will be very glad to read your answer to this letter and look forward to meeting you in N.Y. I expect to sail as soon as my new passport arrives. I hope within 10 days.

Will you please address me care of
The Guaranty Trust Company of N.Y.
1, Rue des Italiens
Paris.

## To William B. Smith, Jr., and Harold Loeb,
## [18 February 1926]

Thursday.

Gents—

Yours Special to hand. I came alone, Men, accompanied only by my moral turpitude.

Youre right I gotta return on the 'veldt. I would flash to Provincetown like a flash but for engagements with Publishers, Critics, and the like. Benchley is flashing Carol-less with me. I will also be accompanied by $\frac{Mrs.}{Miss}$ Dorothy Parker. We will try and get off a quip or so. I'll tell Benchley how you feel about Arlen. Don's in Hollywood. He hasnt written to me, nor to Bob, nor to Hadley, nor to Phil Barry, nor to the Murphys, nor to any body.

Scribner's advance me $1500 on The Torrents of Spring (satire) and The Sun Also Rises (novel) They will pay 15% royalties on everything. No cut on the movies nor dramatics. Have an option on only these 2 books / Say that they pleasing me is all the option they want. God but they are white people.

They will also buy stories for the magazine at from 200 to 250 depending on length. Want all the stories I can give them. Will feature same.

I got loose from Liveright on account him turning down the satire. Scribners say they will back me solidly and loyally no matter how the books turn out financially. So now I dont have to worry. Only to work. Will try and write some swell ones. I'm not going to think any more about what is to happen to the stuff. Just work.

God I'd love to fortify the optic nerve with a flash at you men on your native heath. Give my best to Hutch Hapgood. We'll be over in the Autumn any way.

Hadley's in Schruns with Bumby. I'm going right back there. Stay til end of March. Then Paris for a couple of weeks. Then visit the Murphys at Antibes and go to Spain in May to stay through June, July, maybe August.

I have to get back to hang onto the dough I've picked up. In Our Time seems to have went well with the critics, writers etc. At least Neck and Neck with Doodab. Us writers ought to stick together.

I'm crazy for you to see the funny one [TOS]. It's pretty tough but they're not cutting a word.

Gee I hope you hit them between the orbs at tale vending. I'm all admiration for the achievments of Kate [Smith].

Also [EH drew arrow pointing to "Kate" in the previous sentence] here's the best love of one Wemedge if you got any use for it or would like to have it mounted by a taxidermist and put over the fire place.

So long Boid.

A screed to the boat would materially shorten the passage.

It's President Roosevelt sailing Feb 20th at Midnight from Hoboken. [EH insertion: My cabin is 116—] Just imagine pouring a man aboard at that hour in Hoboken.

Best on the sphere to youse lads.

Always.

E. Miller

## To Maxwell Perkins, 5 June 1926

Dear Mr. Perkins—

I was very glad to get your letter and hear that you liked The Sun a.r. Scott claims to too. We are here temporarily quarantined with whooping cough. I went to Madrid and my wife came down here with the child and nurse expecting to join me in a week in Madrid. Himself developed the whoopings on arriving here [*EH insertion*: so after 3 weeks in Madrid I came on here,] and we will be here another three weeks and then take up our Spanish trip.

As to addresses

Care Guaranty Trust Co. of N.Y.

1, Rue des Italiens

Paris.

is the best permanent address. I will keep them informed by wire of my address in Spain and they have an excellent mail forwarding service.

Between July 6 and July 13—inclusive—I will be at the Hotel Quintana

Pamplona

(Navarra)

SPAIN    if you should want to reach me by cable.

It would be better not to try and hit that address with mail. That is the only address I am sure of but will keep the Guaranty Trust exactly informed. They will re-wire all cables and re-forward letters with no delay.

I believe that, in the proofs, I will start the book at what is now page 16 in the Mss. There is nothing in those first sixteen pages that does not come out, or is explained, or re-stated in the rest of the book—or is unnecessary to state. I think it will move much faster from the start that way. Scott agrees with me. He suggested various things in it to cut out—in those first chapters—which I have never liked—but I think it is better to just lop that off and he agrees. He will probably write you what he thinks about it—the book in general. He said he was very excited by it.

As for the Henry James thing— I haven't the second part of the Ms. here—it is over at Scott's—so I can't recall the wording. But I believe that it is a reference to some accident that is generally known to have happened to Henry James in his youth. To me Henry James is as historical a name as Byron, Keats, or any other great writer about whose life, personal and literary, books have been written. I do not believe that the reference is sneering, or if it is, it is not the writer who is sneering as the writer does not appear in this book. Henry James is dead and left no descendants to be hurt, nor any wife, and therefore I feel that he is as dead as he will ever be. ~~The survival of persons who are a part~~ I wish I had the ms. here to see exactly what it said. If Henry James never had an accident of that sort I should think it would be libelous to say he had no matter how long he were dead. But if he did I do not see how it can affect him—now he is dead. As I recall Gorton and Barnes are talking humourously around the subject of Barnes' mutilation and to them Henry James is not a man to be insulted or protected from insult but simply an historical example. I remember there was something about an airplane and a bicycle—but that had nothing to do with James and was simply a non-sequitor. Scott said he saw nothing off-color about it.

Until the proofs come I do not want to think about the book as I am trying to write some stories and I want to see the proofs, when they come, from as new and removed a viewpoint as possible.

Up till now I have heard nothing about a story called—An Alpine Idyll—that I mailed to you sometime the first week in May. Did you ever receive it? I have another copy which I will send if you did not. In Madrid I wrote three stories ranging from 1400 to 3,000 words. I haven't had them re-typed and sent on as I was waiting word about The Alpine Idyll.

What is the news about Torrents? Have any copies been mailed to me as yet?

Could you send me a check for $200. in a registered letter to the Guaranty Trust Co. address? It was very pleasant to get your letter and learn that you liked the book.

Yours very sincerely,

Ernest Hemingway.

Villa Paquita

Juan les Pins

(A.M)

June 5, 1926

## To Maxwell Perkins, 21 August 1926

69 Rue Froidevaux,
Paris, France.
August 21, 1926.

Dear Mr. Perkins:

The proofs came ten days ago while we were at the Cap D'Antibes on our way home from Spain and I have been over them very carefully with the points you outlined in mind.

1st—I have commenced with Cohn—I believe the book loses by eliminating this first part but it would have been pointless to include it with the Belloc eliminated—and I think that would be altogether pointless with Belloc's name out.

2nd—Roger Prescott is now Roger Prentiss. I believe I went to school with a Roger Prentiss but at least he was not Glenway [Wescott].

3rd—Hergesheimer now changed to something else.

4th—Henry James now called either Henry or Whatsisname —whichever seems best to you.

5th—I do not believe that the blanks left in the Irony and pity song can be objectionable—anybody knowing what words to put in might as well put them in. In case they are offensive the word "pretty" can be inserted.

6th—The bulls now without appendages.

I've tried to reduce profanity but I reduced so much profanity when writing the book that I'm afraid not much could come out. Perhaps we will have to consider it simply as a profane book and hope that the next book will be less profane—or perhaps more sacred.

In today's mail there is an invitation to broadcast Torrents of Spring from the Sears Robebuck radio station W L S accompanied by a short talk and the information that "it gives common people a real thrill, to be remembered always, to hear the voice of a well known, admired author". (And who do you think that would be) The other letter was from the Missouri Historical Society asking for a copy of Torrents to be preserved along with the most complete collection of the books of all Missouri authors, which it seems a very strange thing to suddenly be.

In this same mail I am sending you a story—The Killers —which has been typed by the well known, admired author himself on a six year old Corona. So if the magazine does not want it you might send it to the Sears Roebuck broadcasting station care of Mr. John M. Stahl and maybe he would like to have it to show to a lot of the common people.

I also find, in yesterday's mail, that I owe Henry Romeike, Inc. 220 West 19th Street, N.Y., sixteen dollars for clippings, and as I have no dollars and Mr. Romeike, who is I believe by his own admittance the original Romeike, is very lovely about sending clippings, I wonder if you could have this sixteen dollars sent to him and charged to what must be rapidly becoming my account. If this were done it might be well to tell Mr. the original Romeike that the money is coming from me and that he may continue to send clippings to the same place.

Zelda was looking very well and very lovely when I saw her last week. Scott was working hard. Don Stewart has arrived with a very new and awfully nice and good looking wife.

I hope you've had a good summer. We had a grand time in

Spain. I'm working very hard now—plan to mail the proof the end of the week and will send another story.

With best regards,
Ernest Hemingway.

## To *Maxwell Perkins*, 16 November 1926

November 16–1926

Dear Mr. Perkins:

Thanks so much for sending the reviews and advertisements. The portrait, Bloomshield's drawing, looks much as I had imagined Jake Barnes; it looks very much like a writer who had been saddened by the loss or atrophy of certain non replaceable parts. It is a pity it couldn't have been Barnes instead of Hemingway. Still it is fine to have at last succeeded in looking like a writer. The ads and the blurb seem excellent.

I wish that I could do as you suggest about inserting some of the matter about Brett. It doubtless would be of value to anyone reading the stuff for the first time and there is some very good dope on Brett. On the other hand any sort of a foreword or preface would seem to me to break up the unity of the book and altho it does not show there is a certain rhythm in all that book that if it were broken would be very much missed. It was a complete unit with all that first stuff including the Belloc episode—I could cut it where I did and have it stay a unit—but the hard luck we had with Fifty Grand shows the difficulty of cutting that sort of stuff and further tinkering wouldnt help, I'm afraid.

I am terribly sorry because I would like very much to do it for you but I think we'll find maybe, in the end, that what I lose by not compromising now we may all cash in on later. I know that you would not ask me to put that back in unless you really liked it and I know it would be good in many ways—but I think in the end perhaps we would both lose by it. You see I would like, if you wanted, to write books for Scribner's to publish, for many years and would like them to be good books—better all the time—sometimes they might not be so good—but as well as I could write and perhaps with luck learning to write better all the time—and learning how things work and what the whole thing is about—and not getting bitter— So if this one doesn't sell maybe sometime one will— I'm very sure one will if they really are good—and if I learn to make them a lot better—but I'll never be able to do that and will just get caught in the machine if I start worrying about that—or considering it [*EH insertion*: the selling]. Altho God knows I need the money at this present time and I would so like to see the book really go because you have been so very decent to me.

The other thing is that Brett Ashley is a real person and as long as there were no changes in the way other real people James, Belloc, Hergesheimer etc. were handled I did not mind what happened to my people—but since they (the others) were protected I might as well leave out that stuff so long as it is not actually necessary. That was the only stuff in the book that was not imaginary—the Brett biography.

I see that Mr. Bill Benet is very disappointed to find me lifting a character from Michael Arland and that is rather funny as I have never read a word of Arland but went around, after the war, with Lady Duff Twisden, Nancy Cunard, Mary Beerbohm and Iris Tree who took Arland or Arlen up as a deserving Armenian youth and let him in on a few things and then dropped him as soon as he became annoyingly Armenian and less deserving —but not before he had gotten a little way behind the scenes into various people's lives.

So now it is pretty amusing to have known a girl and drawn her so close to life that it makes me feel very badly—except that I don't imagine she would ever read anything—and watch her go to hell completely—and assist at the depart—and then feeling pretty damned badly about it all learn that you had with boyish enthusiasm lifted a character from the un-read writings of some little Armenian sucker after London names.

What do you suppose it is—that Benet imagines that nobody ever really had a title? Was it the title that offended him? Or do people only have titles in books written for servant girls? But as I haven't read Arland I don't know—and now I'm afraid to—because maybe it is like Arland. That would be awfully funny.

Maybe Arland would write a couple of chapters and it would sell millions. Perhaps Benet could get ahold of him for us.

Komroff finally cut only a couple of hundred words out of Fifty Grand. Maybe you could run it some time between serials or if Mr. Phelps were sick and copy was short. You might offer Mr. Phelps from me that if he will condense and give me the space I'll pay him whatever it's worth a page where I overlap into him. Or I'll split the price of the story with him. I'd like to have that story published sometimes before boxing is abolished. Or magazines abolished.

Everything I publish over here is stolen by Samuel Roth who has never had my permission to publish one word and pirates everything that appears here as fast as it comes out and has never paid me a cent. I've seen the advertisements in the Nation and New Republic of his Two Worlds Monthly.

Joyce is all broken up about it. Roth has stolen his Ulysses without permission, never paid Joyce a cent, is publishing Ulysses in monthly installments and expurgating it. I saw Joyce today and he has just received a copy of an interview Roth gave to some N.Y. paper in which he declares that he is publishing Ulysses with Joyce's consent, that he has a financial arrangement with Joyce greatly to Joyce's advantage which he cannot at present divulge and that Joyce has made large sums selling the book under cover in America. Joyce is in absolute despair. The work of thirteen years of his life being stolen from him by a man who not content with that tries to blacken Joyce's character—and not content with stealing a man's life work and lieing about it then garbles it.

Kenneth Simpson who is in the district attorney's office has promised to nail Roth as soon as he gets back to N.Y. Joyce meantime is trying to get an injunction against Roth.

It is horrible and discouraging business and does not make one love the Jews any better. I feel badly about his stealing my stories—but that is a small matter compared to his theft of Joyce's entire book—but it does seem as though reputable publications like The Nation should refuse to accept his, Roth's, advertising. Isn't there some national organization that can blacklist the advertising of crooks?

Life seems quite complicated today.

Next week I am planning to ride down to the Riviera with a friend who has to take a car down there and I'll see Scott. He's sailing the 12th of December, I believe.

I still have a check for 200 dollars that I haven't cashed because the franc has been too high—but it looks as though it were going to stay there. I hope the Sun will sell so that I may get some more from you when I need it—it seems as though it should—it's pretty interesting and there seems to be a difference of opinion about it—I've always heard that was good. The Times review I had to read to the end before I found whether they really liked it or not. Aiken seemed to like it.

Archie MacLeish tells me he's a good critic—Aiken I mean. Maybe that will encourage some of the other boys to like it. It's funny to write a book that seems as tragic as that and have them take it for a jazz superficial story. If you went any deeper inside they couldn't read it because they would be crying all the time. Life's all very funny today—and this typewriter seems to have run away with its-self

Yours

Ernest Hemingway

CHRONOLOGY

NOTE ON THE TEXTS

NOTES

INDEX

# CHRONOLOGY

1899    Born Ernest Miller Hemingway on July 21 in Oak Park, Illinois, second of six children of Dr. Clarence Edmonds and Grace Hall Hemingway (an older sister, Marcelline, was born on January 15, 1898). (Father, twenty-seven, a physician, will share with his sons a deep love of fishing, hunting, and outdoor life. Mother, twenty-seven, a singer and music teacher, will insist her children learn to play a musical instrument—Hemingway will take cello lessons.) The family lives with Grace's father, Ernest Hall. In September the family travels to Windemere, their cottage on Walloon Lake, Michigan, where the young Hemingway will spend part of every summer until 1917.

1902    Ursula, a sister, is born on April 29.

1904    Madelaine, a sister, is born on November 28.

1905    Ernest Hall dies on May 10. In September, Marcelline and Hemingway begin first grade.

1906    Using her inheritance from her father, Grace designs and builds a new family home at 600 North Kenilworth Avenue in Oak Park.

1910    In April, Grace takes Hemingway to visit relatives in Nantucket, Massachusetts.

1911    Carol, a sister, is born on July 11.

1913    Marcelline and Hemingway enter Oak Park and River Forest High School in September. During his high school career,

Hemingway will write for the school's newspaper, *The Trapeze*, and its literary magazine, *The Tabula*.

1914    Austria-Hungary declares war on Serbia on July 28, sparking World War I.

1915    Leicester, a brother, is born on April 1.

1916    Meets siblings Bill and Kate Smith in Hortons Bay, Michigan. Bill will become Hemingway's best friend and the model for characters in several short stories and for Bill Gorton in *The Sun Also Rises*.

1917    The United States declares war on Germany on April 6, entering World War I on the side of the Allies. Marcelline and Hemingway graduate high school on June 14. After spending the summer in Michigan, Hemingway moves to Kansas City, Missouri, to begin work as a cub reporter on the *Kansas City Star* in mid-October. Enlists in the Missouri Home Guards on November 5. His first bylined article, "Kernsky, the Fighting Flea," appears on December 15.

1918    In early March, enlists in the American Red Cross Ambulance Service. Arrives in Schio, Italy, on June 10. Soon after, volunteers for canteen service near the front on the Piave River. Wounded by an Austrian trench mortar and machine gun fire on the night of July 8; transported to the American Red Cross Hospital in Milan for treatment. Begins a relationship with Agnes von Kurowsky, an American nurse six years his senior. Meets British officer Eric Edward "Chink" Dorman-Smith. Travels to Stresa for convalescent leave at the end of September. Arrives back at the front on October 24 to assist in the battle of Vittorio Veneto but returns to the hospital on November 1 with a case of jaundice. On November 4, fighting ends on the Italian front. The war ends on November 11. In mid-December, accompanied partway by Dorman-Smith, Hemingway travels via Padua and Torreglia to Treviso, where he meets up with Kurowsky, who is working in a field hospital. In late December, visits his former superior Captain James Gamble, field inspector for the American Red Cross Rolling Canteen Service, in Taormina, Sicily.

1919    Discharged from the Red Cross on January 4. Arrives in New York on January 21. On February 24, sends his first story to *The Saturday Evening Post*, which rejects it. On March 30, receives a letter from Kurowsky informing him she is breaking off their relationship and is engaged to be married ("I am writing this late at night after a long think by myself, & I am afraid it is going to hurt you, but, I'm sure it won't hurt you permanently"). In late May, returns to Michigan for the summer. After a brief visit home in October, rents a room in Petoskey, Michigan, in order to devote himself to writing.

1920    In mid-January, begins working in Toronto as a companion to Ralph Connable, Jr., the disabled son of wealthy Canadians Dorothy and Ralph Connable, and contributes freelance articles to the *Toronto Star*. His first accepted article, "Circulating Pictures a New High-Art Idea in Toronto," appears on February 14. In May, returns to northern Michigan for the summer. Following a conflict with his mother, Hemingway is expelled from the family cottage on July 27. In October, moves to Chicago and rooms with his friend Bill Horne, who had served with Hemingway in the American Red Cross Ambulance Service. Around this time, meets Sherwood Anderson and Hadley Richardson. In December, begins writing for and editing the *Co-operative Commonwealth*.

1921    Hemingway and Hadley Richardson, eight years older than Hemingway, marry at Horton Bay, Michigan, on September 3. In early October, they move to Chicago. The *Co-operative Commonwealth* folds the same month. On October 28, Hemingway agrees to write for the *Toronto Star* as European correspondent. The Hemingways sail for France on December 8.

1922    Meets Sylvia Beach, owner of Shakespeare and Company, on January 4. On January 9, the Hemingways move into a fourth-floor walk-up at 74, rue du Cardinal Lemoine, in a working-class neighborhood of the fifth arrondissement. Hemingway meets Ezra Pound and Gertrude Stein in February. In April, covers the Genoa Economic Conference for his newspaper and meets correspondents Lincoln Steffens and William "Bill" Bird. In May, the New Orleans–based little magazine *The Double Dealer* publishes the fable "A Divine Gesture." The Hemingways and Dorman-Smith take a hiking trip through Switzerland and Italy in late May and early June, an excursion that will be commemorated by Hemingway in *A Moveable Feast*. On June 11, the couple visits Hemingway's old battle sites, leading Hemingway to write "A Veteran Visits His Old Front—Wishes He Had Stayed Away." Sometime in the summer, Pound asks Hemingway to contribute a book to his "Inquest" series, which will be published by Bill Bird's Three Mountains Press. From September 25 to October 21, Hemingway is in Constantinople to cover the end of the Greco-Turkish War for the *Toronto Star*; he also agrees to report on the war, using the pseudonym John Hadley, for William Randolph Hearst's International News Service (INS). Arrives in Switzerland on November 21 to cover the Lausanne Peace Conference for the *Star* and INS. En route to join her husband in Lausanne on December 2, Hadley momentarily leaves her bags unattended in the Gare de Lyon, Paris, and the suitcase containing nearly all Hemingway's manuscripts is stolen.

1923    *Poetry: A Magazine of Verse* publishes six of Hemingway's poems in January. The Hemingways visit Ezra Pound in Rapallo, Italy, from February 7 to early March. While in Rapallo, Hemingway meets Robert McAlmon, an American writer and publisher, and Edward J. O'Brien, editor of the annual Best Short Stories series. In late March, Hemingway travels to Germany to report on the French occupation of the Ruhr for the *Toronto Star*. Makes his first trip to Spain with Bird and McAlmon, from May 26 to mid-June. Returns to Spain in July with Hadley to attend the Fiesta of San Fermín in Pamplona. *Three Stories and Ten Poems* is published by McAlmon's Contact Editions on August 13. The Hemingways sail from France for Canada on August 26. Hemingway begins work as a staff writer on the *Toronto Star* on September 10. *The Little Review* publishes "In Our Time," a collection of six vignettes, in the fall. In Toronto, Hadley gives birth to their son, John Hadley Nicanor Hemingway, nicknamed Bumby, on October 10. Hemingway travels alone to Oak Park for Christmas.

1924    Resigns from the *Toronto Star*, effective January 1. On January 19, the family sails from New York to France. They sign a lease on February 8 for an apartment on 113, rue Notre-Dame-des-Champs. Around the middle of the month, Hemingway begins assisting Ford Madox Ford with *The Transatlantic Review*. In January, "My Old Man" appears in O'Brien's *The Best Short Stories of 1923*. Hemingway's collection of vignettes, *in our time*, is published by Three Mountains Press on April 3. "Indian Camp" appears in *The Transatlantic Review* in April. In late May, Hemingway is left in charge of the journal while Ford travels to the United States. In July, the Hemingways, the Birds, McAlmon, John Dos Passos, Donald Ogden Stewart, and others travel to Pamplona for the Fiesta of San Fermín. In late September, Stewart begins circulating a typescript of Hemingway's short stories among New York publishers. F. Scott Fitzgerald, who had read *in our time*, recommends Hemingway to his editor at Charles Scribner's Sons, Maxwell Perkins. "The Doctor and the Doctor's Wife" appears in *The Transatlantic Review* in November. "Cross-Country Snow" is published in *The Transatlantic Review* in December, in what will be the magazine's final issue.

1925    On February 4, Boni & Liveright agrees to publish *In Our Time*. Hemingway accepts the publisher's offer on March 6. In mid-March, the Hemingways meet Pauline Pfeiffer, an American writer for Paris *Vogue*. After Boni & Liveright objects to the sexually graphic story "Up in Michigan," Hemingway sends "The Battler" as a replacement—along with the signed contract—to Horace Liveright on March 31. In late April, meets F. Scott Fitzgerald at the Dingo Bar in Montparnasse, an encounter memorably described in *A Moveable Feast*. "Big Two-Hearted River" appears in *This Quarter* in May. In late June, the Hemingways, joined by Bill Smith, Donald Ogden Stewart, Harold Loeb, Lady Duff Twysden, and Pat Guthrie, travel from Paris to Pamplona for the fiesta; Hemingway will use his friends and some of their experiences in *The Sun Also Rises*. In Madrid, the week after the fiesta concludes, begins writing his novel, then titled "Fiesta: A Novel." On September 21, Hemingway has completed the first draft of *The Sun Also Rises*. Dedicated to Hadley, *In Our Time* is published on October 21. Disappointed by the sales and marketing of his collection, Hemingway dashes off *The Torrents of Spring* in less than two weeks. A parody of Sherwood Anderson's *Dark Laughter* and Gertrude Stein's *The Making of Americans*, the book offends his mentors. Hemingway mails the typescript to Horace Liveright on December 7. From December 12 to January 25, the Hemingways are in Schruns, Austria. Pauline Pfeiffer spends the holidays with the family. On December 31, Hemingway receives a cable from his publisher rejecting *The Torrents of Spring*.

1926    Departs Schruns for Paris on January 25, leaving his wife and child in Austria. Sails for New York on February 3. Between

February 9 and 20, finalizes his break with Boni & Liveright and signs a contract to publish *The Torrents of Spring* and *The Sun Also Rises* with Charles Scribner's Sons. The firm will be Hemingway's American publisher for the remainder of his life. Hemingway spends March 2 and 3 in Paris with Pauline Pfeiffer, before rejoining his family in Schruns on March 5. Revision of *The Sun Also Rises* is completed by March 23. The Hemingways return to Paris on March 29. Hemingway sends Maxwell Perkins the typescript of *The Sun Also Rises* on April 24. Sometime in late April, Hadley learns of Hemingway and Pauline's affair. *The Torrents of Spring* is published on May 28. From end of May to beginning of July, the Hemingways, the Fitzgeralds, and Gerald and Sara Murphy are together on the French Riviera. On June 5, acting on Fitzgerald's advice, Hemingway cuts the opening of *The Sun Also Rises*. In July, the Hemingways, Pfeiffer, and the Murphys attend the fiesta in Pamplona. Hemingway returns the galley proofs of *The Sun Also Rises* on July 20. Following their return to Paris on August 12, the Hemingways separate. Hadley agrees to a divorce if Hemingway and Pauline separate for one hundred days. Jonathan Cape issues the British edition of *In Our Time* on September 24. On September 24, Pauline Pfeiffer sails for America. *The Sun Also Rises* is published on October 22 to generally enthusiastic reviews. In mid-November, Hadley releases Hemingway and Pauline from the separation agreement. She files for a divorce in Paris on December 8.

1927    Hemingway and Pauline are reunited on January 8. They vacation with her sister, Virginia, in Gstaad, Switzerland, for most of January and February. In March, *Scribner's Magazine* publishes "The Killers," the first Hemingway story to appear in a mainstream American magazine. The divorce from Hadley is finalized on April 14. Hemingway and Pauline marry on May 10 and leave the following day for their honeymoon in the south of France. The British edition of *The Sun Also Rises*, titled *Fiesta*, is published by Jonathan Cape on June 9. Hemingway and American artist Waldo Pierce attend the Fiesta of San Fermín from July 5 to 12. The Hemingways spend the rest of July traveling in Spain. Throughout the year, Hemingway works on a novel tentatively titled "A New Slain Knight" or "Jimmy Breen," never to be completed. Hemingway's second story collection, *Men Without Women*, is published by Scribner's on October 14. The Hemingways vacation in Switzerland with American poet Archibald MacLeish and his wife, Ada, in December and January.

1928    Returns to Paris in early February. On March 4, is injured by a falling skylight in his apartment. Around this time, abandons the "Jimmy Breen" novel and begins work on what will become *A Farewell to Arms*. The Hemingways sail for America on March 17, Pauline now six months pregnant. The couple move to a rented apartment in Key West, Florida, on April 4. Hemingway will make his home there for the next decade. Reunites with his parents when they arrive in Key West on April 10. The British edition of *Men Without Women* is published by Jonathan Cape on April 20. During May, the Hemingways host Bill and Kate Smith, Waldo Pierce, and John Dos Passos. The couple travels to Piggott, Arkansas (Pauline's hometown) on June 1. On June 28, Pauline delivers Patrick Hemingway, the couple's first son, by Caesarean section. Leaving his wife and child behind in Piggott, and accompanied by Bill Horne, Hemingway travels to Sheridan, Wyoming; the two men arrive on July 28. For the rest of the month and most of August, Hemingway fishes and writes. Pauline arrives on August 18. Sometime around August 23, Hemingway completes the first holograph draft of *A Farewell to Arms*. The Hemingways spend the rest of August and most of September travelling and hunting in Wyoming and Montana. On October 16, Hemingway drives to Oak Park and spends a week with his family. Pauline joins him during the final week of the month. On November 1, they travel to the East Coast to visit the MacLeishes in Massachusetts and Perkins, Pierce, and American painter Henry Strater in New York City. The Hemingways, the Fitzgeralds, and Strater attend the Princeton-Yale football game on November 17 and spend the night at the Fitzgeralds' Ellerslie Mansion in Delaware. The Hemingways return to Key West on November 27. There, the family moves into a rented house at 1100 South Street. On December 3, Hemingway travels to New York to meet Hadley and pick up Bumby. Clarence Hemingway commits suicide on December 6, shooting himself with his father's Civil War pistol. The news reaches Hemingway by cable while en route by train to Key West with Bumby. Leaving Bumby in the care of a porter, he boards a train to Oak Park to attend his father's funeral.

1929    Completes the first typewritten draft of *A Farewell to Arms*. Perkins travels to Key West to read the novel and discuss publishing arrangements the first week of February. On February 13, Perkins wires offer to serialize the novel in *Scribner's Magazine* for $16,000. The family, including Madelaine, Bumby, and Patrick, sail from Havana for France on April 5. The first installment of *A Farewell to Arms* appears in *Scribner's Magazine* in May. The June issue is banned in Boston. The Hemingways spend most of July and August travelling in Spain, returning to Paris on September 18. Sometime in August, John Dos Passos and Kate Smith are married; the same month Hemingway meets the Jewish American bullfighter Sidney Franklin, whose skills Hemingway will praise in *Death in the Afternoon* ("no Spaniard who ever saw him fight . . . will deny his artistry and excellence with the cape"). *A Farewell to Arms*, with a dedication to Pauline's uncle Gus Pfeiffer, is published in book form in America on September 27. On Friday, October 24, the New York Stock

Exchange crashes, marking the beginning of the Great Depression. Dorothy Parker's profile of Hemingway, "The Artist's Reward," appears in the November 30 issue of *The New Yorker*. The Hemingways vacation in Switzerland with the Murphys, the Fitzgeralds, the Dos Passoses, Dorothy Parker, and Donald Ogden Stewart from December 20 to 31.

1930    The Hemingways sail for America on January 10. After stops in New York and Havana, they arrive in Key West on February 2 and move into a rented house at 1425 Pearl Street. From February to April, the Hemingways entertain the American writers John Herrmann and Josephine Herbst, Perkins, and other visitors. Around the middle of March, Hemingway begins writing *Death in the Afternoon*. After picking up Bumby in New York on June 21, joins Pauline and Patrick in Piggott on June 30. The Hemingways and Bumby leave Piggott for Wyoming. From July 13 to October, they stay at the L-Bar-T Ranch in Clarks Fork for hunting and fishing. The stage adaptation of *A Farewell to Arms* opens in New York on September 22. On October 24, Scribner's reissues *In Our Time*, with "An Introduction by the Author," later retitled "On the Quai at Smyrna." On November 1, Hemingway suffers a severely broken arm in a car accident outside of Billings, Montana. Remains hospitalized until December 21.

1931    The Hemingways move into a rented house at 1301 Whitehead Street in Key West. From January to April, the family entertains many visitors, including Grace and Carol Hemingway, Herbst, Herrmann, MacLeish, Gus and Louise Pfeiffer, and Strater. On April 29, Hemingway purchases a house at 907 Whitehead Street in Key West with $8,000 given to the family by Gus Pfeiffer. Sails for Spain on May 2 to complete research for *Death in the Afternoon*. Spends most of the summer in Spain, returning to Paris in mid-September. Crossing from Cherbourg to New York aboard the luxury ship *Île de France*, the Hemingways meet

Pan American Airways official Grant Mason and his wife Jane. (Hemingway reportedly later had an affair with Jane, who serves as the model for Margot in "The Short Happy Life of Frances Macomber.") The Hemingways spend the first two weeks of October in New York and Conway, Massachusetts. They arrive in Kansas City on October 14. Pauline gives birth to Gregory Hemingway on November 12. After recuperating in Kansas City and Piggott, the Hemingways return to Key West on December 19.

1932    Finishes first draft of *Death in the Afternoon* in mid-January. Spends much of January to April entertaining visitors and fishing. A planned ten-day fishing trip to Havana in April turns into months, though Hemingway manages to write and to revise the galley proofs of *Death in the Afternoon*. On July 2, leaves for Piggott to join Pauline and his sons. He and Pauline leave for Wyoming and Montana a week later, arriving on July 12. Stays in the area to fish, hunt, and write until October 16. *Death in the Afternoon* is published on September 23, to mixed reviews. On November 25, Hemingway and Bumby leave Key West to join Pauline and his other sons in Piggott. The family returns to Key West on December 29.

1933    Meets Thomas Wolfe and sees Perkins and Fitzgerald while in New York for two weeks in January. On the same trip, refuses to give John Gardner permission to marry his sister Carol. Also meets editor Arnold Gingrich at Louis and Marguerite Cohn's New York bookstore, House of Books, specializing in modern first editions. On March 25, Carol and John Gardner marry in Vienna. Hemingway agrees on April 3 to write a series of nonfiction "Letters" on any subject he wishes for Gingrich's new magazine, *Esquire*. Travels to Cuba to fish and write from April 12 to July 20. The debut (Fall) issue of *Esquire* contains Hemingway's "Marlin off the Morro: A Cuban Letter." The Hemingways sail from Havana for France on August 7. From August 17 to October

13, Hemingway and Pauline travel in Spain. Around the end of September, begins writing "One Trip Across," the first Harry Morgan story. Scribner's publishes Hemingway's third short story collection, *Winner Take Nothing*, on October 27. Hemingway, Pauline, and Key West friend Charles Thompson leave Paris for Marseille en route to Mombasa, Kenya, to hunt in Africa, arriving December 9; the trip is paid for by Gus Pfeiffer. The party leaves Nairobi with white hunter Philip Percival for a two-month safari on December 20.

1934    In mid-January, flies to Nairobi to be treated for amoebic dysentery. Rejoins the safari on January 22. The party sails for Europe on February 28. They arrive in Paris on March 19. The Hemingways sail for New York on the SS *Paris* on March 27; on board, Hemingway meets Marlene Dietrich. On April 5, goes to the Wheeler Shipyard in Brooklyn and purchases his own motorboat, the *Pilar*, using a $3,000 advance from Gingrich. Leaves New York for Key West on April 9 with a stop in Philadelphia to meet officials at the Academy of Natural Sciences, who want him to assist in a study of marlin species around Cuba. On May 9, takes possession of the *Pilar* in Miami. Two days later, in Key West, begins writing an account of his safari, *Green Hills of Africa*. Much of the summer is spent fishing out of Key West and writing. Departs aboard the *Pilar* for Havana on July 19. Five days later, managing director Charles Cadwalader and ichthyologist Henry Fowler, of Philadelphia's Academy of Natural Sciences, arrive in Cuba to fish and study marlin with Hemingway. Hemingway spends mornings working on his Africa book and his *Esquire* letters in his room at the Hotel Ambos Mundos. Returns to Key West on September 5, but goes back to Cuba on September 14, remaining there until October 26. Completes the first draft of his safari book on November 16. Hemingway, Pauline, and Patrick leave Miami by car on December 17 for Piggott, arriving six days later. While there, Hemingway hires Toby Bruce to manage the property in Key West and serve as a factotum.

1935    Hemingway and Bruce leave from Piggott for Key West via New Orleans on January 2. Max and Louise Perkins arrive in Key West on January 23 to fish and discuss the publication of *Green Hills of Africa*. On February 19, after two weeks of negotiation, Hemingway agrees to terms with *Scribner's Magazine* for serialization of his new book. While sailing to Bimini on April 7, accidently shoots himself in the calf. After treatment in Key West, leaves again for Bimini on February 15. Bimini offers a quieter location for writing and easier access to the Gulf Stream for fishing; Hemingway will remain on the island until mid-August. The first of seven installments of *Green Hills of Africa* appears in *Scribner's Magazine* in May. Pauline and the children join Hemingway in Bimini on June 24. The Hemingways return to Key West on August 15. On September 2 and 3, a large hurricane hits the Keys, destroying a construction camp on Matacumbe Key and killing more than 450 workers, most of whom are World War I veterans. Hemingway assists in the recovery efforts. His account, "Who Murdered the Vets?", appears in September in *New Masses*. Hemingway and Pauline are in New York from September 24 to October 24. *Green Hills of Africa* is published by Scribner's on October 25 to lukewarm reviews. In lieu of one of his regular Letters, Hemingway sends Gingrich his second Harry Morgan story, "The Tradesman's Return," on December 10 (it will be published in *Esquire* in February 1936).

1936    On or about February 17, punches Wallace Stevens after hearing that the poet and fellow Key West resident had insulted him. In April, has finished drafts for "The Short Happy Life of Francis Macomber" and "The Snows of Kilimanjaro." Sails for Cuba on April 26, where he will remain until May 27. *Esquire* publishes Hemingway's "The Horns of the Bull" (later retitled "The Capital of the World") in June. On June 5, the Hemingway family departs from Key West for Bimini, where they stay at the home of wealthy big-game fisherman Michael Lerner. In late June, Gingrich visits Bimini and recommends that Hemingway expand the Harry Morgan stories into a novel. Hemingway and Bumby return to Key West on July 18. The same day, the Spanish Civil War begins when Fascist leader General Francisco Franco declares his opposition to the Second Spanish Republic. After meeting Virginia Pfeiffer in Miami, Hemingway, Pauline, and Bumby begin drive from Miami to Wyoming on July 30. "The Snows of Kilimanjaro" appears in *Esquire* in August. The Hemingways arrive on August 10 at the L-Bar-T Ranch, where Hemingway will write and hunt until the end of October. "The Short Happy Life of Francis Macomber" is published in *Cosmopolitan* in September. On November 25, Hemingway receives a letter from John Wheeler of the North American Newspaper Alliance (NANA) asking him to cover the Spanish Civil War for the news service. On December 15, accepts the NANA job. Sometime in late December, meets the novelist and journalist Martha Gellhorn in Sloppy Joe's Saloon in Key West. Hemingway and Gellhorn will soon begin an affair, which will end his second marriage.

1937      Accompanied part of the way by Gellhorn, leaves Key West on January 10 for New York, where he assists Prudencio de Pereda and Helene Van Dongen on the propaganda film *Spain in Flames*, which premieres in New York on January 28. By January 22, Hemingway and Sidney Franklin are in Miami. They and Pauline sail the *Pilar* to Key West three days later. In mid-February, Hemingway and Franklin travel to New York, where Hemingway agrees to write the script for Dutch filmmaker Joris Ivens's *The Spanish Earth*, chronicling the struggle of the Spanish Republican government against the far-right Nationalists. In New York, he is reunited with Gellhorn, and the two make plans to travel together to Spain to cover the war. In the midst of filming in Madrid, Hemingway files his first dispatch for NANA on March 22. Gellhorn and Franklin arrive at the Hotel Florida on March 30. By May 6, Hemingway is in Paris, where he gives a talk on the war at the Anglo-American Press Club. On May 12, at Sylvia Beach's Shakespeare and Company, reads from the manuscript of *To Have and Have Not*. The next day, sails for New York, landing on May 18. After a week in Key West, the family travels to Bimini on May 26. Hemingway leaves for New York on June 3 for the second annual congress of the League of American Writers, where he delivers a speech titled "Fascism is a Lie" before returning to Bimini. On June 20, flies to New York to complete the script for *The Spanish Earth*, which is narrated by Orson Welles. While in New York, delivers setting copy of *To Have and Have Not* to Perkins. On July 8, Hemingway, Gellhorn, and Ivens visit the White House to show *The Spanish Earth* to President Franklin Roosevelt, First Lady Eleanor Roosevelt, and Roosevelt adviser Harry Hopkins. Two days later, Hemingway, Pauline, and Ivens fly to Hollywood to screen the film and fund-raise for the Republican cause. In mid-July, Hemingway records his own narration for the film to replace Welles's (after Ivens and others working on the project conclude Welles sounds too theatrical). Fitzgerald and Hemingway meet likely for the last time on July 13. By July 21, Hemingway is back in Bimini working on proofs of *To Have and Have Not*. Returns to New York on August 10 en route to Spain. The next day, gets into a scuffle in Perkins's office with critic Max Eastman over his critical review of *Death in the Afternoon* (Hemingway has "begotten a veritable school of fiction-writers—a literary style, you might say, of wearing false hair on the chest"). Arrives in Paris on August 22. *The Spanish Earth* has its official premiere in New York the same day. Hemingway,

Gellhorn, and *New York Times* reporter Herbert Matthews fly to Spain. Hemingway will remain in the country touring battlefields and working on a play about the war, *The Fifth Column*, until December 28, when he travels to Paris, where he meets Pauline, angry about his relationship with Gellhorn and worried about their marriage. Scribner's publishes *To Have and Have Not* on October 15; it is Hemingway's most successful book since *A Farewell to Arms*.

1938    The Hemingways sail for Nassau on January 12. On March 4, Hemingway meets Gellhorn in Miami. Sails for Spain on March 19, arriving in Paris five days later. Hemingway and fellow war correspondents Herbert Matthews and Jim Lardner depart for Barcelona on March 31. During this trip, his third to cover the war, Hemingway contributes articles on the war to Gingrich's new political magazine, *Ken*. On May 16, returns to Paris briefly before heading back to Key West. After agreeing to publish *The Fifth Column* and his collected stories as two separate volumes, writes to Perkins on June 11 to suggest that they be published as one book. On June 22, arrives in New York to watch the Joe Louis–Max Schmeling fight and to discuss possible production of his play. He is back in Key West by the end of the month. The family leaves for Wyoming on August 4. Hemingway mails his preface to and proofs for *The Fifth Column and the First Forty-nine Stories* to Perkins on August 20. Flies to New York from Wyoming on August 29 and sails for France two days later. Reunites with Gellhorn in Paris on September 6. While in Paris, begins writing *For Whom the Bell Tolls*. On September 26, Pauline and her sons move into an apartment in New York, possibly as an attempt to finally end her marriage. Hemingway's *The Fifth Column and the First Forty-nine Stories* is published by Scribner's on October 14, most reviewers responding negatively to the play. On November 4, Hemingway makes his last trip to Spain during its civil war; returns to Paris three days later. Arrives in New York on November 24 and stays in Pauline's apartment until the family returns to Key West on December 5.

1939    Around January 2, arrives in New York to rewrite *The Fifth Column* and to place it with a theater company. On January 14, Gellhorn arrives in New York. Hemingway returns to Key West on January 24. Meets up with Gellhorn in Havana on February 18. Soon after, she locates a house for them to rent—La Finca Vigía, ten miles east of Havana. On May 17, Hemingway and Gellhorn move into Finca Vigía, which will be Hemingway's home for the next two decades. Germany invades Poland on September 1, initiating World War II. On September 3, at the L-Bar-T Ranch in Wyoming, Hemingway informs Pauline that he is leaving her. After arranging for Pauline and the boys to be driven back east, Hemingway meets Gellhorn in Billings, Montana, and from there the two travel together to the Sun Valley Lodge, Idaho. Gellhorn departs to cover the conflict between the Soviet Union and Finland on November 1. On December 19, Hemingway and Toby Bruce arrive in Key West to pack Hemingway's personal goods and library. They sail for Havana on December 24, marking the end of Hemingway's residency in Key West.

1940    Gellhorn arrives in Cuba on January 19. After a nearly two-year delay, *The Fifth Column*, adapted by Sidney Glazer, opens in New York on March 7 to mostly negative reviews. Scribner's issues Hemingway's play in a separate volume on June 7. On July 15, Hemingway signs a contract with Scribner's for his fourth novel, *For Whom the Bell Tolls*. Delivers the setting copy to Perkins at the end of July and stays in New York the first week of August to work on revisions. From Sun Valley, Idaho, sends the last revised galley proofs of the novel to his publisher on September 10. Gary Cooper and Hemingway meet in Sun Valley on September 28 (Cooper played Frederic Henry in the 1932 adaptation of

*A Farewell to Arms* and will play Robert Jordan in the 1943 adaptation of *For Whom the Bell Tolls*). *For Whom the Bell Tolls* is published on October 21; it is Hemingway's biggest commercial success ("Book selling like frozen Daiquiris in hell," he writes to his first wife, Hadley). The novel is a November main selection for the Book-of-the-Month Club. Hemingway's divorce from Pauline is finalized on November 4. Two weeks later, on November 19, Hemingway and Martha Gellhorn marry in Cheyenne, Wyoming. In early December, the couple is in New York preparing for a reporting trip in China. In Hollywood, F. Scott Fitzgerald dies of a heart attack on December 21. Hemingway purchases Finca Vigía on December 28.

1941    Hemingway and Gellhorn arrive in Hong Kong on February 22. She will report on the war with Japan for *Collier's*, while Hemingway gathers material for a series of articles in Ralph Ingersoll's *PM*. The pair travel extensively in the Far East for the next two months. Hemingway returns to the United States on May 19. By June 7, he has returned to Havana, where he and Martha will spend part of the summer with Patrick and Gregory. On September 19, joins his three sons in Idaho. Gellhorn joins them in mid-October. On December 7, the Japanese attack Pearl Harbor; within four days, the United States is at war with Japan, Germany, and Italy. Hemingway, Gellhorn, his sons, and the director Howard Hawks spend Christmas at Finca Vigía.

1942    Sometime in March, begins editing an anthology of war writing for Crown Publishers. In May, sets up the Crook Factory, a counterintelligence organization to keep watch over suspected Fascist sympathizers in Havana; the Federal Bureau of Investigation begins to monitor Hemingway's activities. The first week of June, with the blessing of U.S. Embassy officials, begins running antisubmarine patrols with the *Pilar*; the patrols, which fail to locate any German submarines, come to an end in July 1943. Crown publishes the anthology *Men at War* on October 22.

1943    Hemingway's oldest son, Jack (Bumby), is inducted into the U.S. Army on February 16. The U.S. Embassy in Havana orders the Crook Factory to cease operations on April 1. The film version of *For Whom the Bell Tolls* opens on July 10. On September 10, following months of arguments over Hemingway's lack of interest in reporting the war, Gellhorn leaves for Europe to cover the war for *Collier's*.

1944    Gellhorn returns to Cuba around March 13. She and Hemingway argue over his continuing indifference about covering the war. On April 23, the couple flies to New York, where Hemingway agrees to serve as war correspondent for *Collier's*. Gellhorn sails for England on May 13. Hemingway flies to London on May 17. On May 22, reporter Mary Welsh Monks is introduced to Hemingway by writer Irwin Shaw (who is serving with Hemingway's brother, Leicester, in a documentary film unit). Three days later, Hemingway is injured in a car accident in London. Gellhorn, who arrives on May 27, is angered over his heavy drinking and carousing. Their marriage is effectively over. On June 6, Hemingway covers the D-day landings in Normandy from aboard the troop transport *Empire Anvil*. Sometime after the Normandy landings, begins an affair with Mary Welsh Monks. On June 21, flies on a bombing raid over northern France with the Royal Air Force. Returns to France on July 18. Meets Colonel Charles "Buck" Lanham, commander of the 22nd Infantry Regiment, 4th Division, on July 28; Lanham, who serves as a partial model for Cantwell in *Across the River and Into the Trees*, will remain a lifelong friend. During August, Hemingway will "lead" a group of irregular forces during the advance on Paris. Hemingway and his troops enter Paris on August 26 and "liberate" the Ritz Hotel; he is reunited with Sylvia Beach on rue de l'Odéon. Two days later, meets U.S.

Army sergeant and writer J. D. Salinger. Rejoins Lanham's regiment on September 7. Viking Press issues *The Portable Hemingway*, edited by Malcolm Cowley, on September 18. Hemingway returns to Paris on September 26 and is reunited with Mary Welsh Monks. From October 3 to 6, the Third Army investigates accusations that Hemingway had violated rules forbidding war correspondents from engaging in combat; the inspector general fails to find sufficient cause to charge him, even though he clearly perjures himself during questioning. Jack Hemingway is taken prisoner by the Germans in the Vosges Mountains on October 28. Gellhorn writes Hemingway on November 3 to say they should divorce. Hemingway leaves Paris for the front on November 9. From November 15 to December 3, accompanies Lanham's regiment during their costly battle in the Hürtgen Forest. Returns to Paris on December 4 to recover from a bout of pneumonia. Sometime in the middle of the month, meets Gertrude Stein and the two are reconciled. Soon after, returns to the front, quartering at Lanham's command post near Rodenbourg. Gellhorn and Hemingway have an acrimonious meeting at Rodenbourg on December 24.

1945    Leaves France for New York via London on March 6. Hemingway and Patrick leave for Cuba on March 15; Gregory joins them at Finca Vigía around March 22. Sometime that spring, Hemingway begins what he calls "The Sea Book" (based on his antisubmarine patrols), which will be published posthumously as *Islands in the Stream*. Jack Hemingway is liberated from a German POW camp on April 30. Mary arrives in Cuba on May 2. On June 20, Hemingway injures himself and Mary when he crashes his car. In late August, Mary flies to Chicago to arrange a divorce from her husband, Noel Monks. Lanham and his wife arrive at Finca Vigía on September 22 for a two-week visit. Throughout the fall and winter, Hemingway continues to work on his new novel. Hemingway and Gellhorn's divorce is finalized on December 21.

1946   Hemingway and Mary Welsh Monks are married on March 14 in Havana. Continues to write through the spring and summer. The couple depart for Wyoming on August 6. Mary suffers a miscarriage on August 19. On September 13, Hemingway, Mary, and Hemingway's three sons travel to Ketchum, Idaho, to fish. Hemingway and Mary leave on November 10 and travel to Salt Lake City and New Orleans. They spend December 1 to 9 in New York before returning to Cuba.

1947   On April 14, stops working on "The Sea Book" (which has reached 997 handwritten pages) to care for Patrick, who has suffered a nervous breakdown, possibly due to an undiagnosed concussion suffered earlier that month. Pauline arrives from Key West on April 16 to help care for her son, leaving on May 10. She returns on May 23, and she and Mary become friends. Hemingway is awarded the Bronze Star at a ceremony at the U.S. Embassy in Havana. Max Perkins, Hemingway's editor since 1926, dies in New York. Pauline returns to Finca Vigía to celebrate her and Hemingway's joint birthday on July 21. Hemingway and Toby Bruce drive from Key West on September 21; they travel to Walloon Lake, Michigan, then to the Red Lodge in Montana, before arriving in Sun Valley, Idaho, on September 29. Mary arrives at the end of October. The Hemingways spend New Year's Eve in New York, then return to Ketchum, Idaho.

1948   The Hemingways leave Ketchum on February 1. A. E. Hotchner, an editor for *Cosmopolitan*, meets Hemingway sometime in June. Maurice Speiser, Hemingway's lawyer for the past two decades, dies on August 5. The Hemingways sail for Italy on September 7, arriving in Genoa on September 21. Following a tour of northern Italy, they settle in Cortina to ski. On October 22, the couple checks into the Gritti Palace Hotel in Venice. Soon afterward, Hemingway meets the Franchetti family, who invite him on a duck hunt at their shooting park. In early December, Hemingway meets eighteen-year-old Italian countess Adriana Ivancich. The Venice setting, duck hunting, and girl will all find their way into Hemingway's novel about World War II, *Across the River and Into the Trees*. On December 15, Hemingway and Mary return to Cortina to ski and stay through early March before returning to Venice.

1949    In mid-March, begins a short story about a U.S. Army colonel that is later expanded into *Across the River and Into the Trees*. The Hemingways sail for Cuba on April 30. On November 16, they fly to New York, where Hemingway finalizes publication plans for his new novel and is interviewed by Lillian Ross for a profile in *The New Yorker* before sailing for Paris three days later. Hotchner arrives in Paris on December 9 to assist in the editing of *Across the River and Into the Trees*. The Hemingways drive to Venice at the end of the month.

1950    *Cosmopolitan* prints the first installment of *Across the River and Into the Trees* in February. The Hemingways return to Paris on March 9. They sail for America on March 22. After a week in New York, they arrive in Cuba on April 8. Scribner's publishes *Across the River and Into the Trees* on September 7 to generally negative reviews. Late in the year, Hemingway finishes a draft of his sea book, now called "The Island and the Stream," but will continue to revise it through the following year. He and Mary frequently fight about his drinking and attention to other women.

1951    Sometime in January, begins writing what will become *The Old Man and the Sea*. Remains in Cuba the whole year. On June 28, Hemingway's mother, Grace Hall Hemingway, dies in Memphis, Tennessee. On October 1, Pauline Pfeiffer Hemingway dies suddenly in Los Angeles. Unable to complete revisions on the work, Hemingway places the manuscript of what will become *Islands in the Stream* in his Havana bank in December.

1952    Hemingway's publisher, Charles Scribner III, dies on February 11. Hemingway submits the typescript of *The Old Man and the Sea* to Scribner's on March 7. Sometime around April 24, begins writing a story based on his illegally shooting a heron in northern Michigan in 1915; the story, published posthumously as "The Last Good Country," is the first to feature the character Nick Adams since "Fathers and Sons" (1933). In late spring, Hemingway begins writing *The Garden of Eden. The Old Man and the Sea* appears in *Life* magazine just prior to the publication of the book edition on September 8. The novel receives generally positive reviews and is Hemingway's biggest-selling book since *For Whom the Bell Tolls.*

1953    *The Old Man and the Sea* is awarded the Pulitzer Prize in Fiction on May 4. In mid-May, Hemingway signs a contract with *Look* magazine to return to Africa and write articles about his safari. The Hemingways sail from New York to France on June 24. On July 3, the couple travels to Pamplona, Spain, Hemingway's first trip to the country since 1938. In early August, Hemingway and Mary sail from Marseille to Mombasa. For the rest of the year, they are on safari with Philip Percival, Hemingway's guide on his first safari in 1933–34 and the model for Pop in *Green Hills of Africa.*

1954    The Hemingways are in two serious plane crashes on January 23 and 24. Hemingway suffers a serious concussion and burns. The couple sails for Venice on March 9. Hemingway and Hotchner leave Venice for Spain on May 6 while Mary flies to Paris and then London. She meets the two men in Madrid on May 14. During this trip, Hemingway meets the bullfighter Luis Miguel Dominguín and his lover Ava Gardner. The American Academy of Arts and Letters awards Hemingway its gold medal on May 26. The Hemingways sail for Havana the following month. Hemingway is awarded the Order of Carlos Manuel de Céspedes by the Cuban government on July 21, his fifty-fifth birthday. On October 28, the Swedish Academy announces that he has won the Nobel Prize for Literature. Sometime in the last part of the year, begins work on an African novel. Becomes increasingly agitated by the stream of visitors and the interest generated by the Nobel Prize.

1955    By January 16, 186 pages of the African novel have been written. Aside from fishing trips, Hemingway remains in Cuba. The first two weeks of June, producer Leland Hayward and screenwriter Peter Viertel meet frequently with Hemingway to discuss the movie version of *The Old Man and the Sea*. In September, assists on the filming of fishing scenes for the movie. By December 29, 748 pages of the African book have been completed.

1956    On February 27, stops work on African book (now at 843 pages) to assist on filming of *The Old Man and the Sea*. In April and May, cruises off the coast of Peru unsuccessfully hunting for marlin, footage of which was to be used in the movie. Upon his return to Finca Vigía on May 23, writes several stories about World War II. The Hemingways sail from New York for France on September 1. They leave Paris by car for Spain on September 17, spending two months in the country. Upon their return to the Ritz Hotel in Paris on November 19, Hemingway supposedly discovers two trunks of manuscripts he had stored there in the late 1920s; the material in these trunks will prompt him to begin writing his memoirs of his life in Paris.

1957   The Hemingways leave Paris on January 22. Hemingway, suf-
       fering from various physical and mental ailments, remains
       on the *Île de France* after it docks in New York and cruises
       on to Havana. From February to June, works on *The Garden
       of Eden* at Finca Vigía. In July, begins writing his memoir of
       his life in Paris in the 1920s. The Hemingways spend two
       weeks in New York from September 22 to October 2. Upon
       his return to Cuba, Hemingway continues working on his
       African and Paris books.

1958   During the first half of the year, works on his unfinished
       projects, mainly *The Garden of Eden* and his Paris memoir.
       In April, the *Paris Review* publishes George Plimpton's in-
       terview with Hemingway. Concerned about the increasingly
       volatile political situation in Cuba, the Hemingways rent a
       house in Ketchum, Idaho. They move in on October 6 and
       stay in Idaho for the next six months.

1959   On January 1, the Batista government in Cuba falls. The
       next day Hemingway decides to buy a house in Ketchum,
       Idaho. The Hemingways return to Finca Vigía on March
       29. Having signed a contract with *Life* to cover the mano
       a mano bullfights between Antonio Ordóñez and his
       brother-in-law Luis Miguel Dominguín, Hemingway sails
       with Mary from New York to Spain on April 26. They remain
       in Spain through the end of September. Hemingway is in-
       creasingly depressed and abusive toward his wife. After trav-
       elling through Aigues-Mortes and Le Grau-du-Roi to allow
       Hemingway to check that his descriptions in *The Garden of
       Eden* manuscript are accurate, the couple returns to Paris
       on October 1. Mary flies back to the United States on May
       4 to prepare Finca Vigía and the Ketchum house, but she
       also rents an apartment for herself in New York. On October
       10, Hemingway is at wealthy American expatriates Bill and
       Annie Davis's house, La Consula, in Málaga, Spain, working

on his story for *Life*. Sails for New York from Cherbourg on October 26, his story of the summer's bullfighting still unfinished. On November 3, leaves the manuscript of his Paris memoirs at Charles Scribner's Sons and flies to Havana the next day. On November 12, Hemingway, Ordóñez and his wife, and Roberto Herrera, one of Hemingway's employees at Finca Vigía, begin the drive from Key West to Ketchum, Mary having flown ahead to prepare the house. She breaks her elbow on November 27, ruining her plans to move to New York.

1960      The Hemingways leave Ketchum for Cuba on January 17. Hemingway continues to work on his *Life* story through May. On March 31, writes Scribner's to withdraw the manuscript of *A Moveable Feast* so that he can revise it. On May 15, Prime Minister Fidel Castro wins the annual Hemingway Fishing Competition, marking the only time he and Hemingway meet. On May 19, Hemingway takes the *Pilar* out to sea, the last time he will be aboard his boat. On June 27, Hotchner arrives in Cuba to help Hemingway edit the *Life* article. On August 5, Hemingway arrives in Madrid; Mary remains in New York. He writes to her on August 15 saying that he fears he is having a nervous breakdown. She sends his secretary, Valarie Danby-Smith, to assist him. *Life* publishes the first of three installments of Hemingway's account of the 1959 bullfighting season on September 5. Hotchner arrives in Spain on October 2 to help and returns to New York with Hemingway on October 5. The Hemingways return to Ketchum on October 22. Hemingway's condition continues to deteriorate. On November 22, Dr. George Saviers has Hemingway flown to the Mayo Clinic in Rochester, Minnesota. There, he undergoes a series of electroshock treatments through January that seem to relieve his depression.

1961      The United States severs diplomatic ties with Cuba on January 2. The Hemingways return to Ketchum on January 22.

Hemingway finds it increasingly hard to write but is able to finish the chapter "Nada y Pues Nada" for his Paris memoir by April 1. On April 21, tries to shoot himself, but is stopped by Mary and Dr. Saviers. Four days later, flies back to the Mayo Clinic for additional electroshock treatments. On June 26, he is driven back to Ketchum, arriving the last day of the month. Shoots himself with one of his shotguns at 7:30 A.M. on July 2. Hemingway is buried in the Ketchum cemetery on July 5.

# NOTE ON THE TEXTS

This volume brings together *The Sun Also Rises* (1926) and a selection of related writings by Hemingway, comprising four pieces of journalism written for the *Toronto Star* from 1922 to 1923 and eight letters dating from 1925 to 1926 that comment on the composition and publication of his second novel. It presents a corrected text of *The Sun Also Rises*, originally published in *Hemingway: The Sun Also Rises & Other Writings 1918–1926* (2020) and prepared for Library of America by Robert W. Trogdon. The texts for all the selections in this volume are described below.

In April 1926, Hemingway wrote to F. Scott Fitzgerald to say that *The Sun Also Rises* was back from the typist and ready to send to Maxwell Perkins at Scribner's. In mid-May, he wrote to Fitzgerald again to say he was eager to hear from Perkins and described his novel as "such a hell of a sad story and the only instruction is how people go to hell." Early in June, Fitzgerald read a carbon of the typescript and suggested that Hemingway make extensive revisions to the opening of the novel. After receiving Fitzgerald's critique, Hemingway wrote to Perkins indicating that he was going to cut the first fifteen pages of the typescript and begin the novel with the introduction of Robert Cohn, not Brett Ashley and Jake Barnes as he had originally intended. Perkins sent proofs on July 20 with suggestions for revisions to material that was libelous or obscene. Hemingway acceded to most of his editor's objections and returned the proofs on August 26, 1926. The novel was published by Scribner's on October 22, 1926, in an initial printing of 5,090 copies. It was reprinted three times in 1926, and five times in the following year, when sales picked up after strong reviews. The British edition, published as *Fiesta*, was issued by Cape on June 9, 1927, in what Hemingway characterized for Maxwell Perkins in a letter of June 24, 1927, as "the cheapest form possible"; three days later he wrote to Cape, complaining about the book's "numerous typographical errors."

This volume presents the text of the first printing of the 1926 Scribner's edition of *The Sun Also Rises*, emended to account for typesetting errors, small errors and inconsistences that require correction, Hemingway's preferred American spellings and his more typical closed-compound spelling of "someone," his terminal punctuation for rhetorical questions, and alterations made for reasons of libel or obscenity. The titling of the chapters and in Chapter Nineteen the treatment of Jake's handwritten telegraph form—in upper- and lower- case letters and not set apart from the text—follow the typescript setting copy of the novel. The published version was collated against the holograph manuscript, held at the John F. Kennedy Presidential Library and Museum, and the typescript setting copy, held in the Clifton Waller Barrett library in the Albert and Shirley Small Collections Library at the University of Virginia. The partial typescript at the Kennedy Library was also consulted. The aim of these labors is to bring readers closer to the text Hemingway would have wished to see printed. Galley proofs that incorporate the original discarded opening exist, but Hemingway's corrected proofs are unlocated.

In his manuscripts and typescripts, Hemingway's punctuation is lighter than what readers encounter in his published books. This is especially true of Hemingway's dialogue. He tended to punctuate dialogue more by ear than by rules, but he was also cursory or inconsistent about the placement of commas. His editors at Boni & Liveright and Scribner's imposed their house style on his prose, regularizing his punctuation. Hemingway was mostly appreciative of these efforts. His most extended comment on the subject of editorial intervention is found in a letter of May 22, 1925, to Horace Liveright, written after he had gone over the proofs of *In Our Time*: "Whoever did the editing on the whole book was very intelligent and most of the changes of punctuation I agree with. Those I don't I have changed to their original form. My attitude toward punctuation is that it ought to be as conventional as possible. You ought to be able to show that you can do it a good deal better than anyone else with the regular tools before you have an license to bring in your own improvements. But don't let this inspire whoever went over it for punctuation to any further action because it is all right now." It is not always possible to distinguish between changes made by Hemingway and by his editors, especially in matters of punctuation. The situation is further complicated by the fact that, in the case of *The Sun Also Rises*, corrected proofs do not survive. No alterations have been made to the punctuation and spelling in the first printing of his novel with the exceptions noted here.

Hemingway's spelling could be variable, but he was fairly consistent in preferring American usage. It was the practice of many American publishers, including Scribner's, to change spellings to British forms, in order to make the books more appealing to prospective British publishers (and by extension to their readers). The idea was that a British publisher might be more inclined to purchase plates from an American publisher if they already contained British spellings. For example, in the published text of *The Sun Also Rises* we find the British spelling "centre" rather than Hemingway's preferred "center." Robert Cohn is shaped into a "rather unattractive mould" in the text of the first and all subsequent printings of *The Sun Also Rises*, and into a "rather unattractive mold" in the manuscript. In the texts of his published books we find hyphenated forms for compound words: "good-night," "to-morrow," "up-stairs," "any-one," and so on, which are not typically found in Hemingway's holograph drafts nor in the typescripts he prepared himself. The text of *The Sun Also Rises* in this volume restores Hemingway's preferred American spellings, with the exception of the British spelling "whiskey," in deference to Hemingway's long-standing habit.

In addition to restoring Hemingway's preferred American spellings, this edition corrects a small number of obvious spelling errors. In Chapter Twelve of *The Sun Also Rises*, for example, American baseball player Frankie Frisch's name is altered from "Fritsch" in the

Scribner's printings to its correct spelling. This edition also consistently uses the modern closed-compound spelling of "someone" (as opposed to the open-compound spelling). In his typescripts and holograph manuscripts, Hemingway was inconsistent on this point, but more often than not he used the closed-compound spelling.

One aspect of Hemingway's punctuation that requires the editor's special consideration is his handling of rhetorical questions in dialogue. Hemingway sometimes chose in such instances to use a period to mark terminal punctuation. In Chapter Four in the published texts of *The Sun Also Rises*, for example, Brett says, "'How do I buck on about this?'"—which is clearly not a question but a remark about her talkativeness. In the typescript setting copy, the sentence is punctuated with a period. Similarly, Hemingway's revisions to the final sentence of *The Sun Also Rises* show he intended it as a rhetorical question. In manuscript, he first wrote, "'It's nice as hell to think so.'", then revised it on the same page to "'Isn't it nice to think so'"(the revision lacks terminal punctuation). And finally, in the typescript setting copy, Hemingway revised the line to "'Isn't it pretty to think so.'" This edition restores Hemingway's preferred terminal punctuation of rhetorical questions found in the typescripts and underlying holograph manuscript of *The Sun Also Rises*.

Fearing libel charges or accusations of impropriety, Hemingway and his publishers made substantive alterations to his texts. The effect of these changes is to soften language or to obscure references to real-life people and places. Most of these changes were initiated by Hemingway's publishers, with his reluctant acquiescence. In a few instances, much later, he revisited these decisions. *In Our Time* illustrates the complex ways in which anxieties worked on both Hemingway and his publishers. Boni & Liveright asked for extensive revisions to "Mr. and Mrs. Elliot" to reduce the inference that the couple was engaging in sexual intercourse, which Hemingway consented to do; however, when Scribner's reissued the book in 1930, Maxwell Perkins agreed to replace the text of the story with that of the original, more risqué version that had appeared in *The Little Review*. In "My Old Man," Boni & Liveright's "son of a b----" became "son of a bitch" in the published Scribner's text, no doubt because Hemingway had been allowed to use the word in *The Sun Also Rises*. In "A Very Short Story," Boni & Liveright's editors changed the name of the shopgirl's employer from "The Fair"—a famous Chicago establishment—to "a loop department store." But for the Scribner's printing, Hemingway let the change stand: While The Fair had been sold to a syndicate in 1925, it continued to operate under that name until the 1960s. In the same story, Hemingway changed the female character's name from "Ag" to "Luz" and shifted the setting from "Milan" to "Padua," to shield his new publisher from a possible libel suit by Agnes von Kurowsky, the nurse whom he had been involved with in Italy in 1918 and the basis for the character in the story. Similar anxieties motivated Perkins to request changes in proofs to *The Sun Also Rises*, detailed in Hemingway's letter of August 21, 1926, to his editor. Perkins feared, for example, that novelist Joseph Hergesheimer would sue for being called a "garter snapper," so Hemingway changed the name to "Hoffenheimer." And Perkins found disrespectful the inclusion of the apocryphal story that Henry James was rendered impotent due to a bicycle accident; Hemingway, grudgingly acceding to his editor's wishes, changed "Henry James's bicycle" to the somewhat puzzling "Henry's bicycle." In another letter to Perkins, Hemingway complained: "To me Henry James is as historical a name as Byron, Keats, or any other great writer about whose life, personal and literary, books have been written. I do not believe that the reference is sneering, or if it is, it is not the writer who is sneering as the writer does not appear in this book. Henry James is dead and left no descendants to be hurt, nor any wife, and therefore I feel that he is as dead as he will ever be." In matters of revisions motivated by fears of libel or for the sake of impropriety, this edition restores Hemingway's original language in the typescript setting copy of *The Sun Also Rises*.

Hemingway began his professional writing career as a journalist. Before he left for the Italian front in 1918, he worked briefly as cub reporter at the *Kansas City Star*. That experience opened the door for him after the war at the *Toronto Star*, where he was given his own byline. In the four years he worked for the *Toronto Star*, from 1920 to 1924, first as a freelance writer, then as a European correspondent, and ultimately as a staff writer based in Toronto, he wrote about two hundred articles for the *Star*. From September to December 1922, he also filed dispatches to the International News Service (INS), under the pseudonym John Hadley, by a secret agreement with INS that clearly violated the terms of his arrangement with the *Star*. The texts of the *Star* pieces selected for this volume are taken from *Dateline Toronto*, edited by William White and published by Charles Scribner's Sons in 1985. White shortened the titles of the *Star* pieces for his collection; here, the original newspaper titles are used. No manuscripts of Hemingway's journalism from the 1920s survive. It was a common newspaper practice to discard manuscript or typescript as soon as a piece was set in type, and the young Hemingway's work was not an exception in this regard.

The letters selected for this volume are printed in the Cambridge Edition of *The Letters of Ernest Hemingway*. The Cambridge editors do not attempt to regularize Hemingway's punctuation and spelling but aim instead to reproduce the flavor of Hemingway's letters "—whether casual, hurried, harried, inventive, or playful (as when he writes 'goils' instead of 'girls,' refers to his cats as 'kotsies,' remarks 'we cant stahnd it,' or exclaims 'Toturletter thanks!')." Missing punctuation and characters are supplied in square brackets only where the original letters suggest the omissions were not intentional or where confusion would otherwise result. Hemingway in his letters often failed to put a period at the end of the concluding sentence in his paragraphs or at the end of a sentence enclosed by parentheses. The Cambridge editors have allowed these instances to stand uncorrected. Square brackets are also used to indicate the conjectured reconstruction of missing or illegible text, to signal where one writer of a joint letter inserts a remark into the text, and to designate interlineations or marginalia where a brief editorial note is required. In the headings, square brackets indicate where the editors provide missing information about the date of a given letter. For a more detailed explanation of the textual policies guiding the Cambridge Edition of

*The Letters of Ernest Hemingway*, readers should consult the Note on the Texts in any of the volumes in the Edition.

The texts presented in this volume reproduce those of the selected sources, altered only in the ways described above. Some of the most significant alterations to *The Sun Also Rises* are discussed in the Notes, and all the substantive alterations to the novel, including the end punctuation of rhetorical questions, are indicated below. The list records, by page and line number, the changes incorporated into the corrected text. A key to the abbreviations used to indicate the source of a particular reading precedes the list of emendations.

## THE SUN ALSO RISES

MS  *The Sun Also Rises*, manuscript, July–September 1925, Ernest Hemingway Collection, MS 28, John F. Kennedy Presidential Library and Museum, Columbia Point, MA.

TS  *The Sun Also Rises*, typescript setting copy, April 1926, Papers of Ernest Hemingway, Series 1.2, Albert and Shirley Small Special Collections Library, University of Virginia, Charlottesville, VA.

A1  *The Sun Also Rises*. New York: Scribner's, 1926.

A1³  *The Sun Also Rises*, third printing (November 29, 1926). New York: Scribner's, 1926.

ed  Editor.

23.8  Roger Prescott] TS; Robert Prentiss

23.27  Roger] TS; Robert

25.3  Aren't I.] MS; Aren't I?

36.10  this.] MS; this?

42.11  she."] MS; she?"

47.13  Hergesheimer] MS; Hoffenheimer

59.15  to.] MS; to?

76.18  eyed] TS; eyes

79.11    terrasse] TS; terraces

82.5    terrasse] MS; terrace

82.22    not.] MS; not?

83.3    in to] MS; into

83.7    it.] TS; it?

88.21    he.] MS; he?

93.13    Gorton] A1³; Grundy

94.9    bought] MS; sought

96.10    go in] MS; go on

120.25    Henry James's] TS; Henry's

132.17    Wednesday?] ed; Wednesday.

141.28    whopping] MS; wopping

153.10    it.] MS; it?

177.7    he,"] MS; he?"

183.23    balls] TS; horns

184.22    balls] TS; horns

184.26    balls] TS; horns

188.14    going on] TS; going in

190.17    pretty.] TS; pretty?

204.19    not.] MS; not?

220.4    damn wind] MS; wind

258.1    bar.] MS; bar?

260.29    so.] TS; so?

# NOTES

In the notes below, the reference numbers denote page and line of this volume (the line count includes headings). Biblical quotations are keyed to the King James Version. Quotations from Shakespeare are keyed to *The Riverside Shakespeare*, ed. G. Blakemore Evans (Boston: Houghton Mifflin, 1974). For more detailed notes, references to other studies, and further biographical background than is provided in the Chronology, see Michael Reynold's five-volume biography, comprising *The Young Hemingway* (Oxford: Basil Blackwell, 1986); *Hemingway: The Paris Years* (Oxford: Basil Blackwell, 1989); *Hemingway: The American Homecoming* (Cambridge, MA: Basil Blackwell, 1992); *Hemingway: The 1930s* (New York: W. W. Norton, 1997); and *Hemingway: The Final Years* (New York: W. W. Norton, 1999); and the ongoing Cambridge Edition of the Letters of Ernest Hemingway, including *The Letters of Ernest Hemingway: Volume 1, 1907–1922*, ed. Sandra Spanier and Robert W. Trogdon (New York: Cambridge University Press, 2011); *The Letters of Ernest Hemingway: Volume 2, 1923–1925*, ed. Sandra Spanier, Albert J. DeFazio III, and Robert W. Trogdon (New York: Cambridge University Press, 2013); *The Letters of Ernest Hemingway: Volume 3, 1926–1929*, ed. Rena Sanderson, Sandra Spanier, and Robert W. Trogdon (New York: Cambridge University Press, 2013); *The Letters of Ernest Hemingway: Volume 4, 1929–1931*, ed. Sandra Spanier and Miriam B. Mandel (New York: Cambridge University Press, 2017); and *The Letters of Ernest Hemingway: Volume 5, 1932–1934*, ed. Sandra Spanier and Miriam B. Mandel (New York: Cambridge University Press, 2020).

# THE SUN ALSO RISES

4.1–2   "You are all a lost generation . . . *in conversation*] For Hemingway's account of this conversation, see "Une Génération Perdue" in *A Moveable Feast*.

5.3   Robert Cohn] Based on American novelist Harold Loeb (1891–1974), cofounder of the little magazine *Broom* and author of the novel *Doodab*, which was published by Boni & Liveright in 1925. Loeb would respond to Hemingway in his memoir *The Way It Was* (1959) and, long after Hemingway's death, in "Hemingway's Bitterness" (1967). Loeb devoted time to boxing in his freshman year at Princeton, but unlike Cohn he did not excel at the sport.

7.17   Braddocks] Braddocks and his wife were inspired by Ford Madox Ford (1873–1939) and his common-law wife Stella Bowen (1893–1995).

7.19   Frances] Inspired by American writer Kathleen "Kitty" Cannell (1891–1974), whom Harold Loeb met in Paris in 1923 and who was a contributor to *Broom* and *transition*.

8.3   l'Avenue's . . . Café de Versailles] In Montparnasse.

8.4   *fines*] High-quality French brandy.

11.12–13   the more practical Alger books.] American author Horatio Alger, Jr. (1832–1899), wrote *Ragged Dick* (1868) and numerous other rags-to-riches stories extolling honesty, hard work, and perseverance.

11.14   R.G. Dun report.] R.G. Dun & Company, the first American credit reporting agency.

15.13–14   Café Napolitain . . . on the Boulevard.] The grand café stood at 1, boulevard des Capucines.

17.11   *fiacre*] French: cab.

18.11   *cocher*] French: coachman.

18.14   rather go to Foyot's.] Pricey restaurant that stood opposite the Senate in Luxembourg Palace before its demolition in 1938.

18.18   *poule*] French: literally, a hen; a prostitute.

20.4   Mademoiselle Georgette Leblanc,"] French opera singer (1869–1941), who from 1922 until her death was in a romantic relationship with Margaret Anderson, founder and editor of *The Little Review*.

20.9   "Connais pas,"] French: I don't know.

22.17   Brett] Modeled on Duff Twysden (1893–1938), a British citizen who was part of Hemingway's circle in 1925. Loeb's brief affair with Twysden was a source of jealousy for Hemingway. Twysden also made an impression on

British novelist Michael Arlen, who purportedly used her as the model for Iris March in *The Green Hat* (1924).

23.8   Roger Prescott.] Thinly veiled portrait of American novelist Glenway Wescott (1901–1987), best known for *The Grandmothers* (1927) and *Good-Bye Wisconsin* (1928). At Perkins's insistence, "Roger Prescott" was changed to "Robert Prentiss" to avoid a possible libel suit. Here, the original allusion in Hemingway's setting copy is retained.

23.14–15   *fine à l'eau*.]: French: brandy and water.

26.4   patronne] French: proprietress.

26.9   "C'est entendu, monsieur,"] French: I understand, sir.

31.8   everybody called Zizi] Zizi is French for cock, penis.

31.25   yellow card] Prostitutes in Paris were required to carry a card with a record of their health examinations to show they were free of venereal diseases.

32.19   Mike?"] Brett's fiancé Mike Campbell, based on Englishman Patrick Guthrie (1895–1932).

32.29   Closerie des Lilas.] Montparnasse café whose quiet atmosphere Hemingway preferred for reading and writing.

32.29–33.2   Ney's statue . . . some date; I forget.] Michel Ney (1769–1815) was the most distinguished of Napoleon's marshals; his rearguard action in the Grande Army's retreat from Moscow earned him Napoleon's praise as "the bravest of the brave." After the defeat at Waterloo, the restored government convicted Ney of treason and executed him on December 7, 1815. The bronze statue of Ney was erected on December 7, 1853, at the place of his execution. See Hemingway's meditation on the statue at the conclusion of "Une Génération Perdue" in *A Moveable Feast*.

39.20   CINZANO] Italian brand of vermouth.

40.14–16   The Dingo. . . . this new dive, the Select."] The Dingo American Bar and Restaurant was one of the bars in Montparnasse—the Select was another—frequented by Hemingway during his Paris years. In *A Moveable Feast*, Hemingway describes meeting F. Scott Fitzgerald at the Dingo for the first time ("a very strange thing happened"). The Select opened its doors for business in 1925.

42.27   V.A.D.] Volunteer Aid Detachments, a voluntary unit of British citizens (mostly women) providing nursing care for the sick and wounded. VADs had shorter training requirements than nurses in the Royal Army and were under the control of the Red Cross. Catherine Barkley in *A Farewell to Arms* is also a VAD.

44.5–6   Café de la Paix] Founded in 1862, one of Paris's oldest and most famous cafés, across the street from the Opera House.

45.18   the P.L.M.] Compagnie des chemins de fer de Paris à Lyon et à la Méditerranée (usually called the PLM) was a French railway company.

46.1   Mencken] Henry Louis Mencken (1880–1956), American journalist, prominent literary and social critic. Though he tried, Hemingway was unable to place any of his stories in H. L. Mencken's magazines, *The American Mercury* and *The Smart Set*.

46.9   Harvey Stone.] Modeled on American cultural critic and horse-racing journalist Harold Stearns (1891–1943), part of the American expatriate scene in Paris in the 1920s.

47.13   Hergesheimer] American historical novelist Joseph Hergesheimer (1880–1954). Perkins insisted the name be changed to avoid libel, and Hemingway made it "Hoffenheimer" for the published text of the novel. This volume restores the original reference, as it appears in the setting copy.

47.21   the Alexander Hamilton Institute."] A twenty-four-volume set of business texts published by the New York–based Alexander Hamilton Institute (1917).

51.4   *Paris Times*] Afternoon American newspaper, published by Cortlandt F. Bishop from 1924 to 1929.

55.21   Look at Hardy. Look at Anatole France.] A writer of late-blooming creative powers, British novelist and poet Thomas Hardy (1840–1928) was in his thirties when he embarked on his long publishing career. French poet, novelist, and journalist Anatole France (1844–1924) was productive well into his seventies.

57.25–58.1   the pelouse . . . the pesage] The pelouse, the grassy area around the racecourse, the least expensive section, without seating accommodations; the pesage, the area where the jockeys are weighed in, the paddock, and the grandstand for the public as well as reserved seating sections.

58.13   Bill Gorton] Based on Hemingway's friend from Michigan, William B. Smith, Jr. (1895–1972), and the American novelist and humorist Donald Ogden Stewart (1894–1980). Stewart accompanied Hemingway to Pamplona and its Fiesta de San Fermín in 1924, and both men were part of the group who went there in 1925.

60.18   *tromper*] French: deceive.

73.5   the Concha] San Sebastian beach.

73.24   Dempsey] American boxer William Harrison "Jack" Dempsey (1895–1983) reigned as world heavyweight champion from July 1919 to September 1926.

74.3    the fiesta at Pamplona.] Fiesta de San Fermín, held annually to honor Pamplona's first bishop and patron saint, Saint Fermín, beginning at noon on July 6 and ending at midnight on July 14. Hemingway first went to the fiesta in 1923 and attended every year (with the exception of 1928) for the rest of the decade.

75.4    Tiger Flowers] Theodore "Tiger" Flowers (1895–1927), American boxer who became the first African American to win the world middleweight championship in 1926.

76.16–17    statue of two men in flowing robes.] Melted down by the Nazis in World War II, the bronze statue honored Pierre Joseph Pelletier and Joseph Bienaimé Caventou, who isolated quinine in 1820.

80.19    Madame Lecomte's restaurant] Au Rendez-vous des Mariniers at 33, quai d'Anjou, near the offices of *The Transatlantic Review* and Three Mountains Press.

85.2    Ledoux–Kid Francis fight . . . the 20th of June.] The fight, a bantamweight bout between Charles Ledoux and Kid Francis (winner by decision), actually took place on June 9, 1925, at the Cirque de Paris.

92.3    snappers] Mackerel-snappers, a pejorative term for Roman Catholics, referring to the practice of eating fish on Fridays.

94.14–16    the cathedral. . . . a very good example of something or other] Cathedrale Sainte-Marie de Bayonne, built from the thirteenth to sixteenth centuries, is an example of Gothic architecture.

94.18–19    Syndicat d'Initiative] French: Tourist office.

97.7    Col] French: Mountain pass.

98.13    Montoya] Modeled after Juanito Quintana. Hemingway stayed at his Hotel Quintana when he was in Pamplona, and the two men remained friends throughout Hemingway's life.

99.17    fifty pesetas] The exchange rate in July 1925 was 19.3 cents to the peseta. The bet is for $9.65.

100.25    Ayuntamiento] Spanish: Town hall.

110.14    posada] Spanish: inn.

111.16    aguardiente] Spanish: spirits, liquor.

114.3    monastery of Roncevalles.] Site of the battle of Roncevaux Pass (778 C.E.), fought between Charlemagne's army and Basque forces, in which Roland, who was leading the Frankish rearguard covering Charlemagne's retreat, was killed. His story is recounted in the eleventh-century epic *La Chanson de Roland*.

114.30    Nuestra Señora de Roncesvalles.] Silver-plated wooden statue of the Virgin and Child (late 13th century), in the Collegiate Church of Roncesvalles.

117.17    look trouty.] Jake and Bill's day of fishing in this chapter is based on a trip that Hemingway and Hadley made to Burguete with Robert McAlmon and Bill Bird in July 1924. A return trip in June 1925 with Smith and others was not successful due to extensive logging in the area, which had ruined the stream.

119.2–3    "The Bells are Ringing for Me and my Gal."] "Me and My Gal" (1917), by American songwriter George W. Meyer (1884–1959), with lyrics by Edgar Leslie (1885–1956) and E. Ray Goetz (1885–1976).

119.8    the Fratellinis] Famous European circus family, best remembered for the Fratellini Brothers—Paul, François, and Albert (respectively, 1877–1940, 1879–1951, 1886–1961)—a celebrated clown act in Paris from 1902 to 1924.

118.18–20    Primo de Rivera. . . . the Riff."] Miguel Primo de Rivera (1870–1930) was dictator of Spain from 1923 to 1930. The Rif War (1921–1926) was fought between Spanish Colonial forces (later allied with France) and the Berber tribes of the mountainous Rif in northern Morocco. The Rif rebels had the Spanish beat; their mistake was taking on the French in 1925, who were both politically and militarily stronger than the Spanish. Spain and France ultimately prevailed, but the war was unpopular in Spain and claimed 38,000 lives on both sides.

120.25    Henry James's bicycle. . . . a tricycle."] Allusion to apocryphal story that James was rendered impotent due to a horseback-riding accident. Perkins objected to the more transparent "Henry James's bicycle," changing it to "Henry's bicycle." Here, the original reading in the setting copy is restored.

121.15    Dred Scott Case . . . Anti-Saloon League.] In *Dred Scott v. Sandford* (1857), the U.S. Supreme Court ruled that Congress could not prohibit slavery in federal territories and that free blacks were not citizens of the United States. The Anti-Saloon League was a temperance organization founded in Oberlin, Ohio, in 1893.

121.16–17    The Colonel's Lady . . . Lesbians under their skin."] Play on the last two lines of Rudyard Kipling's "The Ladies" (1896): "For the Colonel's Lady an' Judy O'Grady / Are Sisters under their skins!"

123.25    McGinty's?"] McGinty, a wet fly developed by American angler Charles McGinty in 1883, resembling a bee or yellow jacket.

125.23    something by A.E.W. Mason . . . waited too] Jake is reading "The Crystal Trench" in *The Four Corners of the World* (1917) by British writer Alfred Edward Woodley Mason (1865–1948).

127.11–12    Bryan . . . the Great Commoner."] American populist politician William Jennings Bryan (1860–1925), known as the "Great Commoner," took part in what became known as the Scopes Monkey Trial in Dayton, Tennessee, arguing against the theory of evolution.

128.11    Frankie Frisch."] Frankie Frisch (1897–1973), infielder for the New York Giants from 1919 to 1926 (and afterward for the St. Louis Cardinals).

128.14    Bishop Manning."] William T. Manning (1866–1949), Episcopal bishop of New York City.

128.27    the Anti-Saloon League. . . . Wayne Wheeler. . . . must go."] Wayne Wheeler (1869–1927) was a lawyer for the Anti-Saloon League, whose motto was "The Saloon Must Go."

130.14    Jo Davidson."] American sculptor (1883–1952) whose work includes "Gertrude Stein" (1922–23), a life-sized sculpture-in-the-round of the writer.

137.12    the pelota."] A Spanish or Basque court game resembling squash, played with a curved basket used for catching the pelota (ball) and throwing it against the wall. Here, the meaning is the pelota court.

137.15    the Villar bulls . . . the Miuras.] Two breeds of large Spanish fighting bulls. In *Death in the Afternoon*, Hemingway writes, "I remember a corrida of Villar bulls in Pamplona in 1923. They were ideal bulls, as brave as any I have ever seen, fast, vicious, but always attacking; never going on the defensive. They were big but not so large as to be ponderous, and they were well horned. Villar bred splendid bulls but the bullfighters did not care for them. They had just a little too much of every good quality. The breeding stock was sold to another man who set out to reduce these qualities enough to make the bulls acceptable to the bullfighters."

137.17    a desencajonada."] Spanish: releasing; releasing of the bulls into the corral.

140.7    SOL, SOL Y SOMBRA, and SOMBRA] Spanish: Sun, sun and shade, shade.

142.9    the night they'd shot Henry Wilson] Field Marshal Sir Henry Wilson (1864–1922) was shot and killed by two members of the Irish Republican Army outside of his home in London on June 21, 1922. After World War I, Wilson, an ardent Unionist, opposed the creation of the Irish Republic and advocated for a harsh crackdown on the IRA and Sinn Fein.

154.6    Turgenieff] Ivan Turgenev (1818–1883), Russian novelist, short story writer, poet, and playwright, author of *A Sportsman Sketches* (1852) and *Fathers and Sons* (1862).

157.10    ANIS DEL TORO.] Spanish: Bull's anise; Anis del Mono is a popular Spanish brand of aniseed liqueur.

157.21 paseo] Spanish: walk, stroll.

160.21 *riau-riau*] Popular local waltz played during the rowdy procession on the first day (July 6) of Pamplona's festival of San Férmin, from the town hall to the nearby Saint Fermín Chapel at San Lorenzo church.

170.18–19 Pedro Romero?"] The name "Pedro Romero" comes from the eighteenth-century bullfighter who introduced many innovations into bullfighting and whom Hemingway in *Death in the Afternoon* calls "one of the first and greatest of professional fighters." Hemingway's character is modelled on Cayetano Ordóñez, who fought under the name Niño de la Palma (1904–1961). Hemingway initially admired the bullfighter's skill; however, by the time he wrote *Death in the Afternoon*, he believed that after "his first severe goring [Ordóñez] developed a cowardice which was only equaled by his ability to avoid taking risks in the ring."

176.14 the death of Joselito] The Spanish bullfighter José Gómez Ortega (1895–1920), known as Joselito, was killed in the bullring on May 16, 1920.

179.24 Marcial Lalanda] Spanish bullfighter (1903–1990). Hemingway offered a harsh assessment of him in *Death in the Afternoon*: "a sad and unemotional bullfighter, although he was technically skillful and completely intelligent, and for once that he was good in the ring he was mediocre and uninteresting a dozen times."

180.12 Algabeno,"] José García Corranza, Spanish bullfighter (1902–1936), also known as "Pepe Algabeño" (1902–1936), whom Hemingway in *Death in the Afternoon* calls "the worst faker of them all."

180.18 Gallo."] The Spanish bullfighter Rafael Gómez Ortega (1882–1960), known as *El Gallo*. In *Death in the Afternoon*, Hemingway characterizes him as "a great bullfighter and the first one to admit fear. . . . A matador is never supposed to run, but Gallo was liable to run if the bull looked at him in a peculiarly knowing way."

182.7 banderillero] A bullfighter who assists the matador, using a decorated dart (banderilla) that is thrust into a bull's neck or shoulder.

183.8 twenty-six arrobas.] An arroba is a unit of weight in Spanish-speaking countries, equivalent to about 25 pounds. The bulls weigh 650 pounds.

184.4 Fundador] Spanish grape brandy.

184.14 Villalta,"] Nicanor Villalta (1897–1980), Spanish bullfighter whom Hemingway in *Death in the Afternoon* calls "the courageous telephone pole of Aragon" and "the best killer." Hemingway named his firstborn son, John Hadley Nicanor Hemingway, after him.

194.29 thousand duros] The duro was the five-peseta coin. Five thousand pesetas was roughly $965 in 1925.

207.5    encierro?"] Spanish: literally enclosing; the running of the bulls.

207.6    cogida."] Spanish: the catching and tossing of a person by a bull.

208.4    Es muy flamenco."] Spanish: It's very flamenco.

222.31    muletas] Spanish: A muleta is a small red cape pendant from a stick, used in the final stage of the bullfight to distract the bull from the sword and to display the torreo's mastery over the animal.

223.25    Belmonte . . . Marcial] Spanish bullfighter Juan Belmonte (1892–1962) was famous for his rivalry with Joselito (recounted by Hemingway in *Death in the Afternoon*); Belmonte had retired in 1922, but attempted a comeback in 1925. Marcial, see note 179.24.

245.14    *strega*] An Italian liqueur made with mint, fennel, and other herbs.

245.15    *vieux marc.*] Pomace brandy.

247.9    the Concha.] See note 73.5.

249.12–13    Bottechia . . . abandoned it at Pamplona.] Ottavio Bottecchia (1894–1927) was the first Italian cyclist to win the Tour de France in 1924. After winning the Tour again in 1925, he dropped out of the 1926 Tour during a severe thunderstorm.

249.27    Paname.] Nickname for Paris.

253.26    chica] Spanish: girl.

255.27    Gib."] Gibraltar, but a "gib" is also a neutered cat.

259.12    *rioja alta.*] Spanish wine.

## JOURNALISM

265.17    *femme de ménage*] French: housekeeper.

266.9    Jack Clifford . . . suitable purse was offered.] Clifford has not been identified. French boxer Georges Carpentier (1894–1975) captured European titles in multiple weight divisions.

266.27–267.2    Soldier Jones. . . . Beckett . . . Harry Greb] There is no evidence that Canadian heavyweight John Horace Beaudin (1897–1942), who fought under the name "Soldier Jones," ever battled British heavyweight champion Joe Beckett (1892–1965). Jones was knocked out in the fourth round by American middleweight Harry Greb (1894–1926) when they fought in Toronto on April 11, 1921.

268.5    Café Rotonde.] Brasserie at the corner of Boulevard du Montparnasse and Boulevard Raspail.

269.28   the "Merry Widow" Period] *The Merry Widow* (*Die lustige Witwe*), an operetta by Austro-Hungarian composer Franz Lehár, was first performed in Vienna on December 30, 1905.

270.24–25   Charles Baudelaire led a purple lobster] Hemingway confuses French poet Charles Baudelaire (1821–1867), the author of *Les Fleurs du Mal* (1857), with French writer and poet Gérard de Nerval (1808–1855), who supposedly had a pet lobster.

272.4   Mike and I decided to go to Spain.] Hemingway did not make his first trip to Spain—in June 1923—with Henry "Mike" Strater (1896–1987), the American painter, but with the American literary men Robert McAlmon (1895–1956) and Bill Bird (1888–1963). All three had roles to play in his publishing career. See also notes 130.2–5 and 628.16–17.

272.6–8   a restaurant in Madrid . . . suckling pig roasted] The restaurant in Madrid is the Restaurante Sobrino de Botín, the same restaurant where Jake and Brett dine in the last chapter of *The Sun Also Rises*.

275.6–17   Gitanillo . . . Chicuelo. . . . Villalta.] Many Spanish bullfighters used the nickname "Gitanillo" (gypsy), making identification difficult, though Hemingway in *Death in the Afternoon* says that Gitanillo "was short, arrogant and really brave; in Madrid, at least." Spanish bullfighter Manuel Jiménez (1902–1967) fought under the name "Chicuelo." Villalta, see note 184.14.

281.19   Joselito] José Gómez Ortega (1895–1920), Spanish bullfighter. Hemingway, who never saw him fight, wrote of his rivalry with Juan Belmonte in *Death in the Afternoon*.

289.27–30   Olmos . . . Tris Speaker. . . . Maera . . . young Algabeno] Rosario Olmos Caballero (1897–1966), Spanish bullfighter; Tris Speaker (1888–1958), American baseball centerfielder who played primarily with the Boston Red Sox and the Cleveland Indians; Manuel García Lopez (1896–1924), Spanish bullfighter known as "Maera" (who appears in *in our time*, *In Our Time*, and "Banal Story"); Algabeno, see note 180.12.

## LETTERS

298.2   Hadley] Hadley Richardson Hemingway (1891–1979), Hemingway's first wife. The couple married on September 3, 1921, and divorced in January 1927 after Hemingway began an affair with the journalist Pauline Pfeiffer, whom Hemingway and Hadley had met in March 1925 at a party in Paris. Hadley and Hemingway had one child, a son, John Hadley Nicanor "Bumby" Hemingway (1923–2000).

299.10   Don Stewarts] See note 58.13.

299.16   Bob McAlmon's] Robert McAlmon (1895–1956), expatriate American author and publisher whose Contact Editions issued Hemingway's *Three
Stories and Ten Poems* (1923).

299.19   the Big Corrida de la Prensa] The annual Corrida de la Prensa raises
money for the Press Association of Madrid. The event on July 16, 1925, fea-
tured matadors Louis Freg Castro (c. 1890–1934), Nicanor Villalta (see note
184.14), Litri, né Manuel Báez (1905–1926), and Niño de la Palma (see note
170.18–19).

299.21   Belmonte] See note 223.25.

301.1   *Clarence Hemingway*] Hemingway's father (1871–1928), a physician,
who died three years later of a self-inflicted gunshot wound.

301.11   my book] *In Our Time* (1925).

301.17   the straights.] The straits of Mackinac.

302.3   Leicester] Hemingway's younger brother (1915–1982).

303.1   *Horace Liveright*] Horace Brisbane Liveright (1886–1933), owner and
editor of the New York publishing firm Boni & Liveright, founded in 1917.
Among Liveright's authors were Theodore Dreiser and Sherwood Anderson.

303.25   Louis Bromfield] American novelist and conservationist (1896–1956)
best known for his novel *Early Autumn* (1926).

303.2   Dear Mr. Liveright:] This is a draft of Hemingway's reply to Live-
right's cable and letter, both of December 30, 1925, informing Hemingway
that Boni & Liveright would not publish *The Torrents of Spring*. In the draft,
Hemingway provides greater detail than in the letter he actually sent to
Liveright. The typescript of *The Torrents of Spring* was sent to Liveright on
December 7, 1925.

304.5–6   a novel . . . called Doodab] See note 5.3.

304.13   I have already received offers . . . from several publishers.] Alfred
A. Knopf, Harcourt, Brace & Company, and Charles Scribner's Sons had
expressed interest.

306.1   *William B. Smith*] William B. "Bill" Smith, Jr. (1895–1972), one of
Hemingway's closest friends. A native of St. Louis, Smith and his sister Kate
spent their summers with their aunt in Horton Bay. The two men enjoyed
camping, fishing, and hunting. Smith served as Hemingway's best man in his
first marriage, to Hadley Richardson.

306.7   the 'veldt.] Transatlantic ocean liner *President Roosevelt*.

306.9–13   Benchley . . . Carol-less . . . Dorothy Parker. . . . Arlen. . . . Phil
Barry . . . the Murphys] Robert Benchley (1889–1945), American humorist

and actor, contributor to *The New Yorker* and *Vanity Fair*, and member of the Algonquin Round Table; Carol Goodner (1904–2001), with whom Benchley was having an affair; Dorothy Parker (1893–1967), American writer and frequent contributor to *The New Yorker*; Michael Arlen (1895–1956), English writer; Philip Barry (1896–1949), American playwright best known for *Holiday* (1928) and *The Philadelphia Story* (1939); Gerald (1888–1964) and Sara (1883–1975) Murphy, wealthy American expatriate socialites.

306.17   No cut on the movies nor dramatics.] Hemingway misreads his contract with Scribner's, which stipulates that non-book income is to be split equally between author and publisher.

307.5   Hutch Hapgood.] Hutchins Harry Hapgood (1869–1944), American writer and journalist. Smith was staying with Hapgood and his wife in Provincetown, Massachusetts.

308.1   *Maxwell Perkins*] Maxwell Evarts Perkins (1884–1947), influential editor at Charles Scribner's Sons from 1917 until his death. F. Scott Fitzgerald was one of his authors.

309.1–2   I will start . . . page 16 in the Mss.] In a letter of June 1925, Fitzgerald had strongly urged Hemingway to cut the opening of the novel: "I think that there are about 24 sneers, superiorities, and nose-thumbings-at-nothing that mar the whole narrative up to p. 29 where (after a false start on the introduction of Cohn) it really gets going."

309.11   the Henry James thing] Perkins in a letter of May 18, 1926, objected to the implication that James was impotent: "I swear I do not see how that can be printed." In Chapter Twelve, Hemingway revised "Henry James's bicycle" to the opaque reference "Henry's bicycle."

311.11   Belloc eliminated—] The original opening of *The Sun Also Rises* included an anecdote in which Braddocks amusingly mistakes occultist Aleister Crowley for the French-born English writer Hilaire Belloc. Hemingway later used the story for "Ford Madox Ford and the Devil's Disciple" in *A Moveable Feast*.

311.23   bulls now without appendages.] Perkins objected to Mike shouting "Tell him the bulls have no balls" in Chapter Sixteen. Hemingway revised it to "Tell him the bulls have no horns"; however, his original line would be restored in the 1954 edition of the novel.

312.18   Henry Romeike, Inc.] Newspaper clipping service.

314.4   Thanks . . . the reviews] Perkins had sent Hemingway two highly favorable reviews of *The Sun Also Rises*, both published on October 31, 1926: "Marital Tragedy" in *The New York Times Book Review* ("a truly gripping story, told in a lean, hard, athletic narrative prose that puts more literary English to shame"); and "Expatriates" by Conrad Aiken in the *New York Herald Tribune Books* ("If there is better dialogue being written today I do not know where to find it").

314.5 Bloomshield's drawing] John Blomshield (1895–c. 1952) was an American illustrator. His portrait of Hemingway was used on the back cover of *The Sun Also Rises* and reproduced in many of the reviews of the book.

314.10 the ads and the blurb] Scribner's ad copy read: "THE SUN ALSO RISES—and with this book Mr. Hemingway's sun also will rise, for this is a novel able to command the sharpest attention even in a season so crowded with good fiction. The publishers advise you to be very much aware of this book from the start."

315.23–316.14 I see that Mr. Bill Benet . . . for us.] Hemingway refers to a comment made by William Rose Benét in his column "The Phoenix Nest" for *The Saturday Review of Literature* that Lady Ashley "had strayed out of 'The Green Hat,'" a 1924 novel by Michael Arlen, in which Arlen based the character Iris on English writer and heiress Nancy Cunard. See also note 387.2.

316.15 Komroff] Manuel Komroff (1890–1974), American writer and former editor at Boni & Liveright. The extent of Komroff's editing of the story is not known due to the paucity of prepublication drafts for the story.

316.17 Mr. Phelps] William Lyon Phelps (1865–1943), professor of English at Yale University. His "As I Like It" column ran in *Scribner's Magazine*.

316.23–317.19 Everything I publish . . . advertising of crooks?] Samuel Roth (1893–1974), an American publisher, was famous for pirating James Joyce's *Ulysses* in his magazine *Two Worlds Monthly*. There is no evidence that he pirated anything by Hemingway.

The text in this book is set in 10½ point Fairfield, an old-style serif font designed by the Czech American engraver and illustrator Rudolph Ruzicka (1883–1978) and published by Mergenthaler Linotype Company in 1940. A half century later Alex Kaczun re-created Ruzicka's font for digital typography, expanding the suite to include additional weights, ligatures, and numeral forms. The chapter heads are Magnesium, designed by Mark van Bronkhorst for his foundry MVB Fonts. He was inspired by the style of lettering often seen on early twentieth-century hand-painted signage.

The paper is an acid-free Forest Stewardship Council–certified stock that exceeds the requirements for permanence of the American National Standards Institute. Text design and composition by Gopa & Ted2, Inc., Albuquerque, New Mexico. Printing and binding by McNaughton & Gunn, Saline, Michigan.